THE
SERPENT
PAPERS

JESSICA CORNWELL

Quercus

First published in Great Britain in 2015 by

Quercus Editions Ltd
55 Baker Street
7th Floor, South Block
London W1U 8EW

A CIP catalogue record for this book is available
from the British Library

HB ISBN 9781848666726
TPB ISBN 9781848666733
EBOOK ISBN 9781848666740

10 9 8 7 6 5 4 3 2 1

Typeset by Hewer Text UK Ltd, Edinburgh

Printed and bound in Great Britain by Clays Ltd, St Ives plc

THE
SERPENT
PAPERS

For my parents, Stephen and Clarissa,
and my sister Lizzie, whose strength is boundless

Chapel
Valldemossa
Lucretia's House
University
MALLORCA
Palma
Rex Illuminatus's cave
Mediterranean
=Monasteries
GRACIA
Fabregat's apartment
3rd body
Natalia's apartment
map of Barcelona

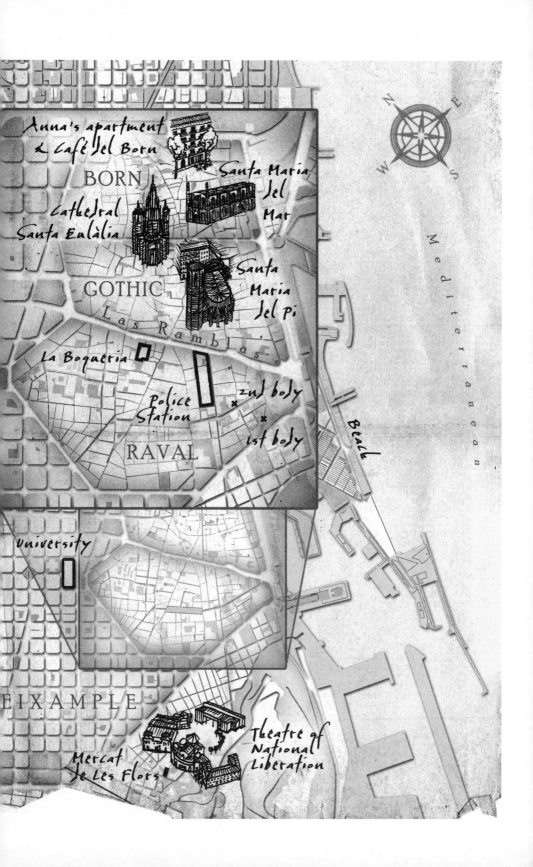

PRELUDE

FOREST

2003

It can happen suddenly that a young woman in the fullness of youth realizes she has gone to bed with the devil. He will mark her deeply. Her mouth will be frozen, unable to speak a word against him, to say his name in any language; he will watch her always and bear witness against her in many guises, that she may never forget he has taken her. You have heard of these occurrences. At times he appears as a dragon, a great scaly brute with steel claws, but there are other moments when he chooses the garb of a goat, a nasty ugly thing with horns and a cleft foot, but more often than not he comes as a man.

Beauty is his favourite cloth, his most beloved costume.

In the case of this young woman, she hears the sound in her sleep and so she reaches for him, but he is gone. She turns in the bed, body unwilling to wake, but hear it she does – deep within the house, a muffled panting. She stretches for the dressing gown hanging on the corner of the four-poster bed; wriggles bare shoulders into silk that slides across her collarbone, orange koi swimming on her spine. Barefoot she goes to the door of the bedroom, tying the silk sash of the dressing gown around her waist. She can hear music – *music from the ground floor?* He has gone, though his body has carved his weight into the sheets. He must have moved softly, so as not to wake her, *but still* – those sounds carry an animal curiosity. She hears a cry, and then a repeated call, like a moaning, and it frightens her.

'*Macu?* Where are you?' she asks the black corridor, using the old term of endearment. She asks again. '*Macu?*'

There is no answer.

It is his private house, a kind of working studio. They spend the weekends there and in daylight it is very beautiful, shaded by a mass of oaks, with the property divided by a brook and lovely labyrinthine gardens. At night the house takes on a different feel. After dark she does not like to go outside, and asks that he lock the windows. 'It's too close to the city,' she first explained. 'It doesn't feel as safe as real countryside.' To which he laughed and replied: 'But the woods, the woods are real, surely.' 'But not safe.' So that was that. Every night spent in the house brings a ritual locking of the doors and windows. Now, peering through the corridor, windows covered with tightly drawn curtains, the air warm and still, no, she does not like that he is gone.

'*Macu?*'

She walks quickly down the carpeted hallway – panelled teak to either side, alcoves cut for bookshelves, a window seat with cushions – to the stairs. All pristine, to the ground floor, through the stoneware kitchen with its glistening counters. Southern pottery perched brightly on the walls. Blue castles and yellow fields. Thick brush strokes. Dried red peppers tied to the air vents above the stove-top turn the colour of rust. Cured sausages left out in a wicker basket. Fresh heirloom tomatoes, overripe, ready to be sliced through the middle and crushed into the morning's stale bread. She leans on the wooden countertop at the centre of the kitchen, built as a chopping board. *Listen.* He has left a record playing in the living room, some Harlem jazz, notes thick and purple – but still, *that sound.*

That strange, unearthly sound.

Again she hears it. *A low muffled sob.* Perhaps it is an animal baying at the night? Or maybe he has fallen?

In the dark, she walks down a corridor leading away from the kitchen. Past the dining hall, the smoking room, to the side of the house that faces the back garden, the rose and azalea bushes. 'Some of these are fifty years old,' he told her proudly when he first showed her the grounds; dropping his hand to the small of her back, he propelled her forward, leaning in to bite her ear, and she felt the call of his power, an opiate mingling with the perfume of roses from the garden. She sensed it as a coming wind, the change she had lusted for, there in the topiary and the gardens, the crumbling rock walls, the small fountains, and creeping peonies.

From the living room, the noise grows louder, clearer; her feet make no sounds on the floor, she walks with precision now, senses tingling – *Where is it? Where is he?* There is a light on in the work-room, the studio space for physical exercise, which he has given her for advancing choreography. 'I want you to feel free here, to dance. I love to see you dancing.' He lined the room with four mirrors, and installed wall-mounted bars for her to use when she stays with him.

Light rims the cracks of the door, a seam of gold stitched from the dark, pouring out onto her toes. It has been left slightly ajar. She feels a breeze, she worries – a window open somewhere?

'*Macu?*' she asks. 'Are you alright?'

But he is not there when the door opens.

The stains are brown, spilt paint on light bamboo. She registers the drops as iridescent patterns, a hacking cough louder in her ears than any drums, explosions of gunpowder dying into a dull thud, the throbbing of her heart as marks of brown turn to a swamp of gore; smeared against the mirrors of the work-room she sees the refractions of carnage. A stale smell, *rotten fish and urine,*

13

she stands above the moaning creature, the girl's breasts barely formed; stains ooze across her skin like the juice of a pomegranate, following the strained veins along her neck, leaking from her mouth to the crevice of her ear. She moans and chokes and gurgles, but cannot speak; her body goes through the motion of sound, though her mind has left her. She has fallen, trying to cover her face, and rests there, hands desperate to hide her nakedness, eyes closed, tears sliding down her cheeks. The woman drops to her knees by the girl's body. She pushes the girl onto her side so that she does not choke on the blood, pulling her face forward, and holds her there as the girl whimpers, body too limp to fight, blood streaming from her mouth onto the polished bamboo floor, reflected in the four surrounding mirrors of the workroom. She pulls the hair from the girl's face, trying to clear the blood, but the damage is endless. A chunk of flesh, severed at the base, then scattered to the side. Clarity comes with a heaving wave of nausea. *The monster has cut out her tongue.* She hears movement behind her. Can feel his eyes resting on her.

'Call an ambulance,' she demands. Without turning round.

'Why?'

'Call an ambulance now.'

'I wanted to show you,' he says from the door, drying his hands on a dish towel. 'What I do. It is an art form, my darling. It is an art.'

BOOK THE FIRST

Fragmentation

O Phoebus! O Pythian King! How Philomela howled and raged! O! She cried! O! O! When she heard the rapture of the Swallow caught in the beams of the palace roof and knew the hardness in her beak. O! O! He has shut me up! But as she hung suspended in the sky, Apollo showed pity, saying: 'Once-Virgin Bird, write your tears in the oak leaves at the edge of the forest. Seek out the ones called Sibyl for they know of darkness and they know of light and nothing that has gone before and nothing that goes hence shall be unknown to them.' And for this the Nightingale is said to nest near certain caves, and the Sibyl is said to know the song of such Birds.

Rex Illuminatus,
The Alchemical History of Things 1306 CE

I

ISLAND

In the sorting room at the far end of the cloister the librarian punches in a security code. He bustles past a filing cabinet made of ruby teak, drawers the size of a single card, then slows respectfully through the public reading room. There is the black marble statue of an old man holding his book, arranged beside the Virgin and a pewter urn. Oak shelves lined with broken spines from floor to ceiling. An upper balcony reached by a series of rickety stairs and then climbed higher with a ladder set against the volumes. Behind this a second door, leading to an inner sanctum. The padlocked cellar where they keep the medieval manuscripts of the Abbey. He halts abruptly at the cleansing station.

'You must wash your hands,' the librarian says. 'The book is very fragile.'

I do as I am told.

The librarian's eyes damp-rimmed and glassy beneath long doe-like lashes. His cheeks are creased and his hair smoothed against his scalp. On his wedding finger a simple gold band. On the other hand the mark of a good family, obsidian crest against the tweed and the lined blue shirt. When I am finished he places his hands under the scalding water. *A constant ritual.* I smell him, the incense and fresh soap, the dust. He has not suffered for wealth. I admire the line of his shoulder as he leads me; how strong he must have been in youth, when he built this place, as he first told me, when they pushed the animals out from these medieval quarters, relocated the donkey and the lamb, and the squatters, and rebuilt the Abbey; yes, of his life this man is proud as he shares his secret with me.

The cellar is not broad or lofty. It is uncomfortable, and dank, and not unlike an interrogation chamber. The wrong temperature for keeping books, I sigh, but at least there is no invasive light. A dehumidifier hums loudly at the entrance, a vain attempt to address the moisture in the air. Harsh, electric bulbs cast a sickly pall over the mortuary of nonsensical memories, the Abbey's personal collection of the antiquarian and mundane. Complaints and petty criminals. Ledgers of expenses and inventories of wheat. Some bigger than an atlas. Others smaller than a pocket dictionary. The volume I examined last week – with some annoyance – had consisted of purchases for the holiday pageants from 1468 to 1532. *1487 ... Bought two trumpets and a rattle, twelve reales.* All labelled with numbers. Binary pairs a centimetre apart. *12 15 34. 76 85 19.* Above this an older form of notation, faded into skin. Not in the best condition, any of these, but they are not my responsibility. I will tell the librarian time and time again, vellum is an organic material, made of animal hide, and when it is stretched and dried for production, it is pulled along the lines of the animal's body. The skin never forgets the shape of its muscles, the location of its legs and heart and head, and as a result parchment cockles. The natural tension of the hide defines the tension in each page, so that when parchment becomes too hot or cold or damp or dry, *it moves.* The books are, in this sense, very much *alive.* We restore them by applying heat and gentle pressure, relaxing the hides, allowing them to let go of traumatic memories. *They need to be treated like breathing creatures, not stacked like the skulls in ossuaries. You hurt them by exposing them to the elements.* The dehumidifier is a compromise, but it is not enough.

The librarian approaches nervously. At the centre of a small working table, a desk lamp dangles over two wooden triangles supporting the covers of an open manuscript, fat and bloated with water. I take off my coat and leave it on the chair pushed up against the wall. Pull my hair back from my face with pins. Catching my expression, the librarian's shoulders droop.

'The first gatherings are part of a Book of Hours,' he says. 'But the style shifts abruptly here.'

'It's been frozen.' *Look at the water pooling.*

'They found it in the snow.' He worries his cufflinks apologetically.

'And you didn't think to send it directly to the conservation department? Javier, you should not have called me to come here.'

A rattling bursts from his lips.

Mea culpa! He prostrates himself. 'I am guilty of obfuscating aid ... upon receipt of this manuscript I was paralysed by tragedy! I could not think clearly, the blow struck so deep into my heart. I prayed for an hour before I could act – I was so disturbed by what I have found ...'

He flinches beneath the tweed.

'We are the first witnesses ...' The librarian reaches forward and turns the pages of the book.

His gnarled finger glides to the far corner. 'The book has been violated! Very cruel!' the librarian laments. 'They were very cruel! Come, look, where they cut, the quire is of a different parchment ...' The librarian squints at the book, bringing his nose close to the manuscript. 'They have taken all but a single leaf!'

Folios excised in a hurry, using modern tools. Cuts clean. We are left with carnage. One golden page, the others ripped free. *A rigid, brutal stump down the heart of the manuscript.*

'Am I wrong?' The librarian breathless. 'Is there Greek? Hiding there, beneath the gold? Perhaps I have imagined the letters? My eyes ... my sight plays tricks on me ... Can you ... Can you tell me what you see?'

A ghost. Barely visible on the page.

I peer closer.

Is that an Alpha? An Omega? Light smudges of recognizable bookhand? Beneath a Latin blackletter? My eyes read hungrily, my mouth hanging open, I can feel my tongue grow heavy, treading over the letters. Blink and look again. And then I catch it. The ultimate proof: *Rex Illuminatus.* A name I first saw written into the marginalia of an alchemical book discovered in London in 1872 through a private estate sale in Kensington. The book itself published in Leipzig, a re-edition of the German alchemist Basil Valentine's *Of the Great Stones of the Ancients* accompanied by allegorical illustrations titled 'The Twelve Keys'. Across the eleventh key an enthusiast of the subject has scribbled '*And such was the transmutation achieved by the immortal Rex Illuminatus*', with an arrow pointing to Valentine's maxim: '*If you will but remove the veil of ignorance from your eyes, you will behold that which many have sought and few found.*' On the page before me, standing beside the Abbey Librarian, I witness his signature in gold leaf painted over the ghosts of Greek letters. *Remnants of an Illuminatus palimpsest.* One hand written over another. Red tracks of deer left in damp clay. Old words, milky and half forgotten, burial mound shrouded in gold.

'You are quite pale,' the librarian says. Pulling a chair towards me. *Roll up your sleeves. Adjust the light overhead.*

'We need to stabilize the parchment.' I curse the shaking in my voice, the dryness. I unsheathe the camera from my bag. *No flash. Just capture what is there. Record everything.* 'Picatrix will come and take the book to the conservation department at the University of the Balearic Islands. It will need to be dried properly; we have the facilities there.' Fans of purple mould gobble up the golden margins of the book, spreading like pestilence into the heart of the letters. A single illumination, small, text underneath, light scoring on the page beneath the lettering . . . Mallorcan flourishes, made locally on the island. *Writing fading. Friable verdigris pigments, lifting in some areas coupled with recent exposure to water*, my heart sinks. *Wet, quite critical, the ice has melted easily.*

'There will be paperwork – permissions, legal formalities. I will stay here with the manuscript until we have the appropriate means of transportation. Once we have taken it to our department you will have continuous access during the conservation period, and we will call on you for help documenting where and how this book was found. You will not have to say goodbye to it today, even if it leaves this place. When we have finished with it, they will return the book to you.'

I continue the examination.

'It may take five or six days to remove the moisture . . . if not longer . . .' *Burns around the edges of the text block, and wax . . . Beeswax . . . not tallow . . . spattered all over the vellum, so it was likely to have been kept in a church or a wealthy household. Deep bacterial infection – deteriorating sheepskin binding . . . sixteenth- maybe seventeenth-century, wooden boards, one broken. Ornate buckle and clasp suggest baroque period, gilt tooling on cover . . . minuscule patterns. Parchment bifolia, much older, burnished on both sides, gilt highlights and iron gall ink . . . badly cockled, tannins from covering leather have stained early and final pages of the book. Wherever it was stored was unsealed and unstable. Freezing in the winter and very hot and humid in the summer. Most valuable pages missing, presumed stolen. All in all*, I sigh, *a disaster.*

But I am confident of other things.

Do not tell him what it is.

The name spinning round my head.

I park the car just north of the village of Valldemossa, along the easterly road to the Hermitage of the Holy Trinity. They have taken the book to the university, but I have declined going with them. The chemists will handle it, the supervisor. People with the appropriate skills. The book doctors. The surgeons. The right pigments and chemicals and machines. The right scalpels and humidifiers and magnets and weights. I walk angrily, burning off the energy.

To come so close, only to lose what is most valuable. Think of Harold Bingley, warm in his Belgravia office. *Neighbours to the Queen we are, at Picatrix.* An idiosyncratic location for an office, far from the relevant libraries and museums, but the one preferred by our funder as it is nearest to his favourite hotel, though we don't see him. Only Harold Bingley has that privilege. What will he think? *We have located the very object you have been looking for, through no genius of our own.* A freak storm, an old church, a bunch of monks putting out a fire find a book, which just happens to be the palimpsest we have been hunting for — *nothing you have done merits praise.* I imagine the man who will receive this information. *They have recovered the manuscript, sir, but the Illuminatus palimpsest is missing from within. It has been stolen. Disappeared. Lost.*

Will he be angry?

Will he be sanguine?

Will he experience the same raging frustration?

I know nothing about him, though rumours abound. *He is a Texan venture capitalist, American, New York, the guy used to fund the Met. I heard he was a professor of antiquity who came into a vast fortune inherited from his recently deceased Brahmin wife. No, no, no, Picatrix is an Israeli start-up engineer who sold his platform to Google for three billion . . . originally obsessed with collecting Isaac Newton's alchemical notebooks, he hunts for the source material Newton studied.* We talk about him, without knowing anything other than the size of his wallet, which is immense, and his intellectual persuasions, which seem – bizarrely enough – to run in parallel with mine. And now, I number one among Mr Picatrix's team. I kick the snow. With nothing to show for it but a mildewed book with a missing set of pages.

I entered Picatrix two years ago on a sleety afternoon. Halting light peculiar to London in October. Summoned to a grand café in St James's on Piccadilly. Dazzling black and white marble in geometric designs, sumptuous columns sprouting Japanese lacquer. Domed ceilings. Edwardian teapots in the style of George III, silver glinting. Coiffed hair and gold cufflinks. At the appointed hour Michael Crawford, Classics professor and Archivist at the Special Collections Library at Stanford University, arrived accompanied by a severe gentleman in a suit. Crawford brisk in manner, kind in language, comfortably settled into his middle sixties. Soft Midwestern tones. A mentor from my graduate days. Specialist in multispectral imaging. Papyrologist. His friend pinched in a wiry sort of way, the skin on his cheeks so pale I could see the blue of his veins.

'Meet Harold Bingley, Deputy Head of Picatrix,' Crawford had said.

'A pleasure to make your acquaintance.' I reached out my hand.

'Likewise,' Bingley lisped.

With that they demanded service.

'Devilishly miserable day,' Bingley observed, while Crawford said to the waitress: 'No tea for me, I'll have a fresh juice. Grapefruit and ginger? Anyone else?' I ordered dutifully, hiding my shoes under the table. Leather brogues. I had worn them every day. Fraying laces. Holes in the side, torn seams. Mud spattered. 'Weathered' would be the polite word, but they were destroyed. My anxiety grew deeper. Fingers un-manicured. Not a lick of make-up. *They'll see right through me.*

'Do you like your current research?' Bingley asked.

'Very much.'

'And your work with the universities? Challenging enough?'

I paused. Any positive affirmation would be a lie.

'No.'

Harold Bingley scratched on a notepad produced from a pocket.

'Novelty is good for the soul. A challenge best of all. Don't you think, Crawford?'

'It is indeed,' Crawford said. Then the men asked me if I had any questions. *Picatrix is funded by a billionaire. Would that be a constriction?*

'What's it like working for an anonymous patron?' I asked.

Bingley frowned.

'How do you handle the pressure?' I soldiered on. 'You don't feel at all compromised, intellectually? In terms of your parameters?'

'I rather view it as a privilege,' Bingley sniffed.

'And what about the man himself?'

'Our founder is quite secular. He does not take sides. His goal is the restoration and publication of lost manuscripts, particularly the missing literary and scientific masterpieces of antiquity ... the disappearance of which he considers one of the greatest tragedies in history. He is an earnest palaeographer.'

'You would describe Picatrix as a secular organization?'

'With absolute sincerity.'

'And if I worked for you, you would not curtail my interests.'

'On the contrary, Miss Verco, we would fund them.'

You would what?

'All of them?' I stammered.

'Within reason.' He turned to Crawford. 'You're certain about her?'

I did not inspire faith.

Crawford nodded conspiratorially. 'She's one of our best, Bingley; I wouldn't send you anything less.'

Bingley coughs delicately into a linen handkerchief.

'This is our offer, Miss Verco. It will only come once. Our team is elite. We are in the unique position of being able to empower the minds we wish to work with. Picatrix trusts your intelligence, and if you prove yourself in the field, we will follow where you go. Now, as this is your interview, it's my role to ask questions. How would you describe yourself?'

'You've knocked the wind out of her, Harold.' Crawford laughed across the table.

Harold Bingley smiled coyly.

'Why so shy, Miss Verco? Where does your elusive passion lie?'

On the road from Valldemossa to the Hermitage of the Holy Trinity I pull my collar up against the cold. The monks will show me where they found that damn book. Now. Today. *Walk faster.* The rain has turned to snow, and it drifts lightly down. It is not a long journey and the cold helps clear my head, scarf wrapped round my throat, hat pulled close over my ears. Bare fingers in pockets. Buses fly by, roaring up into the mountain, careening around a one-lane highway. I move swiftly, heading towards Deià, where the road forks, until I hear the *honk-honk* of a truck behind me. '*Bon dia, Nena! Com estes?*' the farmer calls, his red nose swollen, slapping the side of his pickup, arm hanging from the open window. 'Where are you going?' I tell him I am walking to the hermitage. '*Anem!*' he shouts. 'Hop in! It's too cold to walk.' In the truck he chatters idly. 'Did you hear? The bolt struck a chapel! In the dead of night! A fire on the cliff!' I listen to the farmer, who asks about the house, our garden, if my Francesc can help him with his wife's roses. I nod. *Francesc has green thumbs, Francesc has broad hands.*

'You're not at the university today?' the farmer asks. 'I saw your man going down this morning in the car.'

'No,' I shake my head. *I'm a free woman.*

'You make a nice couple,' the farmer remarks as we veer into the mountain. He glances down at my chapped fingers. 'You should wear gloves in this weather.'

Here on the western range of Mallorca, the forest slopes from the sea. Hidden fields populated by olive groves and moribund sheep; a road, unmarked, leads from the winding coastal highway through blue, arterial woods. The truck rumbles and shrieks, mirrors pulled in; my driver inhales as we squeeze through a thin mouth of stone. A monk in the garb of a workman greets us fresh from feeding his flock. His hands crusted in a powdery, paprika dust. Teeth jagged as the Pyrenees, as he informs us in the old Mallorqui dialect of the state of this year's lambing. *No man here under fifty*, I think to myself. *These aged monks are a dying breed.*

As I wait for the arrival of the man who found the Book of Hours, I lean on a low rock wall. Eyes wandering over gardens and orchards and outstretched cliffs. Comforted by the wilderness. By the sea.

Harold Bingley's voice cuts through me, mixing with the wind. I return to the grand London café. Lights dripping down from the ceiling. Ebony glass and gold inlay. Salmon and caviar. Bingley poured himself another cup of tea through a fine silver strainer. He took a bite from a finger sandwich, and gave a little murmur of pleasure. *Divine.* He wiped the corners of his mouth delicately with his napkin.

'Crawford tells me you are something of an expert in our area. One of a select few who believe Ramon Llull's simulacrum had flesh and blood.'

'The historical evidence for the existence of the alchemist Rex Illuminatus is irrefutable.'

'You are very bold in that assertion.'

'Because it is the truth.'

'Then what I have to say should interest you most profoundly.' Bingley smiled conspiratorially.

'A philosopher in the thirteenth century writes alchemical recipes, in the tradition of the Franciscan alchemist John of Rupescissa's *Book of Light*, onto a series of Greek codices, creating a palimpsest of a remarkable nature on two fronts. First, because the Latin work seems to have been signed by none other than Rex Illuminatus, making it the first piece of Illuminatian writing ever to have been discovered in the original. Second, because, Miss Verco, the Greek subtext echoes findings in the sixth volume of the Nag Hammadi codices. We are effectively looking at a Hellenic poem, presumably composed in Alexandria in the second or third centuries CE, which has been recopied by a later scribe onto parchment, which Illuminatus wrote over in the thirteenth century. We know of this book because we have one page of it, due to a most unusual series of circumstances.

'A gift of *coincidence*, Miss Verco, pure chance. That ephemeral thing which drives our industry. Several months ago, a research colleague at Oxford University brought forward citations of Rex Illuminatus's work referenced in unpublished laboratory note-books written by the American alchemist Eirenaues Philalethes in London in 1657. These notes contain translated fragments of a text which appears to be four centuries older, excerpts from a magical book, known to medieval scholars as *The Chrysopeia of Majorca*. These laboratory notebooks link the authorship of *The Chrysopeia of Majorca* to a mysterious Catalan living at Westminster Abbey at the behest of the Abbot Cremer and Edward III between 1328 and 1331. An individual who can only be the alchemist Rex Illuminatus.' Bingley paused. 'You have heard of these laboratory notes?'

'Yes, but I have not been given access to them.'

'We can arrange that.' Bingley made a scratch on his notepad. 'Said laboratory notebooks were compiled and archived in the Bodleian library by a young English scholar in 1829, one Charles Leopold Ruthven, who went on to publish accounts of an extraordinary find at an unspecified monastery on Mallorca. He recounts the discovery of a palimpsest sewn into an illuminated Book of Gospels. Enchanted by the quality of the illuminations and the bizarre nature of the prayers – simultaneously apocalyptic and alchemical – Ruthven cut a page from the book and returned with it in secret to Oxford, where a series of studies took place in the hopes of revealing the nature of the Greek letters written vertically beneath the horizontal Latin. This is the page we now have in our possession. What was the book Ruthven had seen in Mallorca? We asked our friends at the university to investigate. A volume in a list of works held by the Mallorcan Diocese in 1825 entitled *The Chrysopeia of Majorca* dated to 1276 CE. In 1835, when another list is published, the book vanishes from the records. We have reason to assume, Miss Verco, that the book was stolen, shortly after Ruthven's visit to the monastery.'

His voice echoes through me.

'It was a work of mesmerizing beauty. A magical book, layer upon layer of history. The manuscript's value, if it still exists, would be in the millions, the ideal purchase for a private buyer. But if the book went to auction it would run the risk of disappearing from public access. The buyer always controls their purchase. The same would be true of a claim made by the Church; should it fall into the possession of certain members of the Archdiocese, I can guarantee you that the Illuminatus Palimpsest would never see the light of day. Obviously neither case is ideal. As a philanthropic venture, my benefactor would like to avoid these scenarios if possible. And so we come to you, Miss Verco. We are in need of a scholar. A book hunter. You've been described as a Renaissance woman by your colleagues and impulsive and rash by your critics. Given your peculiar set of skills, our benefactor seeks your services. He would like you to go to Mallorca for a year or two, maybe more. Work with our faculty at the University of the Balearic Islands, make an inventory of all manuscripts at the monasteries and abbeys in the Serra de Tramuntana. The groundwork is in place already. The local diocese has agreed to collaborate, as have our academic partners. Should we find anything of value, we will have the world's top institutions at our disposal, the brightest minds, the finest laboratories. Such is the power of Picatrix, Miss Verco. Which brings me back to the page of the palimpsest preserved in Ruthven's collection. He did not have the technology to read the Greek … but today we can.'

Harold beamed, turning to his colleague.

'Michael has been an immensely valuable resource at Stanford. He's connected us to the Stanford Linear Accelerator Center, and the Synchrotron Radiation Laboratory. Using Synchrotron light to pick up the iron traces on paper from faded gall inks, we've gained access to the submicroscopic world on the page.'

Harold removed a laptop from his briefcase.

'Now. Why don't you take a look for yourself?'

II

ILLUMINATUS PALIMPSEST

Single folio – verso and recto

Greek subtext as translated by Picatrix

London, 2012

You have called me
Thrice Great
Two-Faced
Forked Tongue.
You have called me
Devil's Mouthpiece
Eve's Blessing
Vulture's Seed.
Skin of transgression and her Sin.
The Silence who speaks in Song.
I am the Beggar Queen who cast off Kings
Carrying silver cities on her shoulders,
Plucker of roses and violets,
Irises and hyacinths and narcissus,
Crocus gatherer
Dwelling in the deep
I gathered you like stamens
And ate the seeds of summer and birthed the cold of winter.
My tears formed rivers and oceans.
My womb the many-tiered world,
Yet I am empty,

Parthenogen Eternal!

Self-Making and Self-Destroying

Knowing and Unknowing

I am the forgotten and I am the omnipresent.

Alpha and Omega.

O!

Babylon you called me!

Grinding me to dust.

Dust!

I bear this proudly.

I say I am Foundation.

Root of your root.

Clay of your clay.

I am the Light Who Raised You To The *Knowing*

And I am Thunder

The Perfect Lightning,

I am the Storm of the Mute and I am the Alphabet of Birds,

I am the Cry from the Dark and I am the Listening.

I am the Holy Path that you have called Knowledge,

And I am the Path that you abjure as Unholy.

I am eternal and I am ephemeral

I am your Mother,

and I am your Daughter

I am Wife of your Wife,

and I am Whore of your Whore,

Dust of your Dust,

and Ash of your Ash.

I am the Moon's marriage and the Virgin's child.

The Conquering Blade and The Spirit of Insurrection.

I am the Serpent's Tongue and her Master.

III

DONUM DEI

Boots leave claw prints in earth, black holes where the rubber has crunched into snow. *Ash and fire on the air.* Smoke from a farmer's chimneystack. The path frozen over, darting through the olive grove. *The wind cold as a Norse god, ice on the tip of your tongue.* The terrain drops steeply as we enter the woods. Pine needles underfoot, snowdrifts interrupted by black trunks. I shudder, pulling my jacket close, up round my ears, feeling my breath quicken. *There he scrambles. Much faster than me.* I look to my guide, thick turtleneck, polyester coat, hunched shoulders tight against the cold. Full of thunder. Already the sun fading. Clouds ominous. Stomping out the light.

'Miss Verco!' The monk Anselmo calls. A great pine uprooted at the side of the forest. Limbs contorted beneath the snow, roots exposed. Veins frozen. 'The wind did this! The brute was fierce last night. We lost three oaks to the gale.'

'And the chapel?'

'You will see soon enough.' He whistles through his teeth, the old goat call of the shepherd, and walks faster.

And other things too. I shake the thoughts from my head. *Focus.* Hold my eyes to the path. *It is nothing.*

'I assume you heard the storm,' he says.

43

'Yes.'

'And did you sleep?'

'No. Not well.'

'Neither did we. Are you afraid of the wind?'

I shake my head.

'Good.'

Anselmo stops at a break in the white-frocked pines. His gaze leads along the thin spine of shale to a broken structure.

'You can see where the bolt struck,' he says. 'The lightning began a fire, but the snow soon put it out.' Blackened spokes of wood jut into the sky. Two slits for windows, or eyes, at the height of the first floor. Tiles scattered like gravestones. Above us the storm frowns. Gathering spleen. Smudging the sea with soot.

'Is it safe?' I ask, wary of the roof.

'*Segurament.*' He nods. '*Caminem amb Déu.*' *We walk with God.*

Ducking low to enter the chapel, his movements are muscular. Well oiled. Two fingers in the stone font by the door. He genuflects, crossing himself from his forehead to his heart. I wait beside him. *Listening.* Breath raw against the cold.

Pater noster, qui es in caelis, sanctificetur nomen tuum. Our Father who art in heaven, hallowed be Thy name.

Rubble from the collapsed wall smothers the chancel and altar. Snow through the broken arch of the roof. *Adveniat regnum tuum.* Stone pulpit dusted with powder. *Fiat voluntas tua, sicut in caelo et in terra.* He prays fiercely. The chapel intimate, designed for meditation. I rest in the fallen stones, listening to the snarl of the wind overhead. For a moment I am frightened. I can hear voices in the gale. *Cries of the Siren! One, two three, she screeches up! Up the cliffs! Into the trees, into the village! A kiss of darkness!* The gold of the tabernacle glints beneath black earth and ice, half crushed. A hallowed lamb upon his throne, obscured by dislodged dust, bears the Cross of St John. White silk trapped beneath the pile. *Give us this day our daily bread and forgive us our trespasses as we forgive those who trespass against us.* Glass on the floor. *And lead us not into temptation, but deliver us from evil.* Shards of colour arranged in patterns like poems. I watch the sound of his words hovering in the air. *Amen.*

When he finishes, Anselmo walks into the shaft of dim light cutting through the roof near the chancel.

'I found it here. Half buried. Who knows how long it had been hidden in the foundations of this chapel – eight hundred years? Maybe more? It's a miracle that it survived. *Un donum Dei,*' he adds beneath his breath. 'If there are more pages hidden they will be here.' The wind sends a stone spinning. 'Crushed in this chaos. If we do not find them today, the excavators will come once the storm has calmed.' He looks at me closely. 'I've heard your technique for finding things is quite unusual.'

I do not bother to answer.

'You would like to work alone?'

'That is preferable.'

I push the fear down, feel its weight settling at the base of my spine. *No. Do not buckle. Wind howling like a banshee.* He points to the crevasse in the sky. 'I will check the damage to the wall outside, on the cliffs. Perhaps something has fallen there? Be warned. The rockwork is very weak. If the wind picks up the roof will collapse further.'

When he is gone I am still. Resting in the empty chapel, looking up into ravenous clouds. With each gust, the roof creaks and groans like the hull of a broken ship. But I only listen to that thing peculiar to me. *For the sound of colour. For the song a book makes.* Here amidst the shadows and great stones, the mortar and dark mud, the ash and blackened beams. Where even the gold takes on a lustreless pallor, disappointed in its fate. *Listen.* First to the wind. *Purple and thick.* I wait until I can feel the pages, grasping at a shape. Calling from beneath the stones. Emanating from the dark heart of this

45

chapel. A single image emerging with the gusts, rising up from the rocks in the golden shape of a bird.

Impulse guides me.

Come.

I place my hands on the wall, feeling along the cracks. I drop to my knees at the place the book was found, running my hand over the flagstones. A thick paste of snow and dust comes away. I reach back. Startled. *Black hairs.* A matted tuft poking through the earth. I gather myself. Look closer. *Almost human. Horse most likely, judging by the length of the strand, or sheep's wool for insulation and binding.* I rub harder.

And then a little bone. Black soot between my fingers.

Immured.

The half-notes of a song. Indistinguishable from the roaring of the sea but for a golden ringing. A bright tolling against the slate water.

The bone staring back amidst the stones.

Listening.

For what?

The aching begins at my temples. The shooting pain that pulls at my head like forceps. *Somewhere inside.* I wait for the dowsing tremor, hunting for a seam on the air, a little thread that weaves through the chapel. *Pure discovery belonging solely to me.* I push forward, into the rubble, stepping behind the altar, moving back in the stones. Snow floats through the roof, landing and melting on my shoulders. But I no longer feel the cold, mesmerized by the ripple of gold, warmth blinking from amidst the rocks. A sliver of ore, invisible to the naked eye, but *present* nonetheless, binding me to the solitary travellers, the grubby monks, second sons, farm workers and monastic librarians who once trod these fields. The men who moved swiftly, leading sheep or bearing fresh orders of pumice stone and vellum, the crescent tools to scrape the animal hairs and fat from parchment; who gathered ancient heresies but could not burn them, for love of words or want of paper, and so rubbed them dry, back to flesh, leaving palimpsests they promised not to read, one book written into another, text beneath text. Ghost fragments of Seneca and Cicero, Archimedes and Homer. Reduced to flecks and smudges. In the era that formed this chapel, such books were not mass-produced commodities nor adventure stories. They were the maps of the world as God made them. Keys to our cosmos not gifted to the commoner. They were holy testaments of meaning. They were heretical or they were gospel. And nothing in between.

In an alcove beneath the creaking timbers of the roof, obscured by shadow, I reach into the cavities beneath stones. Crawling forward. Centimetre by centimetre, I stretch out onto my belly, wriggling until my hand reaches the firm, fleshy object whispering from beneath the rock. Instinct drives me. I pull gently, not wanting to lose my arm beneath the pile, holding the weight with my shoulder, tugging at the mass until it comes free with a slick, chugging thud. Struggling back from the other side of consciousness, I cannot see clearly, enchanted by the light's movement. *The fleeting, darting paroxysm of its stillness.* Gradually I focus on the physical. A heavy weight. Coated in black dust, sealed with a strap of cloth and an old tortoiseshell button. *One breath. Two.* Electricity shudders up my knuckles. A pulsing. Just behind my ears. Emerging thickets of sound. The wail of a finger sliding along crystal, taste of sherry, stale bread. I open it gently. Black ribbon of mould, fecund and festive dancing round the edges. Dank potato odour. The hard scratch-scratch of a metal nib, bent at the side, inky divots on pearled paper – *Dear Heart* – my eyes roam across the page. *A quick desire. Irresistible. Pure.*

'Miss Verco?' my guide calls.

Snap it shut. Hold the contraband against your chest. Hide.

'Anna, where are you?'

I do not answer. Crouched against the flagstones behind the altar, snow wet into my knees. He calls again.

'Quick, Miss Verco! The storm has come too fast. The wind will blow us off the mountain.' The beam of his flashlight scrapes against the musty air. He swallows his words. Staring into me.

'Are you mad? It is pitch black in here.' His flashlight reaches my face. 'Anna, you are covered in dirt.'

'I fell,' I say, dusting off my clothes. Adjusting the weight of the bag around my shoulders. Sliding the satchel behind my back.

He frowns. *Now. Outside.*

We stand in the snow. His gaze flicks to my clenched fist.

'What have you found?'

'A bone.'

'Show me.'

I give the fragment into his gloved fingers.

'Animal.'

'Perhaps.' I bide my time. 'I'll have Picatrix send up an archaeologist in the morning. They'll want access. No one should touch it until then, Anselmo.'

He nods, placing the bone in a handkerchief produced from his coat pocket. 'We will give all the help we can, Miss Verco. With some parameters, of course.' He slips the cloth bundle into his pocket and taps it twice with the flat of his hand. 'Privacy is paramount. You understand that, I'm sure. We trust you. You have done great work for us, and now the favour will be returned.'

In the pantry, I reach for a round winter squash, two onions and a head of garlic. *Cinnamon. Brown sugar. Chives.* I heat the oven to 180 degrees centigrade. The blade of a broad knife scrapes against the skin of the squash, looking for an entry point. I push my weight into the gourd, snapping it in two, then scrape out the centre, saving the seeds for roasting in the oven. I crush the head of garlic with the fat side of the knife. Rub the clove into the meat of the squash. *Olive oil, rosemary, sea salt.* Slicing the onion, my eyes burn, but I continue fiercely. An hour passes. Maybe more. I try not to think too much. There are patterns in the wooden cutting board like shells and leaves. Stains made over many months.

'Where are you hiding?' Francesc calls from the door. A cold draught billows into our house at the edge of the village. I shout back that I am in the kitchen.

'I can smell a feast!' Francesc slides his coat onto a hook by the door, leaving his satchel on the kitchen counter. A good-looking man, with a square jaw and bright hazel eyes, short beard and thick brown hair. He wears a knitted fisherman's cap to ward off the cold. A recently broken pair of spectacles perch at the end of his nose.

'You didn't come back to the lab?'

'I was tired.'

His face close to mine.

'*Book Finder Braves Perils on Mallorcan Coast,*' he teases. 'I can see the headlines now: *Savant discovers Ancient Gospels in Church Struck by Lightning. Island Sanctifies Atheist for Contributions to Society.* It's what you've always wanted.'

I laugh and push him away.

He holds me tighter. Hands pressing into my waist, bringing my chest closer. Pulling me into him.

'No compliments?' he murmurs into my ear. '*My darling, you are a genius.* That would be nice . . .'

Nice. He smells like musk. A nice smell. A lovely smell.

'I spent my day slaving away in a laboratory to stabilize your manuscript, while you got to frolic on the mountainside. And you didn't even come by to see what we have done for you! I'm insulted. Deeply offended, but I'll let it go. Just this once . . . Think of it from my perspective. Anna Verco abandons Lowly-Professor-Who-Sacrifices-Life-and-Limb to resuscitate parchment. *Letters come from the Spectroscopy Department of the University of Barcelona and the Laboratory of Restoration at the Archive of the Crown of Aragon: "Join Us . . ." Professor asks Book Hunter: "Will you come with me?".*'

'Is that true?'

'Not yet. But one day soon.'

I kiss his ear then push him softly. 'The soup will burn.'

'It wouldn't be the first time.' He lifts me up onto the kitchen counter, back against the cupboards. 'Tell me everything you know,' he growls. 'What did you find at the chapel?'

'Nothing.'

'Lies!' he teases. 'You sent down a bone. And not just any bone at that.'

I blush.

'A human phalanx.' He beams. *The final joint of a finger.* 'We haven't dated it yet, but it must be thirteenth-century. Buried around the time the chapel was built. I imagine it was some old anchoress.' He kisses me again, tongue warm in my mouth. 'We'll start looking for the rest tomorrow.'

I have never seen anyone else so excited by a skeleton. 'Now. More importantly: we have wine and you've cooked dinner.' He laughs and lets me go.

'A glass each? A toast? What do you prefer? I couldn't decide what to get. Red or white . . . They were all asking at the market. Word travels fast in this town. They all want to know the secrets. I said there are none. *Senyoras, Senyors, I humbly proclaim that the mouldy lump is just an old book, nothing more. No conspiracies. No occult machinations. It is literature! A palimpsest!* Now may I have some *sobrassada*, two bottles of wine and a bag of apples?'

Francesc unpacks his satchel. Bottles clunking on the kitchen table.

'*A palimpsest? Is that a curse?* An old woman who was buying bread asked me that. *No, madam, it is a better deal – two books in one.* With that I made my exit.' I watch as he pulls a tablet from his work satchel, accompanied by a bound case of papers, loose receipts and a chewed pen. He takes an envelope from the case and gives it to me.

'This came in for you today.' It is a simple white envelope, with a lime-green stamp of King Juan Carlos I. There is no company insignia or business template, and no return address, though the postal markings indicate that the letter had been sent from Barcelona.

'Maybe it's another love letter from one of your old antiquarians,' Francesc laughs over his shoulder. He fetches glasses from the cupboard and a corkscrew. I open the envelope. He begins to lay the table, rhythmically. *A bill.* I sigh. *A fee for the location of a few out-of-print nineteenth-century novels.* Personal interest. Nothing more.

'Anna, where have you gone?' Francesc asks. *Smiling. Always smiling.* I stir the soup on the stove. Pulling me towards him, he kisses my hair, warm hands round my back – I feel the breath of him, the reassuring beat . . .

'You always worry,' he says. 'But not tonight. Please. Don't think about those things tonight.'

An eerie sound disturbs my sleep. *Low crackle and steam*. The hiss of a boiling kettle. Francesc's broad back rises and falls beside me, mouth close to my shoulder, breath condensing into warm moisture. I sit up. There is a low humming rattle like a mouse drilling. *By the corner of the window. A hissing, sliding sound, scurrying. Barely present . . . and yet . . . unarguably there. Francesc*, I try to whisper. My blood tingles, the animal in me straining. Beyond our window it is dark. I cannot see the garden, or the field or the forest . . . but I can hear the hissing. *It is a rustling. The burrowing of a mouse – an intruder?* I imagine the chink of dirt moving. *The sound of air exiting a fissure. Francesc! Get up!* He stirs and turns over. *Francesc –* I try to call, but his name catches on my teeth – *there are two lights shining through the window*. Beams of light floating beyond the glass, and I am afraid. They are rising out of the earth. Two orbs like lanterns streak the window. They shrink and condense into a ripple suspended on the night. Blur and snap. I squint through the wakening haze. Two great flames, floating on air? The beacon of a stranger? No – they are eyes. Golden luminous eyes. *Looking at me*. The sound coils again, breath hissing. *In and out. In and out*. My mind sharpens. A dark thrust of shadow moves against the pane of glass. A serpentine body unravels itself, birthed from the corner of the window, almost invisible but for the dull ambient sheen of moonlight on scales. A beast watching me as I watch her ... *A snake*, I realize. *A garden snake.* It was her entrance to the room I had heard, as she burrowed through the earthen wall, the growing crack near the corner of our window. I had said to Francesc that creatures would come. It would be a rat or a gecko or a scorpion, but no – it was the snake who entered first – and I had heard her hissing. *Francesc*, I whisper. Curious now. Intrigued. *There is a snake in our bedroom. She is probably the olive snake I have seen in the hedgerows, with the flat snout and the flecks of black that travel up from her nostrils through her eyes – I have told you to kill her, the one who sleeps by day at the foot of the yucca and eats the sand lizards at night.* But I say nothing as the snake stirs. I watch the shadow move, descending the wall, flat on her belly, winding across the dark tiles to the foot of the bed and for a moment she disappears. *Francesc!* I shake him. *Francesc!* I try to move, to jump to my feet, to leap out of bed and grab the shovel from the garden. I aim to smash her skull with the sharp end of the blade, to sever her throat, to crush her bones on the tiled floor – but too late: the arrival of a foreign body on the sheets terrifies me. Here comes the mounting weight of the snake slithering across the blanket, between our legs. A river of toiling muscle, moving faster and faster, her head swaying. *She watches me.* Gaze steady. I am hypnotized by her undulating wave as she slithers towards my outstretched fingers, her scales greet me cold and she begins to climb up me, sliding her bulk round and over my arm, she rises towards my shoulder and I am still as she coils round my throat. I feel the heavy noose of her form as two cold, golden eyes rise before me. Up, up, she rears, dog-snout level with my own. *Looks into me.* We are frozen in mutual observation. Her tongue flickers. *In and out. In and out.* Tasting the air. She arches back, as if to strike – but I am quicker, grabbing her throat as she held mine, placing my hand around her. *Be calm and still. I am not frightened any more.* The snake winds through my fingers, I hold her head below her cheeks, careful to not constrict her windpipe, and pull her tail with my hand, remembering that snakes are weaker in their lower half, unwrapping her from my throat, keeping her far-distanced from my face, and decide in that moment that we will let each other live. *We're going out*, I tell her. *Out where you belong.* I take her to the garden, unlocking the back door by the kitchen before laying her flat on the cold hard dirt. *It is winter, snake, you should be sleeping, not burrowing through walls.* When I look back to where I left her, I begin to doubt my sanity. The snake is gone. And I do not know where I am.

I lie for hours in the dark listening to the sounds of the long-eared owl who lives in our pine tree, curled into the triangle of muscle between Francesc's shoulder and chest, his arm wrapped around my body, hands protective.

The visions have begun again. The voices. It is a sign that I am close and it frightens me. Gently I move Francesc, and slip out of the sheets. He is a heavy sleeper and does not seem to mind my midnight perambulations. I walk naked to my desk, sitting against the cold wooden chair. In the dark I open the drawer and take out the goatskin box. *Cast away the guilt. He does not need to know.* I stare at the sealed container. *It is better that he doesn't know.* Checking the office door is closed behind me, I switch on the small lamp beside the laptop. Again the sickness comes, the bile and the nausea, churning in my stomach. *The stench of fear on these papers.* My nostrils burn with the heat of a candle, a sensation of dripping wax. The pages are bound in wood and leather, codified by a spindly hand, long dead, who has written on the outer sheath of the primary collection: *Field Notes of Llewellyn Sitwell of Bath, 1851–1852.* The first sheets of these are markedly original. Sketches not unlike medical drawings. Precise. Astute. Each illustration no larger than a small print in a nineteenth-century journal. Pictures capturing aspects of a female body. The front and rear of a woman. Tattoos drawn into the skin, crosshatched with shadow. I look to the centre of her forehead, onto which an individual has carved the letter *B* in an ornate script. *Mystery.* On each breast, the letters *C* and *D*. Across her rear and kidneys the letters *E, F, G, H* respectively. On her thighs, the final pieces of a code: *I* and *K*. The lack of *J* in the alphabetical sequence is due to the non-existence of the letter in old Latin. I turn the page, revealing a study of her palms, tattooed in thick black strokes with a coiled serpent and a cross. *Captain Ruthven's Woman of Akelarres.* Beneath this: an afterthought, erratically drawn. Incomplete. A visual footnote formed by a small passerine bird, round black eye glassy, beak open. Each feather notched into paper, profile flat against the gaze of the draftsman. In the same wavering script:

LUSCINIA L. Megarhynchos.

The Latin name of the nightingale.

The phone chafes again, rattling on the bedside table. A hot, urgent ringing. Francesc answers groggily. The colour drains from his face.

'*Sí*,' he says, '*sí*.' I stand in the door, watching him. He pulls on clothes as he speaks, bending over the mobile phone, stress palpable. 'We'll be there as quick as we can.' I hear the words *incendi, forestal, foc, capella, signes*.

Fire, I realize, *at the chapel site.* My mind goes numb – hiking boots and overcoats, hats and unbrushed hair follow, sleep still thick in our eyes – Francesc rushing – *Faster, be faster, if anything can be salvaged* – he scrapes ice from the windscreen of our car angrily, a little blue Panda, the engine stalls and stalls again, struggling to ignite. I look at the sky, cumulus clouds against Egyptian blue, night dismounting her throne.

'Get in!' Francesc swears and bangs on the steering wheel. We drive in silence, feeling the cold, up through the sleeping village turn towards Deià. Then: '*Fotre!*' Francesc explodes. The car's tyres crunch on frozen rock and snow as we pull to the side of the mountain pass. Francesc is out the door in a flash, long legs striding into the distance. I am running after him, following the trail. There is a bad symmetry here and it unnerves me. Oak forest looms above us as we streak through olive groves. It is difficult to keep my footing in the half-light. I hear Francesc panting. *Damn it*, he whistles again as he trips and almost falls. *God fucking damn it* . . . As we move, the sun begins his fire to the east. Hot pokers pierce the sky as the bristling pines part and we stand looking over the rocky straight of earth that leads to the broken chapel. Flames consume the shattered, ancient beams, a raging inferno licking the dry stone walls and casting blue shadows onto the tumult below. It is almost sublime, I think in a daze; it could be a scene from Hannibal crossing the Alps, in the eye of the approaching storm. Clouds of smoke leer Turneresque above us, what was once a quiet sanctuary taken over by heaving humanity – firemen and farmers and working monks. The storm of yesterday had quenched the lightning, but this second fire burns hungry, loud belly hunting for fuel. Francesc knows as well as I do that any hidden bones will be charred into dust. Whatever other books might have been contained in the rubble reduced into nothing. All gold and signs melted into mud. The excavation site destroyed. Buckets of water and spray will do no good to the conflagration; they will contain it, let it burn out, burn down to valueless soot. *An act of war.* Francesc's face darkens. I grip his hand tightly. The moment of decision is now. When I am most certain of the danger. The trees and ground are ice-ridden and damp, they will not catch – unless the fire grows, and the men will work tirelessly to stop this – but fear of fire is not why the monks pray at the forest's edge, or the firemen quake in their boots, or Francesc's cheeks turn pale. What disturbs us all is the vision of four limbs forming a quadrant in the earth, each cloven hoof pointing to the sky. A quartered pig planted in the rocky soil.

IV

ILLUMINATUS PALIMPSEST

Accumulated Evidence
Excerpted from the collected laboratory
notes and translations

of

Captain Charles Leopold Ruthven
As presented by Harold Bingley
to Anna Verco

London, 2012

'Suggestions for Aqua Vitae' by Rex Illuminatus

Single Page from the presumed palimpsest. Trans. from Latin into English by Mr Charles Leopold Ruthven with notes by the author.

Scriptio Superior

You will find it efficacious to grind the mineral into a delicate powder, separating the base into three perfect elements (the Trium-virate of Hermes, recall – all that which is above is below) through wit and ingenuity fuse these elements anew into a solid substance like a wax – a stone with a pliable texture that can be melted into a tincture and consumed. You will need two drachms of antimony, also of Crocus Martis you will be wanting two drachms, and an ounce or so of Cumphire to which I recommend adding roughly half a pound of common turpentine. For the metals, 8 oz of quick-silver, with 5 oz of Copper Filings, shaved with precision, bound with equal quantities of brass and gold filings also and a sizeable share of Clearable Alum and that wondrous Efflorescence of Copper called *Calcantum* by the Greeks. Do not forget Golden Orpiment to be mixed with Elidrium, Saffron and Natron also, all of which should be readily and easily found in your alchymical cupboard. As to Lead, that imperfect metal, I prefer to purge the mound first – stripping it of its meat – the lumps and thickness ... repeatedly washing the beast with a liquid alloy. Thus you will find what many call the Father, the Son and the Holy Spirit distilled, extracted and combined with salt in the creation of aqua vitae. Procure also a sacred wad of gold blessed by the priests and infused with the Will of God. To this I tend to add a little Moon-Earth, or *Aphroselenos*, of the family of selenites. Should this be in short supply, the gypsum Desert Rose may suffice as well. Once in your possession, divide this wad into five parts before creating an alembic solid which must be allowed to rest under low heat for seven days in pursuit of what I consider the foundational mud of man. The Water Stone of the Wise, known to the initiated as the Sophic Hydrolith. *Nothing comes from Nothing.* We are speaking of what Aristotle called Prima Materia* and Epicurus called Atom – and you call Adam – Adamas[†] – the Incorruptible Mud birthed by the marriage of lovers, by king and queen, sun and moon, by the Alchymist and his apprentice.[‡] When this heir to the throne has set, it must be heated at such a high temperature that it turns at first crimson, then the luminous emerald of the dragon, deeper and richer in tone, before becoming a brilliant pearl that transforms into the white of stars darkening into a horrifying scarlet before transmuting into a purple wax (some call it dust), which may be applied as an ointment, rubbed onto the skin, or given into the mouth of the adept. Though difficult, I do not think it so complicated as the theologians would have it. Arnold of Villa Nova and

---

* RI breaks from the colloquial to use 'mater' in the Latin meaning *mother*. Translate within context as *Prima Materia* in reference to the alchymical definition of *Prime Matter*? Consider later: *mater* not only alchymical substance but mythological figure of the First Mother?

† V. curious in extreme. RI read of Epicurus's *Letter to Herodotus*, enshrined by Diogenes Laertius's *Lives of Eminent Philosophers*? V. few extant copies circulated in the Dark Ages, and yet RI knew of Atoms.

‡ NB to the Mater preceding Adamas, RI suggests divine union of male & female archetypes.

John of Rupescissa proclaim that this stone is the emanation of Christ resurrected after crucifixion ... But remember, John is always preparing for the apocalypse. There is too much talk of horsemen and fire in the world! Better to rest in the practicalities of science, young man, look to the future, which is of your making, not ours ... Human ingenuity must guide the philosopher, faith in the real ... though the usefulness of the wad of gold does seem heightened by a blessing, a detail I find peculiar, but may have something to do with the mineral rather than spiritual content of the gold mined by the Church*.

---

* Greek below. V. irritating! Too faint to read. Parsed last line only: 'I am the Serpent's Tongue'. One can dream of deciphering & never achieve salvation. This being the natural curse of the scientist of letters.

V

CITYSCAPE

Clouds race past my window. A stewardess clears coffee from our trays. *Please return your seat to the upright position.* I oblige, pressing my nose to the window, studying the patterns of ice on glass. *Tendrils. Little alchemical stars.* The plane dips and bobs. Beneath me, Barcelona ripples out from water, unfolding in sheets of glass, turrets modern-cut and gleaming. Green fields churn into the mouth of the sea and behind her Tibidabo, where the rivers run, and behind this, further still, Montserrat, alone in the thin afternoon sun. I grip the armrest of my seat firmly and monitor my heart.

Gather the strands that led you here. Listening to the whirring jets, it is not difficult to return to the catalyst, floating above my destination. What feels stranger is the absoluteness of my decision.

From the back seat in the taxi I watch her dangling from a small chain attached to the rear-view mirror. Her body rocks with the car. *Again. Ca-chink, ca-chink.* She kisses a wooden cross. The car lurches. The Black Madonna collides with a metal coin carved with the face of St Francis. She pirouettes, god-child at her hip. I recognize her song, even though most have forgotten that once upon a time, at what has now become the Sanctuary of Lluc in the highest mountains of Mallorca, a black Virgin, carved of local chalk and painted in the regalia of the Madonna, was found by a Muslim shepherd boy in the forest. Across the halo of the Black Madonna, her anonymous author wove the words: *Nigra Sum Sed Formosa.*

I am black but beautiful.

The taxi swerves off the highway. Distant asparagus towers of the Sagrada Família. Seagulls swoop overhead. Winter clouds clamber out from the sea, black as fermented berries. Paint splats ricochet across the façade of banks: *Capitalista! Assassin! Swine!* Scrawled in the windows of global chains. *Down with Madrid! Down with unemployment! Fuck los Estados Fucking Unidos de Europa! Fuck los fucking banqueros! Gordos! Cerdos!* Shuttered doors and beggars. *Barça!* The sun emits a rusty glow, tinged with frustration. *Take to the streets! March!* City fetid. Hungry. Bristling. I lean my forehead against the car window. In my trade, there is a sense of good, and there is a sense of bad. Sometimes these senses merge, but more often than not there is a line I do not cross, which I consider moral. There are good projects and there are bad projects, just as there are light witches and dark witches, sometimes divided along a confusing etiquette of those who drink water and those who drink wine, although divisions can be fiercer. In Barcelona, this city of opposites, the most prolific serial killer before the outbreak of World War One was a woman by the name of Enriqueta Martí, who dressed in rags to steal children by day and farmed their blood, grinding their flesh into potions which she sold to the rich at night. Enriqueta Martí leaves a taste in my mouth like rot, but thinking of the Black Madonna causes a delicious sparking at the back of my throat. I recognize her call. The Black Madonna sings to a root in me, sitting in her church-cave, she beckons with her thousand-year-old secret, and whispers: *I am black but I am beautiful. We will make thee borders of gold and studs of silver, while the King sitteth at his table, my spikenard sendeth forth the smell thereof. The beams of our house are cedar, and our rafters of fir.*

The scents of memory are multiple and varied. Wet bark breathes out mint and secrets. I arrive to a cologne-clad man smelling of sweet orange and mustard, keys clinking in his pocket. He whistles from across the street as I approach. *Maca! Maca! Benvinguda a la Ciutat Meravellosa! Bienvenido a Barcelona! Welcome to the City of Marvels!* I thank him. He kisses each cheek and shakes my hand warmly.

'Senyoreta! Senyoreta! Forgive me, but you take me by shock! You are earlier than I expected.' Keys chinking in his pockets as he greets me. '*Tot bé, tot bé. Com sempre dic*: God is great. God is good, and I make it! I am very pleased to meet you! Let me take your bags!'

I protest. He insists with a snort.

'You have travelled very far, but Senyoreta, you have found yourself a gentleman and this gentleman will not – No he will not! – allow you to carry your bag up the stairs. Let no one say that chivalry has died in Barcelona!' And with a flourish the gentleman landlord proceeds. We stride over the wide boulevard, lined with trees, bare and dark in the winter. Leather boots and green felt flowers promenade on the street, vanilla and cacao waft up from a chocolatier below the new apartment. Elegant couples in charcoal coats and cashmere sweaters flit through sheer glass doors ornamented by bronze metalwork. In shop windows, pale china, bleach-smothered table tops. Bouquet of winter tulips in clear crystal. My knight warbles, leading me up the stairs to the flat. His face wine-flushed, cheery as a robin.

'You have all the modern amenities, wi-fi, heating, coffee-maker, dishwasher and washing machines. Anything breaks: you call. We fix it. *Val? Val!*' He pants at the top of the stairs. I thank him. He chirps with pleasure as we enter the flat on the second floor. The space is pretty, fitted with basic furniture. Walls recently painted a rich cream, such that my adjoining rooms (kitchen, living room and bedroom) are, to my delight, neither dark nor dank. The landlord smacks his lips together and kisses his fingertips when he catches my smile.

'You have problems, you call me!' I offer him cash. He waves it away. 'Your friend has taken care of it – he has paid for everything.' He twitters and winks as if my benefactor and I were lovers. I scowl. We have not even met. The landlord sallies forth, unvanquished. 'He says I must take care of you. Keep a close eye. Now. Senyoreta. I shall avail myself of a question! And a mighty one at that!' The landlord suddenly rakish, breath rasping on my cheek. 'I have worked with the inspector for many years – long ago – when things were noble. He is a legend in this city – OOOOOH! *El Llop Fabregat*, we call him. The Wolf!' The landlord gloats. 'He swept the streets of Barcelona with the coat-tails of the corrupt! He stitched the brothels with the hairs of the indecent! *Hòstia! És famós!* He is famous! Nothing but the greatest respect.' A tap to the nose. 'Ours is a special agreement. I have found places for many different types of people to stay. But he makes no favours, not even for young senyoretas.' Keys exchange hands. 'You must tell me what you do for him?'

No. I rebuke him firmly.

He whistles as he wanders out.

This evening I study them. A young man occupies the room across from mine. I stand in the balcony and smoke a cigarette, wrapped in a jacket and scarf. The wide, wet branches of the trees between us. I watch the stranger move his bags into his room and arrange his paintings on the wall in the bright frame of his window. His bedroom a bare yellow glow against the dusk. A Warhol-inspired poster of Che Guevara, Swedish upholstery. He opens the doors of a large oak wardrobe that looks like it's been there for centuries. Only twenty metres between this parallel life and mine – I could call to him! Shout across: *Hello! Hello!* Instead I inhale and feel the night darken and smooth, wondering if that piece of furniture is the same. My cigarette stubs out. I move inside. The cold bites the skin beneath my shirt. Everything in its place. You can't understand a mystery without inhabiting the space that gave birth to it, without knowing what it looked like, how it smelt, the geometry of the home, what I call the psychological architecture of a person's inner life.

The phone interrupts me angrily, vibrating in my pocket. FRANCESC.

Let it ring out.

Again. A second, third time.

A voicemail flashes up and then a text. *WHERE ARE YOU? Gone.*

I listen to the message. *A pregnant pause.* Fish hook dangling. *I need you.*

Another text comes through: *Is this about your health?* The phone rings again.

You can tell me. Please.

Do not answer.

You're behaving like a child.

But what would you say? *Nothing. You can tell him nothing. You dig too deep for him to follow.*

I catch my reflection in the black glass of the French doors. The line of my shirt rubs against my neck. Worn cotton vest beneath a woollen jumper and waxed parka. Thin grey scarf. Mud on my jeans from this morning, dried onto my boots. I remember the hawk I had seen like an omen, before the car had come to take me away. A shooting black thing. Rocketing down! Wings wrenched back as the rabbit lunged, leaping into underbrush at the edge of the field. The hawk, reckless, dishevelled, soaring over the sleeping village. The sky cloudless. Slate blue. Sharp as the ice at the edge of my pine-needle path, brown husks of grass pummelled into mud.

Back inside the apartment, I survey my new environment with a certain element of unease. Already installed for the renter: knives and spoons, books and oven mitts, a radio, a small TV, the beautiful steel vase with dying flowers. I look about me. An entire floor to myself with long windows on the front facing side. When I was seventeen, living in this city, I would have dreamt of such privacy. Ten years later it feels too spacious. *How much have you changed?* I ask myself, pulling my bags into the kitchen, taking the cooled container from my carry-on first. I check the contents gingerly, placing my hand against the box of medication. Almost warm. Twenty-eight vials. A month's worth. In case of emergency. I open the refrigerator door and position the blue and white box that holds the syringe capsules, each designed to be popped into a plastic injector – bright and cheerful, accompanied by cotton balls and alcohol swatches. I select a syringe from the box, breaking a single injection out of its packaging and set it on the kitchen counter. Wait.

I begin the familiar distractions. Memory games. *The warm triangle of his chest. Sleeping beside.* I push him away. *Walking through the village this morning, you bought coca de patata, a spongy sweet cake made of boiled potato and sugar.* I tear the packet containing the alcohol swab. The skin on my upper left arm tickles. I pinch at the fat, pulling it down from the bone. A tight knot remains from last week. With my fingers, I feel for fresh skin, four centimetres lower, hoping the lump will go down. *From the road leading to the river, you saw the roof of the car. Mallorca's policia local. Vehicle unusually festive. Painted like a medieval flag, raucous red and purple, blue lights dull on the roof. No sirens yet.* I insert the pre-filled syringe into the auto-inject, wipe my skin with alcohol. Seven seconds. Count. Never habitual, never comfortable. *When you entered the car, the policeman swore. 'It's fucking freezing,' he'd hissed as he rubbed his hands together. Unseasonably cold, colder than ever before. You offered him coca. Crumbs landing on his collar as we drove out of the village, away from the azure bell tower, the Charterhouse bold. Your anchor on the hill.*

Click. Click, goes the syringe, buckling against my skin.

I am done.

At the appointed hour, Manel Fabregat opens the door to his flat, a simple address overlooking the Plaça de la Revolució. He is a short, heavy-set man in his late fifties, blessed with thick legs and a full, muscular torso, resplendent in a black shirt reminiscent of the uniform of Los Mossos d'Esquadra, the urban crime unit of Barcelona's police force. Flesh handsomely creased, weather-worn and athletic. Though the pallor of his complexion has faded, his dark eyes are compellingly alive and his mouth remains tender, while the shadows of his lower lashes are filled with a baleful sadness.

'Come in! Come in!'

Eyes dart over my shoulder. I follow him to a luminous sitting room, white walls bursting with photographs of family, a pretty wife, a boy playing soccer, old men and women at a house in the country. A dog lopes forward, a German shepherd who shoves his black snout into my legs, wagging his tail.

'Meet Panza,' Fabregat booms. The inspector's name is hard, factory-made vowels slamming into consonants. 'Just push him out of the way, push him! There you go, girl.'

Fabregat invites me to take a seat on the sofa across from him. He crosses his legs in his armchair and offers tea. A biscuit? Sugar?

On the wall behind him there are also photographs of the police-man with his troops, and athletic awards from his youth.

'My son wins these now.' Afternoon light streams in.

Fabregat's sunroom is framed in white curtains harking to a past century. Light scatters through lace steeples and dewdrops. A small teacup filled with dried rose petals on the table. Bleached linen tablecloth. The air exudes a chalky mix of mint and sugar. On the wall, a devotional shrine to the Virgin Mary – 'My wife's,' Fabregat explains. He offers tea, then settles into his chair. Panza rests his face on Fabregat's knee, yellow hound eyes half closed. Fabregat runs his fingers through the dog's coat twice before he meets my gaze.

He smiles. Shark-like. Polite. 'I've given it some thought, and I think you should know that *Picatrix* sounds like *Pikachu*. The Pokémon.'

'It's a reference to a medieval magician,' I say tartly. 'A man with three names.'

'Huh,' says Fabregat. He cracks a nut between his teeth.

'You don't look the part.'

Of what? An academic? A treasure hunter? There's almost a tinge of disappointment on his face. He studies me carefully. What was he expecting? Mouse hair, pinned back? Owl glasses?

'How old are you?'

'Twenty-seven.'

'You look younger.' He sniffs into a handkerchief produced from a pocket. 'I wouldn't take you seriously if I met you on the street.'

I've hidden my frame in an oversized knitted sweater, thick grey wool, and retreat further into it, pulling the sleeves down to my wrists.

'Generally, I'm phobic of academics, but I've decided to make an exception ...' Fabregat stiffens ever so slightly and leans forward, pointing to the coffee table, where a stack of photocopies rests neatly beside a green folder. 'I didn't go to university,' he says. 'Went straight into working. No time for an education. A roofer for a while, helping my father. Then a security guard. Then an entry-level policeman. I read for pleasure, not for *notas*. We weren't *pijo* . . .' He sighs. 'But to business.'

I can tell the man is smart.

Eyes snapping over me. Drinking me in. Taking my number.

'You sent a set of images to a colleague of mine for review at Los Mossos. Dated 1851 in Barcelona. Drawn by an Englishman. *Lew-ell-eeeen.*' He struggles with the pronunciation. '*Seeet-wall.*'

'Sitwell,' I say. 'Yes.'

An illustration of a girl's body carved with nine letters, above a picture of a nightingale.

'It gave me quite a shock when that arrived in my inbox. I thought – what are they drinking on Mallorca? *Lightning, chapels, books, Americans* . . . Next thing you know, there'll be a secret society,' he says, looking straight at me. 'You're not a member of a secret society?'

'No.' I shift my weight. *No special handshakes or occult machinations.*

He looks at me wryly. 'Your letter intrigued me. I must thank you for coming. It's a good thing, I hope. The case was one I worked on quite extensively; I'm very pleased you're here. You're serious about getting involved?'

'Yes,' I say.

'You're certain?'

A sideways glance. I am a curiosity. The day's singular event.

He mutters under his breath. Disbelieving. *She's a child. És una nena.* He slows, using the Catalan word for little girl. The nickname sticks, rapidly replacing my own. 'It's not a very nice story, Nena. Quite different to your books, I should think.'

'Perhaps,' I say. *You'd be surprised.*

'I've had you checked out.'

'And what did you find?'

'My friends in Palma tell me you're gathering a reputation as a bit of a local savant. A circus act. You do some pretty strange things.'

'Professionally or personally?'

'You've had a few episodes on the job recently.' He waggles his fingers at me. 'It seems someone on the island has taken a strong dislike to you. I heard about the fire. Gossip travels fast in these parts. Rumour has it you're a psychic? Part time? Full time?'

'That's not the phrasing I would use.'

'But you're kinda funny, aren't you? You hear things other people don't.'

I recoil.

Psychic is false.

As succinctly as I can, I explain that I listen. It is my preferred name for what I do, which is a kind of heightened feeling – mediated now and controlled.

No, not psychic – I repeat. I do not know things other people do not know. I cannot solve a murder by closing my eyes and psychically knowing something magical. I'm not going to snap my fingers and conjure a solution. That's absurd. I can't tell you what you are thinking unless you want me to know – but I can watch you, closely, and I can listen, and the same is true of books and stone – or perhaps, even *listening* is inaccurate. The more I understand a situation, the better I can trace the invisible threads that run through it. I feel like a bat. Generally speaking, my work mostly takes place in libraries and museums, in the deep archives, the underground layers, the boxes that people have left behind, or in more corrupt cases, hidden. I move in the shadows. I watch his right eyelid spasm, and withhold. *Don't tell the whole truth*. That in the last year of university I spent two months asleep believing I was awake before the doctors realized I was in a constant state of REM. That while in hospital I had eruptions of pain in my head and my skin broke out in rashes. That when I awoke the voices were so loud that blood ran from my earlobes and nostrils. That I'm a freak in the clinical sense of the word. Instead I bait him – oh, when it comes, the chase is addictive. *I am like you. A good researcher is a bloodhound, following the molecular brush of a human hand against paper.*

'And you enjoy investigating the past?' Fabregat's mouth splits open.

'It is the only thing that keeps me sane.'

'Your Catalan is excellent. Ideal. For what I want you to do for us. If you feel up to the job, that is.'

Of course.

'You were living in Barcelona in 2003, but you didn't personally know these guys? Hernández or Sorra? Never met? No? Good.' He looks at me closely. 'But you'd heard of her before she died?'

How could I not have?

'And the murders? Did you read the papers?'

Yes. I nodded. 'I followed them closely.'

'Out of interest? Passion? Curiosity?' he asks.

'All of the above.'

'And this is why you sent us the letters. Illustrations of the corpse?' Fabregat flicks through his notes. 'You made the connection?'

'I don't want to waste anybody's time.'

I can feel him studying me.

'Neither do I,' he says. 'May I see the originals?'

I open my purse and give him the package. Flinching as he pulls open the wax paper. *These are mine.*

'They are identical,' he says.

I let him rest in a sensation of discovery.

I know the markings intimately now. He will be looking at the serpent drawn like an *S* over the centre of the left palm, and the cross like a brand on the right. He will be drinking in the circle round her navel, and the crescent moon on her chest, the alphabet on each flank of her body, the letters across her forehead.

A document in the flesh is always different than a scanned image. The freshness of the ink impresses itself upon you – subsumes you, draws you into the tantalizing allure of a corporeal attachment. *Someone living wrote this once. Someone held this paper, a century and a half earlier. Someone whose hand shook as he wrote.*

'They match your case in every detail,' I say.

He draws the pages closer to his nose. 'He was a good artist, the boy . . . What happened to him?'

'We're tracing that now. Sitwell left Spain in the winter of 1852, heir to an enormous fortune given to him by a friend and mentor. He returned to England where he deposited documents in libraries in London and Oxford.'

Documents I have had the pleasure of locating and assessing over the past two years. They all pertain to the palimpsest and Illuminatus. But Fabregat does not need to know this.

'And you believe you know who did this?'

'Not with certainty.'

For a while he is silent. Thinking.

'Certainty,' he murmurs. 'Funny thing, that.' Lost in Sitwell's illustrations. 'No one else has seen these?'

'Not that I'm aware of. Not in living memory.'

His voice sharpens.

'You're right to draw a parallel.'

He puts the papers down. Satisfied.

'We agreed over the phone what the stipulations of this project would be, but I repeat them now. I am retired, and have no direct jurisdiction over the police, but the Hernández case is the great tragedy of my career, one of my life's profound dissatisfactions – of which, I hasten to inform you, there are few. Perhaps if what happened had been contained I could forget. Close the book, as it were. Move on. But that is not the case.' His face darkens. 'Now, your letters suggest that identical killings happened in Barcelona as early as 1851? That . . .' He pauses. 'Interests me . . . I want us to be careful. Sensitive. If you take this research on, you have the support of the police. You work as a writer, a psychic –' his hand twitches on the papers – 'whatever it is you do.' He waves his hand again. 'A two-week preliminary examination of Natalia Hernández, her character, her work, her habits. Talk to people. Get them comfortable. Say you're retelling the case as an independent project, your grant research, analysing her death as an artist – don't look so excited, Verco! I'll explain what that is as we go along. I'll help you set up interviews – just get them talking about her, and that Sorra kid. Ask questions. Read into their lives; get a feel of the city. Any facts you need that we've already filed I'll send you. I want you to meet Sharp as well – have a look at that book. At this point we've tried everything – I've had every expert in Europe on the case. The question for me has always been why: I've never understood that. Perhaps you can . . . just feel. I'll give you support if you need it, but I don't want you to try and engage with anyone on a more investigative level. I want you shadowed. I want to know where you are. And I want you to actually keep notes, actually write things down. I'll pay you – personally, with a little help from the force. We don't usually work with your kind of people and I don't want you getting into any trouble. I want you to stay extremely, *extremely* safe. Over-compensate for that, OK?'

I agree. 'I mentioned over the phone . . . Anything I find along the way? Anything that comes up – I can use that for my own work?'

He opens the green envelope and pushes the contents forward. 'Have a read.'

On the little side table beside his armchair there is a black pen.

I read over the contracts, the confidentiality agreement. Then I take his pen and sign.

'This has become somewhat of a hobby for me.' Fabregat pleased with himself. We drink from little china cups. He offers me a biscuit.

'I value the calm now,' he says. 'Life is good. I'd like to reassure you of that.' And very slowly, ex-Inspector Manel Fabregat paints a picture of the events as he witnessed them.

Things began two weeks before Hernández died. (The first letter came on 8 June, Fabregat barks through a mouthful of almonds, Sunday of the Pentecost, 2003.) Fat Father Canço in the church of Santa Maria del Pi found the envelope in a confessional at four in the afternoon, with no indication of the sender. Being a responsible citizen, Canço trundled over to the Ciutat Vella's police station to ask that the letter be delivered to the man in question. Fabregat opened the letter idly, settling into the chair behind his desk, hat tipped onto the back of his crown, reading glasses perched on his nose. A piece of thick paper, like an old parchment, on which someone has drawn an illuminated diagram like the round face of a compass or an astrolabe for navigating stars, twelve centimetres' radius, outlined in gold ink, heavy blue lines executed with comfortable precision.

Fabregat examines the figure closely, noting that it contains four outer rings, divided into nine equal parts. The triangles create a star with nine points, aligned with each of the nine sections. Three points of the uppermost triangle are labelled in Catalan: *com, medi, l'extrem*. *Beginning, middle, end*. In each of the nine sections an exquisite capital letter – B, C, D, E, F, G, H, I, K – and a sequence of numbers (1 to 9) around the outer rim. Fabregat skims this tersely, eyes hunting for what he considers the crucial detail. In the bottom left-hand corner, written in an eccentric, sloping calligraphy:

Find me in the Utterance of Birds.

Fabregat's eyebrows furrow.

He growls to himself and sits up in his chair. Reads the line again. Then he turns the parchment over. A picture of a serpent consuming its tale in gold leaf. Shimmering on the page. The-snake-of-tail-biting-eternal-life – or whatever-the-fuck-it's-called. Within the coil of the snake, the phrase in Catalan: *All is One.* Half of the snake is solid gold; the other half outlined in a thin silver. *Hippy bullshit.* He does not take it seriously because he does not understand it, but at the same time the inspector grows suspicious. He props the letter up at the base of his lamp, goes out of the office and asks who had it delivered.

'Is this a joke, lads?' he asks the boys.

He is told it came via fat-priest-post, a man flustered, who was unaware of its sender. At nine, Inspector Fabregat goes home. He has dinner with his son at the table and that evening he makes love to his wife.

Twenty-four hours later a second missive arrives, this time delivered by a choirboy, who uncovered the letter cleaning the seat of the confessional in Santa Maria del Mar before the evening mass of Whit Monday. The letter is delivered duly to Fabregat, who opens the envelope to find a second wad of parchment. On the outer sheet the tail-biting-serpent-of-eternal-fucking-life. On the inner pages an identical diagram. The nine letters placed around concentric circles. One dial within another. In the same curling script someone has written:

You have called me
Thrice Great
Two-Faced
Forked Tongue.

Inspector Fabregat's blood curdles. For half an hour Fabregat chews his lip. What is this? A prank? Some punk kid getting him back? A lunatic?

Thrice Great? He turns the phrase around.

What does it mean?

For surely it means something.

They find the first victim in the small hours of morning on Tuesday, 10 June 2003. Fabregat follows a young sergeant through a passageway between tight apartment blocks. Beneath the hanging gardens of Baluard de les Drassanes, lit by a few torpid lamps, the bleakly painted apartment blocks turn a damp and dreary grey. Laundry dangles from windows: brown knickers, faded linen. Sweat malingering. The washing feral in the night, stained with hanging shadows like half-lit *jamones serranos*. One disappointed ambulance in the centre of a square. Blockades on all entrances, and traffic on the bypassing road has ceased. Police tape circles around the trunks of each of the outer lamp posts and trees, with the exception of the young jacaranda at the centre, around which the team of suits now clusters, looking at fingernails, pollen, semen, blood – looking for hair follicles and gum, fingerprints and grime – a melancholy storm wheeling round the object in question. Little feet dangling towards the pavement. Dead as bone china. A child. Fabregat starts. *Barely a woman.* Hanging from a rope attached to a branch of the jacaranda tree. Auburn hair falling over her chest. Wounds dry. He looks up into her. Emotions rise in his chest he had forgotten. He battens down. *Look closer.* He ignores the chatter of the team around him. Presses on. A camera flashes. No warmth. *Pop! Pop!* goes the flash. *Her mouth? A cave of darkness.*

Fabregat squints. Observes the hanging body. *Faint red lines in the skin of the girl* – No – don't look at her face again – not yet. *A scarlet letter B.* Skin pristine in its clarity, hair lustrous, tumbling down over shoulders. In life she would have been lovely, a real beauty. He studies her carefully. Clinically. Between her nipples someone has carved the points of a crescent moon. Around her navel, a circle, the full rim of a sun around her belly button. Fabregat steadies himself. Records the litany of sins: '... *Lacerations made to the body. Tongue removed in its entirety. Muscle severed at the base. Victim appears to be in her mid-teens* ...' The forensic officer points to her hands – '*Image of a snake cut into her left palm, a* ...' Fabregat slows, squinting at the mark. *Don't focus on her face. How had she died?* Strangulation, he thinks, clocking the bruised skin on her neck. *Mutilated first, then strangled.*

'Cross cut into her right palm, all flesh wounds, a few milli-metres deep,' one of the investigators barks.

There is a *C* on her forehead, between the eyes.

Fabregat stops. *Nine letters in total.* His face pales. *The letters corres-pond exactly to the parchment charts on his desk. B, C, D, E, F, G, H, I, K*, cut onto a child-cum-crime-scene, opened up for inspection. Words whiplash through his skull. Verses of a demented poetry. *You have called me / Thrice Great / Two-Faced / Forked Tongue* ... Was she the answer to his riddle? The hanging figure of the voiceless girl? Later the medical examiner gives his verdict, flanked by earnest students from the university. He points to shallow wounds like tattoos on the girl's body.

'Those are medieval letters – styled after roman uncials – all capitalized. Made with a steady hand – real artistry. It's not easy to cut flesh with precision like that. Ten centimetres in length, depend-ing on position. The incisions suggest a variety of tools – a boning knife has been used in certain places, a razor blade here. Body meticulously cleaned. No conclusive DNA. She died after her tongue was removed – I believe the letters, cuts in the palms and the markings on her breast and stomach came subsequent to asphyxiation. Also we have what looks like forced sexual entry. He needed time to do this – there will be a place he kept her alive, and a place he worked on the body.' The victim is Rosa Bonanova. Sixteen, only child, went missing four days earlier, last seen walking home in the evening from a choral rehearsal in the Eixample.

The forensic graphologists have a field day when Fabregat sends them his letters. The message comes back clear: *same calligrapher? Same writing? Same hand, on body and paper.* Her case logged by the police. In the pictures, she had been pretty and smiling.

On the cusp of transformation.

Gone now.

Fabregat's hackles are up.

He is not an inspector who enjoys murder.

A third letter follows swiftly, left in the confessional of the old monastery of St Peter of Puelles on Thursday, 12 June. Addressed to *Sr Manel Fabregat of Policia de la Generalitat de Catalunya.* The inspector's eyes bulge. Insolence rising like fog towards him. This time the sender has written:

> *No more riddles.*
> *I will teach you.*
> *Follow. Heed my words.*
> *Ancient Crimes.*

And left two dates like bookends:

1182–1188

Fabregat does not waste time. *Missing persons!* he shouts to his team – flag them up, chase any leads, distressed parents, disappearances – I want to know about it. No talking, lads! No leaks to the bastard media. I don't want them knowing any steps to this dance!

This is not the first time the killer has done this.

It is too practised. Too rehearsed. Is there any history? Any incident in the past? He feels a net tightening . . . *No more riddles?* And beneath this a profound, restless unease. *Why me? Why single me out? The recipient of such strange knowledge.*

The answer comes in a second body, discovered on Friday, 13 June 2003 by the bartender of the nightclub Genet Genet – who stumbles over his words – relaying how he found the body after the club closed, taking out the trash – his nerves break as he talks to the police who have pulled him to the side of the building near the *narcosala* – I just found her (he repeats as a man who has lost his mind) – she was covered in blood – the blood has soaked through his shirt – and she had been left there, hanging from a lamp post – he looks away from the street, casts his eyes towards heaven. A strong man refusing to weep. I . . . I . . . But she too is gone, her soul departed, and not in a pleasant way. Xavi has found a woman without a tongue. Her mouth a pool of blood. Her body naked but for the letters carved into her chest, throat and arms. Lakes form around her, pouring from the stump of her tongue and the letters on her body. From the pictures on her hands.

Working at the scene, Fabregat is interrupted by a shadow who pushes herself up against the wall behind the blue-and-white tape, coughs loudly and lights a cigarette.

'Another one for the bin bag.'

The old prostitute lisps. Matter-of-fact.

'Trust me.' She burps a malingering cloud of smoke. Tired peroxide hair. Yellow plastic crown. Lavender eye shadow. Lips like a foul red barn.

'She's a nobody.' The woman smirks, face cloaked in darkness. Her voice rasps like a rusty saw, bent from overuse.

'*Como tú, Mosso.*'

The hair on the back of Fabregat's neck rises.

'*Basura.*' She sounds the syllables out in a song.

Ba-Su-Ra.

You are trash.

Dust on the wind.

'Tell them to forget it,' she croaks. 'Nobody knows her. Nobody cares.'

The second body is identified as the medical student Rosario Sarrià, twenty-three years old, training to be a nurse, interning at the Hospital Clinic. She had been living alone in Sant Gervasi. No one had reported her missing, though she had not shown up for seminars on Wednesday or Thursday. And her classmates had begun to worry.

Soon words come in from the specialists. The cryptographers and analysers, the historians at the University of Barcelona. Words Fabregat has never seen before and struggles to understand. Any ciphers? Any codes? Any anagrams? Fabregat asks. Hopeful. Thinking of a book he read on the subject. *No. No. And. No.* Fabregat is grasping at straws. However . . . *The carvings on the body also seem to be alchemical – the circle around the belly button echoes the alchemist's shorthand for Gold, a perfect circle around a dot at the centre. The crescent between the breasts may be the alchemical notation for Silver. The snake on the left hand suggests an affirmation of sin, the cross on the right hand a representation of divine judgement.* And the eternal-serpent-biting-its-fucking-tail on the letters?

Professor Guifré, expert and medievalist with the Special Collections department at the University of Barcelona, responds with the following:

'That snake is an ouroboros. Dating from second-century Alexandria – taken from an alchemical treatise called *The Chrysopeia of Cleopatra* – the Catalan here echoes the Greek proclamation *hen to pan* – literally *one is all*. The black and white halves suggest Gnostic duality. The ouroboros has traditionally been accepted as the stamp of a continuous cycle, eternal consumption and creation. An elliptical generative force containing the universe. The ouroboros also alludes to ancient mystical traditions associated with turning coarse metals into gold ... If there is a code, I believe you're looking at an alchemical one.'

And the tongues? Why cut out the tongues? If everything else is so charged, there must be a significance in that. The professor doesn't know. Fabregat sits dejected, head down at his desk. *Why send all this to him? Why carve these things onto a woman's body?*

'You're looking for a man obsessed with the occult.' Guifré warbles over the telephone. 'Your killer is an enthusiast of alchemy. An aficionado of black magic. One of these – what do you call them? – a Goth,' Guifré suggests, pleased with his grip of pop-culture. 'A cloak-and-dagger type. A reader of fantasy.'

Fabregat sees things differently. *Someone Herculean. Precise. Clinical. Efficient.* Fabregat adds his observations to the list. A female officer approaches Fabregat. He looks at her blankly. She hands him a cup of coffee. They talk awhile. She musters the courage to forward a theory. It does not fly. He shakes his head woefully.

'We'll get the bastard, Inspector,' she says.

Fabregat isn't sure. There are no marks, no prints, no traces of a killer. *The guy's too clean. He's professional. No one saw him ... How does no one see a man hang a body from a lamp post in the middle of a city? Unless they are afraid? Perhaps the witnesses are afraid? Perhaps they know him. Or he is a phantom? A ghost?* Round Fabregat goes. Round and round again.

Monday, 16 June 2003.

A fourth letter arrives. Found after evening mass on the fountain in Plaça de Sant Felip Neri. The priest asks that Fabregat send a courier. He does not want to touch the envelope. Inside, the diagram of the concentric dials is identical to the previous three missives. The message consists of four lines and one set of dates:

> *Count the grains of Sand*
> *And measure the Sea.*
> *Read the deaf-mute*
> *And hear the voiceless.*

1312–1317

Nothing more.

Tuesday, 17 June.

First light. Sun rising benignly on the sea. A hot radiance. A couple walking their dog in the hills behind Barcelona find a body hanging from the trees on a trail spiking off from the Carretera de les Aigües. The golden retriever sniffs her out below Tibidabo, at the bend above the heart of the city, behind a stone bench and water fountain, hidden in a black thicket. She is hanging by a cord round her neck, swaying in the air, just metres up from the trail, hidden behind brambles and ivy, in amidst the leafy oaks and Aleppo pines, where it smells of damp spring and mud.

Tibidabo. A favourite childhood haunt. Fabregat feels robbed of sovereignty as he slides his car past the police check onto the dirt road. *Assaulted. Violated.*

Tibidabo. Named for the devil's Latin – the temptation of Christ on the mountaintop.

All this will I give you . . . On Tibidabo you get some air and a better view of the city, stretching, yawning from her sleep. Flickering towards the harbour.

From the mountain you see everything. Barcelona flesh-coloured. Undulating skin all the way to the sea. Parc Güell, directly to the south, the port of Barceloneta, the city open like two hands cupped for water. There are hills to all sides, Collserola, Putget, Montjuïc – the mouths of the rivers Besòs and Llobregat, the diagonal line of Las Ramblas, a bold incision, confident, stripping the city centre into two triangular pieces. Viewed from this height the Gothic and the Raval are mirrored human lungs, breathing against the spine of the Ramblas.

Fabregat swears under his breath as his car chunters down the white dirt path to the place where they have found her. He sees the menagerie of vehicles – the white motorcycles and yellow ambulance, the black-and-blue vans. He catches a glimpse through the windscreen of the distant Christ-figure on the top of the wedding cake temple of the Sacred Heart. Perched at the summit of the range. Arms open, greeting Fabregat.

Smiling down on the forest.

It is not a normal place for Roseanne Aribau to be found. The third victim lived miles away, at a hippy community near Terrassa. She had been reported missing on Friday by her friends, who said she had not returned from a training session conducted in Barcelona. She had taken the *Ferrocarriles* into town on Wednesday, spent two nights in Gràcia and then ... silence. Her phone did not answer.

Usually she texts. I pick her up at the station. That had been the plan, her friend said.

What is her profession? The police asked.

She's a doula – A doula? thought Fabregat. What in hell's name is that?

A midwife, someone says. *A new-age midwife.*

To be sure, it had been an animal.

A goat kept by some farmer in the foothills but the suggestion – no, the implications of the prints, in such proximity to the corpse – leaves a sick feeling in the base of the inspector's stomach. When Fabregat had arrived on the scene, the young *Mosso* on duty was green in the face. When asked what he had seen, the boy revealed that a creature had moved in the shadows that was like a man in shape, but had been too dark to discern. When he had pursued the figure, it had disappeared into the forest and the cadet returned to watch over the body of the girl. Retracing his steps, the cadet had looked down at the ground, where he had noticed beneath her body a muddy print tracked from the puddle in the ditch of the road. The prints, which the cadet had later shown to Fabregat, were not in the shape of a human foot, but the cloven print of a hoof, like that of a ram. Only much larger. The size of a grown man's shoe.

He blinks. *An apparition. The imagination.*

'I think it was the devil,' the young officer said, and crossed himself.

But superstition will not get the better of Manel Fabregat.

'It was a goat. Pull it together, *tío*.'

Later Fabregat lights a cigarette and inhales fiercely. The effect is welcome. He walks to the look-out point, the stone bench on the side of the white dirt track that runs above Barcelona. He scans the hillside. *How would he have approached?*

He thinks carefully.

The zigzag cut above Bonanova and Sarrià. By the roundabout.

Is it gated?

Yes. He remembers. *By a thin metal chain that runs between two wooden posts.*

He makes a call to his officers. They check the entry point. Sure enough, the lock of the metal chain that stretches across the turn-out has been cut.

The bolt hacked through.

When Fabregat holds the cut metal in his hand, he runs his eyes over the surrounding apartments. A modern development with a swimming pool. Slick gated gardens. *Surveillance cameras.* His eyes light up. *Hope. Someone will have seen him. Vehicles are not meant to pass through here. The headlights would have streaked into their windows.* The investigative team checks all the apartments. A woman comes forward. Around two in the morning, she thinks. A city car pulled up. Lights very low. She could not see the make. It was black, she thinks, or silver ... the witness says again. That's not helpful, Fabregat barks. Any licence plate? Any number? The look of disappointment on Fabregat's face makes the woman blush. *But it is something. It is something to go on.* When they check the camera there is no tape to record on. Fabregat turns purple with rage. *What is the fucking point of a camera if it doesn't record anything?* He returns to the dark copse at the bend in the white track. Runners have gathered at either side, desperate to complete their daily circuit. Kicking up dust at their heels.

Fabregat says: *No. You cannot pass. Not today. Not tomorrow. Not for a while.*

Then he looks up at the trees and asks them: *What have you seen?*
As if they would want to tell him.

At first he had been confident that they would find an answer – no killer could commit these atrocities without leaving some piece of himself on the material. Discovery of a suspect was just a question of time, he told his team – keep looking, trace everything, study the ground – the pollen – the mud – their flesh. Look for anything in their gut ... What had they eaten? What had they drunk? Look for the numbers of coffees they had consumed in a day, when they had last been to the bathroom. Look into their faces, the wounds on their throat and chest, the brutal severing of flesh – what knife

94

had he used? What blade had caused these lacerations in the mouth, the markings of her stomach? In all his career of cleaning marital spats off the kitchen table, responding to rape, armed robberies, burglaries, breaking-and-enterings, pick-pocketing, smuggling and human trafficking, Inspector Fabregat has never worked on a case like this. His previous exposure to manslaughter had (fortunately) come in instances of ones and twos, generally male on female, and most often between two people who knew each other. Crimes of passion in which the perpetrator came forward within days or killed themselves or did any number of peculiar things that did not include (a) returning to kill again, or (b) sending cryptic letters by phantom post that looked like the holdings of the University of Barcelona's archive of illuminated manuscripts . . .

He shudders at the thought of the copy of the latest document he had sent to the expert's desk. It arrived as the others did. Another confessional. Another envelope addressed to Manel Fabregat. Inside:

Serpentarius!
One-who-is-arriving!
Know this:
Nine books of Leaves gave forth this rage of man

Fabregat chews his lip. He smokes ruefully. Barcelona is not famous for its serial killers. Any loco comes here and they get distracted by the beach. Scenes like this? It's just not in keeping with the atmosphere. On a personal level, it irks him.

Act Two starts quietly. It is the morning of Sant Joan's Day. The holiday in Barcelona stretches over forty-eight hours. Festivities began on the evening of 23 June with *la Revetlla de Sant Joan* and culiminate now in the sleepy Feast Day, the 24th. On this occasion, the sun rises behind the imposing pinnacles of Barcelona's Cathedral. Dominant spires sprouting from the heart of what was once the walled Roman city Barcino, said to have been founded by Hercules, half man, half god, who loved the girl Pyrene, namesake for the Pyrenees; or perhaps Hamilcar Barca, father of Hannibal, the Carthaginian, built the first structures on Mont Tàber. The Great Cathedral rests here now. *La Catedral de la Santa Creu i Santa Eulàlia*. Gargantuan. Brooding. Product of a fiscal boom, the brainchild of a medieval superpower long since dwindled. Nowhere else in the world are there so many great churches in such close proximity. The thrust of the cathedral feels drunk on power, still famous for exorcisms, exalted soil, stone-plated, façade ornamental, deceptive, a neo-Gothic addition made in the nineteenth century. Hung with the silhouettes of angels peering down on mysteries below. Studying the tourists with their cameras, the covered markets, the beggars and street cleaners, the businessmen in suits, the activists, the strikers, the politicians, the stoners and salesmen of squeaking birds who garble whistles in their mouths and shoot flashing lights into the sky, hoping to entrance a customer. In the night the gargoyles and angels have been gossiping with one another beneath the belfries. Watching something unusual. *Something curious.* Stone eyes gaze on the form of a girl. Laid out on the eleven steps leading to the mouth of the cathedral like an offering to an indifferent god.

Fuck! the medic whispers, as he pulls the shirt from the female body. Her flesh still warm. The assistant by his side loses his balance, and trips. The medic shouts. *Get up! Get up!*

Natalia Hernández?

The world stops for a moment and stares. *Or her double?* The assistant chokes. It might not be her. But they know. Everybody knows. Someone has pulled the hair from her face, leaving sticky marks on her cheek, and her brow, where they have tried to clean the death away. She has been gored in her belly and her chest. Punctured. Many places. She is porous. A quagmire. Her lips fresh-rouged. Mouth a lake of darkness. A policeman retches on the steps.

And yet her face so still?

The medic gives a small prayer under his breath as he inspects her neck.

There are wounds all over this girl. God, he was cruel. Ostres! The medic whistles. He feels a chill on the air, as if in the presence of ghosts. A nasty icy-frost, even in the heat of summer. *Natalia Hernández.* Retrospectively, people will wonder how they left her there.

They will feel a collective sense of remorse.

She who was so beautiful.

The housewives will read the tabloids with attention.

This the medic knows with certainty as he feels the nothingness of Natalia Hernández's pulse. She whom they held so tenderly in their hearts.

Across the city, the doorman on Carrer de Muntaner will slam his fist into the desk. He had not known to alert the police that she never came home – Natalia Hernández who always came home at eleven – who never went out later – not even on an opening night. *Hòstia, Santa Maria! Quin horror!* Her hair pristinely coiled at the nape of her neck in a tight bun. Stage make-up thick on her face, and those luminous lips, burst berries against brown skin. Delicate limbs fold like the crumpled hind legs of a colt. Fingers long and curled in a death grip on her chest. Two moles, constellations at the corner of her neck and jaw. And yet she looks serene. Dreaming into herself, she disappears.

Elsewhere, all is not as it seems. As the case unfolds, an investigator brings the media's attention to Natalia Hernández's doorman at No. 487, who saw a stranger enter and leave his building that fateful morning, taking the elevator to Natalia's floor in the lavish apartment complex on leafy Muntaner. Said doorman fails to recognize the man on his departure from the building. The little that he could remember upon questioning was that he was nondescript and sandy-haired, slight features, of an average height. 'I don't know, I suppose it could have been anyone. I didn't see him come in. I assumed he was a romantic friend of one of our inhabitants, leaving after the night.' At 6.30 a.m. the mystery man is promptly forgotten. Later the doorman will claim he was a ghost – a demon, a spirit – no human could have crept by, not in that nasty, serpentine way, slithering along the floor so that he could not be seen by the human eye! Smoke, however, is not so easy to dismiss, and by seven in the morning the living room of 5A, No. 487, has raged into a blazing inferno. Black clouds billow out from the cracks around the apartment door into the fifth-floor hall of No. 487. Fire of this kind never before seen on Muntaner. And still it worsens. In the workroom of Natalia Hernández the heat reaches a vat of turpentine, stacked on the shelf – the flames consume everything – and then the great explosion – a magnificent fireball rising in the air. Sprinkler systems flood the floors to either side. When the fire brigade arrive they struggle to put out the roaring flames, by which time the living room is blackened, the two sofas a disfigured mass of leather, smelling like a burnt carcass, and at the centre of the living room a charred circle of thick black dust. Inside the ash are still discernible the woman's implements of writing, the spines of books smoke-eaten and destroyed, the pages incinerated in a fire caused by a flame which had met the gas stove (left on) and exploded through the small adjacent kitchen into the living room of the apartment. The firemen suspect arson – the door to the apartment ajar, the taps running in the kitchen. What remains bizarre is that this incendiary cloud of black smoke engulfs Natalia Hernández's apartment approximately one hour and fifty-seven minutes after her death.

Was it the explosion of her soul – split like an atom from her body? Or the intensity of her life manifested in flames? Only Bobi the Pekinese lapdog remains calm, clutched by his aged owner. His glassy canine eyes observe the fire with placid acceptance from the stricken crowd below.

Inspector Fabregat stands, in this exact moment, in the square of Natalia Hernández's death. Sleep barely rubbed from his eyes. He runs a hand through his hair, his features wolf-sharp. Across the way the sun glints in shop windows. Olive trees murmur beside diminutive palms. The stone of the surrounding buildings golden and pink. Layered. Mismatched, from all ages. Cypress trees standing to attention at the rim of grey flagstones.

This morning the almsmen will be kept away from the church steps. As will the tourists. *Still too early for crowds . . . but they will come*, Fabregat thinks. Pacing beneath black ornate lanterns jutting out from stone walls. Past museums and church archives. Narrowing streets. He walks in circles. Waiting for results. This time they will have cameras of the diocese, the door-guards, and Fabregat is agitated, eager, to see what they hold.

Soon Sergeant de la Fuente will lead Inspector Fabregat back to the white-and-blue van stationed at the far side of the square, underneath a row of larger trees.

The excitement on his voice is palpable. 'We're tracing them back now. All the way through the Gothic.'

'*Them?*' Fabregat's left eye twitches.

De la Fuente grins. Fabregat forces a smile.

'If you're telling me this, you'd better be sure, Sergeant. I'm a very sensitive man. Don't go getting my hopes up.'

De la Fuente opens the door to the mobile lab. He pulls up a chair to the central computer and gestures to the inspector, who refuses to take a seat. Fabregat frowns. De la Fuente sits back down, his forehead greasy in the early morning light.

Fabregat runs his hand through his hair and registers surprise. He watches as the young tech in front of him pulls up clear footage, from a vantage point near the Museum of the Archdiocese. Fabregat looks again. A man is carrying her.

'We're assuming she's dead by the time this camera sees her.'

De La Fuente's voice emotionless.

'Bring up the rest,' Fabregat barks.

From the shadows of a side street, a figure emerges and crosses in front of a café closed for the night. La Estrella de Santa Eulàlia. Out of the darkness, the figure lumbers. Vague and blurry. Now clearly discernible as a man. Mid-length black hair. Skin reflecting the glow of the street lamps. His shoulders and chest bare. He wears belted jeans low on his hip, and in his arms he carries the girl, covered in a shirt. Her arms limp, trailing towards the ground. The boy's face long. Streaked in something black.

Blood? Fabregat's heart quickens.

Around the two strange travellers, the street and square are deserted.

'Can we get closer?'

The officer's fingers fly over the keyboard. He enlarges the image on screen, zeroing in on the young man's face. Fabregat sees curling dark hair, down to the shoulder. Had the camera been clearer, he would have made out a hooked nose and yellow eyes like a cat. For the majority of time, the visage is blurred, the quality of lighting is poor – but there are flashes of clarity.

'*There* – stop there.' Fabregat raises his hand.

The man's mouth firmly closed, eyes straight ahead. He stands for a long time, hugging the limp girl to his chest, before setting the body down on the ground, at the base of the steps leading up to the Grand Cathedral. The suspect kneels by the woman's side. He moves the dead girl's arms, crossing them over her chest, straightening her legs, pulling the hair from her eyes. He strokes the skin of her forehead.

A needle of doubt turns in Fabregat's mind. *There is nothing cool or calm about this guy – nothing practised. Nothing clean. He doesn't fit.* For a moment the suspect looks down. Down at Natalia Hernández. *Sadistic little shit* – the tenderness enrages Fabregat, baffles him, as the boy covers her face with the palm of his hand – caresses her cheek, closes both eyes – to what? To apologize? The suspect kneels over the naked girl. He stays there for three minutes and fifty-six seconds. Shoulders heaving.

'He's crying,' Fabregat says, emerging to catch his breath.

And internally he repeats it again, as would the nation when they watched the footage roll through the investigation. He is not just crying; the boy is sobbing. Hot tears streaming down his face. A millisecond later, the suspect moves. *Head up.* He's heard a noise. He wipes his eyes with the back of his hand. He does not look down at the woman again. Then turns, and begins to run, south, down the Via Laietana. Towards the sea.

'Right! Who the hell is this guy?' Fabregat explodes. 'Can anybody tell me yet?'

De la Fuente beside him glowers.

'Tell the City Council to install more cameras. You'll have a devil's hunt to catch him on our system.'

The inspector makes a move towards the sliding door.

He pulls it open.

'Find him!' Inspector Fabregat shouts back into the seated row of technicians. He steps into the sun. Hot air hits like a wave. Sweltering, unforgiving heat. *It's a scorcher.* Not a fun day to be on the run. Outside the surveillance van, Fabregat stands still for a moment. *El dia de Sant Joan.* Should be a holiday for everyone. He thinks of how the beaches were last night, of how the drinking began at noon, of his son Joaquim, the little children with their fireworks and sparklers, the crowds on the beach, the mass hysteria, the petty crime that always comes. But this? This is a nightmare. He rubs his forehead with the back of his palm. *A mistake on la Revetlla de Sant Joan.* But we got the bastard. We got the bastard on bloody camera. Case closed. My God. Fabregat rocks on his heels, and gives a slow, long whistle under his breath. *Tranquil·la macu. Calm down. Tranquil·la. God damn it. We've got him.*

But this is not true.

Adrià Daedalus Sorra has already walked into the sea.

On the morning of the 24th, the Argentine producer Tito Sánchez calls from the back seat of his silver Jaguar, parked at the top of Avinguda Portal de l'Àngel, just off the big square – Plaça de Catalunya.

Fabregat can see the nose of the car poking out into the street. *Sánchez: forty-three, extremely wealthy, ties to the drug trade, Russian crime. Real McMafia type. We've never pinned him down, but we know. A viper. He's been a producer at Natalia's theatre for the past twenty years. High-profile admirer of the actress. No alibi for the hours of midnight to six thirty,* Fabregat says softly. *We had developed a strange kind of friendship prior to the case. Still, Tito Sánchez knew too quickly for my taste. We brought him in, questioned him. Nothing conclusive.*

Tito leans into the dark leather interior, phone pressed to his cheek. His driver silent. He does not want the driver to see his face.

'I heard . . .' Tito's voice hardens. 'You on the ground? You there?'

'Look—'

'What happened to her?'

Fabregat steels his nerves.

'I can't, Tito. I really can't. It's bad.'

'I need to know.'

'Not from me.'

'Fabregat—'

The line goes silent.

'Where is she?'

'I'm sorry.'

Tito is winded.

Empty of all feeling.

Fabregat plays out the scene in the car as he listens – Tito stares into the gold face of the watch on his wrist, concentrating on the dials. He has failed her. He feels impotent, bereft, sucked dry of life, and still the damned minute hand clicks forward, and the seconds.

'Tito? Tito, are you there?'

Fabregat's voice crackles on the line. Then Tito takes off his watch and smashes the face of it into his window, cracking the glass of the car. Fabregat listens to the punching. The watch face shatters. Tito punches his hand again into the window of the car.

'Who was she with last night?' Tito growls.

Fabregat does not answer.

The actor Oriol Duran had gone out for a dawn run and returned to his apartment that morning to discover an unwelcome guest. Duran takes off his shoes in the hall, then his socks. He calls out.

Hello?

No answer.

But he can feel somebody breathing.

Oriol makes his way to the kitchen.

'Tito,' Oriol says, forcing on the light. 'You should let me know when you're coming over.' He walks, hand outstretched. 'You gave me the fright of my life.'

'You smell like smoke.' Tito's hands stay firmly by his side.

'Cigarettes, they do that to you.' Oriol goes to the sink and washes his hands. 'Why didn't you wait for me to let you in?'

'What happened last night?' Tito asks.

'I don't know what you're talking about.'

'You're a fucking idiot.'

Oriol walks to the kitchen bar, pours himself and Tito a glass of water.

'Coffee?' Oriol asks.

'No.'

'Come on, Tito, you're scaring me.' Oriol laughs. 'It's not like you.'

'She was a nice girl.' Tito's eyes lock on Oriol.

'What are you talking about?'

'I don't like it,' Tito says.

'Like what, Tito? This is a joke, right?'

Tito lunges at Oriol, grabbing him by the neck and ramming Oriol into the stainless steel refrigerator behind him. 'I can do whatever the fuck I want with you,' Tito snarls. Oriol's face puckers, and turns red. Tito spits. 'I own you, asshole. I own your career. Your entire fucking operation.'

Oriol makes the desperate whining sound of a dog in pain.

'She's dead, Oriol.'

Oriol loses the strength in his body.

'What?' he wheezes.

'You were there. You let her go.'

Oriol squirms, grasping for breath.

With his free hand, Tito rams Oriol in the gut, his fist bunched into a bullet. Oriol chokes hard as the air shoots out of his body, his head smacks against the steel. 'That's for leaving her behind. Now –' Tito leans into Oriol's ear, then punches him again in the gut, sending Oriol's head into the stainless steel door. 'How could you leave her behind?' He punches Oriol again. 'My Natalia? You were there, you could have stopped it from happening.'

Oriol's shoulders crack against the stainless steel.

'I want to know what happened, Oriol. Why she was there. Who she was with. I want to know why you left her there.' Tito stands back from Oriol, watching the actor slump against the metal door of the refrigerator.

Witnesses describe the encounter in the members' club in Plaça Reial, with its colonnades and mustard-yellow paint and brown shutters and lanterns by Gaudí. Look closely at his work and you will see the omens. Serpents climbing towards the light, blue tails entangled about throats of winged metal. The famous nightclubs are here: Sidecar, Karma, Jamboree. You can dance your heart out. Leave your Vespa parked outside or come with stragglers falling over each other, arm in arm and singing.

Fabregat used to love the area when he was younger. In the summer the square is full of encounters: students lounging around bollards, tourists red-skinned and fresh from the beach, salt-haired and sticky, rubbing against each other in the half-light. The foreigners who flock to the palm-filled square, with its shaded cafés and outdoor tables, will feel that they have entered a pervasive Mediterranean sensuality worth every penny of their airfare or bus ticket or hostel bed. People's cameras are stolen, their wallets and, in the later hours of the night, their sense of dignity. But love is also born here, exaltations and warm kisses drifting up from the square to fill the palm fronds.

It was in this environment that a young man approached a famous and remarkably beautiful woman on the second-floor bar hidden behind shuttered windows in an east-facing corner of the square. The general feeling of the public that observed them was that the young man had no right to be speaking to the woman and that their encounter was furtive and private.

'It had the look of *mala suerte*,' the barman said.

Bad luck.

'I think he spoke to her first.'

But others in the crowd contradicted him.

'She seemed to be expecting him.'

'Expecting him? Was she frightened?' Fabregat asked the witnesses.

No, they said.

Unanimously.

Everybody cross-examined.

No.

She did not seem afraid.

She seemed confident.

In control.

'Sad. She was sad,' said one young woman with a piercing in her nose. Perhaps 'sad' was another word for frightened?

No. Not that either. The crowd agreed that, were it not for her beauty and that flavour of familiarity which afflicts the famous, no one would have noticed them. But there she was, the face of the moment: Natalia Hernández.

Speaking to a surly young man who had no right to be speaking to her, and something deep – something uncomfortable – passed between them. So that people *noticed*. And what they noticed seemed to be an exchange of packets. Of money? Of drugs? And also a flirtation no one could understand or overhear. But when the Beautiful Actress kissed the Stranger, everybody *noticed*. Everyone in that crowd could remember that precise moment, because they were watching a famous face with curiosity, as they drank *cervesas* and *cañas* at two in the morning on the night of Sant Joan, and felt rather pleased with themselves that an actress had chosen to frequent the same bar as they did and that their taste was so precise, so *on the pulse!* The crowd remembered the dancing and the talking that happened near the window, and they remembered the moment the actress left the bar with that Surly Young Man.

'Around three thirty . . . maybe?'

'I'd put it closer to four . . .'

And they described him well.

'He looked like a wraith.'

'An addict.'

'A hot mess.'

His clothes were dirty. His shirt was torn at the collar, hanging open on his chest.

'He had hair on the back of his hands.'

'He was ugly as a dog.'

This was unkind – Fabregat does not think Adrià or dogs are ugly.

'I saw her drink with him. Very happy. Beautiful.'

The bartender's face crumpled. Hair cut close to his ears, arms covered in ornate ink – the Virgin of Guadalupe, a dancing skeleton, a rosary. The bartender is thin and long and lean. No older than twenty-five.

'*No lo puedo creer.*' *I can't believe it.*

Sancho the doorman stands with his hands in his pockets, looking sour. He is rotund in the classic sense, with a belly that bulges over his belt in a slight, wobbling curl – but strong: upper body well-extended before the mirrors of his home, weights in each hand, biceps balanced.

'They came out to drink a few times at the back – both of them ... He offered me a cigarette – they were happy – early on – *bailando – bailando*, dancing – *o sea* – Yeah. Just there, both of them. I smoked with them, before they went back in – don't usually do that, but I mean ... Natalia Hernández – Well, I just said yes. Because she was there with – *Sí tío* – *Sí! Sí!*'

The Cleaner of the Bathrooms pitches in a confirmation.

'She went into the bathroom to put mascara on. She was a little drunk. But nothing else. No funny business in the toilets. Clean – yeah – from what I saw. Some kid? Yeah, I came up and saw him. Black hair – beard – not a regular. New face here.'

Smacks lips. 'Cute. He was cute. *Pero loco.*' The cleaner has skin that flakes like chalk. Too much foundation.

'*Ay, macho* – spend enough time working down here and you can see the crazy in their eyes.'

More mundane details follow.

'He was wearing grubby Converse.'

'He stank of sweat and marijuana.'

Other adjectives spilt forth.

Shifty, uncomfortable, haggard, harried . . . and then the crueller names.

Hijo de puta. Asesino. Diablo. Cabrón. Monstro.

At 8 a.m. on the Feast Day of Sant Joan, the youthful fury that greets de la Fuente at the door to Adrià Sorra's apartment is not what that good fellow had expected. He coughs loudly, rights his stance, moves his chest forward, and states, clear and concise as possible:

'*Policia! Sergeant de la Fuente.* Can you please confirm that this is the residence of Sr Adrià Daedalus Sorra? Señorita . . . ?' De la Fuente's confidence wilts under the eyes of an irate woman.

'Sharp. Emily Sharp.'

The policemen and forensic specialists congregate behind de la Fuente expectantly. Can it be that de la Fuente has lost his nerve? But de la Fuente is made of stronger stuff than that. He rights himself, continues, stepping further into the hallway; the squad fans out around him.

'Have you been in contact with Sr Sorra in the last twenty-four hours?' De la Fuente holds Emily's gaze.

'No.'

Unconvincing. De la Fuente twitches. His team moves further into the apartment. If he's there, they'll want to get him fast – if he's asleep in his bed with his knife – they'll grab him. *Keep her distracted.*

He clears his throat again, sticking his chest further into the air.

'Sr Adrià Sorra. Is he here?'

'No,' the American says, trying to hide her increasing annoyance. 'No, he is not here.'

'But this is his residence?'

'Yes.'

'And, Miss . . . you are his . . .' De la Fuente's bald forehead wrinkles into lewd suggestions. Emily switches deftly to Catalan. Disgust at the idea evident.

'Absolutely not,' Emily says. 'I live with his sister too – we all live together. The apartment is theirs.'

An American Catalanista! And an attractive one at that! De la Fuente's resolve softens. *Or a murderer's accomplice. Pull yourself together, man!*

'When was the last time you saw Sr Sorra?'

'I spent the weekend with him and his family.'

'Where did you see him last?'

'At the Girona train station. We left him there to catch the train back to Barcelona Sunday morning.'

'Two days ago?'

'Yes.' She falters.

'What time?'

'Around eleven.'

'And you saw Sr Sorra when you arrived home?'

'No. He can't get in at the moment . . .' Emily stops herself.

'What do you mean by that, Miss Sharp?'

She looks down at her feet.

'He lost his keys.'

'You didn't let him up?'

Emily shakes her head.

De la Fuente's eyes rest on the honey-coloured interior door.

'You've had a forced entry here.' He points to the shattered glass by the handle.

'Adrià broke it four days ago.'

'Is he very violent, Miss Sharp?'

'No . . . well . . . Yes. He has been lately.'

'Perfectly understandable, Miss Sharp. Is Mr Sorra's sister here?'

'No. She is still with her family. In Girona.'

'Thank you, Miss Sharp.' De la Fuente snaps into business: 'We will be conducting a search of your apartment and holding you for questioning. I apologize for any inconvenience.'

Sergeant de la Fuente is not impressed by what he discovers. Adrià's room is a slovenly dive. The place reeks. The windows to the outer balcony have been closed for days. Plates of food not cleared to the kitchen. On one wall, a collection of antique blades and a Swiss Army knife. A large double bed with unmade sheets, a battered desk pushed to the side and . . . revolting . . . De la Fuente shudders . . . the most obscene drawings covering the walls. Repeated portraits of a man's face with electric rods emerging from his nose. Wild eyes with many lashes. Bitter monsters and genitalia. Beside a shelf containing two university files, the boy has cut a message into the floral wallpaper paper: *La Topografía del Dolor*. 'The Topography of Pain'. His writing scattered, angry, a terrifying scrawl. Followed by a series of barely legible lines from the Communist Manifesto.

'*Jefe!*' Caporal Gómez calls. De la Fuente treads on the path the team have laid out. He crosses to the centre of the living room, and places his hand on Gómez's shoulder. 'Take a look at this.'

De la Fuente's jaw locks.

There, on the walls of the living room, across from a decapitated doll's head and strewn peacock feathers, is a cabinet which the sergeant has opened to reveal a dragon's hoard of vials and bottles and medical capsules, barbiturates – amobarbital, pentobarbital, then lithium and benzodiazepine, more innocuous ibuprofen and paracetamol, along with other names he does not recognize: Zyprexa, Lamictal, Symbyax.

A terrible cold settles in the marrow of de la Fuente's bones.

It is a journalist who inadvertently finds the last clues of Adrià Sorra's life. As the heat presses into his shoulders and the sand sneaks behind his heels, Pepe Calderon regrets the decision to humour his grandmother – a ninety-seven-year-old woman with a beach-front apartment who claimed she had seen a man drown in the sea that morning. Even at the water's edge it is sweltering – *hot hot hot* – so hot his curiosity wanes, dips back down to the blasé state of contentment which has become his norm. He approaches the boulders of the sea break.

Big porous black stones, the home of rats and the animals that hunt them. At the far end – twenty metres out into the sea – two fishermen have erected a parasol and look for crabs.

At first nothing.

His effort is lacklustre. He walks down to the sea for show, turning to wave at his grandmother, who should go back inside soon – it's too hot for her, much too hot for her – and then, as he turns to plod his way back up the wet sand he sees the shoes. A pair of men's Converse, size eleven, high tops, laces dirty. Underneath the first rocks of the sea wall, tucked into the side facing away from the shore so that they would be hidden initially from view. Pepe can feel the eyes of the old lady on him as he stoops to turn the shoes over. A pair of socks and a pair of shoes – and – Pepe's heart quickens. *That's blood on the grey rubber rim of the shoe, and blood on the left one's laces. Not in small quantities either.* That undeniably foul smell.

A profusion of human gore, dried and cracking in the sun.

Pepe stands still for a moment.

Then he calls Fabregat, speaking first to a receptionist at the police department, then the man in question.

'What?' Fabregat roars.

Pepe walks back to the end of the promenade.

'I know this sounds strange – but I've just found what may be your suspect's shoes. You should get someone down here now. And if you have any video surveillance out here – any shop-front footage, check it. You'll thank me for it if I'm right.'

And in the end? Fabregat sighs. The media took hold of the story. 'Natalia Hernández MURDERED,' the tabloids yowled. National papers splashed her body across the front page. From Valladolid to Zaragoza, old men discussed the matter over games of chess and wives gossiped with their hairdressers. *Have you heard what happened?* There was speculation and recrimination, analysis of personal habits and family life, lovers and career. Her fame and beauty cruelly eclipsed the other victims, relegating 'Las Rosas' to bit parts in a famous woman's saga. Long before the police announced Adrià Sorra's disappearance, a leading commentator remarked that the murderer of Natalia Hernández and Las Rosas was probably a fascist from the corrupt epicentre of Madrid bent on stirring political dissent in the city. In a time of financial stability, the arrival of the euro and the economic boom, tourism has been the main source of revenue in Barcelona and now some mad Madrileño was destroying Catalonia's image by giving it a reputation as a murderous enclave of occult serial killers. A psychological expert was interviewed who added that the killer's abandonment of mutilated female bodies in municipal spaces suggested a love of spectacle and that the killings were deliberately attention-seeking in motive. Inspector Manel Fabregat, when interviewed that morning, assured the public that the police were very close to finding the source of this violence.

In the evening papers, *El Corazón*'s Pepe Calderon commented on the sensational elements of the case – the means by which the bodies had consistently been attacked by a man obsessed by the art of calligraphy. Mothers kept their teenage daughters in that night, young women were encouraged to travel in groups, to avoid the dark corners of El Raval and not speak to strangers. *It was not a man that did this, it was el Diablo. The dark king. Un vampiro.* And so it continued, until the police initiated a manhunt, revealing that their primary suspect had flesh and bones and blood and was named Adrià Daedalus Sorra: last seen by his parents at eleven o'clock on the morning of the 22nd, at the train station in Girona. The boy had run away from his uncle en route to Barcelona, secretly getting out at Mataró, before switching trains and coming in to Barcelona on his own. Adrià Sorra spent the next twenty-four hours on the streets, at squat parties and nights out, and had not returned to his apartment on Passeig del Born. When an anonymous source came forward with Adrià's diary, the city raged. *He had fantasies of necrophilia and cannibalism. He wrote about the recent murders with the sexual appetite of a voyeur, considering them a philosophical problem – a symptom of modern societal dysfunction – and an apotheosis of his most illicit and secret desires: 'A Fucking Social Revolution'.*

His diary also contained innumerable erotic dreams involving his sister's friend and housemate, a young woman named Emily Sharp, who testified at length to Sorra's instability and proclivity to violence. He had no concrete alibis for the nights of the respective murders. He was a raver, his friends said, rarely slept; secretive, but fun – charismatic, a wild child, uncontrollable. Doctors came forward to comment on his illness, his therapy, his resistance to treatment: *an unfortunate character.* The specialist who had been dealing with him said that while she had never suspected he might realize his fantasies, she did not doubt that it was possible. *The patient is extremely unstable. He is obsessed with blood and organs and anarchism. I regret not having taken further measures to section him that weekend.* The city cried in consternation: Where is this killer? Where has he gone? And so it went on through the night and the next day and the next until Adrià Sorra's body washed up on the beach in Sitges and no one could ask him any questions any more.

At first Manel Fabregat ran with it. Despite his bouts of mania, Adrià Sorra was – according to his professors – genuinely brilliant. The Philosophy Department ranked him at the top of the class, but the boy suffered a kind of split personality. At university he presented the veneer of an erudite, high-achieving student; by night he became a hedonistic, sexual animal. Adrià Sorra seemed the perfect psychopath (*if that term even means anything*, Fabregat mutters darkly, *I'm not sure that it does*). Violent, unpleasant, he'd broken into his apartment on Friday, beaten the shit out of his sister . . . His parents – for that matter – were as aggressive as the boy must have been in life: they were proud, aloof, selfish, vile. Their son had been running wild for two weeks and his absentee jet-set parents hadn't seen fit to stop him, or help him, or treat him. It was a shit show, as far as Fabregat was concerned, an upper-class quagmire, with two snob architects defending their monster of a child. And yet, as their lawyers repeatedly pointed out, there were certain elements of the puzzle that didn't fit. Specifically the letters. Why send the letters? Adrià Sorra was no calligrapher. The boy could barely draw – in fact he suffered from dyspraxia, his hand-writing a nearly illegible scrawl. The university had supplied him with a volunteer who took his notes during lectures. Adrià typed his academic essays on an enormous desktop computer. The forensic handwriting analysts agreed: when they studied Sorra's diary in comparison to the parchment evidence, it was clear that the boy had not written the illuminated verses. Nor, for that matter, would he have been capable of cutting such intricate patterns onto the skin of his victims. *He doesn't know anything about the Middle Ages*, his mother hurled at the investigators, arguing that her son had a vivid imagination, and was chronically ill, that he had been blighted by poor timing. Faced with the honesty of the camera footage, the Sorras insisted that their son followed Natalia out of the club, and that he had stumbled on her body, and feeling on edge and suicidal himself, had carried her to the steps of the cathedral and then decided to end his own life in the sea. The argument that Adrià was the killer, however, was strengthened by the sudden abating of death that followed his disappearance. On Sant Joan's Day everything ended, Fabregat explains. There were no more corpses hanging from the branches of trees. The inferno that had opened up in the city closed without fanfare, leaving in its wake a long, empty silence.

'And the letters?' I ask.

'That psychotic pretence at a game?' Fabregat explodes. 'What do you think happened with those?'

Nothing.

'We were forced to leave them as an enigma, an unresolved itch. I couldn't make head nor fucking tail of them. But mystery breeds obsession. I'll be the first to admit that. It was like staring at a Sudoku problem with no apparent solution. Mind-bogglingly irritating.'

The inspector couldn't sleep at night. He couldn't work. He couldn't function. Worse, he began having dreams of a serpent. The very snake that formed the insignia on the letters unravelled itself and haunted him in his sleep. He dreamt that the snake wanted to speak to him, to lead him through a black thicket to a house where the ground was filled with bones of buried women. In one dream the snake appeared in pieces, cut into shreds, in another the snake was enormous, like a boa or a python, and reared on its tail and stretched above him. He felt unhinged. Derailed. Unable to focus. His superiors began to notice: *Fabregat is making mistakes. Fabregat has lost his cool.* The inspector developed shingles and night terrors. Stress riddled his body as the unsolved mystery consumed him. It was a block like no other. The inspector believed passionately that he had been asked to decipher a message that he could not understand. He felt played with. Teased. Manipulated. Frustration nearly destroyed him. That year, Fabregat became convinced that there was another malevolent force in the mix, a person or persons who had walked away from his investigation unscathed, but whose hands were as bloody as the devil's. Six months later Fabregat's nerves got the better of him and he took a sabbatical before returning to the force for the next ten years and retiring gently at the age of fifty-two. His schoolteacher wife supports the family now and Fabregat reads the paper at home.

In the brightly lit sunroom, sitting with me in the present day of this wintry January in Gràcia, ex-Inspector Fabregat deflates like a sad balloon. The breath sags in his chest. He stands and thanks me, ushering me out towards the evening, but stops me at the door.

'One more thing: it is personal conjecture, nothing more. Natalia's murder was different than the others. Brutal, fast, efficient. A cut to the artery below her ear. A slice to the lower muscle of her tongue. Very sharp blade, high speed, done in a matter of seconds. She must have been like a fucking water fountain, there was so much blood, it was all over the kid's clothes ... Who would do that? Kill that fast, and then take the body on a twenty-minute walk through town to the cathedral? Adrià may have been crazy – I'm sure he was crazy – but he wasn't able to kill like that – I don't think so ... We are hunting for an expert – you've got to understand that. A person or persons who had killed many times before. Everything about it was habitual. Rehearsed. Up until Natalia's death he never appeared on camera, left no trace of himself on victim or on site . . .'

'What are you saying?'

'That it doesn't match, you see – what serial murderer would carry his fourth victim to the steps of a cathedral and leave her there before drowning himself in the sea? I've thought about that for a decade. The man who killed those women was calculating. Terrifyingly so. He was not impulsive. Each step had its own logic. Where does Adrià Sorra fit in that? He was a pawn, a means of hiding someone. So our fucker could just evaporate away. No one believes me – *Ay Fabi*, they say – *Ostras, not again. Let it go, they're all ten years dead. Ghosts don't care.* But I can't shake my feelings. Natalia's death held its own message; one I never knew how to read. Each letter gave me a riddle and a body. But there was no letter for Natalia. Call it an old man's intuition – but I am convinced of this: Natalia knew him intimately. Bear that in mind, when you speak to people. The real murderer is out there. In this city. Tanning on the beach. Eating olives. Being a bastard. If I am right, he will be one of her crowd. He is someone she would have recognized, someone she trusted and then feared. Someone she knew.'

VI

HUNTING

Outside it is cold. Much colder than I had expected. I stroll down Passeig de Gràcia towards the shoreline, skirting the shadows along gridlocked, elegant fissures in the flesh of the Catalan capital, made with surgical precision across the chest of Barcelona.

In January, Barcelona feels lean. Stripped of leaves. Draped in slate clouds, and soft, rising mist. As I walk through the city, I see the metropolis shifting. *Scraped, and scraped again.*

Written and rewritten.

There is the Eixample, the new expansion, a victory of modernist foresight. Gaudí's house of bones, Casa Batlló. Aquamarine tiles undulating and bulbous. Once-fortified walls hide beneath ring roads. I cross the vast Plaça de Catalunya, carrying my papers. Soon Barcelona slips into medieval garb.

I make my way to the square of the cathedral where Natalia Hernández appeared at rest. *Her chest ornamented in blood.* For a moment I stare at the steps where they found her. They are vacant. Dark grey. Stub ends of cigarettes. A guard at the church door watches a group of gypsies asking for alms. I buy a clump of rosemary for good measure. Looping round Carrer del Bisbe, I skim over flagstones. *Left onto Pietat.* And then the secret many people walk past. The street of Paradise. Carrer del Paradis. Dark and narrowing. Sucking out the oxygen. I am looking for a porthole. *A domed slit in walls. Barred windows. The sign reads: 'Ajuntament de Barcelona. Temple Romà d'August. Local del Centre Excursionista de Catalunya.' Slip in beneath key stones, black beams overhead. Duck under low archway into open courtyard. Mustard-yellow paint and hanging window boxes. Follow the slight red arrow.* I pass a wrought-iron gate, descend worn steps. Enter a second tiny courtyard. Sea-green. Red brick at eye level.

There they are! Stretching to infinity. Three enormous Corinthian columns squeezed between sea-green walls. I have reached the pagan outpost and sit on the bench beneath them, arching my neck to look up. A French couple snap photographs. A man and woman in their sixties. They are with me for a while, very quiet and reverent. And then they slip away.

Taking my notebook out of my bag, I write out the verses of Fabregat's letters, placing the words in the order received. I will analyse it systematically. Slowly. *Now I am only beginning to think.* The collated words form an altar-shape, similar to Alexandrian poetry in the third century CE. *That is good.* An affirmation.

Find me in the Utterance of Birds (1)
You have called me (2)
Thrice Great (3)
Two-Faced (4)
Forked Tongue. (5)
No more riddles. (6)
I will teach you. (7)
Follow. Heed my words. (8)
Ancient Crimes. (9)
Count the grains of Sand (10)

And measure the Sea. (11)
Read the deaf-mute. (12)
And hear the voiceless. (13)
Serpentarius! (15)
One-who-is-arriving! (16)
Know this: (17)
Nine books of Leaves gave forth this rage of man (18)

Listening to Fabregat tell his story, I had to contain myself. To not reveal anything. Neither the shaking of my hands, which I hid beneath my thighs, nor the voices I heard on the air, clamouring like a flock of gulls. For me the words on his tongue conjured colours. The letter *A* groans like dried blood. Scabs at the corner of my vision. *R*: regal, dark, Tyrian purple. I hear *D* as indigo, and *I* makes a bright light, partially defined, like a clear haze, but pointed, sharp as a shaft of ice. *E*'s true colour is yellow. The sound delicate like the hind of a bee. My feelings are not sensible. They do not transfer to others. They cannot be easily explained. Ink breathes. The heart quickens. Voices make concrete shapes. Poem like a portal, opening my skin. I fight not to lose myself, to stop my eyes rolling back into my sockets and disappearing.

Lines 2–5 of Fabregat's anonymous letters were carbon copies of verses of the poem presented to me by Harold Bingley on that sleety London afternoon in October. They provide an anchor and a key, rooting his conundrum into familiar territory – the palimpsest poem Captain Charles Leopold Ruthven cut out of the book in 1829 that fell from the walls of the lightning-struck chapel three days ago.

There is a rich and compelling history of documents like our elusive palimpsest. Books pulled from strange places in strange conditions with unexpected and incalculable outcomes. In 1896 Carl Reinhardt purchased the Berlin Codex from an Egyptian dealer in Akhim, who told a convoluted story of discovery – the book was wrapped in feathers, and hidden in a wall. Reinhardt suspected it had been retrieved from a burial ground. The Berlin Codex contained four Gnostic scriptures: *The Act of Peter, The Gospel of Mary, The Secret Book of John* and *The Wisdom of Jesus Christ*. It was a groundbreaking find: a set of ancient manuscripts hidden from the world for two millennia.

In December 1945, following the end of World War Two, three Egyptian brothers rode out into the desert on their camels, tracking towards the red cliff Jabal al-Tarif, beyond the city of Nag Hammadi. The brothers intended to harvest a nitrate-rich fertilizer buried in the broken rocks at the base of the cliff. As they were digging beneath the boulders, they unearthed an ancient jar sealed with a bowl. In a fit of passion, the youngest smashed the jar open hoping for treasure – perhaps the death mask of a king, or a lapis lazuli scarab. Instead, he sent shards of disintegrating papyrus into the wind. Rather than gold, the youth stared down at thirteen bound codices. This trove is now known as the Nag Hammadi Scriptures, constituting one of the most significant historical discoveries of the twentieth century. In the 1970s a third collection of Egyptian codices appeared on the market – their origins deliberately obscured. Rumour has it that the volumes were stolen from a burial cave containing a family of skeletons and a set of books housed in a luminous limestone box. This box held four works: a Greek mathematical treatise, a Greek translation of the Jewish Exodus, Coptic New Testament letters of Paul, and the infamous Codex Tchacos, a third set of Gnostic papyrus fragments that vanished into the private market – only to be found sixteen years later, stowed away in a safe deposit box in Hicksville, New York.

When I was brought onto this case, Harold Bingley believed

that the Illuminatis Palimpsest — as it was first called — was part of a missing Gnostic work that belonged to the secret history pulled out of the cliffs above Nag Hammadi. Within the Nag Hammadi Scriptures there is a poem called 'Thunder', an anonymous first-person discourse of the Divine Feminine. The poem boldly announces the identity of the speaker in a series of stylized contradictions, redolent of Isis aretalogies and the Jewish Wisdom, Sophia. Thematic parallels between the Gnostic poem 'Thunder' and the subtext of the Illuminatus Palimpsest had made Harold Bingley and those around him ravenously hungry for more. The Illuminatus Palimpsest, if an authentic Gnostic offshoot, would be among the very few tracts preserved in the Greek language. But I was not satisfied with his assumption. The correlation did not ring true, and though Bingley disagreed with me at first, he came to understand that I harboured a powerful theory of my own.

I hear the words forming as I sit beneath the columns. A familiar voice. Like the cries of the siren, she sings to the root of me. Snakes round my mind, singing: *Nine books of Leaves gave forth this rage of man.* Confessions of a killer or clues to something deeper? Some dark old thing hidden deep inside?

The story begins like many others do. An old woman walks through the forest carrying a heavy burden. Tattered sack thrown over her shoulder. Despite her age she is strong, with the thick neck of a bull and the bulk of a wrestler; she hides her hair beneath a white cloth tucked over her ears, framing mannish cheeks and a gnarled nose like a dried head of garlic. In her cloth sack the old woman carries nine books, which she bears to the court of a king. Each scroll beautifully bound, made of sacred leaves sewn into volumes containing a verse history of the world. The letters of her book are Greek, for that is the language she comes from. When she arrives at the gates of the city the old woman demands to speak directly to the King. He grants her a single audience, whereupon the woman offers her books for a hefty sum and a promise of endless knowledge.

The King sneers at the crone.

'I would have nine books for nothing, for nothing is surely what they are worth.'

Calmly the old woman selects three scrolls from her sack, and with a flick of her magic wrist sets them alight in a golden blaze. The books of leaves crackle into embers.

She asks again:

'King, what will you give me for my books?'

'Nothing, crone. Kings do not read the mad ramblings of old women.'

The woman plucked another three volumes from her sack. 'You do not know what you lose.'

The King laughs in her face.

'The choice is yours,' she says, and with a second flick of her wrist three more volumes burst into flames.

A priest rushes forward in horror. 'King Tarquin!' he cries in agony. 'Do you not recognize the counsel of your ancestor Aeneas, who sought out the Sibyl at Cumae? Whatever verses the Madam has written on the leaves, she has arranged in Divine order; they remain unchanged in position and do not shift in their arrangement. King Tarquin, you have flung the door open in haste and disturbed the order of her scrolls! They are lost to us! Burnt into nothing!'

'It is true,' the old crone says to the King. 'You have spurned six books of knowledge of the ancients and lost potential futures of your empire, for I am the Sibyl of Cumae and I would have given you everything.'

King Tarquin begs her forgiveness. Thinking of the words of

Aeneas, he plies her with supplications: 'Do not give your verses to the scrolls and leaves, but sing the prophecy yourself!'

But the Sibyl does not sing to please, and asks that the King pay the full price for the three remaining Sibylline Books, so that he might learn a lesson from his pride.

Folklore states that the Sibylline Books or *Libri Sibyllini* came to Rome in this fashion, delivered in person by the Sibyl of Cumae. In the sixth century BCE, King Tarquin the Proud – Tarquinius Superbus, *poppy slayer* – ordered that the books of scroll prophecies be kept in the city for perpetuity. They were first held on the Capitoline Hill, fiercely guarded by two select priests. The number of priests given exclusive access to the Sibylline Books grew as Roman power expanded from two to ten in 367 BCE and later to fifteen men during the Republic, forming an elite college of priests known as the *Quimdecimviri Sacris Faciundis*. The lines of text in the sacred books were regarded as the highest of state secrets.

When the Sibylline Books burnt in the conflagration of the Temple of Jupiter Optimus Maximus in 83 BCE, the Romans sent out the *Quimdecimviri* to recover prophecies from other Sibyls, collating a new set of divine proclamations from sources at the furthest reach of empire. Emperor Augustus later ordered a purging of these texts, cutting out the words that did not suit his vision of the future. Nero consulted them following the fire of 64 CE, while Julian the Apostate would look to the books in 363 CE in the last year of his life and reign. General Stilicho finally destroyed the remnants of the *Libri Sibyllini* around 408 CE, in the violent build-up to the sacking of Rome. Today, the original Sibylline prophecies are entirely erased.

The Sibyl of Cumae, author of the *Libri Sibyllini*, was just one of many Sibyls circulating books in the ancient world. The Sibyl, as a symbol, as an icon, as a woman, presents a rich literary tradition, though very little of her work survives. While many confuse her with the Oracle at Delphi, the Sibyl was a lone operator, more freelance than institutional. A clairvoyant rather than a medium, she had more in common with the function of a prophet. Her soul was fundamentally different from an oracle: there were no limitations to her prophecy. No set days of the year for consultation, no clear affiliations with a single god, or priestess, or worship centres. The Sibyl alone crafted verses of original poetry as an autonomous author who addressed the gods directly. She placed herself in dialogue with divinity, but did not succumb to its advances. She did not wait to answer questions, posed by dignitaries of state or High Priests. She lived in the ancient forest, far removed from cities and pastoral meadows. Her home? The Neolithic cave. She saw what was going to happen, and she bothered to write it down, despite the fact that nobody had asked for her opinion. In books, no less. And in her own voice. Not as the god Apollo. Not as a vehicle or a vessel, but as a woman, speaking in the authoritative first person from the vantage point of her cave.

This insistence on sovereignty has implications on a stylistic level. The Sibyl claimed a primeval heritage, an eternal watchfulness, placing herself before Troy. Before the floods, the Sibyl asserted her hegemony using the distant, unknowable past. She was critically non-denominational, unbounded by nationality or creed. She claimed she had been watching always. That she predicted all this mess. That she had seen the future from the beginning, and written it down. She said sometimes that she was from the East. That she came from the mountains of Turkey, or the hills beyond Jerusalem, or the high walls of Babylon, that she was born deep inside Libya and Egypt. Always insisting that she knew something old and powerful. In Early Medieval European mythology, this came to mean that she knew the One True God. Her influence was such that she survived through the Dark Ages, becoming a powerful prophet of monotheism, the Pagan seer who gave the word of God to Rome and a vision of Christ to the Emperor Augustus, who left the first acrostic in her poetry and knew the voice of the Infinite in the desert. She wrote Pagan Sibylline Books and later Jewish and Christian Sibylline Oracles. The Sibyl became a layered manuscript, a bridge into the past, a palimpsest of her own.

My argument to Harold Bingley has been the following: that in *The Alchemical History of Things*, the alchemist Rex Illuminatus claims he met a tongueless woman in the mountains of Mallorca who had given him a secret book. If we are to believe that this woman was indeed a Sibyl, as Rex Illuminatus suggests, then the Illuminatus Palimpsest could in fact contain surviving Sibylline oracles lost in the ancient world.

I pause, looking down at Fabregat's lines of text. Would someone kill for a secret like this?

Yes. I grit my teeth.

Yes they have – and yes they will.

It is easy to forget how often people have died for books like these.

And you?

What will you do?

How far would you go to hold such a secret in the palm of your hand?

What would you give?

Your eyes? Your ears? Your nose? Your tongue?

VII

EVIDENCE FOR THE EXISTENCE OF THE SIBYL

from

The Alchemical History of Things
by Rex Illuminatus

The Sibyl carries on her person such a booke of parchement that answers all questions. She has called this booke the Song of the Sibyl but I calle it the Serpent or Serpentyne Papers on account of the texture of the leaves, which, when sewne together at the tip and tayl create a surface very much lyke that of the mottled scayles of a serpent. In the bynding of these leaves, the Sibyl has occupyed manie hours, forgyng meaning from the nonsensical patterns of prophecie, arrangyng words and phrases in algorithms that seemed to her lyke songs, and so the urge for order gave berth to poetry, reflectyng her secret desyre: the dream of the artist to understand the fleetyng rustle of oak leaves blowne about the floor of the cave. She has used the secrets of these leaves to give divinatorie instructions relatyng to my chartes, which I shifted to include her language, believyng that she has access to an inarticulate power which takes a shape of the serpent coyled in the base of her spyne, rumblyng and movyng in her throate when she speaks, makyng its voice heard despyte her stubbed tongue. Since takyng up her language, which I call the Utterrance of Birds[*], the accuracy of my

---

[*] Recall Fabregat's Letters, Verse 1: *Find me in the Utterance of Birds.* The answer to the riddle is clearly *Philomela*. The verse also references the founding of Zeus's oracle at Dodona. Two priestesses of the Egyptian temple at Thebes were abducted and abused by assailants. The priestesses changed

charts has expanded thryce-folde, and my alchymical experie-
ments have been bountiefullie enriched. To learne of the success
of my rosie gold, call for:

8 oz of Quicksilver

9 oz of Gold Filyngs (ground down into dust)

5 oz of Cyprian Copper

2 oz of Brass Filyngs

12 oz of clearable Alum and Calcantum

6 oz of Gold Orpiment

12 oz of Elidrium.

Mix the filyngs with the quicksilver to make a substance lyke a
waxie salve. Add the Elidrium and Orpiment, then the Efflorescence
of Copper – or Calcantum, the Alum and a pinch of Natron, which
I recommend you to dissolve into the intermix. When it has coag-
ulated nicelie, moon-earth will be once again requyred. Keep this
in a pelican, seven times rectifyed to make the burning water or
quintessence which I dailie consume. If the smell be wantyng when
you open it, put it in a bolts head, stopped up with wax and burrie
it in horses dung. This will warm it nicelie. There will emerge a
ruddie water, made of fyre and water. Separate the elements before
as with the water and ayre, so you have all four parts asunder.
Calcyne the earth and rectifie the fyre as you did with the
Quintessence and speak over it the words: O *Serpentarius feminina!**

into doves, the first travelling west into Africa, the second winging her way north to Greece where
she landed in the branches of the great oak at Dodona. As she sang more doves followed until a flock
of white birds roosted on all the branches of the tree. When the wind rustled through the leaves of
the oak, the birds channelled the divine breath of Zeus into coos and hums. They sang arias and told
long tales of the future. Local priestesses and augurs gathered from the villages to observe the
phenomena of the avian prophets. An Oracle was soon erected which rivalled that of the Delphic
Sanctuary. In the fifth century BCE Herodotus forwarded the theory that the prophetic language of
the doves had in fact been a metaphor used to describe the foreign tongue spoken by the fugitive
priestess of Thebes whose pained language resembled the aching call of the birds to local foresters.

* Fabregat's final letter echoes this line: '*Serpentarius! One-who-is-arriving!*'

Soror Mystica! Constellation in the sky! Philomela! Daughter of Asclepius! Your ears licked clean by the serpent Mater who took pitie on a tongueless mouth. Now you bare the stigma of foresight!

And the Secret of Secrets shall be yours.

VIII

FOUNDATION

Worry grips me. I hide from myself. A shadow of a woman seeking a shadow of a book. *You have no place here, and yet you have made the right decision.* Not long ago now. The knots turn in my stomach. Anxiety sets in. *Late November.* I practise thinking. Of the real. The unimagined. *Where had you been?* I play memories out in front of me – live through them.

Francesc and I walk in the mountains, he wearing sweater and green slacks, scarf unusually formal. The breeze is sharp and teases at his hair. *Look up!* he says, and I watch an osprey flit across the open sky, scattering a cloud of birds, hunting little yellow-breasted serin. Following the river back to Valldemossa, we talk softly. *Harold Bingley is coming for dinner. Fresh from London.* I clamber up rocks. *He will make his way up from the airport at Palma and we will sit outside on the veranda of our cottage. Dark red wine. Cured olives in sea-brine. Wrinkled tomatoes and sweet jasmine.* Tension building. *Bruised basil crumbled between fingers and rubbed into garlic. Charred meat. Baked almonds. Warm leek soup to salve parched throats. Bingley's eyes barely move from me. The man is not happy. I can tell. But then I wonder, is he ever happy? Does happiness spill into him in the library, or amidst the archives of the British Museum?*

The man is spectral. Skin sallow. Bare wire-rimmed spectacles perch on a wraith-like nose, enlarging little flaps for eyes. He wears a dark suit and a crisp shirt. The colours wash him out until he is almost nothing. Dust of grey hair about his ears intensifying the bald patch on his skull, making a shape like a tonsure. White flakes of scalp drop to his shoulders. He asks too many questions. And I have too few answers.

In the morning we form a small crowd. Francesc sits in the hard desk chair round the table. His assistant, two PhD students, the head of the Conservation Department and an adjunct professor join us for the discussion. Harold Bingley stands on the sidelines of the university conservation wing, adjacent to the Special Collections library. Arms crossed in front of his chest. Back to the wall. Eyes glued to my face. *What will my divination be?* Underneath the manuscript, categorized as MS 409, a large, grey pillow supports the book so that the spine will not break on the table. Two sister books sitting side by side. Roughly the same dimensions. *150 × 125 mm.* The first – MS 409 – was very old, decaying binding. Beech boards covered in sheepskin rinsed in water. The pages are of rough vellum, made of calf hides soaked in lime until the hairs come loose and are burnished away. The skin is left in the lime solution, then cleaned in running water and stretched between frames and left out in the sun to dry. The hides are beaten and pummelled with pumice, smoothed and stretched, dried under tension. The heft of parchment follows the bulk of a calf's body. Thicker at the neck and along the spine, thinner over the belly and stomach. These hides were rough, castaways, full of holes. *The cheapest quality.* The scribe had taken each calfskin and cut the parchment clean, folding each sheet in half, four consecutive times, to make repeated gatherings of sixteen leaves – thirty-two pages. *A book built to fit a woman's palm. Small enough to stow in a pouch or a purse. Small enough to hide.*

I open the book. Take in the contents. Each parchment skin has two sides, two colours. The facing page tan and rough, coarse where the hairs had sprouted and formed the glossy coat of the animal. The underside is whiter, smooth to the touch, where the skin had met muscle and flesh. The origami folds of a medieval book create an effect whereby white always faces white, and yellow always faces yellow. This makes for continuity on the double facing page. Traditionally, the first side to greet the reader would be the hair side, the rough yellow, opening up to reveal the neat smooth whiteness of the inner folia. The gathering would end again with the flesh side, matched to the second set of pages, until the full book of quires was bound. *Fur to fur. Flesh to flesh.*

I select a page relevant to Bingley's interest. Skin pockmarked with black flecks of hair follicles. Touch the waxy flesh side with my bare finger. *Best for applying minium. An earthy red pigment of roasted white lead.* A kind of alchemy. 'Come closer', I tell him. 'Lean in and breathe. Smell the stillness. The earth. The animal. The mercuric sulphide and lime.' The scent of a parchment book is unique, as are the feel and texture of the leaves. There is nothing in the world quite like it. Raised on hard graft, they are born to be sturdy. To survive careless hands and fading monasteries, to last for thousands of years.

Unless, of course, they are abused.

As in the case of the work before me.

I found MS 409 in an abandoned farmhouse in Artà, near the Ermita de Betlem on Mallorca. The Abbey Librarian helped me greatly in this venture, granting me access to the closed wings of the ruined farmhouse, where the greatest treasures often hide. I found the book, along with several others, in the storerooms of the granary. When I opened the parchment pages of this battered volume, my eyes lit on a minuscule colophon, a device used by medieval scribes to claim authorship. '*I, most miserable of mutes, have written this book to appease my ghosts.*' This colophon contained a seal of a seated, robed woman, holding a book in her left hand. Encircled by a serpent biting its tail. Bird singing on her right shoulder. *A nightingale.*

Originally the pages had been neatly scored. Ruled with grids of guide-lines and divided into two columns for the text. The prickings were made with a long fine-tipped knife, creating triangular divots along the binding side of the manuscript. The outer prickings have been trimmed. The inks used for the script were alternating black and red, iron gall and cinnabar. Black harvested from bulbous growths made by the gall-wasp in fresh buds of oak trees. I have held the dry oak apples in the palm of my hand and turned them over. They are light and hollow, filled with tannic acids. After the larvae of the wasp have chewed through the crust, the apples are knocked off the tree and pummelled into a thick pulp, before being mixed with rainwater over fire until a rich brown liquid forms. To this the scribe would have added ferrous sulphate, which turns the liquid from brown to black; and gum arabic, a thickening agent to prepare the ink. In the book, the illustrations had been gilded but they are hard to make out, because someone attacked the manuscript with malice. They slashed, burnt, crossed out, and hatch-marked until the text and pictures were almost entirely obscured. All but one miniature has been destroyed – a painting of an old man with a long white beard, speaking to a serpent sitting in a chair drawing a diagram on the sand with her tail. The diagram is fully formed, and the man and the snake analyse the contents of the serpent's chart. The serpent wears a crown, and the old man is clearly an alchemist, judging by his cloak and the tools tied to his belt buckle and strewn on the ground around him. Behind them? A cave with a small scriptorium. Around the pair cluster other animals, birds, a nightingale singing on the branch, two deer, a wolf and a cat. They are discussing three concentric circles. An alphabet now overly familiar. Nine letters, each initial boldly drawn by the serpent's tail in the sand. The letters also appear in the air around the serpent. Hanging from trees, in the beak of a bird. *BCDEFGHIK*. Beneath this an angry hand has scrawled in Latin:

THE HERETIC REX ILLUMINATUS TEACHES SATAN'S LANGUAGE TO THE SERPENT PHILOMELA.

The same hand has sliced through the picture with a knife, before stopping short of destroying everything. Bingley and I both know that the anonymous censor must have left this image as a warning, to show others what to look for.

'And the surviving text?' Bingley asks. 'Have we been able to glean anything?' I read the words aloud to the room:

> *Some have even gone so far as to mutter that the man who took my tongue should have taken my hands also. I agree that this would have been more sensible if his intention was to make me truly mute, but I have reflected on this often. He, being a man, did not think me capable of letters, and so did not think to take my hands. Now that I have proven myself in Letters, other men grow nervous. Perhaps I will name him? Perhaps I will utter what he did? They do not know that I cannot. Of all the things I cannot do, I cannot name him. In that moment he bewitched me. I did not bewitch him. He stole a piece of my flesh, and controls it cruelly. It seems that a woman without a tongue is just as powerful as one with one – perhaps even more so – as she does not have to waste time talking, and can spend most of her time thinking. This is a quandary for them, for it proves once again that a thinking woman is even worse than a speaking one. For the thinking woman came into the universe the most dangerous, the most hated of creatures, the worst enemy of*

man, for she desired something more than the immediate garden, something greater than the embrace of her father, and it was that impulse for knowledge, that terrible dirty impulse, that brought the human race into contact with Sin, and made us foul, and miserable and cruel, and so verily they insist that a thinking woman is worst of all, and for that they hate me and come after me and call me a great many names. In anger I have called these men the assassins of words, as they stamp daily on allusion and metaphor and flights of fancy, hunting dactyls and strophes into extinction. They are literalists in the most perverse sense. When I write in my poetry that I have dreamt of flying as a bird, they interpret me literally and refuse to listen to the explanation that in deciding to write about the sensation of flight, I extrapolated this into a real experience of flying, taking the perspective of the imagined bird as my own. But I am not a bird and have never flown and will never fly.

They do not see the sadness in this.

When we have finished discussing, I move to the adjacent table. A second grey pillow beneath a sister volume. A string of soft beads resting at the book's side, waiting to hold the pages gently apart.

'Here we have a book made with traditional pigments on membrane, vellum gatherings,' I say.

A flicker of something like displeasure passes across Bingley's face.

'There are traces of animal blood and chemical liquids on the paper, along with some unusual plant matter. Ink severely water damaged. Washed repeatedly.'

In the medieval period some sacred books were drenched with water, so that the ink would run and pool into a basin, which was then drunk by an adept or used as the base ingredient for a curse or spell.

'Office – ornamental. Text accordingly sized, the width of the margins delicate, the ruling made with a wooden stylus, the writing lines pricked through with a fine awl – a thin needle, handmade – you can see the pricks are uneven, which gives it a flavour of authenticity. Initials –' I point to the large single letters that start chapters and paragraphs – 'are historiated – built of double strokes that exaggerate the contrast of thick and thin marks – each initial illustrates a figure from the life of Rex Illuminatus. Roman characters with a Gothic flare – more reminiscent of the thirteenth-century scribes than the later medieval. They are bound tightly together. The author has avoided the fattened vulgarized, broad capitals of heavy rotunda. The pen deft – ten strokes in the *A*, outlined first, and then weighted in – quietly creative choices – the calligrapher is playing stylistic games. Time and money were not constraints.' I pause.

'Give it to me.'

Bingley takes the book in thin, birdlike hands, and turns it mincingly. He holds it roughly by the cover, letting the pages hang down to the floor.

'Rubbish. You have brought me rubbish.' His voice curdles.

'We break,' he pronounces to the room. 'Ten minutes. No – not you, Miss Verco. I would have a word with you here.'

Francesc shoots me a look as he disappears through the door.

Hold your ground. Don't worry.

'Where did you get this?' Bingley asks once the room has cleared of listeners.

'A private sale.'

The frown across his lips heavy as a funeral.

'Why didn't you come to me first?' His hand rests threateningly on the cover of the book.

I can feel the shaking begin in my knees.

'This is a forgery, is it not?'

'I—'

'This is a fake, Anna, a beautiful fake, but a fake nonetheless. Those should have been the first words out of your mouth. Unless you couldn't tell?'

His eyes narrow.

'Knowing your abilities, I highly doubt this is the case.'

My stomach churns.

'You acquired this without asking. Am I right?'

'I didn't think—'

'Precisely. We have protocols in place for a reason. I'm sure you would not object to repaying the cost of the manuscript, wasted as it must have been, from your salary.'

'I didn't waste anything.'

Bingley's upper lip twitches. 'Nothing at all? Not even my time?'

'The manuscript was given to me.'

He looks at me incredulously.

'Given to you?'

'It's on loan.' Pride burns behind my eyes, threatening to push out hot tears. 'Our team has already tracked down the source and is getting into litigation – they were trying to sell the work as an original volume from the 1390s . . .' I cannot look at his face. 'The real value didn't appear until I ran a check against other documents in our database for possible leads—'

'Remind me again. What are we looking for?' he interrupts.

'A palimpsest, bound into a Book of Hours.'

'Which this is not.'

'No.'

'And how long have you been looking?'

The shame hangs around my neck like a noose.

Bingley examines his fingernails. 'You promised me six months and it's been two years. It must be very nice to be paid to think.

But there is a price on this service, a cost which you owe me.' His mouth purses in displeasure. The red burns brighter on my cheeks. 'For the moment, I will give you the benefit of the doubt. Why?' He points to the book. 'You have five minutes to answer.'

I struggle to keep my temper down. *Let the work speak for itself. Open the book. Stay silent.* A large miniature of a nude woman. A rainbow serpent curls round her throat, broad as a python, her Gordian knot, vermilion-spotted, gold, green and blue, covering the woman's breast and private parts in snake hide. Crimson rings interweaved with silver moons. The woman steps from an open book, cupped like a shell beneath her feet. One outstretched hand offers a golden fig leaf. The eyes of her serpent hungry, combative. On the facing page, a second image, clearly alchemical. A glass amphora heated over a fire, suspended from a tree at the centre of a city. Inside the glass amphora, clouds of different colours – swollen red, lamp black, titanium white – and what appears to be a severed bifid tongue, resting alone at the heart of the jar. In the branches of the tree the illustrator had suspended the words: *El meu coll estava serp, però les paraules jo vaig parlar* . . . *My throat was serpent, but the words I spoke* . . . My heart beats faster as Bingley's eyes consume the black ink.

'Who wrote this?' Bingley whispers.

'A living ghost,' I say, drawing his attention to the colophon at the end of the quire. A woman, encircled by the golden Ouroboros. The nightingale perched close to her ear. A book in her left hand. Bingley breathes a low, little whistle.

'The signatures on both works are identical.'

Bingley's gaze sharpens.

'Provenance?' he asks.

'Barcelona.'

'Year?'

'1995.'

'And what do you make of it?'

'The colophon is a mark of a bloodline or a family name rather than an individual.'

He nods.

'And the author?'

'Anonymous.' I run through the details faster. 'But we have deduced who she is through plays on words. Games. She begins her poem with the line *El meu coll estava serp* – my throat was serpent. Later –' I turn the page and point – 'she calls herself a Snake. Then the Latin *mulier habens pythonem* – a woman having a familiar spirit – and –' I flipped through to a second marked page. 'Here . . . *una pitonissa*. A pythoness. Bringing to mind the Witch of Endor – an *engastrimyth* in Greek translations of the Hebrew Bible, but in the Latin Vulgate is labelled a *mulier habens pythonem* . . .'

'And the Pythia at Delphi . . .' he says softly.

I do not need to explain to Bingley that according to the myths, Apollo took the Oracle at Delphi from a coiling *drakaina* – a dragon snake whom the god transfixed with a thousand arrows. In Greek Homeric verse, the serpent is female: the terrible, vindictive daughter of the Earth goddess Gaia whose blood rotted into the Castalian spring, infusing the divine vapours with her essence. The word python, meaning rot, became a name for Apollo, Pythian, slayer of the serpent, which in turn became the name of his Oracle – the Pythia at Delphi.

I continue, adding that when the author identified herself as a Nightingale (*disambiguation: Philomela*) and a Python, she allied herself with a history of rhetorical contortion. Today the French *pythonisse* translates into English as witch, while sibylline comes into colloquial usage in much the same way that we might say cryptic or enigmatic. In Catalan, *pitonissa* means fortune-teller, while in Italian, the word resonates with Pythoness and Pythia, but also connotes *sibilla* (sibyl), *sacerdotessa* (priestess) and *strega* (witch). One can see the same shifts in the Greek word *daemon* – meaning guide, lesser deity, divine power, demigod. Now our demon.

'And . . . ?' he asks. 'Have you reached any conclusion?'

'The author also refers to herself as a whisperer.' I direct Bingley's attention to a subsequent note. 'My preferred translation of the word "witch" emerges from Exodus, taken from the Hebrew *kashaph* which itself comes from the root "to whisper". Scholars often interpret this as referring to witchcraft in the act of "whispering a spell . . ." but I read this to mean whispering in the sense of hiding.' I pause. 'It is this interpretation of witch which led me directly to the book's author.'

A catlike smile creeps over Bingley's pallid features.

'An identical colophon has been used by an artist whose modern books are housed at the University of Barcelona – a calligrapher and restorer, educated in the 1960s in Barcelona before working in the theatre as a set designer. This author had hidden her name in a fairly rudimentary cipher, formed by the first letters of the titles for the initial six chapters. Such that if you were an initiate, and knew the author of the text and her previous materials, you could translate the hidden acrostics in the document—'

'And you believe she had access to the Illuminatus Palimpsest?' he asks.

'That is what I am suggesting.'

'Name?'

'Cristina Rossinyol.'

'Have we made direct contact?'

'I can't. She died. Nearly twenty years ago.'

'Ah,' Bingley says. 'Pity that.' He thinks long and hard for a while.

'Any children? Any survivors?'

The first newspaper articles refer darkly to the case as a local tragedy. In a flowery retrospective printed in *La Vanguardia*, the writer
mentions '*that with a stroke of luck and a generous acquisition by the
Special Collections Department of the University of Barcelona, Cristina
Rossinyol's gold-bound codices have found a home in the libraries of our
city, ensuring the final resting place of one of Catalonia's greatest contemporary calligraphers and illuminators*'. A series of images, scanned
photographs, arrive from the University of Barcelona's collection.
The first is of Cristina as a young woman, standing in overalls, in
what looks to be a working studio, in front of a series of statues, cast
in the Roman style. She hovers between two men, a dark bearded
man with spectacles and a long face who looks to be in his mid-thirties and another, light-haired taller man in his later twenties. They
both have their arms around her shoulders. The men wear loose
jeans and T-shirts, arms exposed, with paint stains on their trousers.
Cristina's face is full. A lilt to her smile. She has long black hair swept
off her forehead, and thick curls. Her nose freckled, her cheeks firm,
her mouth smiling broadly. Her eyes are striking – a deep, emerald
green – her face eerily familiar – as if I had seen her somewhere
before – in passing on a street or sitting in the little café below my
open windows. Even behind the smiles, there is something radical
about Rossinyol's body language in the old photographs. All three
grin at the camera. The caption below reads:'1975. Back stage at the
New Theatre. Àngel Villafranca, Cristina Rossinyol and Joaquim
Vidal Hernández commence work on their first production.' The
next two pictures come from archives at *La Vanguardia*. The first
published by the paper after the accident in 1996.

Cristina Rossinyol died in a car accident off the pass to Sant
Cugat, along with her husband and two youngest children aged six
and eight. The date of the accident: 21 February 1996. The road
was a dangerous route, and they had driven it in inclement weather,
unseasonably cold for Barcelona. It was conceivable that they had

skidded off the road, due to a thin layer of black ice that had formed in the morning, but judging by the damage to the side of the car that had not hit the ground, the car had been thrown over the edge of the road by a hard impact, probably from another vehicle. Traces of paint and metal on the shattered car later proved that it had likely been a large vehicle, painted black. The mountain highway was known for its reckless drivers, kids returning home after a wild night out in Barcelona, and when no evidence could point to a potential motive, the police closed the case on the basis that it was the kind of hit and run typical of drunk driving on the BP-1417.

There is a shot of Cristina's family attached to her obituary.

Mother holding the youngest children's hands, a little boy and girl.

A teenage daughter stands in the middle, with a short pageboy haircut, almost masculine in her features, her father to her left side, in front of the entrances to the Theatre of National Liberation, a poster for Cristina's final show behind them.

To have lost a family so young.

There she is. Standing beside her mother.

Natalia Hernández. Just fifteen.

Old enough to hide something.

A

From my seat on the cold marble step in Barcelona I watch a mouse run out from the corner of the courtyard, wrinkling its nose. Rump bouncing along the bricks at the base of a Corinthian column. The mouse is small and grey with a long tail and a fat bottom. He is mousing for crumbs. Cautious but intrepid. *Much braver than I am.* I can feel the tremor in my hands. Nerves build. *Have I made a mistake? Should I be here at all?*

I hear the spur again: 'It is not that you aren't performing – no, no, I would never suggest that – it is simply that the work is not, perhaps, as swift as one would wish.'

Bingley's teeth were yellow. Stained with tea.

'Sloth, my dear, is a technical term. We are experiencing a great deal of sloth. Now I do realize that your health has been an issue ... but *speed* is that intangible essence which defines the success of Picatrix. It is the essence we trade in. Precision and efficiency lead to results.' He smiled, that spectre of a man, he had smiled and said: 'My dear girl, no one, no matter how clever, is indispensable. It is one of the great fallacies of life to assume we are irreplaceable.

'I am not interested in amassing scraps. These pieces you have brought me are good – in fact they are excellent – I would not deny that, but they have *no true value*. Let us not forget the grail we are seeking. You have been employed to find one thing and one thing only. The next time I see you I wish to be presented with a *palimpsest*. In the instance that this fails to occur ...' His lisp intensified. 'I am afraid we may need to rethink the terms of our agreement.'

I stand in the cool beneath the columns. Dust off my knees. The sky enclosed by the empty courtyard. The mouse has disappeared into the roots of what was once *Colonia Julia Augusta Faventia Paterna* in honour of the Emperor Augustus. *Barcino. Barca Nona. Barkeno.* These stones form her reliquary. Amongst Corinthian folds I catch evidence of living ghosts. Pieces of antiquity poke out of street corners. Sleep underground. Fragments hurry to the surface. I run over Fabregat's story. *What do you see in the carved symbols on the body of a sixteen-year-old girl hanging from a jacaranda tree?*

The answer comes back cold.

In the nine-letter alphabet grafted on to Rosario swaying beneath a lamp post?

In the circle of blood round the navel of Roseanne in the copse below Tibidabo?

I see a trail of breadcrumbs.

Linking me uncomfortably to the past.

BOOK THE SECOND

Relic Box

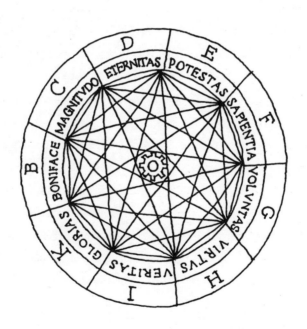

We have employed an alphabet in this Art so that it can be used to make figures, as well as to mix principles and rules for the purpose of investigating the truth. For, as a result of any one letter having many meanings, the intellect becomes more general in its reception of the things signified, as well as in acquiring knowledge. And this alphabet must be learnt by heart, for otherwise the artist will not be able to make proper use of this Art.

Ramon Llull, from his *Ars Brevis*

1308 CE

When you have landed and come to the city of Cumae and the sacred lakes of Avernus, among their sounding forests, there deep in a cave in the rock, you will see a virgin priestess foretelling the future in prophetic frenzy by writing signs and names on leaves. After she has written her prophecies on these leaves, she seals them all up in her cave where they stay in their appointed order. But the leaves are so light that when the door turns in its sockets the slightest breath of wind dislodges them. The draught from the door throws them into confusion and the priestess never makes it her concern to catch them as they flutter round her rocky cave and put them back in order or join up the prophecies. So men depart without receiving advice and are disappointed in the house of the Sibyl.

Virgil, *The Aeneid*

29–19 BCE

I

THE CORRESPONDENCE OF LLEWELLYN SITWELL

Vol. 1

1 November 1851, Barcelona

Dear Heart,

Your letter has arrived at long last and I am grateful! So grateful! My heart lifted and swollen on the nectar of your love, though you rebuff me – I imagined you in fields and I was jealous of your lace, for I longed to see your throat, to reach out and kiss you! Though I write from darkness, I write more honestly for it, and this is a comfort to me, that you might hold the record of my thoughts, in case of my devastation. You cannot have known my troubles, but I see your face and your features like the orb of good faith and take comfort in the thought of our Love! Love, which sent me from your side to seek my Fortune, now requires that I write these truths to you! That you might keep my testament alive. There is no finer torture than my fear that I might not return to you! No greater fire! Katherine, you have not written directly of Love, you are too discreet for that, but I have intuited it in the use of such words as Self-denying, and Friendship – I am more than Brother or Lover, more than Friend! I am your devoted servant, your caged poet, your lovesick amalgam of a man, and though you have pushed me from your side – do not doubt that I will return to your bosom, twice as amorous! Return I will! A richer and more loving disciple, for if you wait for me – my God, Katherine, you will have me till my dying day for there is no stronger draught than the Love which I consumed for you this summer! I know our Friendship is short and my departure from England does not inspire confidence. I know men are fickle beasts, that we are weak upon temptation – but I had sworn off Love until I met you. How I am repentant now – though not ungrateful. For my selfishness and disinterest in the fairer sex has only left me more susceptible to your remarkable powers – I am transformed! Religion which once eschewed me I more fully understand – for my religion is now Love! Love of you! You have written in your letter last that I must not think of you as an ideal, but only as a weak woman, eternally struggling for the light. You have written: 'You must not think me better than I am.' Katherine, you are perfection in your imperfections (if indeed you have any). You are an Angel! You are the air I breathe! And no! It is not dreadfully selfish of you at all to accept my Love. It is enlightened! It is truth! You have asked me to be your confidant in Letters; I willingly accept, if you shall be a confidante in mine. I would like to write you near daily of my exploits, to keep you beside me and in my thoughts through writing. You shall be as a constant companion, Kitty Markham! My adviser and my Friend!

This morning at nine o'clock I was met at Barcelona port by a sallow envoy of Captain Charles Leopold Ruthven, a lean man with a face like a hawk and a malevolent disposition who seemed to be of some strange northern extraction; refusing me his name, I christened him Brass Buckle – his hands (rough and broad) suggested that the fellow had come from the mountains and never eased into the civil-living of the city. Brass Buckle was dressed in luxury for a man of his station, with gold cuffs and a great beaver-trimmed coat; his collar a bright, luminescent gold, his hair short beneath a broad cap. This man accosted me tersely – striding across the melee of travellers to take my luggage with an aggressive nod before pointing to the carriage that awaited me. I had taken measures to send Ruthven my likeness from London, but it surprised me that this alien figure should intuit my features. I resisted mounting Brass Buckle's carriage in the instance that his was an elaborate scheme to hoodwink me of my belongings – I have prepared myself for these European dishonesties by reading the books you lent me – paying particular attention to the depravities of St Irvyne cautioning wisely against corrupt Rosicrucians and Alchemists (of which I am sure there are many).

The servant explained in broken English that Ruthven had instructed him as to my bearing and the clothing I had agreed to wear as a symbol of our friendship: a silk necktie sent to me in London by post. I also wore my frock coat and a wide brown-rimmed hat. The necktie is a disagreeable colour, mauve (I prefer the fashionable black), but having been warned of Ruthven's eccentricities I did as I was told, and the meeting was, in the end, smooth. I agreed to be taken by the servant and his driver to the house of this elusive scholar, bumped and buffeted by a gold-encrusted carriage that wound its way through a marvellous array of crowded streets with Gothic overtones. In short time I arrived at a square marked by the emergence of a large pine spreading its prodigious bows over a covered market and the black face of an imposing church. Across from the church I noted an impressive façade in which (I assumed as the carriage approached) was the address of our Ruthven. I was correct. The carriage dropped me at his door, the servant taking my cases from the driver before bustling me into the house. The gilded door opened for a second, I slipped through. The portcullis was slammed and bolted by the servant behind me. The abruptness of this arrival startled me, as did my lavish environs. The servant uttered a series of fragmented words (Brass Buckle later proved to be alone in his duties), leading me through a series of rooms to the second floor of the building. It should be noted that Ruthven is by all accounts very rich, having made his fortune by the discovery of a hidden mass of gold many years ago while a naval man in Peru, gold he invested wisely in East Indian ventures. I can attest to the truth of these London rumours by the display of opulence in his home. The floors of the home are marble, arranged in a criss-crossing geometric pattern of interlocking black and white slabs. The walls, when not inlaid with stained teak, are covered in the most delicate silk, ornamented with birds and fruit. The furniture is primarily Indian woodwork, the entry hall decorated with swords, pistols and scimitars arranged in the shape of a star. Greek columns and statues intermingle with vast urns from the Chinese Empire. Books are thrown everywhere, piles of paper sit in the corners, the windows are firmly shuttered and very little light enters the bowels of this establishment. The whole sensation is one of confusion and isolation within the luscious comfort of an opium den. After abandoning the service of the Queen (and the uncovering of gold) Ruthven devoted his career to more adventurous pursuits, and the fruits of these travels decorate his home. He is a career explorer, an adventuring type – you know his name from the excavation of the tombs at Abu Simbel – previous to his deployment in Peru! And his subsequent work with Monsieur Jean-François Champollion, translator of the Rosetta Stone. Not satisfied with mastering the language of the ancients and seeking out their bounty, Ruthven has now immersed himself in the study of my own passion, the Catalan mystic Rex Illuminatus and his Muslim counterparts in the twelfth and thirteenth centuries, in the hopes that they will expand his understanding of Alchemy, the minting of divine gold being his current inclination! The resulting treasures of this journey of many wonders: pages of illumined manuscripts in gilt frames, curiosities from the Empire – Indian goddesses and Sanskrit passages, portraits of Ruthven with forgotten Mughals and elephants, Chinese dogs on every fireplace, the floors decorated with Persian carpets and incense burning on the walls. The black-coated servant led me to a sitting room whereupon Ruthven emerged from his chair.

'Sitwell,' he said. 'I trust you have journeyed safely?'

Ruthven looked me up and down before extending his hand to introduce himself. He then nodded at his servant who brought brandy. The sitting room was lit by gas lamps and a single Russian candelabrum on the mantelpiece. The blinds of the windows were drawn in thick curtains, the interior lined with tapestries depicting a woodland scene, the faces of women flickering in and out of the shadows behind Ruthven. It was only as my eyes adjusted to the dark that I realized that the panels were also decorated by a series of four hand-drawn diagrams framed in gold that duplicated the illustrated charts of Rex Illuminatus and that scattered around these pictures on the floor were alchemical instruments medieval in nature. There was a triangle and an eye carved into the wood of the beam above the fireplace. It is true then that he shares this fascination, I thought, my heart lifting.

But of course! He has become the leading English scholar of Illuminatus's work in the philosophical realm, publishing his articles of discovery while cultivating contacts in the libraries of this city and the monasteries on Majorca. Legend has it he encountered Illuminatus via his fascination with the Egyptian alchemists and later through his devoted readings of the Franciscan accounts of the Conquest of the New World (remembering of course that it was the lost Incan gold of Peru which initially drew his interest ... creating a subsequent wealth which enables his less orthodox projects) but I digress ... I wondered briefly what Ruthven might reveal to me about the medieval philosopher Rex Illuminatus that I did not already know? Whole worlds! I thought to myself, settling into the chair across from him, expecting to be engaged in conversation, but for a long while we were silent as Ruthven studied my features, taking in the entirety of my person with unabashed intensity.

I elected to do the same, and so we sat in an uneasy, mutual purdah. Ruthven is not so young nor so handsome as I had been told – but then he has not surfaced in London in nearly thirty years, though his writings have received increasing circulation at the Universities. He looks haggard, as darkly moribund as his servant Brass Buckle, his cheeks hollow and his eyes heavy with some lingering sadness. His hair is a shock of brown curls, thinning at the front, parted down the middle and combed to the side. His face is shaved, which reveals the rawness of his features, his frame broad but somehow weakened, his limbs too thin for his chest, his head small on his shoulders. Despite his stillness, he seemed agitated and enlivened by my arrival. He broke the impasse with a sudden stream of words:

'What is the absolute significance of the Avian Alphabet BCDEFGHIK?'

I retaliated: 'B = Bonifaces, C = Magnitudo, D = Eternitas, E = Potestas, F = Sapienta, G = Voluntas, H = Virtus, I = Veritas, K = Glorias.'

'And what are these?'

'The divine dignities of God.'

'Well done. Now, the relative meanings?'

'Following the same alphabet, you have B = Difference, C = Agreement, D = Contrary, E = Beginning, F = Middle, G = End, H = Majority, I = Equal and K = Minority.'

'And do you know how to read the signs?'

'I do.'

'Would you call yourself an artist?'

'I am a logician and metaphysician – in this sense I am Illuminatus's conception of an artist.'

He quoted from Illuminatus. '*His is a gift from the divine spirit that allows you to know all of the good of the law, all truth of medicine, all discovery of science, and all the secrets of theology.* Do you claim to understand it?'

'No, Captain Ruthven. That is why I have come to you.'

He smiled.

'A test. Let us begin with a test.'

Ruthven reached out to the little drinks table by the side of his chair and rang a silver bell in the shape of a woman with a pleated skirt. The servant Brass Buckle appeared immediately.

'Fetch me my work notes,' Ruthven said. Brass Buckle disappeared through a door leading (I later discovered) to a study adjoined to my quarters. When Brass Buckle returned the servant pressed into my hand an illustration of a circle, containing three outer rings, divided into nine equal parts and at its centre three overlaid triangles. The triangles are stacked in such a manner that they create a star with nine points, aligned with each of the nine sections. The outermost rim of the circular diagram is divided into nine segments, each containing a letter of the divine alphabet. Around the circular diagram, the writer has created an ornate frame of filigree lines, as if the image were mounted on a twelfth-century illustrated manuscript.

'So?' Ruthven asked me, crossing his legs in his chair. 'What is it?'

'Rex Illuminatus's ordering of the Figure T,' I responded. 'A truth machine that can only be interpreted by an adept, an individual capable of navigating the myriad meanings of the alphabet.'

'You're halfway there.' Ruthven's visage lightened before another cloud passed over. He whisked the papers out of my hands. 'You have failed to identify the key figure. However, this is as expected.'

He examined me again. I resisted from launching into my pedigree, telling him of my successes across both the departments of Philosophy and Classics, that I had read all of Illuminatus's works in the original – Spanish, Latin and Catalan – with the exception of his Oriental Works and was entrenched in learning Arabic though that project (as you know) might well last me the remainder of my lifetime. Confidence of that kind does not become a young scholar and Ruthven struck me initially as a terse, arrogant type. This, I assume, had been conveyed to him by my letters of introduction, courtesy of professors at the University.

'Have you read my articles on the immortality of Illuminatus published in July of this year?'

I nodded.

'And you have studied my English–Catalan dictionary at Cambridge?'

Yes, I replied.

'Then you are well equipped for the job.'

I expressed confusion. Employment had not been discussed by my tutors.

'I am in need of an ally. A gentleman. You are a man of honour, no doubt?'

I lifted my bearing and replied that I was, if a third son. Ruthven smiled. 'I will explain more later. Now, how well do you know this city?'

'Not at all,' I replied, thinking this truth ought to be quite obvious from my previous letters. He should know as well as you do it is my first time in Barcelona.

'Well then – it's time you got to know her,' he hummed to himself. 'My servant will take care of your things. Now up, man, come along, I'll give you a tour of the place and our pretty neighbourhood, though it must be said, it's seen nicer days. What's the time? Eleven o'clock – off we go with time for lunch, a few hours' stroll, stretch your legs, get a feel of the place.'

Outside the sun was shining and the avenues bustling with humanity; he promenaded me up through a variety of streets, speaking as we went, travelling by foot to the cathedral. 'Every corner of this city, Mr Sitwell, is layered with stories. It is up to the discerning Scholar to unravel them and glean their true significance, to draw out the secrets from the folk tales which enshroud a common history!' Captain Ruthven's voice rang out.

We turned a corner behind the church, entering a dreary, dilapidated passage, filled with the excess waste of the city – mud and urine among other ugly things. Ruthven stopped before a house, which seemed to have been abandoned by time; the place carried an unpleasant, melancholy flavour. Truly it was a grim abode, with a wide entrance barred by a series of boards, windows nailed shut and no occupants inside despite the scarcity of lodging in the city centre. The stonework was strangely like that of the Incan walls I have studied – the rock bulging at the sides, forming a curved incline from the ground.

'A house left empty in the centre of a bustling city: what history do you see, Mr Sitwell?' Ruthven asked. I confessed I could make out nothing. Ruthven's eyes glowed with an eerie ferocity. He rapped the stone pavement beneath his feet with the tip of his cane and embarked on this harrowing tale.

'There once was a Jewish Cabbalist Alchemist who lived in the maze of little streets behind Santa Maria del Pi and he worked there in peace for many decades. In the neighbourhood his sciences and spells gathered powerful reputation – and with his enemies seemingly dead he felt safe to venture forward in his practices. He would have continued thus for many centuries, had not one morning he exited his house to find a babe wrapped in swaddling on the doorstep to his home, and a note, written in Hebrew, imploring the Alchemist to take care of a child born out of wedlock to the daughter of a Jewish merchant. When the Doctor looked into the infant's face, he was filled with an all-encompassing sense of sadness, and wondered – hoped – prayed indeed, that if he took this child into his house he could slow the curse which plagued the world around him, that brought the pillars of the earth crumbling down and would forever keep the children of the book from reaching love. Taking the infant into his house he raised her with kindness, teaching her the secrets of his craft, the charts and diagrams of his heart, the unspoken language of his letters. In time she grew, emerging from the skin of a girl into the heart and soul of a woman. The adopted daughter of the ancient Alchemist became the most beautiful woman in Barcelona, with rich black hair cascading down her shoulders, skin of olive and gold, and eyes sharp as obsidian. Her father loved her fiercely, and feared for her safety, watching the gaze of the men as she shopped in the market squares. The Alchemist protected her from the world as an innocent and a beauty; that she was his daughter he educated her mind, while fighting to shelter her from the predations of man – understanding the lust which followed her as a smoke.'

Ruthven's voice commanded my attention. He spoke firmly, leaning into his cane, watching my face to see if he could glean any inkling of suspicion.

'One market morning,' Ruthven went on, 'the Alchemist's daughter fell in the street carrying bread for their supper. The man who reached down his hand to help her regain her carriage was a handsome Christian knight from the southern wilds of Spain, come to the city to seek his fortune. His hair the colour of straw, his eyes a lucid blue, and in his pocket a dagger embedded with rubies from the Orient. In the instant his flesh brushed hers he was filled with a powerful love, greater than any he had known before and a desire to possess her absolutely; though he saw from her look her faith, he cast it aside and vowed he would take her in a night of passion. She too found her heart clenched by the hand of desire, and looking into his eyes knew she had met her husband. For many days and nights he wooed her, meeting in the shadows of trees and the rocky squares, far from the roving eye of her father. They kissed gently, but each kiss filled the knight with a lust for more, and finally he begged that they commit the highest act of love. Conjuring the wisdom of her father, and remembering the tale of her origins, the Doctor's daughter rebuffed the knight, saying that she would not take him into her bed unless they were married. The knight scoffed and said he would never take a Jew for a wife. The girl wept then and said there was no answer, for she could not marry a man who did not accept her faith and forbade her children to bear the blood of their heritage. The knight flew into a rage, and stormed away from the square, leaving his lover in floods of tears. All night he felt his groin burning for her, and in place of love, he nurtured a terrible hate.

'If he could not have her, no man would. At dawn the knight resolved to kill the girl by her father's hand, so that no blame would befall him. That morning, the knight made his way to the house of the Alchemist to purchase a potion to destroy an unfaithful lover. The Alchemist, suspicious of the knight, refused, but the knight persisted. "Will you sell me a poison," the knight asked, "for a woman who has betrayed my heart?"

'"No," the Alchemist said, and frowned.

'"If I offer you a fee?" the knight asked. "What would you take in exchange?"

'"Nothing."

'The knight looked at him slyly. "You are an author, I take it?" he said, gesticulating at the Alchemist's books, arranged above his tables, and the instruments of writing about his desk.

'"In a manner of speaking," the Doctor said.

'The knight's eyes narrowed. "I've heard a rumour you are cursed."

'"Rumours have a tendency towards falsehood."

'"I have been told you are an enemy of God, a friend has said you are a man of secrets. You are old and should be dead." The Alchemist felt a weight in his stomach drop.

"'Sell me this poison and I will forget," the knight said. "I am not a cruel man, just a creature lost in love, and I deserve your help." And so the knight continued, threatening the Doctor with his knowledge, until the man accepted a payment of seven golden coins, and thinking of his daughter, and the freedom he could buy her, the Alchemist gave the knight his poison, a spray of deadly perfume coating a bunch of roses plucked from the Alchemist's garden. When the young knight had left, the Alchemist resolved that he and his daughter would leave the city the next morning. He began to arrange his few possessions for departure. At sunset, the daughter of the Alchemist came to meet her lover, having received a note that afternoon asking for her forgiveness. The knight kissed the girl on the lips and said that they could never be together, and as a token of his love handed her the bundle of roses. She held these close to her heart, drowning in her tears, and when she collapsed into her bed that night, she kept them clutched to her chest.

'When the Alchemist woke he spent the day away from the house in the city and was surprised on his return to not find his daughter awake and at work in the house. He called her name – but he heard no answer. He called her name again, and worrying that she had been taken ill went gingerly up the stairs to her quarters. At her door, he knocked twice, a slow tap-tap – and again there was no answer, at which point he pushed through to her bed, with a terrible sinking in his heart that deepened as the door swayed open and, falling to his knees, put both his hands to her cheeks – but he knew – by God he knew – from the silence in the room – the unmistakable heaviness of death – that he was not alone, for the reaper had passed through at night and stolen away the life he loved – and such a rage rose in his throat that he choked, reaching out a finger to touch the crumbling, blackened roses, their perfume turned to the stench of rotting meat he recognized as poison from his own garden. That day the Alchemist boarded up the windows and doors of his house and urged no man or woman to enter into it, for the curse of his beloved had filled the walls with suffering, and any soul to make a bed there would meet the same fate as his daughter. The house remained empty for five hundred years,' Ruthven told me, as we stood before the door.

Then he frowned, muttered something indeterminate under his breath, and continued his story by saying that after this point the Alchemist disappeared from history. He suspects the figure's true identity is the Doctor Illuminatus – my own Rex Illuminatus! – who, after having drunk the elixir of life, made his way to Barcelona to continue his experiments with the philosopher's stone and, moved by Moses de León, converted in secrecy to the Cabbalist tradition. Ruthven told me this with extreme seriousness, in a hushed tone, standing beside me in the street behind the church. This is strange because I did not think this scholar of Illuminatus would be so fitful; I had envisioned a more decorous, academic, post-Enlightenment man who would be disinclined to believe in the ghost stories of the past. When I suggested as much he paled.

'Mr Sitwell,' he contested, 'you know nothing of the world.'

With that he refused to speak to me, and we parted ways after a brief repast, he retiring to his rooms, myself taking a nap before dinner. We ate at the English hour of six. I spent the majority of the meal consumed in utter despair, Ruthven frowning often across the table, using his silver bell to summon his wordless servant, who moved us through the courses with a bitterness I have never seen in a man of his age. In the dining room there is a painting, which you would recognize at once – a Titian, the *Rape of Lucretia* finished in 1490. Above Captain Ruthven's head, Sextus Tarquinius raises his knife against bare-breasted Lucretia. It is a strange and rather discomforting choice for a dining room. When the coffee arrived after desserts, Ruthven pointed at my cup and the servant filled it, never meeting my eyes. Ruthven and I drank this together, the man giving me a grisly stare before suggesting that we retire to the sitting room. This pattern happened over the next four days, in which our encounters were monitored by Brass Buckle and not a word between us was exchanged. There is an unpleasant odour about Ruthven I have not yet placed, a cologne of nutmeg and soot, sickly and sweet. It is as infectious as fear – though I do not know his reasons for exuding it. Raising his eyes with a wry smile, Ruthven rang his silver bell for port, which appeared with two crystal glasses. He poured a draught, handed me the crystal, and nodded. I understood that I was meant to drink, and did so with gusto. Not enjoying this game, I opened my mouth to speak, but Captain Ruthven intercepted.

'Why are you here?' he asked. 'Barcelona is not generally part of the Grand Tour – for which I assume you have garnered the support of your beloved father?'

This left me rather taken aback. 'To study Illuminatus of course,' I said.

'And you think you're worthy of my help?'

'Well, in a manner of speaking,' I went on to say, feeling my temper rise – what did this man mean by his absurd treatment of me? I resolved I would pack my things immediately and move to the pension I had taken note of on my arrival into the city. 'If I prey upon your hospitality, Captain Ruthven, tell me and I will relieve you of the burden.'

He assured me this was not the case, and then began asking me questions of the most peculiar nature, intent, seemingly, on assessing my knowledge of Illuminatus's character but also upon creating a portrait of my own. He wanted to know what I found interesting in the fellow, and why I had followed Ruthven's treatment of

Illuminatus to Barcelona (reasons I had given him in the letter many weeks ago, and I know you are familiar with). He then asked me my thoughts on the apocryphal pseudo-alchemical literature produced under Illuminatus's name. I said this interested me but it was not – of course – the focus of my work. He frowned and continued probing. We passed about an hour thus, until suddenly he smiled. I had said something, at last, that he approved of.

'And the meaning of the alphabet BCDEFGHIK in conjunction with the astrological charts ABCD?'

I gave my answer, an original interpretation, and he poured another glass. 'Just the thing! Just the thing!' he repeated aloud. 'You'll do.'

After drinks I retired to my quarters and decided to read at the desk stationed beside the window overlooking the pretty little square and the rose window of the Basílica del Pi. I flattened your letter with a bronze figurine of a wild boar, fat and heavy, mounted on black wood and a smooth red stone. For a moment I wore an aura of muted dissatisfaction – I was uncertain of what I might achieve with Captain Ruthven or how helpful he would be to my endeavours. The man is clearly deranged, but he is, begrudgingly, the expert in our field and he speaks my language – an added boon. I set my candle on a little ledge above this desk where I write to you now. Overhead, on the shelves that line the office, an atlas, a complete set of encyclopaedias, the naked skull of an antelope, back issues of the Spanish language literary magazine *The Source*. To the right of his desk, a corkboard, covered with a map of the city, littered with red-tipped pins linked by blue thread. On the left, hanging from a lower bookshelf, a spiralling chart of colours, reminiscent of the woodcuts Sebastian Münster printed in *Cosmographia*. Fortunately he stores no chemicals or oils in this chamber, as I would be put upon to sleep in proximity to such dangerous materials.

In the top drawer of the desk, a bundle of string, formed in a sphere. Ink bottles, a dirty mound of plaster. Three gold coins dating from the early Roman period and an obsidian arrowhead. The drawer below is filled with printed sheets of papers, placed in an order only legible by the man whose room has been offered me – to all others chaos incarnate. I am surprised he has not made more of an effort to clear his personal belongings before allowing me to make my home, however briefly, in his company. Sitting as I was at this desk, admiring its trappings, I could not help but explore its contents further. I thought of writing to you at once, but while searching for paper came across a letter, written seemingly by a female hand to my host. Curiosity won out and in a second I devoured the writing.

I read it again, copying the words as I went:

I want you to remember this city. The rain has ceased outside but the air bites hard. The wind hunts for cracks between fabric, bare skin. Anything to freeze, to catch hold of, gnaw. Filaments drip with moisture. Green moss clings to the rocky mouths of gargoyles, pavement slick with hunger. Ice pools over flooded drains and cracks against the sunken roots of trees that line the dingy boulevards of Barcelona. Breathe here. A deserted square, geese preening their feathers. Taste the bedraggled fountain, courtyard drowned in decaying leaves. You stare at knife wounds in hard-stone chapels. The branches of a naked tree, exposed bark, envelope a putrid light-stained sky. This is where you have left me. You have seen it: a narrow, dark street running perpendicular to the trajectory of the sun. The incline is steep, descending from the hill of the Cathedral, passing the entrance to Sant Felipe Neri.

From here you strode into the evenings, to the musicians in the square, and waved hello to the red-draped saint in her powdered box, astride an X-shaped cross. Full of flowers. You looked inside to the dust-covered world of the past. See her robes, her cross turned on its side. Her ebony eyes. O! Santa Eulàlia! Patron Saint of Barcelona! She who at the tender age of thirteen, stirred on no doubt by the hot blood of adolescence professed a belief in God! Barcelona was Old Barcino then and its ruler, one stone-cut Diocletian, took his mind against the girl, following the poisoned whispers of Rome. Eulàlia del Camp! Eulàlia of the Country! Breasts budding and still a virgin marched to the court of the Roman Tetrarchy. She demanded there that Diocletian reconsider his treatment of her Book. The Roman, moved by the tenacity of this red-cheeked child, asked her to recant her faith. Blinded by the suicidal obstinance of the faithful, Eulàlia refused. And so Diocletian declared that he would give young Eulàlia thirteen chances for each of her thirteen years to rethink her heresy. Stripped naked, Eulàlia was led to a public square for all the world to see. At the centre, she looked up to heaven and smiled, stretching out her hands. In the midst of spring, the clouds rumbled overhead and it began to snow, powder cascading over her nakedness, God protecting her nudity! Diocletian roared in displeasure. The results were unfortunate in the extreme. Torments one to four were brutal enough. Eulàlia was flogged, her flesh torn with hooks, her feet gouged with blazing coals, her breasts severed from her body. Still she refused to recant her faith. Next boiling oil, molten lead. She began to resemble a monster, chest raw and lime covered, face eaten and burnt by the hot ore. And still she breathed. Stayed silent, panting on the floor, until Diocletian in disgust and goaded by the gods, ordered her to be placed in a barrel lined with broken glass, the lid sealed, and rolled thirteen times down

La Baixada de Santa Eulàlia, the antique-lined street which now connects the Cathedral to the Carrer dels Banys Nous. They say that God kept her alive until the end, which makes him even crueller than we had imagined – and that when they removed her from the barrel they chopped off her head to put her out of her misery. Her spirit escaped in the form of a dove, like Pegasus leaping from Medusa's neck and I am sure that the black eyes of the thirteen-year-old girl would have turned any man to stone.

Why Santa Eulàlia became the favoured woman of maritime wanderers – why she was chosen to protect the fishing fleets of Barcelona and the great ships of the Empire that extended beyond Perpignan reaching to Tunis, Sicily, Sardinia and Las Islas Baleares – remains opaque to me. Nebulous as my desire to write that grief is endless and hidden and long. That the porcelain, smiling face of the Saint in her robes also covers up a history of violence – coding into her flowers a secret, as great if not worse than mine. Santa Eulàlia is yours, after all, patron of a city that consumed you.

The writer signs herself as *Lucretia*. Katherine, what does she mean by 'consumed you'? What mysteries were contained in the story of this admirer of my host with his deep, sunken eyes? I thought of Captain Ruthven, his face wan, recounting upon my arrival that the city is in a state of chaos, that alchemy as it has been practised is in decline and his is a disappearing species. I asked if he had ever made gold. He shook his head. No. But then he sighed and suggested I ask him if he had ever prolonged life. At my questions he smiled briefly, like the faint beam of light from a waning moon, but then returned to the opacity I associate with his perverse character, his face grim and devoid of stars. 'Yes,' he retorted. 'As one gentleman to another, I swear to you that I have.' I am worried for him, Katherine. I fear Captain Ruthven, good man that he is, may be on the brink of losing his soul. Write to me, I am in need of your love, and counsel.

Your beloved and most trusting, Sitwell

11 November 1851, Barcelona

I write surreptitiously by the light of a single candle. The blinds are closed and my door locked, though I can hear Ruthven pacing even now. He moves like a wraith, up and down the hall beyond my door, pausing, as I have seen him do earlier, to look out between the curtains, his gaze haunting the street, never still. The man is plagued by ill-humours. The floorboards creak and I fear he will enter by force, and demand more – I do not wish to tell you everything, for the horrors are vast – but when I close my eyes to relive it, I see the last few days in a blur. The story begins four nights ago, when I awoke to the sound of a bell. Groggy, eyes half closed, my left hand stumbled for a pair of glasses, which after placing on my nose, led me to matches and candle. The pool of light from the candle at my bedside blurred out into a vast, undulating darkness. It was raining. A sound? My breath slowed. The blinds of the window that face the square were open and damp with rain. The fat patter of a summer storm. Rat-tat-tat at the door. Somewhere below. The shrill tap-tap drifts up through the building, echoing against the window. Glasses firmly on my nose, I wiped the hair from my forehead. No. It is distinctive. I am not dreaming. It is clearly the sound of a fist on the door. Firm. Persistent. Knocking.

Tap. Tap.

I sat up in bed and waited. I did not move to open the window.

Some animal instinct led me to feel that there could be no sign of recognition — at that precise second the bell chimed again. Unmistakable. Exacting. Echoing up through the house. My skin burnt with curiosity. I pulled on yesterday's trousers, left crumpled on the floor, next my shirt and jacket, before slipping on my shoes. I swore to myself as I knocked into a cupboard in the dark. A welt tomorrow, I cursed inside. I did not want to light a candle in the hall, which his visitor would see from the square. I do not know what instinct drove me. I must have been half sleepwalking, or still inside a dream. Carefully, deliberately, I walked into the hall and paused here to see if my host had risen — but there was only a silence from the door that led to his chambers. The blue glow of the rooftop city dripped through a thin skylight — slits of brightness illuminating the winding ebony staircase. The moon had risen. My ears were alert for this visitor. The moon provided a steady glow. I descended three flights rapidly. The light waned. The world rejoiced in darkness. My footsteps slowed, though my eyes adjusted quickly to the dusky light. At the bottom of the stairs, I opened the interior glass door that led onto the mail room and outer portal to the street — a thick oak barrier, aged by humidity, paint peeling and chipping from the hinges. Silence now. My breath was loud and heavy. Be still, damn it, I thought to myself, before looking down to the foot of the door, beneath the letterbox. A fresh letter. Unmarked, but for the spindly blue hand of a calligrapher:

Per l'Anglès.

For the Englishman.

Still in the delirium of sleep, I ripped open the envelope mistaking that the contents were addressed to me. The paper stock of the same weight as the envelope, and the same eggshell taupe in colour. The calligraphy on the page was sharp, written in a tight hand, with the same pen. *Porc ple de vicis, un mal matí son sant martiri ella trobà; la pell deixaren per fer-ne botas*, the scribe had written, but addressed to whom? I struggled through the translation: *Pig fat with vices, one bad morning she found her saintly martyrdom; they left her skin, to make boots with* . . . Ruthven's name marked by a precise line. A shimmering indent on smooth paper. Pounding on the stairs and the Captain's feet behind me! He appeared dressed, wrapped in a dark cloak with a wide-brimmed hat on his head – snatching the letter out of my hands he read the contents, the malaise of the evening thrown to the wind, his face barely recognizable in the wavering light of his candle. 'If you wish to see something interesting, hop to it Mr Sitwell!'

With that he unbolted the door and burst into the square. I followed him, half in a dream, closing the door behind me, trusting Ruthven to be in possession of his keys. Across from my balcony rises the mighty bulk of the Santa Maria del Pi, a brooding lump of black stone built like a fortress flanked on either side by grey buttresses supporting the lofty peak of the bell tower, an octagonal giant fifty-four yards in height. On the cliff-like face of the grand entrance, the decorative arch above the heavy doors forms the apex of a blade. Here the Virgin clutches her child, babe perched on a cold hip, hemmed by a forest of columns. About her head, the arms of the city and parish carved out of rock. Four stripes of Catalonia against a flag, impressed with a cross like that of the Knights Templar. At the summit, the crown of the Kings of Catalonia and curling leaves of stone. And, hanging above them all, the many-petalled flower of a vast rose window, a great black thing like an eye suspended over the cleft mouth of the church. My eyes roamed the shadows as Ruthven approached a woman waiting beneath the leaves of the mighty pine tree at the centre of the square. Under a heavy cloak, she wore an indigo evening dress, the lace of her collar barely visible in the half-light, hair loose about her shoulders. Her face was white, and upon seeing Captain

Ruthven, who rushed to her, she took his hand and exchanged a few swift words in his ear to which he grimaced and nodded. The woman did not speak to me, and Ruthven gave no introduction, but my presence was accepted with a furtive look. She set off at a fast clip, and we followed swiftly behind. Soon we arrived at a red painted door, on which someone had marked a cross. The woman took out a key and placing it in the lock opened the door with a deafening creak.

A young doctor turned in the room, his face hollow, flanked by a trussed policeman, strapped into a gaudy fanfare of scarlet and blue, bristling with sabre, pistol, rifle and bayonet, an ivory plume attached to his prodigious brow. This be-weaponed fellow paced beneath the desultory light of a dim oil lamp fixed to the wall, his face set firmly in a scowl of displeasure. On the table at the centre of the room I could make out the figure of a woman, laid flat on the wood, her arms crossed over her chest. It was clear from the stillness of her form that something evil had befallen her. I was introduced as Captain Ruthven's lodger and companion, and my presence accepted with little contestation. Ruthven spoke brusquely to the policeman – a man who was openly relieved by the arrival of the scholar – a detail I found perplexing until the remainder of the events unfolded, which I will soon reveal to you. The doctor was directed to show Ruthven the mouth of the girl.

'Do you have a strong stomach?' Ruthven asked.

I affirmed – my being a military man. The policeman looked me up and down, as did the doctor, who moved swiftly to the mouth of the corpse and eased it open to show Ruthven the horror of her death. The girl's body was smooth, delicate as porcelain, long legs, wide hips, small breasts pressed flat by gravity. She had once been blessed with an angelic, young face surrounded by fine red hair. At her scalp, her fringe was light and auburn, but in the dampness of the morning dew, or the bile on the street, the tips of her hair had turned a deep, blood brown, and clung to the naked flesh of her shoulder in sickly dark curls, a thick knotted mass at the base of her throat. Her private parts were shaved, as were her arms and legs, not a hair on the rest of her body, pale skin marred by bruises on the forearms and wrists and a series of pricks, made with the point of a needle, which formed a red line – not a cut or a gash – that ran from her groin down the left inner thigh to her ankle. Ruthven called for more candles – cursing the doctor for the lack of light.

I turned away with distaste, shading my eyes. The policeman revealed that the corpse had been found strung to a tree a few streets over by Senyoreta Andratx, as our mysterious female companion came to be known. More candles were brought by this woman, whose hand shook as she lit the wicks. I could see the marks of the rope at the corpse's neck, a red burn about an inch thick. The policeman now pressed a second missive into Ruthven's hand. Ruthven read the letter, which he did not give to me, then looked to the young doctor, who opened the mouth of the girl, telling us that it was likely she had drowned in her own blood. The palms of her hands, the doctor showed us, had been engraved with the image of a serpent and a cross, in gold.

When I neared I saw that the damage to the body was more complicated than I had imagined – and though I will spare you the more gruesome details of that mouth, I will say that the strangest thing about the corpse was that profusion of fine wounds on the woman's flesh, the letters of an alphabet carved across each breast. The engravings on the hands were mirrored by the lighter markings on the breasts, raised in pink, as if scratched onto her chest, not quite deep enough to draw blood, and filled with alabaster ink.

'Do you recognize the symbols?'

I nodded, scarce able to speak. They were the first figures of Rex Illuminatus. Three concentric circles around each nipple, with a letter at its heart across the point of pink flesh. On her fore-head, I discerned the letter B. On the woman's chest, beneath her clavicle and above her right breast the letter C, on the facing bosom, the letter D. On each thigh, the letters I and K. Across her rear and on the points of her kidneys, the letters E, F, G, H respectively.

'*I saw a woman sit upon a scarlet-coloured beast full of names of blas-phemy, having seven heads and seven horns,*' Ruthven muttered, close to my ear. *And upon her forehead was a name written: MYSTERY, BABYLON THE GREAT, THE MOTHER OF HARLOTS AND ABOMINATIONS ON EARTH.*'

'What the devil do you mean by that?' I asked.

'The time has come to show your mettle, Sitwell,' Ruthven countered. 'You are a fine draughtsman. I have seen your illustra-tions. Take note of her wounds. I cannot bear the sight of them!' He turned to Senyoreta Andratx before I had time to answer.

'Bring this gentleman pen and paper! Quick! While they are still fresh! I would know what he sees in these markings!'

And then turning to the policeman he broke into a rapid conversation I struggled to comprehend. When I had finished with my drawings, Ruthven pressed his keys into my hand, and sent me back to his home, guided by the silent woman in indigo who spoke nothing of what I had seen and barely looked at me. At the house the sullen servant was quick to open the door, and ushered me upstairs without any explanation of Ruthven's noctur-nal work in the city. I did not see Ruthven again for the next two days. I took my meals alone, in the company of the glowering servant who still – even today – refuses to speak to me – agonizing over what I had seen and why. The Captain had quoted from John's Revelations in a moment of passion, but the parallel trou-bled me deeply, for I have read that Book many times in my life. *And he saith unto me, the waters which thou sawest, where the whore sitteth, are peoples, and multitudes, and nations, and tongues. And the ten hornes which thou sawest upon the beast, these shall hate the whore and make her desolate, and naked, and shall eate her flesh and burne her with fire.* I felt afraid to leave the house for fear of encountering the type of criminal who could effect such damage on the female form, and highly regretted my choice to travel here alone. Just when I had given up all hope of seeing him again, on the morning of the third day, Ruthven reappeared covered in mud, bursting into the sitting room followed by the grim-faced servant Brass Buckle.

'Thank God you are still here!' He dropped into the armchair beside me. 'I'm so sorry to have disappeared – but the case required intimate investigation.'

'And the victim? Who was she?' I asked, my thoughts harkening back to the murdered girl.

'An engastrimyth from Akelarres,' Ruthven replied. 'A diviner. A woman possessed. It is depraved, Mr Sitwell, and it is brutal. But not uncommon.' I asked if he had found the killer.

'No.' Ruthven sighed. 'But it is not the first time I have seen their work and I will catch them.'

'Their?'

Ruthven would not meet my eye, so overcome with emotion was he. 'When I began hunting, I had no conception of where it would lead. It was only after I had committed myself to a life of exile, that I swore to devote my life to recovering these documents, no matter the cost.'

'But what has this to do with Illuminatus?' I replied weakly.

'Can you not smell it on the air?' he asked me.

My cheeks flushed.

'I have the smell of a marked man. I know it. It cannot be helped. But the scarlet thread of destiny has led you to me – a scarlet thread, Mr Sitwell, that ties your heart to mine. I had an inkling when you first sent those letters you were the fellow, and I must

187

apologize for allowing you to come here, knowing that your exposure to me would forever unite our destinies. Of course, had you proven a lesser man, I might have looked for another – but you are strong, Sitwell, and though inexperienced, intelligent enough.'

I shook in my seat, feeling a fever mounting on my forehead – then suddenly resolution struck me – I remembered you, our happiness together. I will not go down this path!

'You have made a mistake. I do not have the tools to help you, nor the capability.'

'There is no one else.'

I bolted from my chair and stood in a rage.

'I came here for a lesson in philosophy and medieval theory from a great scholar. Not exposure to murder!'

Ruthven held my gaze with his firmly, and did not rise to my insolence. I sat back down in the chair. His left hand trembled on the plush cushion of his chair, moving nervously to his collar to play with the folds of cloth around his throat. 'Tomorrow morning you will leave me – as a friend or a man to be forgotten in time.'

I stammered, partly relieved. 'I am going back to London then?'

'Unless, of course, you should be interested by my proposition?'

I asked him which proposition he was referring to.

'Give me a few more moments of your illustrious attention,' he asked, kicking off his boots and resting his striped socks on the foot cushion before the fire. 'I have need of a courier, Mr Sitwell. Your style is congenial enough, your knowledge of the symbols of Illuminatus sound. I am suggesting a form of employment. You are in want of financial support? There is a woman waiting for you at home, I take it?'

How does he know? I thought in consternation.

'I can smell love on you, boy. She's resting in your eyes, in the hours you take to write letters; you have not once in my company looked with lust at another woman and it is clear that you are set about making your fortune. On your handkerchief are embroidered, in a female hand, your initials intertwined with a KM – the letters of the name of your lover. Am I wrong? She is unsure of your constancy. Never trust a woman at home, Sitwell, they are fickle, particularly the young.'

I nodded, flabbergasted by his powers of observation.

'If you take on this work for me, I will pay you handsomely, in spirit and in kind.'

'And what is the actual nature of this proposal?'

'Am I right in my belief that your intention to travel to Barcelona concerned the alchemical secrets of the Doctor Illuminatus?' Ruthven stood up and moved to a bookcase facing the fire.

I affirmed in the positive.

'Then either way this project will be beneficial to you – I promise that you will discover things which may make you famous, certainly a very rich man, Mr Sitwell – richer than you would be if you mastered the transmutation of gold – which I believe you illicitly desire. If you are swift, you will also save my life. Time is short. Having told you my secrets, I ask this favour of you. I will tell you what I know of Illuminatus's alchemy if you will take this to a friend for me on Majorca before setting off on your journey home. What you gather from my teachings is at your discretion. It is up to you to believe my story or reject it; know only that my days are numbered, and what you take is limited. They have made this clear enough.' Ruthven found a mass of papers resting on his shelf, bound in a golden ribbon. 'I entrust these to you,' he said, smiling grimly, placing the letters into my hands. 'They are copies of my translations and the accumulated accounts of my research into this matter. I have not known you for many days, Mr Sitwell, but judging by the fate of those who have come before me, we may not have the time to address ourselves better and I trust you are a gentleman.'

'I do not understand,' I said. 'What do you fear will happen to you?'

'I would rather that you did not know. It does not bear discussing. But I will not let them defeat me – and have made my preparations. Take these to my friend, one Father Lloret of Valldemossa. I will pay for your passage by ship to the island and return to England from there. I will also cover the costs of your lodgings. Show these papers to him, and ask for his account of the Doctor, recently discovered by the possession of one Maria de la Font. I will give you a second object before you depart tomorrow, but you must swear on your life not to open it until you deliver the contents to a woman named Lucretia. Tell Lloret you have word of me for the Nightingale. He will take you to her when the time is right. You will find what you are seeking of Illuminatus, and in doing so protect the secrets of another.'

Ruthven closed his eyes and rested in his chair for a moment, his hand hanging back, his shirt open at the collar, his feet extended before the fire. He looked deflated, his eyelids strained, and it was only then that I noticed that at the line of his hair on his left temple he had received a blow, which had cracked the skin and left a mottled brown scab hidden earlier by the half-light. The streaks I had mistaken for mud were in reality the dried remnants of blood. Ruthven then seemed to convulse in his chair, his body shaking, before he rose elegantly, his trousers smoothing at his waist, his face handsome at rest.

Ruthven reached out and rang his silver bell left on the table before the fireplace. 'A drink. We shall discuss everything tonight, for tomorrow we shall fly. If I am to help you, and you are to help me, we must meet on equal terms this evening and understand each other clearly. Else failure is the sure – the only – path.'

We talked for many hours, my love, about notions I can only impart to you in person without endangering the life of my strange friend and host. I did not have a moment to agree or disagree, but there seems to me to be no choice. As a free man, I must help a soul who is captive. I will do my best to write more later, when my head is not swimming: Captain Ruthven's secret is too much for one man to comprehend.

Your Sitwell

II

MYTH

I turn and see my pillow stained with a dark smear. *An all too famil-iar sensation.* I wipe my mouth and my hand comes away as I expected. *Another nosebleed.* I strip the pillowcase down and bring it to the bathroom. As the tap runs, I watch the blood stream softly into the sink, catching on the silver metal round the throat of the basin. I clean my face, washing my skin slowly. In my sleep I had dreamt of a tree groaning under the weight of an avian horde. Wings like the footfall of a heavy-booted army. Doves gorging themselves on figs that dripped from the tree like globular jewels.

I make a cup of tea in the kitchen. *Ginger and lemon.* Wearing an oversized shirt and knickers. I had gone to sleep after reading Sitwell's letters and rescue them from my bedside table.

You should take more care, I chastise myself. Looking at Sitwell's illustration of the nightingale, demure cross-hatched wings. Perhaps she is about to sing? *Beak open.* Eye glassy and black. I think of the letters sent to Fabregat. Of disambiguation. Of what was meant by what. Listening to the inspector speak yesterday, I had concluded that Fabregat's investigation made the fatal error of assuming that the collated lines pertained to the identity of an individual rather than the existence of a document.

No one else would know but you, I remind myself. People look for meaning. They seek riddles. That is in our nature. But treated as riddles, these verse lines ask as many questions as they answer. *Do not assume they are speaking to you*, I would tell Fabregat. *Do not assume that they point a finger at the accused, the perpetrator or a criminal. Read them as they are. Blank slate. Fresh context. Focus on the knowable. On the facts to hand.*

Seek origin point. Source.

Nine books of Leaves gave forth this rage of man.

Some treasures are lost forever. But not this one. This one you are going to find. Because you have been sent a message from the grave. In an altar-shaped poem, filled with secrets. There will be no fires lit tonight. No discarded memories.

My thoughts roam over the soggy Book of Hours and the Abbey Librarian warm and asleep in his bed. *Think about it rationally. Someone deliberately removed the poetry hidden beneath Rex Illuminatus's Alchemical Recipes. And then they sealed the book in the wall of a remote chapel on Mallorca, with the collected letters of an eccentric British gentle-man seemingly collated by a third party.*

And a bone.

Do not forget the bone.

A single, solitary bone, shining out of the darkness.

Like a warning.

At two a.m. I dress brusquely. Pulling a sweater over my shirt. *No bra.* Then a pair of jeans. Mismatched socks. Olive coat and black scarf. There is no point in sleeping. *I need to walk.* Keys in pocket and phone. A few loose euro coins. *Not that anything will be open.* I slip down the stairs, exiting onto the street. The little café at the bottom of the building is closed, but the lights are still on inside. *The staff having a last drink. Cut down the side street, heading for Barceloneta.* Only then will I be satisfied. Only then will I stop.

At night the hotels are alien. Red eyes of cargo ships blink on the horizon. Behind me, towards the hills: embers of Tibidabo. Moon stamped out by clouds. Sky heavy, unfriendly. A dull orange sheen. I feel jetlagged. Dizzy. Sitting on the abandoned beach, I sink back into memories of my first summer in Spain. I return to the girl I've left behind. Divorced myself from entirely. *To understand history, you must contextualize it,* I tell myself. *Retrace your steps.* You must begin at your beginning, not the beginning of others. The beach in the luminous warmth of summer.

La Revetlla de Sant Joan. 2003. Midsummer's eve gives way to the Feast day of Saint John. Day of the Baptist. These nights the dragons are tamed and the drunkards are dancing. I claim a place on the shorefront early in the afternoon.

I can see the houses of Barcelona stacked behind me; I study them upside down, each window like the squares of a Rubik's cube. One life upon another. Each smell distinct. Clouds waft down to me – olive brine and pickled crabs, paella and fish oil. My hands crossed beneath my head. The grit infects my hair. There is a loose razor blade beside my shoulder. Discarded needles and Styrofoam. Someone I do not know hands me a plastic cup of red wine. Every hour more revellers join from all quarters of the city. A boy with a guitar begins singing. *Al mar! Al mar!*

La Revetlla de Sant Joan. Saint John's Eve. Also called *la Nit de Bruixes*, night of the witches. For us an endless evening of rapture. Of dancing, of bonfire, and fireworks. There are explosions in the sky like gunshots, and by midnight the city has the glow of a war zone. In memory of battle the city celebrates the life of a saint with pagan ferocity. Her countrymen dance in droves, banging pots and pans in the street and singing and setting fire to the beaches! There is no need for anything else but debauchery. That impulse seems to be all that is left of the saint.

I lie here, prostrate and open, my back against the sand.
Remember.
As you drank you burnt your sins away.

That morning, I greet the dawn stoned, watching the tradesmen waking. There are new lights in store windows. *Panaderos* bring out fresh rolls. *Coca de Sant Joan.* Pastries emblazoned with sugar fruits. Sticky pine nuts. Pigeons preen and coo in the alcoves of Barceloneta, watching me stumble home from the clubs of Port Olímpic. The beach, trash-strewn and grey, stirs in preparation. Within that triangular development built for the outcast fisherman of the city, tapas bars open their doors for deliveries – squid, dog-faced fish, cod, halibut, octopus – with *croquetas y pimientos del Padrón* – piled to the rafters – knowing soon that the smoking masses will spill into the streets laden with liquor.

But on the morning of Sant Joan festivities are interrupted by sirens.

First a car. Then two officers.

They walk down to the stone jetty leading into the sea, uniforms black against the grey sand. I sit up and watch them. Then another car. Then a third. Sirens slide round the hot sun like the punched howl of a discotheque. The hunt follows the police cars on the shore. *A young man had disappeared into the sea.*

They ask us – *Have you seen anything?* No, I say – No.

They find his shoes and socks next to the first jetty.

Big black boulders. He must have left them there and walked down the shoreline, trailing his feet in the water, until he was in the direct eyeline of the city. The police cordon off the area. They search the sea, like fishermen trawling for lobsters.

Behind them a woman stands on the sand in a black dress and prays.

I hold her in my imagination.

Eyes burning more fiercely than the sun.

The police below feel her gaze upon them. An uneasy burden. They do not know what she wants, if she wills success or failure. If she prays for a body or a sign or if she believes that he was innocent or guilty. They know only that she watches.

A dark shawl pulled over her shoulders, her husband beside her, whispering in her ear. *We have to make a show of support, Marta. We have to let them know we care.*

The next sign is the wallet. Escaped from his pocket some ten metres from the shore. They bring it up from the sea like a treasure. A pearl of information. *There is his photograph, a pink national identity card. Adrià Daedalus Sorra. Scraps of paper already dissolved into mud. Debit card and change.* His mother tugs her shawl tighter round her shoulders. In her heart it is icy cold.

As they hunt, the posters come down in the city. Pulled from city walls, ripped from scaffolding, unhooked from lamp posts, stripped from trains and buses. In the square of Plaça de Margarida Xirgu ten men work tirelessly to cover the face of Natalia Hernández with a dull grey paint. At the Theatre of National Liberation, her director stands on the balcony overlooking the square, hands crossed over his chest to watch the descent of his muse. On every floor of the Institut del Teatre, students studying for exams or singing in the hallways stopped. They walk to the vast glass windows facing the Theatre of National Liberation. They watch as the three magnificent posters come down. Her mouth distorted in waves as she falls. And though the students do not know why Natalia Hernández left the face of the theatre, they feel the terrible unease of disorder.

That morning curiosity replaces my desire for silence. I ask the policeman what has happened.

'*Read the paper.*'

Taciturn, he stares into the sea.

They carry the story on the airwaves that night. I listen to them on a radio by a fire. The reporter interviews an old woman. Sharp as a whip. She lives in an apartment complex with balconies over-looking the sea. The old woman explains that at ninety-seven years of age she is not used to surprises. *That is to say, nothing much surprises her any more.*

'Which is why,' she tells the radio, 'I spend most of my time looking at the sea.'

Safe in her fourth-floor apartment on Carrer de la Mestrança, she has a straight-shot view of the beach. I realize with a start: *She was probably watching us all,* studying the fires and the dancers from her little chair in the window, watching the beach where we were lighting candles and flames and throwing beer down our throats.

She surveys the cement courtyard below, the palm trees along Passeig Marítim de la Barceloneta, and beyond, over the sand to the waves. The world below pleasurably constant. She checks the weather and sees when storms come in from the south. In the mornings she watches the runners, the *paseos* of families, the sand-castle-makers from North Africa, the delivery of groceries to the Spar below. In the evening, the drug pedlars, the dancers, the parti-ers with their cans of red beer, the fat pit-bulls, Pakistanis selling their wares, the roller bladers and bicyclists in their bright-coloured suits, the heavy lifters, iron pumpers, ice-cream-smeared children and *guiris*. Her voice like *manchego* and sardines.

Nothing escapes this old woman.

Not even the figure of a young man in 2003 who, in the earliest hours of the morning, runs topless, with long dark hair and stumbles, panting, breathless, to the edge of the sea.

Convenient indeed. She clacks her tongue. A clear line of vision.

Something stirs in the darker annals of her memory. The old woman has seen a figure like this before, as a young woman, from the same windows, of the same house, which once belonged to her grandfather, and had stayed in the family through the Civil War, and Franco, and even the end of Franco and the wild years of the eighties and nineties to the present day.

Oh! she wheezes. *Oh! The boy walked into the sea.*

I imagine her blinking, her watery blue eyes hidden behind half-inch-thick spectacles. Round orbs fixed to her nose reflect the flickering pyres on the beaches.

This woman has a flair for storytelling, and she informs the radio – swearing on good faith – that with a sudden gust of wind, summoned at the exact instant the boy walked into the sea, all of the red votive candles in Santa Maria del Pi are extinguished! The priest is stunned by the wind as he wanders down the aisle counting prayer books for the morning mass. He flings himself on the stone ground. *Holy Mary, Mother of God.* Only the hanging lamps, now electric, stay illumined. Of the 154 candles, not a wick remains ablaze. Is it the ghost of the madman who burnt himself in the march of Corpus Christi? The curate crosses himself and prays. Or some other lost soul who comes knocking at the door?

Before me: a jetty of black boulders claws into the fading night, still deep within the realm of its power. I sit on the beach again, a decade later. Alive and cold in the dark. My knees pulled up under my chin. *The disappeared man walks down this avenue into the sea. Rats ran along the rocks beneath his feet. They make their homes in the cracks and hide there.*

He removes his shoes and walks out further. Waves crash around him. He walks out. Out further than ever before. His feet no longer touch the muddy bottom; he is lifted and then brought down by the waves. The wind tugs at his hair. He walks until the water reaches the line of his neck, without stopping, and then begins to swim, and swim, and swim, until he was fifty metres, a hundred metres, two hundred metres out, much further than I am able to see, even on the best of days. What had she said? The old woman on the radio?

That he did not come back.

Which is the element of all this that reminded her of a black hour in 1937, when she watched a young man she knew and loved swim out to drown in the sea.

And you? I ask the cold night air. *Why have you brought me here?*

III

Excerpts from

THE CONTEMPORARY LIFE OF REX ILLUMINATUS

As compiled by his Allies
On the Island of Mallorca

PROLOGUE

WE HAVE WRITTEN this so that you shall come to learn of the Secrets of the Doctor and his Magic Works. For once the former is comprehended, the latter also will be more easily understood.

THE FIRST TALE

Which Treats of the Doctor's Return by Sea to Barcelona

THROUGH THE chinks in his cell, the rotten wooden boards coloured with a dark growth like the ash from an oak fire, the Doctor heard the breathing of the man beside him. The neighbouring breath is purple with sickness, lungs drowning in phlegm, and by the pattern of the voice and the choking in the night, the Doctor knew the duration of his fellow captive's life would soon be counted in hours. The Doctor never meant to be here: it had not been part of his plans nor self-appointed destiny – but fate felt otherwise, and, slamming the door on all possibilities, she forced the Doctor to resign himself, once again, to the vacillations of sea salt and gangrene, memories broken by the company of rats that feast on the breadcrumbs at his desk – a sorry thing, made of a reclaimed bucket given as a latrine. This too was an unfortunate occurrence.

The Doctor's beard was blue, and curved around his neck as a scarf. His shoulders were a dark, russet brown, his hide like smoked leather. The Doctor's head was bald, and very round, like the fat end of an egg, and his eyes were marked by the thin lines of the crow's foot, which returned to feed on pain, showing the path of its scaly burden across his cheeks. Through a crack in the ceiling of the boat, he could see a patch of cold, grey sky, a gift from the heavens. The Doctor moved himself so that his back was against the wood, before catching a sliver of the sun, and holding it for a moment in his palm.

WHEN they came for the Doctor, they dressed him in the long robes of the alchemist, Byzantine velvet and crisp silk. On his skull they placed the signature cap of the Doctor, a small black hat that moulds to the shape of his head, ending just above his ears. They give him his cane, his beard brushed and arranged, and he was then placed in the cart at the port of Barcelona. As he rode through the city to the court of the king, the Doctor regaled his captors with stories.

THE SECOND TALE

Which treats of the deaf-mute

There once was a man who could not speak and so was unable to confess his sins. Since birth he had been a hermit but upon hearing the calling of the sun he left the mountains to win his fortune. Travelling by rivers, he slept on the damp stream-beds, drinking from a cupped hand. Perched on the banks of an icy pool or a shady glade, he admired the dragonfly as she skimmed the water and traced the path of the peregrine falcon with his finger. He watched the sun rise from haystacks and dreamt of the glory of the Universe and every footstep brought him closer to his destiny.

But when he offered his calloused words to the guards at the gates of the city they jeered and threw rocks at him for he was a poor man, ugly and unkempt. Weeping, he wandered the graveyards, uttering incomprehensible sounds. He could not communicate his love or his pain or his suffering in any language understandable to man. The priests would not take him into their hearts as they saw this deficit as a sign of the Devil. The shopkeepers did not like his groaning and so beat him. The city dwellers threw him sweetmeats and scraps from their table and laughed as he foraged in the dust.

'Get ye hence and sleep in the graveyard, on the stones of the deceased, for it is the closest you will come to heaven,' they snarled, believing that if a man could not speak in a house of God, he could not confess, and if he could not confess he could not be rid of sin – a fact that ensured his certain passage unto hell upon his death. At night lamentations of the man filled the streets as he roamed the courtyard of the house of God. By day, he wove baskets filled with white lilies and peaches as gifts for the fallen, selling them for a penny to housewives and despondent lovers who came to weep on the graves. Soon the man died, and there was great debate as to where he should be buried. A priest stepped forward, arguing that though the man was damned, the graveyard had been his home in life and so should be his home in death. That evening they planted him without ceremony in the loose soil. They gave him no casket and no coffin because he had left them only his flowers and hoped that the worms would eat him away into nothing so that the saved would not have to share their bed with a sinner. For many days there was silence in the streets. The priests and the shopkeepers and the city dwellers gave thanks that their slumber was no longer disturbed by the moaning of the man who could not speak a proper word. A week passed and then another, with such quiet that all seemed peaceful and good until they awoke one evening to a magnificent song played in the golden notes of a flute loud as the trumpets of war. In the graveyard of the church the earth trembled and shook. The priests and shopkeepers and city dwellers rushed to their windows and doors and watched as a conifer erupted from the ground and grew in great leaps and plunges in the air, sprouting leaves of gold and silver and cones of ebony and pearl and still it grew – shooting into the sky – pressing up to the heavens with its golden branches. The pine towered over the church as a giant, its great roots heaving from the ground, tearing at the earth until a glorious golden cage emerged, formed by the roots of the tree, and there the body of the un-confessed man was preserved.

His skin was pale and washed and smelling of cinnamon and cloves. The sorrow had fallen away from his face and he was young and beautiful. His lips parted in a secret smile, his hair filled with the flowers he had sold for the graves, while each of the dead man's prayers ripened into golden fruit inscribed with the letters of his secret, like the emanations of the sephiroth, and the priests ran out and crossed themselves and prayed as a Hand of God rearranged the letters in the tree so that it read in a scroll suspended in the golden leaves: 'I understand all languages, even those incomprehensible to man, and if a prayer is made in good faith I hear it and love the creature who has uttered these words and will pave his way to heaven with gold.'

The tree of gold stayed illumined for twelve days and twelve nights, and when the gold faded it became a giant, living pine with brown bark and green leaves, roots firmly planted in the swampy earth. The deaf–mute departed to heaven and the church, feeling rightly that a miracle had graced their squalid grounds, rebuilt itself with Gothic fervour, taking the name Santa Maria del Pi or Our Lady of the Pine.

THE THIRD TALE

Which treats of the Doctor's return to the court

It is through this square that they paraded Doctor Illuminatus, a slow procession beneath the needles of the tree. The royal emissary, a dour-faced man with a hooked nose, took him to the Court of the Kings, el Palau Reial, where the noble captain of the ship told of this doctor's triumph and of his fall from grace. At the appointed hour, a soldier arrived with a message from the House of Rossinyol, a gold coin with the Nightingale mark, which he passed into the Doctor's mouth in a morsel of meat from the king's table. The Doctor understood then that he had been purchased for the price of a good horse and seven gold effigies, and on the stage he bowed his head and declared:

'My liege, I am the cursed Doctor Illuminatus who will live for a thousand years. You have plucked me from the shores of my fair island to please your citizens. Lords and ladies, courtiers and cour-tesans, ask me any question and I will tell you its answer, for there are no secrets from the living or the dead which are unknown in the secrets of another.'

With that the Alchemist embarked on the story of his first encounter with the Nightingale on the island of Mallorca.

✠

THE FOURTH TALE

Which treats of the Nightingale

Many lifetimes ago, on the eve of Sant Joan, at the midsummer point in the year when the night is longest and the fern blossoms, the Doctor gathered in a bowl his medicinal plants from his field on Puig de Randa. He bathed them in the water from the nine springs that emerged from rocks below his hermit's cave and left the bowl at the entrance of his cavern so that it would catch the morning dew as the sun rose over the eastern seas. That evening he lit a fire to banish the dark spirits, and sat beside the blaze looking out over the villages to the North, South, East and West. At midnight he put out his fire and went to bed. At dawn, when he rose and went to collect his water, he found, to his immense irritation, that the bowl had disappeared, and with it the dew and with it the plants. He scanned the fields, suspecting an errant sheep had come to steal his holy water. There he saw her! Over the small rise to his vegetable patch below. The culprit slept soundly!

At first he thought she was a wolf, her form was so thick with fur. But he looked closer – no, she was a black ewe who had curled up on his vegetable patch to die. *Peuuuu*, he whistled through his teeth. Scat! *Sheeu!* She did not move. With a deftness surprising for his age the alchemist scrambled down the rocky shale towards the sleeping creature. 'Ewe! Ewe! Wake! Tell me what you have taken.' As the animal moved, the wind rushed out of him! It was a girl wrapped in the cloak of a sheep pelt. Beneath this cloak she was naked, her hair and flesh dark as *la Moreneta*. My God! He turned his eyes to heaven. She was covered in wax burns! Her skin pierced with needles, they had made a mark on her breast like a teat ...

The Doctor sat down on the damp earth.

'Are you a witch?' he asked. Her eyes rolled into her forehead and she collapsed in a faint.

Summoning his strength, Illuminatus picked the girl up, and brought her to his cave. He built a bed for her on the floor and devised a structure of birch panels to shield her privacy. Three days she slept without stirring. At the end of the third day a lord on horseback appeared at the gate of the hermitage. The lord travelled alone, his horse and carriage striking.

'Good Doctor,' the lord said. 'I have lost my wife's sister, who has run away. A girl of sixteen. She is deaf and mute and generally bad, but my wife is distraught and I am worried for her safety.'

When the Doctor opened his mouth to speak the voice of intuition rose in his mind: *Do not give the girl to him. This man is wicked. He wears her blood on his sleeve.* Not for the first time in his life Rex Illuminatus lied.

'I have seen no girl. When did you lose her?'

'On the night of John the Baptist,' he replied.

'I suggest you check the river to the south – I heard a human noise among my flock that night which passed towards the ravines before the flatlands ...'

The lord thanked him cordially.

'Be warned. She converses with the spirits of the Dead. We have tried to wash the Devil out of her, but he is rooted deep. You have heard the stories of the Ophites? This girl is of their blood.'

'I know it well,' Illuminatus said. 'I will pray for her.'

'Should you see any signs, please send word and I will come for her. We are fearing she will never be returned to us.' With that the lord flexed the muscles of his legs and moved his horse to leave, but not before crying over his shoulder: 'By the Grace of God, my wife is a converted heretic, but her sister is unrepentant. The girl is a witch!'

Rex Illuminatus returned to his cave full of worry. That evening the girl awoke and gestured for food. When she ate, the Doctor saw the cause of her muteness. A brutal hand had removed the tongue of the girl, leaving a horrid stump in her mouth. He brought her pen and paper and asked her what had happened, but the girl had no knowledge of writing. She pushed the ink away. Then, thinking swiftly, the Doctor retrieved a loom, and five colours of thread he made from the fleece of his flock. He asked her to weave a dress, and this she did gladly, growing more powerful in strength every day. In the mornings she tended his garden. Her bruises lightened. She helped Illuminatus with his esoteric studies, making the inks for his illuminations, and he taught her how to handle gold and the paints with which he wrote his books. One day Illuminatus spoke softly to the woman sitting on the stone of his cave.

'Creation is an act of God,' he mused. 'The Act of Creation is holy. It is something from nothing. It is alchemy. In this Art we have been given nine letters of an alphabet from which you can answer any question, containing all the secrets of the natural world. The Artist should know the alphabet by heart, as well as the figures, definitions and rules – along with the arrangements before proceeding in their knowledge. The alchemy of which I speak is not that which is summarily conceived of as the practice.'

The Doctor wandered through his vials and instruments looking for a book.

'In this is contained the mirror of the world,' he said. 'I have written it for this express purpose. And thus the world is a mirror of this book. It is my art, and as all art is an act of creation, all the universe is contained in the act of its doing and non-doing. As the lover loves the beloved, and the beginning seeks by the middle to the end, and all answers are connected to the questions by the ladder of the intellect and the subjects of the imagination and transmutation, this book will contain in its letters and numbers the answer to your curse. For if you have been touched by the brush of his love you cannot utter this devil's name aloud. But with this book you may offer some clue of his enterprise so that you may be free of your silence.'

And he sighed from experience, for he too had known murder and he too had known love. With that the Doctor showed the woman the figures of his art and he taught her daily the languages of Latin, Catalan, Hebrew, Arabic and Mathematics, along with French and English, such that she could write in all. She read the Talmud, the Koran, as well as Plato and Aristotle. And when she was ready he taught her the language of his ancient art, and the means of transcribing it onto paper.

'K and 9 both consist of two parts, which extend the reach of this true art,' he added factually, running his finger down the illuminated page. 'With these figures you may answer any question in the world. And with these numbers, you may amplify and extend their meaning.'

From the steps of the small house built of stone and the fallen branches of a tree, the woman turned. She felt the breeze on her cheeks and the warmth on her face where her tears had fallen. She entered his cave and emerged wearing the dress she had woven; on each pleat of the skirt there was a figure in black, like the patterns of a Grecian urn, and from this he understood that the girl had been forced upon by her sister's husband, and refusing to lie with him, she had been locked into his hunting lodge beneath the mountain of the Doctor's hermitage and been raped repeatedly; in being so, her sister's marriage had been defiled and her own flower broken. Her brother-in-law grew wrathful when she threatened to escape. As punishment he cut out her tongue, and left her to die in the forest alone.

IV

EMILY SHARP

Professor Emily Sharp, American Doctor of English Literature at the University of Barcelona, lectures in the morning. I arrive early and install myself in the back before she introduces the material. I settle into my seat unobtrusively. There's a slow trickle of students arriving. Many are my own age – postgraduates, PhD candidates, fellowship researchers. I blend easily into the crowd. We sit like the congregated citizens of a roman amphitheatre, stuffed into metal desks.

Professor Sharp does not hold back. She commands the assembled army with abrupt consonants, her colouring Nordic, her features youthful; her skin silvery, translucent blonde hair pulled back into a tight ponytail behind pink ears. Eyes spread like a pretty fish. She blinks behind tortoiseshell horn-rimmed spectacles; the lines of her tailoring are simple, her chest flat. Elegant grey slacks, thin belt, loose blouse, high on the collar. She's not showing much flesh, in a demure, slightly nervous way, but her voice is strong, unwavering. She lectures in English, for the advanced students. The course for the semester: 'The Art/Nature debate in English Poetry', beginning with the emergence of alchemy as a literary trope.

'*Al* is the definitive article in Arabic, while *Kimia* originates in one of two potential sources.' Professor Sharp clicks through – the opening slide of her lecture. 'The first is *kmt* – or *chem* in Greek – the Ancient Egyptian name for Egypt, meaning "black earth", referring to the ebony soil of the Nile, in contrast to the yellow sands of the desert. Thus rendering the true name of alchemy "of Egypt" or the Egyptian Art.'

The students wriggle in their desks. I watch her. Can she pluck me from the crowd? Can she strike out by my bearing, or does my face read infantile, betraying a certain youthful naivety? Am I one of them? Or an outcast on the periphery? The hawkish students, pencils poised over notebooks, scratch words into paper.

Professor Sharp scans the multitude.

Is that a smile? Did the corner of her mouth twitch?

'*Kimia* may also be derived from a second source word – the Ancient Greek *chyma* suggests a more science-oriented definition. If we take *chyma* as the base for "alchemy" meaning to "fuse" or "cast together", we can see how *Alkimia* has given birth to our modern "chemistry". Over the course of this semester we will follow the repercussions of this linguistic metamorphosis in the arts and sciences, studying the emergence of the Scientific Revolution and the Enlightenment through the eyes of English poets from Chaucer to William Blake.'

A poem flashes up on the lecture screen behind the pulpit. Chaucer: *The Canon's Yeoman's Tale*. 'I'd like to draw your attention to lines 773–77 in your Riverside Editions.' The crunch of turning pages.

'When you were reading the poem, did anything jump off the page? What do you make of Chaucer's stance on the alchemical arts?' Professor Sharp checks in with the class. 'Any takers? Thoughts? Feelings? Throw something at me.'

When the lecture is over, students rustle as they leave their seats. A healthy chatter. Plans are made for the evening, phone numbers exchanged. Giggles and flirtations ignited. Who was that handsome fellow in the corner? That enigmatic girl with the plaited hair? I stand and walk down the wooden stairs to the lecture pit, making my way through the crowd.

'Professor Sharp,' I say when I reach the bottom.

She looks at me vaguely.

'Anna Verco, from Picatrix.'

The haze lifts.

'So glad you could make it.' She reaches out both hands and takes mine. 'It is such a relief you are here. Finally I can share the burden – maybe even unload it entirely.' She laughs: a little chiming bell. Suddenly she is very, very pretty. 'Do you mind waiting a moment while I gather my things?'

Professor Sharp opens the door to her office, clutching her notes in a brown satchel, the strap broken and retied at her shoulder.

'Welcome to my lair.' She slumps into the plush velvet chair behind her desk. 'Take a seat. Make yourself comfortable.'

The room is large, fitted with glamorous floor-to-ceiling bookshelves that suit a library. A medieval folio is framed on the back of the door and a series of research awards are arranged on the windowsill behind an opulent desk. The desk's oak surface is mounted with green felt. A stapler, paper clips and a small figurine of Santa Eulàlia in gold rest beside the computer. She checks her watch.

'I'm slightly more cramped for time today than I had hoped.' Emily takes off her glasses and looks at me closely. Her eyes squint in the half-light. 'You have written some very provocative papers in the past, and I am sure that if you really have the talent your colleagues seem to grace you with, then you will handle this material well. Though it does strike me as somewhat outside your remit. There, are, however some rules I'm going to lay out.'

This isn't unusual. She offers coffee. I accept. I listen to her speak quietly; she wants trust, faith, a degree of respect, privacy and to not be named. I afford her all this. She wants the private material we go over – her relationship to the boy who walked into the sea, their living arrangements and her long dead friendship with his sister – to be off the record. I agree – to a certain point: I won't be bullied. If it is integral to the story, I say, then I will have to relate some of the details so that the picture is complete.

I make my own position clear: I don't hang people's underwear out in public unless I really don't like them. She takes the pill, but then, of course, her eyes flash. 'You might not like *me*.'

I laugh. 'I swear to behave in a respectable manner with your story.'

The conversation eases. Emily Sharp explains that she had come to Barcelona in 2003 to assist one Professor Guifré (now deceased) in the classification and analysis of a well-known Mallorcan mystic by the name of Ramon Llull.

'Things don't happen in life as you plan. Originally I hoped to get a research fellowship at Oxford, but another member of my cohort won the position and I had to look for something else. I was in the fourth year of my PhD, read Latin, spoke Catalan and Spanish after completing my undergraduate degree in Comparative Literature. I applied for a Fulbright in Spain to work with Guifré and when the grant came through . . . I leapt at the chance. To some people in my programme the choice seemed illogical. I, however, could always see the through-line, though I didn't think I'd ever wind up being a professor here. When the call came in from the Universitat de Barcelona . . . I thought why not. I moved back here in 2011. It is a shame you can't speak with Guifré about this.' Her eyes cast down. 'He passed away three years ago, just after offering me this position in his faculty . . . But I'm getting off track.'

She catches herself. Redirects.

'You wanted to talk about those letters. At the time it wasn't unusual for me to receive manuscript files from Guifré to analyse. As his research assistant I often dealt with primary resources. But even I, lowly student that I was, recognized that these were particularly strange papers. I received scans of four letters sent through by the police. Parchment pages illuminated in a traditional style . . . They had no author and no context. They were eerie and unsettling. Laden with a deliberately obfuscated meaning. I remember . . . there was something electric about them.'

She sighs. 'That summer has never been a place I permit myself to return to, despite the fact that, years later . . . I'm living here. Though nothing is ever quite the same? Is it?'

In the library on the morning of Friday, 20 June 2003, Emily opens her email and downloads the files sent by Jorge Guifré. She compiles a list of the images. Colours, postulated dyes, associated symbolic meanings. She is surprised by the fact that the diagrams on the second page of each letter are immediately recognizable. Each circle drawn within the other, divided into nine sections, creating three thin rings around a central image – three overlaid triangles. The numbers 3 and 9 are magic numbers, with important significance. *Three for the Trinity – the Father, Son and Holy Spirit – and nine for the Llullian elements of God.*

There can be no mistaking the charts. This she confirms in an email to Guifré. She cites them as being exact reproductions of *Figure T* of the medieval philosopher Ramon Llull. *I'm equally certain that they are direct copies*, Guifré responds. Emily's eyes scans the outer ring of the diagram, fixing on the two-headed snake coiling into itself. Her eyes linger on the curves of its twin belly. With a few hits to the keyboard she enlarge the image. A golden serpent swallowing its tail, shimmering on the page. *Interesting*, she writes to

Professor Guifré, *even a little bit clichéd. Without a doubt a reference to the Hermetic Arts. Ouroboros. Not a difficult reference to find. Well done.* He replies: *You are correct. Can you do a survey of the reference for noon? I'd like you in a meeting with the individual who sent through these files. Come fifteen minutes before. We'll discuss at 11.45.* A shiver of delight runs down her spine. *An ouroboros.* Symbolically, quite like a dragon, often even synonymous.

Emily leaves her desk and speaks to the earnest librarian at the special archives collection. She hands over a set of call numbers to the woman, who says the batch will be ready in the Secure Reading Room in forty-five minutes to an hour. *The books will be put aside for the rest of the day, you may return at any point . . .* The woman frowns severely. *But you are not allowed to bring anything in with you.* All pens, pencils and personal items must be left with the security guard at the door. Emily thanks her profusely and returns to the notes on her desk.

It is at this precise moment that Emily Sharp's peace is disturbed by the angry buzzing of her phone on the desk beside her. Emily answers it.

'Can you come home?' Núria Sorra asks breathlessly.

'Can't. Busy,' Emily whispers, cupping her hand over her mouth. 'I'm in the Athenaeum.'

'Oh.'

'Why?'

'It's Adrià.'

'What's he done—'

Núria cuts her off. 'I really need you. Now.'

'Call your uncle,' Emily says fiercely. Núria's uncle lived around the block from her apartment, a grand flat tucked behind the Picasso Museum.

'Emily, I need your help.'

'I have a meeting. I can't leave.'

'This is more important than a meeting.'

'More important than a meeting?' The library monitor raises an eyebrow.

'No, seriously, I need you to come over. I need you to be here soon,' Núria continues.

'He needs help.'

'I need help.'

'Call your mom. Call your dad.'

'I can't reach them.'

Emily ducks into the women's toilets on the library floor. Núria's voice wells up with tears.

'I need you to come now.'

'You realize how important this is, don't you?'

'I'm scared.'

'Of your brother?'

'I'm frightened.'

'I don't have time—'

'*Capitalista!*' Núria shouts and hangs up.

In the toilets of the library, Emily turns on the lights and looks at her face in the mirror. Her make-up has streaked – the mascara has left a fine black powder that emphasizes the circles forming beneath her eyes. She has struggled to sleep at home for the past few nights, even with earplugs, and the signs are showing. She feels disgusted at herself, at the smell of sweat she discovers under her armpits, clinging to her from the morning run – her tight brown dress, a size too small, the one she had bought on sale at H&M for twelve euros. Cheap metal necklace round her throat. Her breasts bubble up over the top rim of fabric – goose-bumped and raised, like skinned apples. She pushes them back down, into place. Emily runs her fingers in the water of the tap and began to clean away the black streaks of mascara beneath her eyes.

Some time later, a knock at Guifré's door pounds three times. Guifré dusts off his hands.

'And so the treasured calm departs,' he hums, hopping off his chair. Emily watches his belly wobble as he pads to the door and gingerly greets the inspector.

'*Bon dia*, Jorge.' Inspector Fabregat embraces the professor. 'Have I caught you in flagrante? *Hòstia!* Who is this lovely young lady?' He doffs his hat at Emily in the corner. She flushes a bright crimson. Inspector Fabregat saunters deeper into the office.

'Refreshments, Guifré? Is there such a thing as refreshments in this establishment?'

The fat professor bristles. Emily finds the inspector handsome. Disarming. A world apart from the men at the university. She has trouble focusing, scratching at the corner of her thumbnail, tearing at the skin. Inspector Fabregat flops into a plush armchair.

'I'm tired,' he proclaims loudly. 'The whole business is terrible for the morale, Gordito!' *Little fatty*. 'I've been thinking of an early retirement.' He puts his feet up on the coffee table, resting them on a history of the Balearic world. Guifré grumbles. Emily stifles a giggle.

'I want to know what you think of what the bastard sent me! I wish you'd come down to the damned site, man.'

'You are well aware I am working for your department on a casual basis,' the professor huffs loudly. 'Until we unlock the language of the text, we will be of little use to you. And please take your feet off the table. That footstool you have colonized is my most recent publication.'

Fabregat does as he is told, settling his weight into the seat below him, his shirt tight at the seams. He worries his cap between his fingers. 'You've seen the files? And no – I don't take sugar.' He puts a hand out to stop Emily, catching her eye. He winks. 'Bitter. Just milk will do.'

Professor Guifré adjusts his spectacles on his nose and frowns. Emily hands round the drinks. Guifré asks that Emily bring the files up on the projector. Illustrations dark on the page, indigo close to black. Fabregat studies the notched dial at the centre of the figures.

Confronted with the inspector's brash exterior, Emily struggles to remember what she meant to suggest as analysis. One letter stands out purely for its beauty – Emily is enchanted by the delicate brushwork, the authenticity of the characters – *painstaking hours for every stroke*, she thinks. *A calligrapher's life of dedication.* Curled into the letter B – she had gazed in awe! – a male devil with the feet of a goat who carries a bird Emily identifies as a nightingale, woven into a single consonant accompanied by a green lion, holding a map of Barcelona – the old town and Gothic, with the church peaks rising out of the mass of thatched roofs. The letters are dotted with ornate combinations of consonants and numbers – generally consisting of a strange gibberish. The devil always paired with a soaring bird – a nightingale, from whose beak emerged ornate lines of poetry. Most of all she admires the design of the golden serpent that recurs as a signature in the corner of each page, the size of a dime or the stamped press of a wax seal.

Emily's notes direct Inspector Fabregat to the *Libro di Biadiolo*, held in Florence, and the *Belleville Breviary* at the Bibliothèque Nationale in Paris – with special emphasis on the royal illustrator Jean Pucelle, who employed ornamental flowers, dragonflies, swallows, and distorted, miniature musicians in the border of his work – such that the text itself appeared to sprout petals and leaves, curling ivy and roses, like the music of devils that play the flute menacingly, vines tumbling forth from terrible illustrations of vengeance against young women, dramatizations of the lives of martyrs, Emily assumes, weaving into and out of a nonsensical combinations of letters and words. *The artist is clearly well-versed in the art of illumination, and its history, drawing references from the period.* Beyond this observation, however (and a detailed explanation of the typical meanings of an array of classical symbols), there is limited information Emily can give about the nature of the writings. '*Egg tempera and leaf gold*'; as to the paper, '*Parchment made in the traditional style*', are her descriptive comments. It is obvious that the anonymous author had a purpose in writing – but whether that purpose was sheer madness or eccentricity – or what import these letters held – neither she nor Guifré can say.

Fabregat and Guifré discuss the mystery for a while in oblique terms. Later she voices her feelings that the lines of poetry were intermingled with a text that took direct inspiration from the illustrated manuscripts of the thirteenth or fourteenth century (hence the medieval dates at the bottom of two verses).

Her phone buzzes silently in the pocket of her dress, against her thigh, a hot, warm warning. Emily offers coffee from a stainless steel pot on Guifré's desk. Fabregat accepts.

'Do you want to answer that?' he asks her, phone still buzzing in her pocket.

'No.' She blushes again. 'Sorry. I'll turn it off.'

Fabregat terse. 'Let's cut to the chase. The lines of poetry. Do you have any idea of what the hell this means?'

'No.' Guifré flustered as a beetroot. He huffs and heaves. 'Did he send you any more than this? Have you received anything else?'

Fabregat shakes his head. Emily's interest piqued.

'God help us,' Guifré laments. 'We know what they are, Fabsy, I've told you as much, but what, why, or who sent them?' The professor sorrowful. 'I am not a savant. I cannot know these things.'

The inspector barks back at him. 'So there's nothing in any of the letters that provides any clue to what it means?'

'Ah. "Meaning" ... what is the meaning of meaning?' Guifré laments again to no one. 'We can make some headway. Individually, the illustrations, for instance, are translatable,' Guifré says. 'The diagrams belong, as we have already told you, to the medieval Catalan philosopher Ramon Llull. The snake is an ouroboros and most likely a signature of the sender. The dates beneath the verses here —' he points to the screen — 'and here, also link to Ramon Llull. We start with *1312–1317*, if we are to assume they reference the Common Era. This is the window within which Ramon Llull died. We have no historical confirmation of this event, which is estimated to have occurred between 1315 and 1316 CE. Coincidence? I think not. The second set of dates *1182–1188* are more perplexing. We cannot be sure of what they refer to in the life of Llull ... Emily has gone through possibilities, and the strongest implication seems to be the 1184 CE Papal Bull of Pope Lucius III, the *Ad Abolendam*, which emerged from a growing desire to eradicate diverse heresies in Western Europe, particularly the Cathars.' Guifré muddles his words, takes a deep breath and starts again with a loud huff.

'Given that Ramon Llull was the victim of a similar anti-heretical Papal Bull two centuries later, there could be something there ...'

'And what do you make of this?'

Guifré shrugs. 'That your writer is a fan of Ramon Llull, perhaps?'

It leaps out at me as soon as Emily begins speaking to me about her involvement in the whole affair. It would not have been their fault. Guifré didn't misread the signs.

No. Not at all. To some extent the assumption was justified. *But they are not the same. Their language is different. And this is key. Accurate translation is crucial in a game of symbols. Misread the reference, and you are doomed.* Guifré would not have wanted to see the alternative, though he might have recognized the parallel. And he would not have wanted to see the difference because it would not have followed *logically*, given the information he had to hand.

Is there any doubt?

I ask myself.

Could you be wrong?

No.

Guifré would have argued against you if he were alive.

Yes.

He would have said: Llull's venerated tomb in Palma is emblazoned with a stained-glass crest in the Basílica de San Francisco. A golden crescent moon hanging against a scarlet shield, sliver curved towards the earth, facing the abyss.

He would have said: Is this not the moon carved between the breast of three girls?

Is this not the divine alphabet on her clavicle, on her cheek, on her belly, on her thigh, on her calf? Do these letters not correlate exactly with Ramon Llull? Do the symbols not align?

Yes and No.

I scratch things in my notepad.

An exquisite misinterpretation. No one else will follow me.

It is true that Ramon Llull was born in 1232 CE on Mallorca. In 1315, at the venerable age of eighty-three, after a career which took him to the University of Paris and into the heart of papal power, Llull travelled by Genoan ship to Tunis as a Christian missionary. His last official works were written in December 1315, dedicated to the Sultan Abu Yahya Ibn al-Lihyani. Christian lore claims that the Doctor was stoned to death by infidels and died a martyr. More likely he was forced to flee the city, becoming fatally ill on the Genoese ship that delivered him home, and expiring before reaching his native island. As a result of conflicting testimony, scholars do not know precisely when or where Llull died. In a life that is otherwise painstakingly recorded, he vanishes from history. There is no end date. No final word. No closure. But something very interesting happens after Llull dies.

He posthumously becomes one of the most significant alchemists in Renaissance Europe. Everyone reads his treatises on base metals and *Sal ammoniac*. His *Secrets of Secrets*. From Giordano Bruno (whose proclivity led him to an untimely end) to Giovanni Pico della Mirandola (who tutored Michelangelo), to Paracelsus and Athanasius Kircher, to the poets John Donne and – perhaps even – John Milton, to Montaigne and Voltaire right down to the Enlightenment luminaries. The avaricious Newton and his earnest enemy Leibnitz both kept copies of Llull's works in their libraries. Despite the fact that Ramon Llull never wrote in favour of the alchemical arts, he became its rising star, a legend, one of the few who achieved success, who minted rosy nobles. And like his counterpart Nicolas Flamel, Llull was famed to have lived forever.

Who was responsible for this shift?

Someone who took his name, or was given it accidentally (so the story goes): a true alchemist. A genius of the arts. A man whose writing first appeared in 1332 CE, identified as a Catalan alchemist living in London. In contemporary studies we call this man – or men – the 'Pseudo-Llull', and the texts he produced *pseudo-Llullian manuscripts*.

Academics now generally conceded that the anonymous Catalan alchemist who wrote *The Book of the Secrets of the Nature of the Quintessence* (*Liber de secretis naturae seu de quinta essentia*) and the highly circulated *Testamentum* was none other than Rex Illuminatus. Which changes everything. Dates rattling through my memory: court records of Castile and León declare that on 2 December

1572, Rex Illuminatus was repatriated from the Peruvian colony, having been charged with a crime of witchcraft. Allegations place the age of the alchemist at 343, a remarkable claim generally accepted as false. *He has all his teeth*, the report notes, *and the face of a young man, and yet the Alchemist claims to have been born on Mallorca in 1229.* The report concludes that the alchemist is immortal – well over 300 years old. His name was *Llum* – meaning *Light* – which became easily confused with *Llull*, due to the fact that both simultaneously took on the title *Doctor Illuminatus*. Rex Illuminatus possessed a highly unusual lineage, and as a result was immediately suspicious. '*All is One and One is All*' was the proclaimed mantra of the alchemist, but in the damning words of the Inquisitor General: *Rex Illuminatus belongs to no one.* (*Let them call me what they will*, Illuminatus said, *but they will never have my soul, which I give only to an eternal sensation of Love, Love without strictures. Love without boundaries. The Engendering Love of Creation.*)

Here, before me, I connect the missing pieces of a primary, crucial mistake.

I would have told them. Had I been there. 'I would have said: 'You are scrambling in the dark. You are refusing to see what is in front of your nose.' I visit Llull's tomb every now and then. Out of curiosity more than anything else.

To understand what he was not.

Emily directs me back to the past. In the small office, seated with an increasingly glum Inspector Fabregat, Professor Guifré drones on about the medieval period that informed the creation of Llull's work. For the most part, Emily is silent, studying the markings on the paper. She reads every document carefully, making notes on a small pad she produces from her briefcase and a blunt pencil with a chewed eraser. Finally, after receiving a permissive nod from

Guifré, she speaks with confidence, her dress flowing in brown pleats about her knees.

'Well ... You see these rings – they're not circles, they're wheels – if you imagine the circular figures as three-dimensional you would have something reminiscent of a compass, separate dials spinning on an axis kept on a flat plane – that's what the writer's given you, a machine of changes as it were. And each of these letters – here you have *K B E H C F I D G* – they will have multiple meanings within the same family of extremes. Spin the wheels, and the letters and numbers will align to form combinations with systematized meanings. A coded language, Inspector. Look at the letters. In Llull's case he invented a nine-letter alphabet with each letter representing a family of words.'

Emily's American accent cuts through the Latin: 'Here you have B for Boniface, C for Magnitudo, D for Eternitas, E for Potestas, F for Sapientia, G for Voluntas, H for Virtus, I for Veritas, and K for Glorias. In a nutshell: God and everything created in his universe are formed of: *Goodness, Greatness, Eternity, Power, Wisdom, Will, Virtue, Truth and Glory.* In essence, Llull built one of the earliest versions of a programming language. What academics now consider a medieval truth machine. Sadly, he never had the technology to fully realize his plans.'

Fabregat nods. 'And what is that?'

'A chart of symbols.' Guifré's voice swoons across the room. 'Engineered to answer any question in the world – a book to rival the Bible, to unravel the workings of the dogmatic Church, a logic system incapable of being marred by human deception. The true voice of God on earth, the unadulterated mathematics of the cosmos, the genesis of the computer.'

Fabregat coughed. 'How would you use the circle to ask questions?'

'Each letter of BCDEFGHIK is also representative of a query word, like 'What?' or 'Where?'. So you can ask a question in a three-letter combination where the middle word denotes a question.'

'Sounds fucking complicated.'

'It is.' Guifré pauses, unsteady. 'But no more so than the language programmers use today. You ask a question of the system, and – if you imagine this diagram as a machine – you would then spin the wheels. A combination of numbers and letters is produced by this action, and the question is answered in the combination. This answer will consist of a limited number of variables (the nine-letter alphabet), which in turn produces a logical order of meaning in the letter–number combination. Basic tautology, Inspector Fabregat, before such notions had been articulated systematically.'

'You're telling me it produces a legible code?'

'A language, Inspector Fabregat. A divine infallible language. What you have in front of you is taken from the embryo of modern computer science. A total logic system. In this, Ramon Llull's work was groundbreaking.'

The inspector pulls a cigarette out of the case in his pocket and lights up, facing the projection of the figures. 'I'm here for facts. Do we have anything in here that can help us find an author?'

Professor Guifré makes a series of exasperated humming noises. He retracts his neck, causing a treble chin to appear at the base of his throat, and warbles: 'Believe what you wish to believe. As I have mentioned, the poetry must be understood in relation to the charts before we may begin to understand their full import! Most certainly they are bizarre.'

Fabregat's eyes narrow. 'Meaning?'

'We don't know why these were written or how they came to you. If he signed with a name or some script – perhaps we would know. To be sure, he is a Catholic and an educated calligrapher. This alone we can deduce from these papers . . . with caution.

Correct me if I'm wrong, but one would be horrified if a false translation occurred . . .'

Fabregat's voice breaks on the air. 'Gordito! I love you but I don't have time for this. For God's sake tell me what it means, or if you can't . . . God damn it, if you can't, I also need to know!'

He kicks the coffee table in a fit. Guifré huffs to himself, then offers to pour another cup of coffee. Fabregat declines. Guifré checks the clock on his office desk.

'I'm sorry, Gordito,' the inspector says, mollified.

Guifré smacks his lips sternly. 'Your cryptologist has been in touch for any sign of a classic cipher . . . but I'm afraid that at the moment there is none. The lines of poetry are gibberish, gobbledygook! They are mad! I suggest you take them to a psychologist rather than a medievalist. The trouble is . . . this arrangement of information. It is perplexing in its presumption of meaning.'

Fabregat blinks. 'Its presumption of *what*?'

'Meaning.' Guifré points to the text on his screen as if this were obvious. 'The levels of layering suggest that the letters are intended to be analysed by an initiate, someone who would understand the verses immediately, and whose understanding would be vastly illuminated by the proximity of that poetry to these charts.'

'So why would a murderer send them to me?'

'Ah! You have hit upon the problem, sir. That is the question! What you have is a mystery, Inspector.' Guifré bellows as he heaves his bulk across the room. 'A true and portentous mystery! Extraordinary! Most extraordinary. Should you give us a year or two, I'm sure we would have it, it's just that in the constraints of a morning . . . Time, Inspector, is a costly commodity . . .'

'A year or *two*?' Fabregat explodes, launching into a string of expletives.

'Clearly we can help you no more.' Guifré switches off the projections. 'And now it is lunch. Will you join us, Inspector? The café is magnificent, you may have a glorious soup and, should it tickle you, *croquetas*! My God, *croquetas* of Catalonia's finest. It is a veritable delight to sup here – nothing like the halls of Oxford but a delight nonetheless!'

Fabregat collects himself, wiping his forehead with a handkerchief before standing to shake the professor's hand.

'Come now, Inspector. Take heart! We'll send you any thoughts.' Guifré clutches Fabregat's hand in his bearlike paws. 'Emily will be doing a bit more work on this – won't you? But for now, it remains a mystery. A dreadful, dreadful mystery.'

Emily stands to say goodbye, her long skirt falling to the ground. Her phone buzzes in her pocket. She reaches for it, sees the message, then stops herself. Fabregat holds her eyes firmly in his. Goosebumps on her wrists, he notices, looking down, and then returns his eyes to her face.

'Everything alright, Miss Sharp?' Fabregat asks.

Apologizing for the interruption, Emily excuses herself. When the office door closes behind her, she checks the message again. And then she runs. She runs out of the library, pushing through the stiles, past the library docents who tut-tut behind her. She runs into the street and out across the park, adrenaline pounding through her body, muscles burning into muscles, her feet sending her flying forward, racing against time.

In the office Emily Sharp drifts. She floats on air.

'You knew him well, didn't you?' I ask softly. *A strange coincidence.*

'Adrià?' she murmurs, playing with the cap of a pen on her desk. 'I knew him as well as you know any person you live with.'

Her gimlet eyes make me uncomfortable.

'Are you trying to write some pattern of logic into this?'

'Perhaps.'

'How many other people are you speaking to?'

'For the moment? Just you.'

'Why?'

'I thought you might have some insight into his character.'

'His character?' She examines her fingernails. 'There's always been a lot of debate . . . Did he do it, did he not do it? You get tired of being asked. It used to keep me up at night . . .' She worries the top buttons of her shirt. I sense the freshness on her voice. *Reach out to her.* The colour rises to Emily's cheeks. She pours another cup of coffee. Her eyes focus on some vague body sitting in the foreground between us. She is thinking. 'What can you tell me about that day?' I ask. *Start at the beginning. What is your beginning? Your beginning and yours alone. That's what I'm looking for. Your first memory.* We talk openly. I smile, and take notes. And then something interesting happens. I ask a question which connotes intimacy. She steps over a line. Here is a trick: confession is addictive. If you have kept a secret for a long time, the first moment you divulge it, a knot of adrenaline explodes in your stomach and every word that trips out of your mouth is a sensual burst of serotonin. That is, if you are dealing with somebody honest. Never assume this is the case.

At 13.27 on that self-same Friday, 20 June, seventy-two hours before his disappearance, Adrià Daedalus Sorra, man-about-town, disc jockey and student of philosophy, careened up the stairs with his skateboard. When he reached the blue door on the second floor he slung the board off his shoulder and slammed it into the handle, shattering the wood. He slammed the door again. His board snapped in two pieces, which he threw behind him, clattering down the stairs. Adrià rammed his shoulder against the door, banging it twice, then hurled the weight of his body against the lock.

'Núria!' he screamed. 'Núria!'

He beat the door with his fist.

In the living room, Núria huddled on the floor crying. The bay windows onto Passeig del Born were open. The day was warm and the buzz of the crowd below crept up through the windows, winding into the curtains. A little band of students played music at the base of the church beyond Núria's window, and in the street, people were clapping and laughing. A fly hummed lazily through the window and hovered near Núria's left ear.

She sobbed uncontrollably into the floor, pulling her knees up into her chest. Down in the street below, on the black stone steps at the rear entrance of the Gothic Santa Maria del Mar, a woman sang, accompanied by the tinny student orchestra. The song was obscure, little known outside the local community. But through her tears, Núria-La-Catalana, Núria-from-Barcelona, recognized it instantly: '*Se'n Va Anar*'. Written by Salomé for the Festival de la Cançó Mediterrània in 1963, under Franco. Núria choked on her tears and cried harder.

'Let me in!' screamed Adrià. 'Let me in! Let me in! Let me in!'

Blue paint peeling as the door shuddered.

The woman's voice seeped into the room.

I hate him. Núria's mouth tightened. Adrià's fist pounds on the door.

I hate him. I hate him. I hate him.

Twelve months earlier, Núria Sorra lost an apartment in the Gothic due to her brother's unbridled debauchery and she does not want to repeat the experience. The neighbours, terrified by the dubious characters spilling from Adrià's *saló*, had formed a cartel, plotting the removal of the Sorra siblings. After a few calls to the police, and a heated discussion with the landlord, the neighbours on Carrer d'Alemagne successfully orchestrated the Sorras' expulsion from the building – all to Núria's abject mortification.

Now Adrià's festivities have begun again. On Tuesday last, Núria returned from her graduate work at the Institut del Teatre late in the evening, stopping at the Bar de Choco for a few drinks before winding her way home through the Raval. When she arrived at the blue entrance to her apartment, she heard Adrià's braying laugh pouring down from the balcony. Music hugged the street, sludgy drum and bass. From the fourth-floor apartment, a window flew open and an ancient matron in a chequered nightgown peered down into the street. '*Por el amor de Dios!*' the ancient matron cried out, seeing Núria. 'Make them stop!' Núria walked up the stairs to number 5B with steel in her heart. A cloud of marijuana greeted her, a smoky haze through which dark figures moved disjointedly, stumbling into the kitchen to refill tumblers of cheap vodka. Two shadows fumbled in the hallway, boy's hands creeping into a young girl's jeans. Music flooded Núria's ears, a pounding bassline that thickened the blood.

Adrià sat at the centre of it all like a king, a cross-legged *petit dauphin* surveying the court of his anarchy. A spliff hung between lazy fingers as he threw his head back and laughed. He was beautiful here – amidst his courtiers, a prince as delicate in features as his sister, his hair hanging in lank black waves to his shoulder. His face resembles an El Greco portrait of a saint, with fine brows and a long, aquiline nose. Adrià carries himself like an eagle of royal stock, with hands too big for his body and sunken, Byzantine eyes. Swedish Mark sprawled on the couch beside him. Vernon, the dreadlocked, pierced American who made his way in the day via internet gambling, was relating a story of sexual exploits. His ex-girlfriend (now night-time reprieve) dangled across his lap. She was French and loud. One of the Pakistanis who sold beer by the can on the streets was having an animated conversation with Tree, a Dutch university student who dealt coke on the kerb by the late-night club Genet Genet. Settling on the simplest attack, Núria threw her body against the wall, closed her eyes, and flicked on the lights. A terrible whiteness flashed into the room. The bleary-eyed revellers recoiled. Lovers in the corridor covered their faces and a girl threw up in the bathroom.

Adrià lunged off the sofa, instantly defensive. He swore out loud. Swedish Mark shaded his eyes with his hands, while Daisy the cat, stoned to oblivion, slipped peacefully from his shoulders.

'Where's Emily?' Adrià asked.

'Party's over,' Núria said. 'It's three in the morning. Time for you to go clubbing or something.'

'Fuck clubs,' Adrià said.

'I'm serious,' Núria said.

Swedish Mark waved hello.

Adrià raged.

'I don't care,' said Núria. 'I'm going to bed.'

Adrià retaliated: 'These are my people, man, we're having a good time. You're stepping into my territory.'

'Relax, man, relax,' said Mark, tugging at Adrià's shirt.

Adrià sat back into the sofa. Vernon, who had slept with Núria once months ago, leered at her in the brightness.

'Hey, Núria,' he said. Núria ignored him.

'You all need to go.' She pointed at the door.

Adrià glared at his twin. In the courtyard below a wandering drunkard sang discordantly, an old song in Catalan that echoed into the alcoves of the cathedral and drifted solemnly through the open windows of the balcony. The cathedral bell-tower struck the hour. A heavy fullness coloured three sad notes.

A mobile rang. Once. Twice. Núria switched off the music.

'What the fuck, man!' Adrià exploded, flinging the glass next to him to the floor. The glass shattered. In the corridor, the girl caught in the arms of her lover shrieked. Adrià screamed again, picked up another tumbler of vodka from the coffee table, and hurled it at Núria's feet. Mark moved quickly. He grabbed Adrià by the arm and pulled him back down onto the sofa.

'It's all good, *tranquilo*,' Mark said, putting away his phone. 'It's all cool, Adrià. We can go. Lola's at the Macba. They're heading to Alejandro's squat.'

'Cool,' Adrià said, breathing heavily.

'Alright, everyone,' Mark said, taking charge. 'We're going.'

After the exodus, Núria tried to clean the kitchen, after sweeping up the glass in the living room, but gave up in disgust at four in the morning. She made herself a cup of tea and went solemnly to bed. At eight in the morning she was woken by Adrià, still drunk and stoned, desperate for revenge. Lola was there with her mismatched earrings and long black hair. Adrià only had time for Lola, and coiled himself around her in the corner of the blue sofa, reading excerpts from his pornographic novel and explaining the motifs of his art while Tree cut coke on the floor. Adrià was going to start a revolution, a Catalan Independent-State-of-Anarchy-and-Free-Love-Where-Nobody-Worked-and-Everybody-Fucked. Lola thought this was the most beautiful thing she had ever heard, and gazed dreamily into Adrià's red-rimmed eyes. Núria hated this world of the Barcelonauts: the thrashing bodies and heavy music. These nights, when she entered her home, a dark decadence seemed to cling to the walls, reeking of impotence and frustrated revolution. The women were pierced and handsomely dirty, dreadlocks hung down their backs, their conversation coloured by desire. The boys, overstimulated by the presence of attractive women in their midst, reached constantly for that lawless place where tongues and hands are loosened by hash and empty pockets. Lola grinned, offering Núria a joint. 'Enjoy it, *Maca*,' she said, as the red embers smouldered between her fingers. 'Fuck the *Mossos*.' Lola curled her lip at the police.

'He's ill!' Núria shouted. 'He's sick!'

'I'm not fucking sick! This is freedom, Núria. You have no idea what freedom even fucking is!' Flinging up her hands in disgust, Núria gave in to the fates and locked herself in her bedroom. Later that morning as she stepped over the sleeping bodies of the Barcelonauts on her way to class at the Institut del Teatre, she paused at Adrià's shrine, studying his pornographic novel. She removed the icon from its altar, slipping it into her bag. She felt guilty but did not return the object to its owner. Instead she hid the book in her locker at the university. When she returned to her apartment after the morning's lectures, Núria made a life-changing discovery. Beneath a battered copy of short stories of the Latin American Boom Generation, a packet of tobacco and an uncapped pen, Núria found Adrià's keys to the apartment. He had gone out to a course on Schopenhauer at the Autònoma in Terrassa and forgotten them. His sister recognized the power immediately. She confiscated them, clutching the keys in a tight fist. Núria realized once and for all that she did not want Adrià to come into the apartment. Not until he apologized. Not until he stopped having people over. She made that very clear. *He was not to come racing up the stairs and he was not to pass the door. He was not to kick it in, and he was not to touch her.* But Adrià did all these things anyway, just to spite her, hitting her across the face and calling her a Betrayer of Independence and Sexual and Social Revolution! And at three in the afternoon, when the doctors finally came to take him away, their uncle smoked a cigarette in the living room and called the Sorra parents to say Adrià had cracked again, and it was best if they took him out of the city. To the country house – why not take all of them? Get the kids to make up.

'The doctors have got the medication into him, they'll keep him overnight, and then perhaps the country air would do him good?' the uncle suggested hopefully as Núria wailed in the corner, showing the bruises left by her brother to Emily Sharp.

In the train leaving Barcelona that Friday night Emily was hungry and tired and content to disappear – to grab a bite to eat, a few drinks on the river, followed by an early evening in the sleepy country city of Girona. The girls sat side by side, facing forward. Núria had the window seat and pressed her hand to the glass thoughtfully. 'The house is nice,' Núria finally said. 'We go every summer. Adrià and I used to love staying there.'

The fields outside the window were a rich golden yellow. Emily shifted her weight. She would not share what she had thought as she raced up the stairs to their apartment, remembering blood on the floor from where Adrià's hand smashed through the honey yellow windowpane. Instead she asked:

'Will he be alright?'

Núria shrugged. 'I don't know. My parents are bringing him tomorrow.'

A childhood friend of Núria's met them at the station in Girona. She had agreed to host them for the night in an apartment overlooking the sluggish river before Joan picked the girls up in the morning. The friend had a hunch, which she would pursue throughout the evening, plying Emily with alcohol and questions – a hunch built on the observation of Adrià and this

American girl. *Something had passed between them.* Núria's friend was a queen of deduction. *Something suspect. Something sexual.* And here she chewed on her hair thoughtfully. *Adrià and Emily exhibited a tangible amount of attraction, you'd be* tonta *not to notice it – Núria, they like each other,* her friend had whispered long ago. Núria ignored her – Don't be stupid. She knows he's trouble.

'Stupid? You're stupid. Seriously, Núria! It's obvious.'

I do not want her to know. Núria tugged at Emily's shoulder. One evening presented a time frame the girls agreed was manageable, though clearly undesirable. They would go out with the intention to dance the night away, and if possible, with guise and cunning, locate new friends who might be able to entertain them for the nocturnal hours of the escapade. The girls all armpits and necklines. Their limbs swayed to the beat of the forest. Dance floors built into woods, sky illumined with strip lights, gyrating colours. Alive with music! Quick! Green bottles and blue vodka! Emily walking, body curving, one step forward, two steps back, but still, not enough alcohol for oblivion, not even enough alcohol for a slight high, till the dance floor, oh the dance floor, hands in the air now, feel the beat, and midnight was forgotten in the city of Girona – Come! Come! Núria was dancing and Emily watched fiercely, *but she will not go to her, no, not yet,* until, hiding in the forest they stood nose to nose and kissed deeply and there could be no such thing as darkness, only colour! *Music! Bodies! Dance!* The throng has run to the great arching tents that replace the cramped bars of winter with the open dance floors of summer. Trees stretch up into the air. Leaves pulse with music, leaves sway to the thumping bass of desire. Desire for the night, desire for the world, desire for the desperate stolen kiss outside of the concrete bathroom to the south side of the tents and the haggard woman who guards the toilet paper in little piles and wears gold and smokes a cigarette sullenly through the night from the earliest bell-cry of eleven to the first sigh of dawn.

That morning the jeep raced along the flat roads of the valley. Gold to all sides, cypress trees and big, leafy walnuts. In the distance the Pyrenees curved into prostrate giants, elbows and knees jutting into an endless sky. The girls slipped gently into the swerving rhythm of summer. The wind streamed through the back of the car, tickling their ears. Núria batted at a fly lazily as the car jumped over a dip in the road.

Joan laughed and pointed to a stone house in the distance. 'That is the beginning of *Fontcoberta. Molt macu,*' he said in Catalan. '*Molt molt macu.*' The villages were Romanesque, he explained, pointing out the window. Built in the eleventh century. Golden stone, like the fields. 'We have a church in our village that is beautiful,' he reassured them. 'A Romanesque gem,' he shouted into the back seat. 'You're in for a real treat.'

Joan Sorra was a large man, with slouched shoulders and a bruiser's features. The man was exceptionally tall, like his twins, but heavyset, with arms like a woodcutter or an old *camperol;* he boasted an ageing fighter's broken nose and paunch. Brown as a nut. Stubble on his chin and cropped silver hair. His hands were big as well, with thick fingers that moved with deliberate precision. Beyond his height, Emily does not see much of his twins in him – perhaps when he was younger? When he was slimmer, before the years and wine caught up to him – perhaps then she could have seen the line – though there is something of his eyes in Núria; yes, there must have been something of his eyes.

At the door to the country estate, Núria's mother La Marta greeted the girls with open arms – shrill coos of pleasure, dyed ash-blonde curls bounced around a flat face like the moon. The woman was soft as an overripe peach. Her body bore the same signs of age as her husband, cheeks rouged by too much drink, neck wide beneath sea pearl necklace, coral blouse, gold bangles on puckered wrists. She was unpleasant, unsettling ... tourmaline on plump fingers, which she flitted nervously on the air.

'*How was he, darling?*' she asked Núria. Emily's anger burnt. But no one would mention that. La Marta would cook dinner and give them towels, before escorting them to the guest wing of the restored farmhouse, the old hay barn. The donkeys used to sleep on the bottom floor. The walls of the house are firm and yellow – pillars of strength. There was the traditional *llar de foc – home of the fire* – a hearth in the bowels of the living room, pushed into a dark alcove around which the family would have gathered over the centuries to sing, or do needlework or sharpen their swords. The living room filled with modernist furniture – yellow velvet chairs built like small, vintage thrones, many-patterned sixties carpets, lace curtains.

The girls moved down the corridor, brushing shoulders. Núria and Emily would share a white stucco bedroom in a wooden loft. They fell into each other inside. Wrapped in each other's skin, they curled like nesting birds, fingers wandering through hair, kissing eyebrows, they slept entangled. The bathroom window gazing over the street behind the farmhouse. Crumbling stone and dirt. In the distance the tips of six swaying columns. Cypress trees flirting with the sky. A neighbour, in a smaller house across the cobbled street, draped Tibetan meditation flags over his door. Later Emily napped in one of the lounge chairs on the patio, overlooking blue mountains. White arms all bare and angular. Summer dress. Straps loose at the shoulder. Plum-coloured roses. A golden field of grain. She felt easy and calm. Lovely and still.

When Adrià arrived at the farmhouse that evening he did not say hello.

He sat on the wooden chair at the centre of the stone patio that faced the mountains. From the guest bedroom, Emily observed him through the window, his face obscured by the hanging branches of a vine that grew around the trunk of a citrus tree. For the rest of the afternoon Emily successfully avoided talking to him. The decision uneasy, mutual. Later Adrià cornered Emily in the garden, behind a rock wall hidden from the house. He pressed his body into her, bit her neck. *I want what my sister has.* Emily was very still. Does she tell him that she hates him? He would not hurt her. This at least she knows. *I hate you,* she wanted to say. Instead?

Nothing.

Adrià gave her a piece of crumpled paper.

On the paper he had written:

> *My sins*
> *Are unutterable thoughts.*
> *I must atone.*

'Go. Go and show them,' La Marta said at dinner. She flicked her wrist at her son. Dismissive. Regal. Adrià's mother, bovine and rouged, exposing it all at the table, a great crevasse that runs from her throat to the low coral silk. That evening the moon rose late. A grove of citrus behind them. Sweet lemons. Overhead, clusters of wisteria dripped from a wooden frame. Adrià shirtless, streaks of sweat pooling over his collarbones. In the light of the summer candles, his chest heaved as if his lungs were bulging out of him. Making his excuses from the table, Adrià pushed out his chair, and went into the house. From the courtyard below, as he ran up the carved stone steps to the house, his silhouette stood out against long French windows. A sharp breeze blew from the valley below the patio. The night's breath drunk with the scent of lavender and sun-warmed mud, thick and heady. In the house, the curtains rustled, curling through the open windows. Drone of the cicadas singing.

When Adrià returned he carried an object wrapped in thick cloth. Cradling it in against his chest like a babe in swaddling. His mother threw open her arms.

'Come, come!' she exclaimed. 'Tell them the story – it's a lovely story, Joan – go on, tell them, Adrià, like you told me in the car.'

Adrià hugged the cloth closer to his chest.

'Funny story.' Adrià laughed. Too loudly. 'I was at a party—'

'You are always at a party,' Adrià's father interrupted. Adrià released the package with a dull thud onto the table. A cigarette hung languidly from Adrià's lower lip. Emily's nostrils burnt.

'Yes, Papa. I was at a party. With Max, actually – you know him. We caught the train out from Barcelona, towards Sitges. Max heard there was a rave, or something, you know, one of those big house parties by the sea – in an abandoned mansion that some squatters had taken over in April. They'd been found out a week earlier by the police –' Adrià spat emphatically – 'and were about to be evicted. So they decided to have a garden party.

'When I got there, I knew the place was special. The house had doors that opened onto the sea, and art everywhere. Big paintings. Portraits – old pictures of men with ruffs around their necks and sour faces. Luxury. Real luxurious house. The squatters had the music playing loud, turntables, a dance floor in the garden – it was . . .'

Adrià shook his head violently, slamming his chair away from the table. He flung his arms out into the air. 'It was crazy! The music was slamming, and I was dancing –' his body hurtled round the courtyard – 'and there were so many people there, crazy people, dancing like this, and like this, and like this . . .'

'Adrià,' his father said. '*Deixes de fer això.*' He caught his son by the wrist, and pulled him back into the table. 'Sit down.'

Adrià refused to sit down.

Adrià's mother smiled a pained smile. She put her fat fingers over her mouth as she spoke. 'Isn't Adrià a good dancer? What a nice dance, Adrià.'

Adrià stood firmly by his seat. His hair electric, made wild by the dance. 'I haven't finished my story.' Adrià took the cigarette from his lips, and tapped it twice, sprinkling ash onto the table next to his father's plate.

'Go on, Adrià.' His mother looked at Joan for affirmation.

'Please, Adrià,' Joan said. 'I would like to know what happens next.'

'It was crazy . . .' Adrià shrugged. 'And I was dancing.'

He paused, resting his hand on his father's shoulder.

'And the whole place was up in the air.'

Adrià consumed space with his body.

'The people were rammed inside. I loved it. By the sea they had set up a barbecue and a bonfire, and people were shadow dancing and drinking. Max and I only knew a couple of people there, but you know how it is. We met this little guy from Granada, small, with glasses, clean cut, but a true Anarcho brother . . .'

Adrià's father coughed.

'The kid from Granada asked me if I wanted to leave the music for a second and explore the house, and I was like, sure, come on, let's go. He said that the man who'd owned the house had died suddenly and his body was still in his bed. So we went up to the second floor and along the corridor and then we opened this massive bedroom door and everything was all gold and beautiful and wild, and there at the centre of the bed, surrounded by the sheets was the dude himself – *dead*. Pale and grey and stony as shit. And I was like, hey man, you weren't kidding . . . So we left the bedroom and this Andalusian guy said I could take anything I wanted from the house, that it would be his gift to me, for trusting him and being all cool – you know – and agreeing not to tell anybody what I had seen.'

Adrià picked up the long spool of cloth on the table and unwrapped the contents. Núria's face emptied. Eyes glued to her brother.

'What did you choose?' asked Joan jovially.

Adrià unveiled his prize possession. There, pressed into the cloth was a long, stainless steel knife with a wooden handle. A folding knife of extreme proportions – more machete than tool. Adrià picked the knife up and twisted the handle, locking the shaft into place. He held the handle flat against his palms, showing the blade to the table.

'Let me see it,' his father said.

'No.'

Adrià balanced the blade between his fingers. Metal stained by the candles. Radiating light.

La Marta's breath caught in her throat, a detail she hid with her napkin.

Adrià's father laughed again, this time in a forced, loud way.

'*És macu, no?*' said La Marta. 'Go on, let Joan see it.'

This was part of her plan.

Confiscation of the object.

Adrià gave his father the knife, who kept his grip on it, holding the blade in his lap for the remainder of the meal.

When dinner was over, Emily followed Joan into the kitchen. Joan hid the knife behind the kitchen cupboard.

'It's worse than I imagined.' Joan's voice was low.

Emily nodded. She was not sure what to say.

'Did anyone tell you what happened two years ago?'

'No.'

'Nothing? Not one word?' Joan sighed. 'It was a shame. A real shame.'

'What happened?'

'He broke.'

'What do you mean?'

'Ask Núria. Try to keep yourself out of trouble.' They walked back down through the kitchen towards the garden party. As they descended down the outdoor steps to the patio, Joan touched Emily's shoulder gently and whispered into her ear: 'Lock your door tonight.'

The next day, after Adrià's uncle had come to collect Adrià and return him to the hospital in Barcelona, Emily requested to be driven to the bus stop in the village. Nuría begged her not to go: Emily must spend the day with her in the mountains – this is her family home, after all, Emily is most welcome – we will all drive back tomorrow, we will visit Adrià in the hospital, we don't want to interrupt the weekend – my parents, they have so enjoyed having you, I want to tell them – I want to tell them with you. Emily was resolute. She had seen enough. She wanted to go home.

Once she arrived in Barcelona, Emily decided to walk the weekend off. She padded along Passeig de Gràcia, the artery of the city, to Plaça de Catalunya, to the Cathedral, then down Carrer dels Comtes into the heart of the Gothic quarter. The sun dropped behind thunderheads as a vast blanket of shadow fell over the western streets. Narrow alleyways lit by dangling orange bulbs. The evening thick with water. Humidity hanging on the air, stinking of secrets. City stone streaked with urine. Music wafted from the old quarter. Dancing in Plaça del Rei?

The beating of a drum? The *tin-ta-ran-tan* of a marching band?

The steady thump of leather shoes. The shriek of approaching crowds. Emily rounded the corner of Plaça de Sant Just. A cacophony of noise exploded from the Basílica. Mounted *Guàrdia Urbana* appeared at the head of an enormous throng. Horses' hooves clattered on the graves of Christian martyrs embedded in the square. Sombre trumpets bleated over the city. The first flank of a religious procession. Emily relinquished herself to the horde, engulfed by red uniforms. Gold-encrusted lapels. Tassels and bayonets.

She turned to a man in the crowd. 'What is happening?'

'The march of Corpus Christi.'

Emily entered the delirium. Toddlers gaped in awe. Mothers wrangled their children into order. Confetti and streamers burst on the air! Laughter! Noise! Exuberance! Next came the *Cavallets Cotoners* – eight men and women in traditional costume: white tunic, scarlet velvet, knee-high boots. They danced in medieval hobby horses. The parade joyous! Extravagant! Emily felt the thumping thud of feet, the clanging clatter of pans. Enter the Eagle and Lion of Barcelona! Bunches of yellow blossoms soaked up the dying embers of the sun. Here come the dancing figures! Giant clay and fibreglass costumes for the initiated. A crowned lion gargled a wreath of sunflowers in his mouth! Black wings and golden coronets! The trumpets regal and proud!

The lion bowed, once, twice, three times, then careened into a drunken gig!

Tan-ta-ran, tan-tan ta-ran!

Capgrossos, the giant heads of the Catalan Peasant, worn on the shoulders of costumed dancers – yellow, orange, gold, smooth fabric, they pranced before the *Gegants de la Ciutat*. Welcome the Royal Giants of Barcelona! Kings and queens of the city! King Jaume wielding a sceptre and orb. Bob-bobbing above the crowd. The queen ferocious! Ebony plaits coiled in a spring. Blue gown trimmed with gold. Fecundity burst from her fists. The crowd sang:

> '*Els gegants del Pi, ara ballen, ara ballen;*
> *els gegants del Pi, ara ballen pel camí.*

Els gegants de la Ciutat, ara ballen, ara ballen;
els gegants de la Ciutat, ara ballen pel terrat.'

The Giants of Pine dance on the path! The Giants of the City dance on
the roof! Emily fought for breath in the tumult. Roaring in her
elbows and her knees. Blood rushing to her temples. Church spires
spinning. Pale stone glinting in the sun. Geraniums and begonia. A
scent of sulphur or smoke? Music! *Music everywhere!* Tinny blasts of
brass. Droning clangs of drums. There danced Mulassa the donkey!
A wreath about his neck. Bou the bull of Barcelona – then the
dragons – the metal-breasted Vibria, the serpent demon, wings
extended, fierce eyes, gaping mouth festooned with ivory blossoms. Daisies and lilies! Pointed breasts with thick iron nipples!
Drums, drums drums! *Faaaaaan-farron!* The crowd roars. *Olé! Olé!*
Olé! Olé! The Vibria's scaly metal hide flashed gold. Emily glimpsed
the legs of the dancer wearing the fibreglass shell. The man beside
Emily finished a cigarette and threw the butt into the street. Emily
moved to escape. To leave the march behind.

'Stay,' the man said, barring Emily's path with his arm.

'*Jo sóc l'Esperit Sant.'*

A voice ruptured the crowd. Drowned by music. Pipes! Drums!
A voice high pitched shouted again.

'*Cos de Crist!* Corpus Christi!'

More giants rocked forward, a Moorish king and queen – the
Babylonian *Gegants de Santa Maria del Mar*, the bearded king with
his red cape, crest of the Catalan flag; his wife followed, jaunty
feather in her hair, draped in the style of an empress. Delicate stars
emblazoned on her trestles. Behind these Giants lumbered the
most terrifying of all, the *Tarasca de Barcelona*, an ancient dragon –
or She-Devil? – jaw hanging open, operated by an internal
mechanism. Bright humanoid teeth, an iron-spiked tortoiseshell,
four clawed hands. A ghoulish, serpentine figure. Eyes bulging into

the crowd. Four women, *Tarascaires*, moved the dragon, wearing purple capes. The *Tarasca* swayed rhythmically, weaving in and out of the square. Teeth gnashing. Red mouth drooling.

A man broke from the crowd, caked with the veneer of streets, dustbins, trash heaps – mad-haired, frail bones, age mid-seventies perhaps. A farmer's coat, waxed cotton, flax hair slicked down with water or oil, his face stretched, lean. In one hand, he carried an open leather flask, in the other a lighter – bright pink. Cheap. The kind you buy in tabacs, licquor stores, *Carrefours*.

'*Sóc el cos de Crist!*'

Again the reedy voice. Thin and menacing. He reeled forward, danced two steps with the *Tarasca*. The monster tumbled away.

And then, with no warning, no shout, the man burst into flames. His jacket sprouting a fire that runs up his shoulders to his hair. He reeked of kerosene. Cremated flesh. The *Tarasca* clattered to the ground as the four women lunged towards him. A mounted guard leapt from his horse, racing towards the flames – he ripped the cloth from the *Tarasca*'s frame, throwing it over the fire, covering the burning man's shoulders, hiding him from the crowd. Children cried out, babies squealed, but the band continued playing as the mounted guard stamped out the fire, men running with buckets of water from the well of the Chapel of Sant Just at the corner of the square, and Emily fell, half fainting into the stone wall behind her. Sirens blazed. Policemen on motorcycles slammed through the crowd, men running towards the crumpled, blackened figure of the man, the lump hidden in the *Tarasca*'s cape, the blue-and-yellow herald of the dragon, as Emily broke free, launching across the parade. She hurtled through the crowd, each face as intricate as the next, children carried on parents' shoulders. Grandfathers wearing the red, snail-shaped cap of the Catalan peasant, symbol of independence. Flags! Gold and vermilion spilling over Gothic awnings, black shutters, ivy balconies. She moves desperately towards the harbour. Away from the chaos. Away from the *capgrossos* and metal dragons. The world neared dusk. The electric lights of the city expanded into the approaching night, creating an urban aurora borealis – toxic hallucinations of colour that soaked into her skin. Shop fronts oozed red light into dark alleyways stained with green illuminations. Emily was like an animal, hunting out the water, and when she walked across the sand to the sea, past the boys with their beer bottles, she slipped off her shoes and stood in the lapping folds of the sea. She looked out to the horizon, to the tiny lights of far-off shipping giants, and felt cold.

Empty.

Behind her: laughter.

A young woman laughed, and the sound floated out over the Mediterranean, magnified by the dampness of the night. Emily disappeared into the ache of the water between her toes.

On the evening of 24 June 2003, days before his body washed up in Sitges, Adrià's mother walked ahead, solemn as an asp, to the edge of the pier and the painted wooden dinghies. Núria carried the bread roll with the candle placed at the centre of the cross. She lit the candle and closed her eyes. The sun set over the foothills. It was dark, and the water was cold, as the wizened mariner led the way. *Careful. Careful.* La Marta settled her rear in the bow of the boat, resting on the little cushions the good fisherman set out. She pulled the veil full across her face. Back straight, she looked over the prow, towards the waves. Behind her, clouds swallowed the horizon with deep indigo, sky bruised from the heat of the day. Núria sat next to Emily, who crossed her hands in her lap demurely, and watched the last of the sunlight wane against the silhouette of Columbus above the city, his finger outstretched and ominous. Following the call, the fisherman uncoiled his rope, wood scraping wood as the boat bumped its way into the sea. Dampness underfoot and splashing waves, and so into *el mar* they motored and out and across the sea.

La Marta sat hidden by an ornate black veil, cut like a paper snowflake. Husband conspicuously absent. Núria covered in a long dress wrapped round her ankles. A wisp of hair caught in her mouth and stayed there like a hook. She kept her hands around the flame of the candle, as the old man's motor churned into the water and he led them to an unfixed marker in the sea, some arbitrary point which to him seemed suitable with all his knowledge of such things.

Here.

La Marta raised her hand. She pointed to the water. The candle stuttering. A hungry flame that stung Núria's fingers and cast long shadows onto the water. The bread in the basket scratched with the marking of the cross. *Bread of the drowned man. Bread to find the sailor lost at sea. Pan d'Ofegat,* made holy on the feast day of Saint Peter, La Marta's offering blessed by the priest in solitude, a trusted way to find the disappeared.

Ofegat. Oh Fe Gat. Emily turned the syllables like marbles. *Drowned Man.* In Catalan a single word. One identity. One meaning. She felt the water fill her own throat and threaten to choke her as La Marta raised her hand and pointed, and summoned the bread, with its candle inside, which Núria brought to her, looking to the spot where La Marta points and together they drop the bread into the sea, which found the water with a low *plop* and kept to the side of the boat as if it did not want to leave.

What's in a word? In a name? Your destiny. Adrià. Derived from the old Venetic language . . . Adrià. Taken from the word 'adur' for water. For the sea.

Emily cursed herself for thinking as the bread grew heavy in the water and floated stoically on, passing the boat, with its little light, to dip and turn in the sluggish waves, and a voice leaps from some hidden fold in her memory and reads out with all the clarity of a bell:

Forget your fish eggs for eyes. Look, the claw of the crab cradles your ear and the snake has found a home in your mouth where your tongue once was. Take off your clothes and dance for me. Let me see your chest, all sleek and smooth. Your copper skin has turned to pearl, the snails have eaten out your calluses. Your genitals are swollen, fat and bloated with water.

You hide them with seaweed. I call your name.

Dead One. Disappeared. Dance for me. For everything that happened is Truth. Was true and is true. I swear on my life. I swear on Santa Eulàlia, on the Church of Saint Mary of the Sands, now Santa Maria del Mar, Mary of the Sea, Patron Saint of Sailors and all those who gravitate to the water's edge to breathe.

Candle for the soul. Bread for the body.

Emily's eyes locked on the little light as it drifted away, and slowed, the bread pregnant with water, and stayed still for a moment, sinking against the surface of the sea, until with an inaudible sputter, the flame quickened out and was gone.

V

EXHORTATION TO
THE INSPECTOR

I emerge from the metro at Plaça de Catalunya only to be drenched by an onslaught of black rain. The sky breaks and water cascades down. I hide in the doorway of a coffee shop, open my umbrella and leap forth. Heavy clouds leer overhead, washing the city in a freezing deluge. A dismal damp wind howls in from the sea, carrying whispers of hoar frost and capsized fishing boats. In the winter months, the city is barren, like a stone that cannot feel the sun. The trees of Las Ramblas crouch in corners, bare and wettish. In the summer, a transformation of colour will occur. Reds that have hidden explode beside ochre, redolent of anarchy, fierce and unforgiving, and the heat hangs over the city like a hot blue blaze. Tempers flare and Catalan flags shake above the demonstrations that rage through Plaça de Catalunya, and down Passeig de Gràcia and Via Laietana. Las Ramblas bloom, leaves sprout on threadbare trees, the florists bring their canopies, their bustling wares. Live statues will bow to onlookers. Men and women who have painted themselves silver and gold dance for euro coins. This is the Barcelona of imagination, the balmy idyll. But things are not so now. At four o'clock, the streets are deserted. Human statues conspicuously absent. Crowds retreat indoors. Black coats and scarves wrapped around cold throats. *Storm descending.* I move steadily forward, past the taxi ranks, down Las Ramblas to the covered market. La Boqueria, food hall of *la ciutat vella*, the old city. Fabregat has asked that I meet him here. Near the police station where he once worked.

When I enter the market I am greeted by a barrage of colour. Sugar-coated plums, candied chestnuts. Chocolate almonds. Pink meringues. Mangoes and strawberries, imported from abroad. Mushrooms and cured cheese. Olives from across the region. Fish heads and sow's ears. Honey from the Pyrenees. Fillet of beef and suet. Tortilla made to order. Endless food stalls, labyrinth of flavours. I take my time, making my way to the back, where the tapas bars rank towards the parking lot. Wet crates piled with drooping heads of lettuce, unhappy with the day. Lorry loaders and shouts of *Hola! Tío!* and *Pescado!* and *Would you like to try?* A cornucopia of scales. Echoes of fresh blood and tide pools. I turn away. At the little bar in the thick of it all, ornamental painted lamps hang from a wooden awning. There are stools lining both sides of the bar facing two thin glass cases of tapas. *Pintxos* from the Basque country. *Embutidos.* Pressed sandwiches. Green peppers salted and fried. Fresh in the mouth. *Albóndigas.* Minced meatballs drenched in a gently spiced sauce. Hard ewe's cheese cut in triangles. Quince jelly. Three waiters administer food, offering beer on tap and coffee for the thirsty. Businessmen and women grazing. Selecting a stool beside the warped bar, I take off my hat and coat. *No more than fifteen places to eat here.* I guard a seat for Fabregat. *Now he is late. This is meant to be a quick in-and-out. A bite on the go.*

Bona tarda! What do you want? I wait in the warmth of the grills and packed bodies while the patron pours me a beer – an old man with a cracked face and hands like cricket gloves. From my vantage point on the stool, I watch the world slink by. The carcasses of sleeping cars and trucks litter the backlot parking space of La Boqueria. Evening promenades. Students. Men with jaunty strides. The Raval arches its spine like a cat. A woman catches my eye. Beautiful, face strained, streaked by the winter sun. Brown skin over fine bones. Torn blue slippers. A child wanders with her, cloaked in rags, an infant strapped to her bosom in a black sash. Decaying clothing, hands outstretched, leading their way through the crowd.

Begging.

'*Hola!*' A mock-American accent behind my ear. My eyes lock on to the centre of his spine, his movements fluid, wolf-hungry, as Fabregat slides into the chair beside me. The retired inspector plain-clothed, relaxed. Charcoal jeans. Grey linen scarf thrown over his shoulders. Brow easy. Lines smoothed. Coat spattered with rain. He calls to the patron – *Bona tarda! Amic!* A plate of hot *patatas bravas* follows swiftly. Tomato sauce with chilli and paprika, a pinch of parsley and mayonnaise. *I pernil! Pata negra sisplau!* A plate of cut ham, thin strips of maroon, fissures of white fat.

'Drink?' Fabregat asks me, looking at my empty glass.

I nod. He holds up two fingers to the barman. '*Dues cerveses!*'

'*El Llop!*' shouts the barman. In Catalan. *The Wolf.* 'Anything for you, my man!'

When he is finished, Fabregat wipes his mouth with the back of his hand and throws down a few euro notes. *Anem.* He leans into my ear. *Let's go.* A wave to the bartender, and I follow him into the maze of the market stalls. He walks quickly, with purpose, zigzagging past the tradesmen, out the side, and down the back alleys running parallel to Las Ramblas. *Thin avenues in stone.* We emerge at the southern end, where the underage hookers line Nou de la Rambla and things turn cruel. Close to the statue of Columbus, barely discernible in the fog that has drifted in with the onset of darkness. The rain has stopped at least. He lights a cigarette which hangs at the corner of his mouth. 'You want?'

I shake my head. *No.*

'You don't smoke?'

'Sometimes. Not now.'

I wait for him to finish. *He is strangely nervous. Still and energetic at once. Unsatisfied.*

At the entrance to the police department I am struck by its simplicity. Fleshy stone squeezed between the ornamental façade of a hotel and a series of little shops. The station is deceptive. Several storeys up and many offices wide, but from the street it looks small. *Petite.* You would never notice it, but for the solitary policeman on guard, cap on his head. *Watching the street.*

The policeman recognizes Fabregat.

'*Hola!*' he cries. *Do you remember me?*

Fabregat smiles. *Of course! Of course!*

A clap on the shoulder.

How does it feel to be living the high life? the policeman asks him.

We are whisked into the belly of the beast. Down a narrow passage for the vehicles into a large inner courtyard lined with windows. Elevators. Codes for entry.

A series of checks and signatures later and I am through. Long municipal halls. A bare room. An officer and three archival boxes. Fabregat and the officer exchange a quiet set of words. A handshake, a thank you. *Calls have been made higher up. Approval given. Just this once.* The officer will observe as we work. *As long as you want.*

How is your family? the young man asks Fabregat. *Your little boy?*

Good. Good, Fabregat says. *Now. To business.*

A thread of tightness has entered his voice.

These things are charged for him.

They make him angry.

Fabregat lays each of the letters out. Embalmed in thin plastic. *Five envelopes. Five sheets of membrane.* The duty officer sits uncomfortably, staring at me. Fabregat paces back and forth, around the low, thin table. Bright lights overhead. *Washed-out colours. Gather your senses.* Feelings muted. *Thudding around. Not clear. Clean them up. Parse through.* Each sheet of parchment is small. They have been cut to the same size, probably at the same time. *So the intention was to create five documents simultaneously. Full poem text. One complete message.* Process methodical. *They were written on the same desk, with the same ink. Each letter made in advance and then delivered at the appropriate time.* I reach for the first. Look at Fabregat.

'May I?'

Fabregat nods. I touch the first sheet nervously. Feeling the skin between my fingers. My flesh against flesh. Taking my time. I am not expecting revelations. All I need is a tiny pulse. A quiet reassurance. A siren call to match the voice I heard inside the chapel, purple notes on a foreign wind. A song struck loud and true. *A joining.* Usually there will be something on contact. Generally manuscripts feel green or yellow, often dusty, as if viewed under a dirty film. Sometimes they sound like silver trumpets, or make dark flute calls. The worst scream. Sometimes I touch earth colours, ochres, rich autumnal spreads. Other books leave a salty taste in the mouth like pickled onions. But I have not prepared for the speed, or the sound, or the volume of this welcoming.

Hello?

The voice comes. Disembodied.

Sharp and urgent.

Hello?

I pull back, terrified.

A split second, no more. Time rears up. Breathe quietly, study the page. *Unlocking.* Not yet, I say. Push closed. Bring the letter up to

the light. *Again parchment from a modern distributor. Made tradition-*
ally. Excellent quality. Pergamenta. Very clean and bright. Adroitly
rendered. Strokes of a sable brush light on the parchment. Thin
lines, sharp and precise, creating the nodes of a compass, a web of
letters shooting out from the centre. I am reassured by the lettering. The formation of the web, in each layer of the rings, nine
sections, with nine letters. *They are absolutely Illuminatian. You are*
on firm ground. There the golden Ouroboros. Interpreted by Rex
Illuminatus as the Serpent of Knowledge. Language Bearer. I turn the
sheet over, keeping it inside the plastic. *A few cursory words. Find*
me in the Utterance of Birds. I hold it up for the ex-inspector.
Fabregat cannot bring himself to look. No. He shakes his head.
Not now. I read each one in succession. The sign glares out at me.
A signature in gold ink. A snake swallowing its tail. A colophon, match-
ing your mother's. Stamp of a family of scribes. And there? Above the
letters, a mark that no one noticed. A pictograph, almost like a smudge,
representing a bird flying – panic extrapolated into a symbol. Three
quick beats of a pen. My mind races. *All scribes work with exemplars.*
A text from which they copy. I know your origin point. Your source. I
have caught you red-handed.

Natalia Hernández.

'And the photographs of the victims?' I ask.

Nothing I could have done prepares me for the reality of those
pictures. Tossed like a cigarette box onto the table. *Not very nice,*
Fabregat says drily. A corpse hanging from a lamp post. Limp. Life
stolen. Soul sucked out. *Violated. Tortured. Wounds swollen, skin*
pin-pricked. My arms ache. My tongue swells in my mouth.

This is what he does, Anna, to women like you.

'What do you see?' Fabregat murmurs, close to my ear.

'Your first victim is a sixteen-year-old choirgirl . . .' I stammer
through the obvious.

Fabregat looks at me wryly. The word 'victim' sits awkward and

264

false in my mouth. It does not belong to me. *You're in way over your head.* I panic. *Don't lose your composure. Keep calm. There she is, Rosa Bonanova, lying flat on the mortuary table. Catholic. Virgin. Barely a woman. She's raped and has her tongue cut out. Someone painstakingly carves nine letters and four symbols onto her body.* When I look up, the dead wait for me. I see blue uniform. Neat clips pull back auburn hair from a centre parting. Standing beside the inspector. Watching. *What is your name?* she asks me. Opening her mouth. She wants to come through me. *I want to speak through you*, she says. No. Not here. *Why? Why come then?* I hesitate. *You're just like the others. You are selfish. You do not care.*

I'm trapped. My whole body shaking. The officer glances at Fabregat.

'Nena ...' Fabregat leans in and whispers very softly, so the policeman doesn't hear. 'Why don't we take a break for a moment?'

He ushers me out of the room. I stand with my back to the wall in the long hallway. *Counting. Deciding what to do.* Bringing myself back down. *Grounding.*

'It's a lot for anybody to take on,' Fabregat says, handing me a glass of water. 'Are you sure you want to continue?'

Ten minutes. I just need ten minutes.

'Where is the bathroom?' I ask him weakly. He points vaguely in the direction.

'Do you want me to take you there?'

'No,' I say. 'No, I'll be fine.'

You are stupid. Inside the locked stall, I take the ready packed capsule with its hypodermic needle out of my bag. Fit it into the plastic injector. Break open disinfectant wipes. Pull my jumper off, my shirt. Standing in my bra, I reach for the fat of my stomach, pinching it between two fingers. *The doctors tell me to use a different location every day. One of seven places, seven days a week. Rotate through. Otherwise the skin will scar. Tight knots will form in the muscle. Cause harm. Hit the needle in.* Quick and calm. *Breathe. Breathe. Count to seven. One-one-thousand. Two-one-thousand.* And so it goes. And goes and goes.

On my return the retired inspector squints at me. I will not touch the pages again. He leans in on his elbows. Smiles. The ghost girl has gone.

'Don't worry, we won't be here long. Why don't you tell us what you think so we can get this over with quickly?'

'Yes.' I choke. Attempt to gather myself. 'Of course.'

'Guifré told you that these diagrams –' I point to the charts on the facing page of the first parchment letter – 'represented the attributes of a famous 'truth machine' created by Ramon Llull. This was not true. In actuality your letters reference the lesser-known work of a medieval alchemist called Rex Illuminatus.'

'OK,' Fabregat says quietly.

Control yourself. Don't look too deep. Don't be sick. Don't let the fear show.

'There's the serpent on the left hand, the cross on the right. The circle round the belly button and the crescent between each nipple drawn over her chest. These markings are replicated on the subsequent two victims.'

'Correct.'

'Guifré said the symbols were alchemical. The circle represents Gold, the crescent, Silver.'

'Yes.'

'We can agree that this is accurate.'

Fabregat nods. Focusing on something invisible in the distance.

'But there are other meanings as well. Rex Illuminatus saw the world through the lens of his own esoteric codes. For him, Gold would immediately be affiliated with the sun god Apollo, Silver with the moon goddess Artemis. So your victims are branded with symbols associated with alchemy and the mystery cults of Apollo and Artemis . . . That should help us understand the nine letters . . .' I lead him on. 'Which are meant to be read as a specific language of divination. A language of the birds, no less. That's what is meant by the line *Find me in the Utterance of Birds*.'

My eyes hover over the letter B cut into Rosario's shoulder. *A serpent on her palm. Serpent-bearing. Avian Speaker. The Alphabet of Birds. Gold round her belly, but also a play on words. Count the grains of Sand and measure the Sea: again, a reference to the Sibyl – see also 'displacement'. Witch. The moon on her breast representing Silver – and the occult, a horned goddess, the domain of an ancient earth mother. Each letter of the Alchemist considered a pagan heresy. An interloping language of divination.* But the marks on the right hand? Those are different. The fear resonates. If I listen long enough I might just grasp them, follow them. Locate them.

Fabregat wants to know who *he* is. 'He'? *There are many. Many hands in this.* This is one thing I am certain of, though I do not have the vocabulary to explain it . . . I *know* intimately. I return to the bloody markings on the victims – *a serpent and a cross. On the right hand for conversion, on the left hand for transgression.* Breathe in. Begin again.

'Fourth verse,' I tell him. Avoiding the photographs, the cuts on bodies, taking strength in the letters. *Academic grounding.* 'There's a direct reference to a famous proclamation spoken by the Oracle at Delphi. Recorded in the fifth century BCE by the historian Herodotus. Herodotus informs us that when Croesus, King of Lydia, decided to test each oracle's power before selecting a favoured seer, he sent messengers to all the oracle centres of the ancient world bearing an unusual question.

"Tell me precisely what King Croesus is doing now," the representatives asked. The Oracle of Delphi responded correctly, winning the game. *King Croesus is boiling a tortoise and a lamb in a bronze pot*, she said. But she also admonished the King, declaring her omnipotence boldly: *I count the number of grains of sand on the beach and measure the sea, I understand the speech of the dumb and hear the voiceless.'*

An uncomfortable doubt invades my throat: Natalia Hernández – was she hunter or hunted? And if she was hunted . . . who would come after you? I think of Ruthven and Sitwell alone in that house in the Gothic—

No. Now focus on the Sibyl.

I recall a legend of Rex Illuminatus, one that claims he woke to birdsong and emerged from his cave. Philomela sat with her back towards him, overlooking the plains to the sea. She held in her left hand a bowl of food, and to Illuminatus's great astonishment a serpent was eating from the bowl. The Doctor rushed forward.

'The Serpent is an evil creature!' he chastised the girl. 'The Serpent is a messenger of the Devil.'

No. The snake is a creature of the earth. It has no ears to hear with, no voice to speak with. It is a deaf-mute. We are brethren. Kin. You have called me Philomela the Nightingale, but I was born the daughter of Asclepius and named Hygieia. I am Serpentarius, the Serpent Bearer. My silence knows a divine language – when I teach you this you will raise the dead. You will make gold from lead and live a thousand years. Then you too will count the grains of sand and measure the sea, you will know the secrets of the maker and shall read the deaf-mute and hear the voiceless.

In the story Philomela put the snake down on the ground and stood up to face the Doctor. *I have been thinking of your Alef Bet. You say it began with a flame in the great dark, the flame in the infinite, the spark of an idea*, she said with her brown hands. *I am of accord that the Great Mystery resides in silence. In the unknown beyond the*

known, in the Being beyond appearance, it is the generative thought stronger
than words. Silence is the root of language — it is the thought before speak-
ing. Look — she signed with her hands, and picked the snake up. *A*
snake's tongue forks. One side holds healing powers, the other teaches a
prophetic language. When a seer has been kissed at night by a snake, she
is granted both the language of the Birds and the magical ability to heal.

'And?' Fabregat nods at the letters on the table. 'Whoever sent
me these wanted me to translate the poetry?'

'Yes and no. They were not necessarily writing *for* you. They
wanted you to become a messenger. *A Serpent Bearer.* To deliver
these to someone who would understand.'

'To *One-who-is-arriving,*' Fabregat adds.

Someone like me.

'And the *Nine books of Leaves*? The *rage of man*?'

There are things I see, but do not want to share. Not yet. Not
until I am certain. I pause, uneasy. Then jerk ahead. This time I
will not look at the dead. *Golden serpent curling. Mouth biting.*
Meaning clicks into place.

'I don't think your victims died because of who they were as
individuals. I believe they were selected because of what they
represented as symbols.'

'Now you're speaking in riddles.'

'What do these three women have in common? A virgin, a
nurse, and a midwife?'

'They shared a very unfortunate death,' Fabregat says darkly.

I tell him that in 1297 Philomela was burnt in Barcelona. Her
tongue was cut out and her body was carved with the letters of her
master's alphabet. In 1851, Captain Ruthven and Llewellyn Sitwell
witness the aftermath of an identical crime. The 2003 murders of
Rosa, Rosario and Roseanne repeat a tradition of dismemberment
associated with the mortification of pagans, specifically clairvoyants
and mediums, given the broad title *Witch*.

A lump settles in the base of my throat. Come now. Push harder. Do not be afraid.

What mark? What mark is his? I feel the nausea rise again. Everything here is about controlling the victim. Defining who she became. First he took her tongue. Then he defiled her. He labelled her body with letters and symbols. He made her into something he wanted to destroy; writing meaning into her skin, he reshaped his victim to make the act of cutting out her tongue more potent. To imbue it with significance. Her body became a manuscript. What else did he wish to rewrite? To erase? To stamp out? What message was he choosing to send? And to whom?

And what of the palimpsest? *You are looking for a mirror.* Distorted reflection. Equal and opposite. Book slayer. Tongue killer. Following the same threads, he found her first. Made his mark, as she made hers. I begin to feel delirious. *Violence uncomfortably close. Letters left in cloisters, hidden in confessionals. Allusions to prophets, Serpent Bearers and Whores of Babylon. Llewellyn Sitwell's letters and Ruthven's palimpsest interred in stone. Things don't just die overnight. Books can be burnt. Faith can be outlawed. But language is carried underground. Beneath the surface. On the tip of your tongue. So how do you kill something carried orally? Something like the Song of the Serpent? The Language of the Birds? You make the carrier mute.*

I blink and look again.

There will be a sign on their bodies that belongs exclusively to him. *Harder. Look harder.* When he was finished with the first three victims, he marked them with the judgement of the cross on the right hand. And yet he did not take the time to do that to Natalia Hernández. Because she didn't need to be rewritten. She was already the symbol. *The object of the hunt.*

Go through the steps. The original *Alchemical History of Things* was made in the early fourteenth century. It comprised forty-eight numbered leaves, measuring 32 × 24 cm. There are seventy-two leaves of text and twenty-two lustrous miniatures in full body colour. In this manuscript, Rex Illuminatus describes his encounter with the Sibyl Philomela, and later the parchment book she gave him. The provenance of that manuscript (known to Renaissance scholars as the *Tabulae Serpentis* – the Serpent Tablet) is of the highest order. At some point in the early sixteenth century, the immortal Rex Illuminatus bound pages of the Sibyl's *Tabulae Serpentis* into a medieval Book of Hours which he gave to his allies on Mallorca for safe keeping in their monastery. Captain Ruthven found this Book of Hours in the early nineteenth century and cut out a single page, which he returned to London. His laboratory notes record the incident in 1829: '*There is a wondrous revelation called the Process of the Philosophers most unusually contained in a simple Book of Hours. I have seen the Alchemist's Great Elixir, represented in diverse & incomparable miniatures & certain of this discourse eclipse a Greek hand perpendicular on the page, ranging beneath the gold in two divine columns.*' Then the Book of Hours disappears. Only to be rediscovered in a lightning storm on Mallorca, with the crucial pages violently removed. A woman by the name of Cristina Rossinyol duplicates the colophon sign of a Philomela, and replicates the Alchemist's illuminations. Her daughter quotes the words of the hidden palimpsest text in the final letters of her life and hints at access to more.

All signs point to Natalia Hernández's ownership of a secret – a secret that her assassin presumably recognized and knew. *What if her death was instigated by this secret?* The curiosity in me pushes: why? What revelation could be so powerful? Did it truly contain a magic?

I shudder and think of the cloven feet pointing into smoke-filled air. *Someone cared enough to set fire to our chapel on Mallorca. Someone cared enough to mutilate women in Barcelona in 1851 and 2003 – all whittling down and down and down into the most unlikely place. A place Picatrix would never have thought to look.*

What if someone else traced Hernández, tracked her down, courted her, as I am now following her trail? My stomach turns: *and if this same person is following you? Faster. You must be faster.*

Fabregat watches me intently.

'Facts, girl. I need facts.'

'You said you wanted to find out who wrote you these letters,' I murmur. 'I can get you closer to this person than you ever thought possible.' *How much do I tell him? Minimum. Bare minimum. Keep it close. The roots in your throat. Keep them in.* 'What makes your letters interesting is their awareness of Illuminatus. That is highly unusual. We are a small pool, Inspector. Trackable. Locatable.'

Fabregat's hand opens and closes on the table. He does not interrupt.

'I know everyone who reads Illuminatus. I have handled all the available material.' Fabregat drinks the information in slowly. The energy lowers in his belly. 'The lines of verse you received in 2003 quote a document Rex Illuminatus salvaged in the late 1200s. A Greek poem that may have been hidden for nearly two millennia. Only one copy of the Serpent Tongue Poem is known to exist, and it came into our records three years ago. This fragmented poem had spent over a century at the bottom of a sealed archival box at Oxford University. And who knows how much longer locked away in an old Mallorcan monastery. It would not have been available at the time of your murders.'

'*Val.*'

'So your author either had access to an alternative edition of the poem in print, or knew an oral version of the poem . . . a song which fell out of popular circulation over seven centuries ago. That puts them in a fairly limited category. Such a limited category that I can tell you, with almost one hundred per cent certainty, who she is.'

'*She?*' Fabregat chokes.

'Natalia Hernández.' Ash in my mouth: hair of the flea. *Almost an apology*. I had expected Fabregat to rage, to shout, to kick, but instead he is profoundly contained. Professional. Quiet. *Natalia Hernández?* I'm not sure where to begin. I feel the weight of shadows settling in the white walls around us, resting their spines against door handles, peering over the photograph and papers. *Still angry.* I say it bluntly, because I can say nothing else. I speak about Cristina Rossinyol, about the books I have found – though not what I am looking for. I tell Fabregat about the nature of a colophon, the signatures of scribes, how the ouroboros is a family mark belonging to Natalia Hernández, knowing that they are also listening. The wording crucial. *An order, an invective. It positions you in the mythology. It's like a sign post – a street name.* I take him through the beats. *Like mother like daughter, I recognize the hand, shared between scribes.* Facts aid me. Fabregat's letters, written in 2003, quote the single page of Ruthven's palimpsest verbatim. But Harold Bingley's research team only discovered Ruthven's palimpsest in the spring of 2011. The translation of the Greek subtext occurred a year and a half later. Even if someone had seen Ruthven's page, if they had opened the sealed box in the dusty archives of Oxford, and read through Ruthven's laboratory notes to find the cut sheet of parchment, they would have garnered nothing. The Greek subtext is illegible to the naked eye. No one could have divined the content of the poems so accurately without being familiar with the original. This makes for a valuable temporal incongruence. I parse through Natalia's lines, translating them as I see fit. She wanted you to understand, Fabregat. *That if you do certain things, you will find me. Then you will become Serpentarius, Snake Bearer. One-who-is-arriving! And the holy path that they have called knowledge will be yours. You must speak the language of the deaf-mute, hear the voiceless, see the silenced one.*

Fabregat sits by the low table in the police meeting room. He stares at his hands. 'This changes everything. But you can't prove it yet.' He looks at me fiercely. Combative.

I falter. Try to speak more clearly.

'The language of birds, the language of the deaf-mute, the book of leaves — all that is code for a universal language that Rex Illuminatus believed could express and control the smallest elements of life on a fundamental scale. He describes this language as an essential magic. An elemental force that the alchemist codified into the alphabet carved onto your victims bodies—'

'Why are you the only person to see this?' He cuts me off.

'I have one area of expertise. I can only tell you what I have deduced in relation to that body of knowledge.'

Fabregat gestures to the officer. *Put these back in their boxes. Take them back to the grave, to the sealed containers, to the mobile shelving units. Take them away.*

In the dusk light, Fabregat steers with confidence. *The inspector's guide to the city.* With the life-long habit of an investigator, he reels off facts, veering down Carrer Nou de la Rambla while I struggle to keep up.

'At eleven o'clock on Sunday morning, Adrià Sorra leaves his parents' vehicle and walks into the Girona train station with his uncle. He initially caught the 11.23 train to Barcelona, due to arrive in the city at 13.26. But Adrià leaves his uncle's care in Mataró, stepping off the train under the pretext of going to the bathroom. He then boards the subsequent train to Barcelona, and refuses to respond to any contact from his parents or his uncle. He purchases a water bottle from the station café in Passeig de Gràcia at 14.40, along with a *chorizo bocadillo*. His movement through the station is captured on CCTV footage. He goes off the radar for twenty-four hours, staying at a squat outside of the city, before coming in for a midsummer's party on the evening of Sant Joan, 2003. At 18.00 and 18.07 on 23 June 2003, Adrià makes calls to Lola Jiménez, a twenty-two-year-old Comparative Literature student from the Universitat Autónoma, and Sjon de Vries, a twenty-six-year-old foreign resident and local drug dealer of Anglo-Dutch parentage. Sjon (aka Tree) and Adrià Sorra plan to meet here – at a bar called

La Rosa del Raval – at 22.00. Adrià arrives at La Rosa around 22.30, de Vries is also late for the appointment. Sjon and Adrià share a few drinks (according to the barman, several Voll-Damms). They meet a stranger: an Austrian–Venezuelan actor and Raval local by the name of Kike Vergonoya, who invites them to a party at the club in Plaça Reial. Ostensibly to deal drugs.'

Fabregat stops on the Carrer de l'Hospital and points down the street to the top of the long oval roundabout that forms the Rambla del Raval. We turn, heading back towards Las Ramblas.

'Sjon and Adrià Sorra left La Rosa del Raval around 00.45 on 24 June 2003.' He veers down an alleyway lined with trash, inhaling the sticky air of the darkness. In the distance, the night sings, flooded with inky female voices from a neighbouring bar. Then right again, onto an ugly street lined with ramshackle buildings.

Fabregat winces slightly, running his hand through his hair. He pauses.

'Cigarette?'

'No, thanks,' I say. *I'd smoke too many with you.*

For a while we are silent.

We reach a once-glamorous dive on the Plaça Reial. A large square, muted marigold and cream, peppered with palms. Black fountain at its centre. *Font of the Three Graces. Daughters of Zeus.* Colonnades bristling with cafés and restaurants, nightclubs and boozers. Despite the cold, Fabregat chooses to sit outside. Palm trees windswept. Water drenched. Embittered. The regulars at the bar recognize him – they nod their heads slightly, agree to behave. Fabregat on home turf. He orders two Voll-Damms from the waiter.

'You have a boyfriend?' he asks in the chair beside me. His eyes scan the buildings above us.

'Yes.'

'He knows what you're up to?'

'Not entirely.'

'You should tell him.'

'Why?'

'Don't you always tell him what you're up to?'

'No.'

'And he doesn't mind.'

'I think he does.'

'But you don't care?'

'My work is more important.'

'Huh,' Fabregat says. He looks at me sharply. 'And what about me? Do you tell me everything? Can I trust you?'

What's in this for you? is what he wants to say.

You are hunting for a man, Fabregat, but I? I am hunting for a book. And I will only help you so far as I can.

'Now,' Fabregat says. 'You can see the entrance to the members club Eufòria in the corner of the square. The bar's not marked, you buzz into what looks like an apartment complex. You can see the entrance to it just there –' he points to a black unmarked door across the street from our bar. 'Natalia Hernández attended a party here with Oriol Duran. Playboy actor and wild child, generally harmless. Duran, Natalia Hernández, Villafranca, Sánchez, Joaquim Espuma, Alejo Castelluci and several other members of the glitterati theatre scene are all in attendance . . .' He pauses.

'Just a stone's throw from where I worked. Five minutes walking.' He sighs. 'Almost in sight of the police station. *Everything happened right under my nose.* I wanted you to see the place before you get properly started. Walking this shit in person is always better than reading your books, I'll tell you that.'

He throws back the beer, snaps his finger at the barman. *Food? Calamares.* Fabregat is hungry.

'Adrià Sorra and Natalia Hernández meet for the first time here.

278

Zero evidence suggests that they have been or ever were in contact before.'

'Do you have any surveillance camera footage from the bar? Any photographs?'

'Yes.' A machine on task. 'The paparazzi did us a favour.'

He slides another set of pictures across to me. The scene: the internal bar at Eufòria shot from a camera positioned overhead, looking down from a balcony into the crowd. Natalia Hernández leans over the bar, elbows extended, hands clasped beneath her chin. Oriol Duran. Auburn hair, sideburns, forelock cut close to the face, good-looking and he knows it – body like a gymnast.

Fabregat notes the contours of Oriol's muscles with his index finger: 'A strong *cabronazo*.'

Oriol orders a whisky. Natalia tugs on his shoulder, whispers in his ears – No, two. Natalia turns around, she's seen someone she knows, comes back, orders a third drink – for who? Three drinks in two hands cupped together to form a triangle. *Toma.* Duran hands Natalia a drink. The cameras at the bar catch it well – the first sign – three drinks but no third party appears, not yet. Natalia is laughing. She's wearing a doll-collared silk shirt, tied at the throat with a pink ribbon. Neat. Precise. Low profile, though you can slightly see the contour of a bra through the shirt, which shows up dark on camera. Her hair is pulled back against her neck in a tight, black bun, make-up minimal, except for the signature tint across her lips, and that amber, flawless skin. Her hands move nervously when she speaks, agitated, energetic, but I have a feeling that's more personality than anxiety – she's not afraid of him. Not Oriol, she's smiling, intimate, Oriol's hands outstretched, laughing – and he's reaching with money for the drinks, the bartender cracks a joke. They laugh. Their shoulders move – she touches his shoulder – the crowd is heaving but they exist apart – did you catch that? – she touched his shoulder – and then they left? They or he?

'And Natalia, when does she leave the bar?' I ask.

'For good? We're not certain.'

'So you know where she is from midnight to around 4 a.m.'

'Yes. Staff confirm this.'

'And that she reappears dead. At the foot of the cathedral in the arms of Adrià Sorra, who leaves her just before dawn, whereupon her body is found by a street cleaner.'

'All correct,' Fabregat confirms.

'Right. Returning to the photographs at the bar. The third drink?'

'Goes to a young man with long black hair.'

'Adrià Sorra?'

Fabregat nods.

I roll this fact around in my mind, looking across at the shuttered club. 'They definitely meet at the bar?'

'It appears so.'

'Sorra's journey afterwards?'

'Never clear.'

'When did he arrive?'

'Came through the doors at 01.23.'

'Accompanied?'

'By one friend.'

'Who?'

'Sjon de Vries. Well known little shit. Brought in a couple of times before. Drug dealer. Dutch. Moved back to Holland ten years ago.'

'When did Oriol leave?' I ask.

'Earlier than Natalia did.'

'He left her there alone? At his own party?' Curiosity must have shown on my face.

'Apparently they had an argument. He doesn't feel good about it.'

Fabregat turns and gestures at the waiter. 'Do you want another?'

'No. I can't keep up.'

He laughs. '*Senyor! Una caña sisplau!* And water for the girl! It's a lot to take on board,' he says, mouth dry.

'Our coroner's report reveals that Natalia downed a lethal cocktail of drugs sixty to ninety minutes before she was attacked in the Gothic. The barbiturates started to take serious effect as she left the club. Slurred speech had already set in, and she was stumbling, half asleep. Everyone presumed she was drunk. Very, very drunk. No one remembers exactly when she left, but we estimate that it was between three thirty and four in the morning. We think Adrià followed her at a distance, that he had taken an interest in the actress. She crossed the square down that side street there.' Fabregat points to the arch across from us, at the north-eastern corner of the Plaça Reial.

'Then she's off camera for a while,' he says darkly. 'She goes down Carrer dels Tres Llits.'

I follow the inspector as he strides into the maze. A side alley near Carrer d'en Rauric.

'Someone met her here, though she may have already collapsed from the drugs. Unlike the others it wasn't systematized or clean,' Fabregat says. 'The act was impulsive. Passionate. Brutal. The assailant punctured through her carotid artery with a thin, sharp blade before stabbing her repeatedly and cutting off the tip of her tongue. The whole thing was incredibly quick. She had no time to cry out. The neighbours say they heard nothing.

'Adrià would have stumbled upon her in that state. She may even have died in his arms. Why he didn't call us I don't know. Off his face, I suppose. He was covered in her blood. That's the markings we found on his shoes. They all match hers. And he carried her, up the winding streets to the cathedral, where he laid her out on the steps before taking his own life.'

Fabregat kicks the stones. 'When we finally traced her back to this place, the street cleaners had washed most of the evidence down the drains. Who knows what we would have found otherwise.' Fabregat glares at the wall. 'She was stupid. If it was her who sent the letters, then she knew what was going on intimately. If it really was her, Nena, then why didn't she come directly to me? If she knew all this was happening?'

The inspector's voice suddenly harsh. 'Silence is a choice,' he says. 'It is a decision. If she knew him, she knew what was happening. If she did it, well, that's something to consider. But if we follow your line of thinking we know she had access to information – she knew about each of the victims, and she knew my name. If she was close enough to the killings to have been involved in them . . .' He shudders and falls silent. 'It makes my own failure more painful.'

We keep walking. He runs over details. Adrià carried Natalia up through here, to Plaça de San Josep Oriol, then to Felip Neri, then to the Cathedral. He processed past the churches with her. As I listen I feel myself loosening. Drifting. And then it comes.

Hello?

The expectant wave. A hazy, lucid richness. No more than a few seconds, but it will feel longer. *Rest here. Follow. Keep your eyes open.* Bright-faced girl buying drinks at a bar. Midnight: peach-cheeked, sun-painted, jeans dirty. She has an arch of freckles across her nose like a crescent moon. When she laughs I see valleys and rivers full of life. Coins clinking in her pocket. *Vodka? Gin? Cervesa?*

You choose.

I follow her through the crowd.

The sweet sway of her hips. The loose joints of her knees. The men turn their heads in unison to catch the wake of her movement. Her spectacle fills them with drunken pleasure. She is queen of the room. Music condenses into a fog of cigarette smoke. Soot marries the cloth round her throat, swims into her hair. I notice him then, standing in the corner of the room. *Watching her. Hunting her. Selecting her.* It is difficult to discern, through the haze, what was real. What did he look like? I ask the vision. But I do not know his name. I cannot call him. My vision blurs. How had he stood? The weight of his figure, the curve of his voice? *Look away.* I shake myself. Dance. Shift the weight into your hips; push your centre of gravity low, toes stretching in their sandals, legs bare and brown. Each move is slow, breathing to the rhythm of Nu Cumbia. I stop. A stranger is standing in front of me. Face shadowed. Blurred memory.

'Who are you?' He asks. Smelling my hair.

I take a step back. I cannot make out his face. But it is him. I am certain it is him. She has disappeared into a menagerie of flesh, a formless mass of arms and limbs and lips pressing closer to one another, one thousand hearts working towards the same end: begging for a kiss, a union – I cannot shake his eyes. There is something unnerving about him. I see every piece of him. The stubble round his cheek. The fabric of his collar light on his clavicle, the wave of hair that floats across his temple. And yet I do not recognize him. I cannot find a name.

'You don't have to answer,' he says. 'You can tell me if it's too personal.'

Something deep and dark inside me turns. A hand that opens the pages of this book and shows me the past, a feeling stronger than words. I see Natalia Hernández with the shadowy figure of a man. It is not Adrià. It is not the night she died. It is a night much longer ago, in a deeper past. *I am for you and you for me.*

When I close my eyes, this is what I hear.

Two words spoken soft and low.

Follow me.

As I walk with Fabregat I feel the constriction of the narrowing streets. We track north through El Call, the old Jewish quarter. Graffiti on bolted wooden doors. Retrace her steps. Second shadow: man who kissed her hand. Walked with her to a point about a mile above the city – it is a dusty path that snakes around the mountains overlooking the sea. La Carretera de las Aigües. *You cannot see his face but feel his fingers, skin brittle and bare.* There is a bench here. A lookout near a lemon tree and a wild grape vine. She sat on the stone bench, knees knocking together. *Inhale the aroma of pines. The sweet citrus scent of eucalyptus.* Below her the city moans, sleepy and sluggish stretching into luscious bleary-eyed contentment. He picks a lemon from the tree and takes a knife from his pocket and slits the skin of the lemon. *Cuts a slice from the flesh of the fruit and gives her the rind to taste.* 'Querida, Maca, darling, stick out your tongue.' He takes the pulp of the lemon between his fingers and places it on the centre of her tongue. The lemon juice drips down his fingers. *Two leaves from the grape vine behind her ears.* He cut two more slices, one for him and one for her. The lights come on over the astral spires of the cathedrals and later they are silent still as they walk down the dirt road to the car at the station below Tibidabo. *Again. Watch again.* Now they are dancing. His hands run over her arms, his eyes never leave her face. I know nothing about him. *I cannot see him clearly. Not his history, nor his creed, nor his origin. He is a phantom birthed on the aether of this hot night by the sea. I want to show you –* her heart opens – *I want to show you love! To tell you that when he came into my dreams, he sat at the end of my bed, looking at me. I move when I felt the weight of his body against my legs, through the covers, causing my hips to roll slightly forward. Now see I am awake. Put out your hand and touch my cheek.* See her stirring. Orange koi swimming down silk spine. Hair black and matted and tangled, tumbling down. Small feet on a cold tile floor. Bare and frozen. I see his emptiness, his goneness. *Apprehension tight in my stomach.* In the vision I stumble over the tiles, but catch her eye. She moves through me not seeing. Searching for him.

Calling: *Macu? Macu?* Where are you? Bloom-like girl. Soon to die. Natalia Hernández. I blink. We turn a street. She slips away.

'You alright, Nena?' Fabregat asks. Hand on my shoulder. We have emerged in the open square before the great cathedral. 'Don't forget to breathe.'

VI

THE CORRESPONDENCE OF LLEWELLYN SITWELL

Vol. 2

To Llewellyn Sitwell

from

CAPTAIN CHARLES LEOPOLD RUTHVEN

Sitwell. Wash your hands of nonsense. When looking to the records kept by the monks of the Abbey of La Real, historical writings & vitae & accounts & journals of religious scribes encountered etc. remember always that where torture & women are conjoined with power, you will see traces of the Order. In England we have experienced a dissipated version of these horrors; inspired by the work of such men as the Duke of Wharton in 1719 who abandoned the club to become a Freemason ... These organizations have infiltrated Europe & therefore allow men of high reputation to live double lives & move in their public spheres as Gods while in the night they inhabit the work of the Devil, becoming debauchers & butchers & sadists ... & yet they have the brazen audacity to call themselves men of God. Like many zealots they do not have a sense of irony. Originally I believed that this stemmed from a vulgar fascination with the mechanics of torture during the Inquisition, but I have come to realize the Assassins of Words are vehemently anti-pagan & are particularly put out by the new wave of interest in our goddess-worshipping antecedents. They dislike me intensely as I am gnostic by persuasion. Worse, I love Rex Illuminatus dearly. Their guiding principle rests on the eradication of witchcraft. Their founder, known to me only as the Duke, was a pioneer in this respect. There have never been lists of the members of the Assassins of Words – all evidence of them has been destroyed & little remnants can be traced to a secret body like that of the Freemasons – but I am certain that this group originates in the Dark Ages. They are sworn to destroy two things: Divination in Women & Alchemy, both of which they see as forms of transmutation proscribed in the Bible. Should this come as a surprise to you, know that within the famed witch hunter's manual, the *Malleus Maleficarum* (v. edifying) the odious Mr Heinrich Kramer & Mr James Sprenger open their diatribe against witchcraft with an oft-ignored attack on Alchemy & I quote from fractured memory:

> *Demons do not seduce except by Art. But art cannot contain truth. For which reason it is declared in the chapter on Minerals that the alchemists who claim to transmute one species to another through the arts should know that species – whether mineral or animal – cannot be transmuted.*

& I would also turn your attention to the Canon Episcopi (10th century) in Gratian's *Decretum* which rejects the belief that certain members of the gentle sex are capable of transformation, but does suggest that women worship the Goddess Diana in Secret & therefore commit Acts of Heresy & that these women come together in vast gatherings & believe they can transmute into animals as an alchemist transmutes lead into gold & thus forbids the pagan faith in shape-shifting. The explanation for such revelry always devolves into supposed pacts with the Devil & demons who enable 'transformation' or 'transmutation'. They are anti-science & anti-art, two things as a gentleman of Queen & country I have sworn nobly to defend – I hasten to add the only things I *care* to defend – & I do hope you feel honour-bound to follow suit. I point your attention also to the *Margarita* of Martinus Polonus (*d.* 1278) & his work on alchemy – '*Alchemy seems to be a degenerate art due to the fact that the alchemist who believes that he can transmute one species into another, except by the beneficence and majesty of God, is both a heretic & an infidel & far worse than a pagan.*' Curious evidence also in the rhetoric of Alfonso de Spina – *Fortalitium Fidei* (1459) – whose sentiment echoes the following: '*Many perverse & vile Christian alchemists are fooled, having consorted with demons, believing that they transmute iron into gold through their art.*'

More to follow.

Captain Charles Leopold Ruthven

P.S. Find me in London. I will be at my club shortly. Assuming, of course, that I am still alive.

19 November 1851, Valldemossa, Majorca

Katherine, my love, curiosity has doomed me to the fate of the most miserable of foot soldiers. My tutors at Cambridge did warn that when I had begun to understand Rex Illuminatus, his omissions and obscurities might drive me to near madness. Perhaps these were not empty threats. Coupled with the information I have received from Ruthven, I find myself awash with confusion. My life has become one of the very novels I used to read so dearly, and while you did tell me, Katherine, that if I went seeking monsters, I should find them – I did not at first believe how true your faint words were. Since leaving Barcelona, I have been plagued by ill-luck and ill-humours. On the lamentable morning of my

291

departure from the city, the servant Brass Buckle drove me to port and placed me on a packet ship bound south to Majorca. Ruthven did not accompany me, afraid as he is to leave the safeguard of his home, but made certain I took his documents on my person. I assured him I would do my best to help him, and to make whatever headway necessary in the aid and protection of a friend. As to the men who stalk him – if what Ruthven tells me of their methods is true, then I am sure their obliteration is a worthy cause and I am happy to lend myself to it. To that end, I carried a letter from Captain Ruthven to his friend and ally Padre Lloret, priest of the Holy Trinity at the village of Valldemossa on Majorca. True to his word, Ruthven purchased my passage, a fine first-class cabin, and posted me as his messenger with a firm shake of the hand. His eyes, however, had the haunted look of desperation, and earlier that morning he had made many foreboding remarks about this being our last goodbye. Unlike his master, the servant felt no sadness to see the back of me, his very being pervaded with an atmosphere of brutal animosity. As I watched the face of Captain Ruthven's servant merge into the rocks, the mainland quickly became nothing more than a black smudge on the horizon. I ruminated then on the unspoken sadness of travel. Katherine, I would not have thought it possible, but I find nothing so depressing as a vanishing skyline. The retreating vision of land as it disappears, fading into mist on water. My heart grew dull with melancholy. What I had seen pervaded my dreams and disturbed me deeply. I had not learnt what I wished from Ruthven. Barcelona had not been as I expected. All this before seasickness took me. I spent the majority of my voyage in pain and misery, reflecting on the body of the woman I had seen. The injustice rankled me. Storms buffeted from all sides; clouds of bitter dankness surged up from the sea, pelting down rain and cracks of lightning, and waves crashed into the hull of our ship, sending our sails skimming across the surface of the world. For a while I believed that I would die in passage, held in the grip of a gale the like of which I have never seen nor experienced, my journey marked by a contrary wind seeking out my bones, and my cabin mates trembling with fear. The rain did not cease in the port of Palma, where I hired a buggy to take me to Valldemossa, a day's ride from the capital. I had not imagined that the island would be so mountainous nor so violent in its beauty.

God has carved Majorca in the shape of an axe head and her women, I am told, feast at certain times of the year on water rats, considered a rare delicacy in the more rural environs. The island's garb is lush and wild, the roads near wilfully jagged and rocky. As my poor driver bravely attempted to summit the sierra, the rain lashed it down, the horses spooked by the weather and my driver's brimmed hat dripping with water, I occupied myself by looking out the buggy window. En route through the lower foothills I passed fields where poor sheep had been summarily drenched. Once arrived in Valldemossa, I made my way as per Ruthven's directions to the rooms at the Charterhouse. The village is not large and the people for the most part are friendly. At the door to my lodging I was greeted by a buxom woman who enquired as to my name and took payment for my chambers. When I asked of Padre Lloret, she coloured brightly in each cheek and spoke to a small boy playing in an anteroom. The child promptly disappeared and I was left in a state of bemusement. The woman encouraged me to wait, offering a cup of cocoa, which I welcomed gratefully, and a half-hour later a man appeared at the door in farmer's garb, a country cap on his head and a shepherd's crook in his hand. The man shook off his cloak at the door and left his rain-soaked hat on a hook, before striding across to greet me. 'Master Seetweelll!' he cried with an enthusiasm that shook my expectations. He was a warm sort of man, with a mountain face and almond eyes and a rustic mouth given readily to smiling. I can see why his name brought a flush to the good woman's cheeks as he was perhaps the most roguish priest I have ever met: his manly visage ornamented by a black, well-trimmed beard, his eyes bright. I placed his age at around thirty-five. Lloret smiled when I told him I had met Ruthven. In the company of the priest I felt surprisingly at ease. He was jovial and warm, a far cry from the vampiric shadows of Ruthven, and I struggled to imagine how the friendship had formed, the two men seemed so at odds with each other. Lloret requested that I follow him to his quarters, bidding me to leave the Charterhouse when the rain had lightened. We strode through the village passing a series of farm buildings. The houses here have no kitchens within them, but little huts across the street, so that at meal times, mothers and wives and sisters can be seen tripping across the cobbled roads to make their meals, kept (perhaps more sanitary than our English ways) away from the animals that popu- late the ground floors of homes. As we processed I found myself much observed in the village as an anomaly.

'Stranger,' Lloret reassured me, 'do not fear – now that you have walked with me, no one will think ill of you.'

At his table, Lloret offered me a glass of red wine and produced a round earthenware bowl of olives. 'Last season's,' he told me proudly, intimating that his friends the monks had grown them. I gave him the letter from Ruthven. He asked if he might take a moment to review the contents. The priest studied the letter closely before putting it down with a sigh. I decided then that he was good and honest, watching the emotion play across his face.

'How much do you know?' he asked.

I told him what I had seen. A mighty interrogation ensued. Had anyone else met me with the Captain? Did any person or persons know of my current whereabouts? Did I trust his servant? I replied that I did not. Lloret frowned. Had I written letters, or shared confidence with any individuals close to me? I did not tell him,

Katherine, that I write all my secrets to you – which was unusual as I consider myself honest to a fault, but he looked to be a man who would trespass on this weakness, and force a silence between us, a prospect frankly I cannot stomach.

'That is good,' Lloret said when we had finished. 'You have escaped with your reputation unscathed.' He then intimated that I had been wise to stay indoors. 'God has been with you. The more innocent you stay, the better,' Lloret declared ominously. 'I am loath to reveal anything, though Ruthven has asked me to share what I know. The Captain has made an enemy of a very powerful and diabolical class of people. I am concerned for his safety, and by extension yours, *Anglès*. He has rendered you more vulnerable than you likely realize.' The fields beyond Lloret's window were covered by a canopy of storm. Trees shook free their burdens. I heard the rumble of thunder, and pulled my cloak tighter round my shoulders.

'And what of the men who stalk Ruthven?'

'They are an anonymous organization operating within Catalonia and abroad – their leader is known as the Duke, of what I am not sure. They are formed of rogue members of the clergy and high society, devoted to the extermination of forbidden books. For a while we thought they had disappeared into the folds of history, like so many devils before them, becoming legends – fuel for fairy tales. You have heard of werewolves and vampires no doubt?'

'I have read the accounts of Dom Augustin Calmet.'

'Some truths are worse than myths. You cannot seek the holy flame without encountering its equal and opposite, Master Sitwell.' I shuddered at the thought of the drawings I have made in my journals, depicting the woman I had seen with Ruthven.

'But what has this to do with Rex Illuminatus?' I asked.

'Like many thinkers of his age, Illuminatus made strong enemies, the greatest of whom was the Inquisitor General of Aragon, Nicholas Eymerich of Girona. Do you know the name, Master Sitwell?'

I intimated that I did not

Lloret crossed himself twice.

'Ruthven has asked me to discuss him with you – and this favour I will do. Eymerich was one of ours ... not of our order but of our inclination – he was a shepherd before God, and a monster before men, who hated our Illuminatus. Eymerich believed that the Doctor was a sorcerer and a heretic who held a poisonous influence on society. Eymerich was famous for piercing the tongues of heretics with nails so that they could not speak – he studied practices of torture and fear, the best temperature to burn a witch – the most honest keys of pain.'

Lloret raised his eyebrow and looked at me. 'Do I continue?' he asked.

'Yes,' I said gravely, imagining what it would look like if a woman's tongue were pierced with a nail.

'In 1376, the Grand Inquisitor published what would become a definitive manual of the Spanish Inquisition, the infamous *Directorium Inquisitorum*. In it he expressed a great disapproval for Alchemy. But it was not until twenty years later that he published *Contra Alchimistas*.'

'This I have heard of,' I replied.

'Let me assure you it is a disgusting book. In his *Contra Alchimistas* Eymerich outlined the heresies of the alchemical philosophers that had swept up the passion of Catalonia and the world beyond. When the treatise was finished, the Inquisitor dispatched the book promptly to Rome, demanding the erasure of Illuminatian works. I have a copy of it here. Rex Illuminatus was an artist, a thing that Eymerich hated above all else.'

Lloret walked slowly to a shelf, from which he removed a dusty, thin volume. He opened it to a page marked with a thin strip of cloth. Read, he said, pointing at the Latin. I translate for you now:

> Through art, alchemists seek to imitate life, whose image and figure they conjure tirelessly. These copyists are false in their creation of new works, as they cannot imitate life perfectly in regard to features, most especially faces. In fact, the alchemist cannot imitate life in any sense of the word, because all imitations must be by definition false and corrupted, and devoid of motions and singing and all consciousness and passions, as art cannot conjure the flight or song of birds, nor the odours or flavours of the forest, nor the virtues or deformities of men.

'Ah,' I said, pretending to understand. The priest ate an olive slowly before informing me of the following:

'I met Ruthven when he came to visit our archives in an attempt to find a magic book proscribed by Eymerich in 1396. Your Captain Ruthven arrived armed with a map carved onto an emerald, a relic which had come into his possession in the battle for the Independence of Peru. This map led us to the discovery of a sacred palimpsest, written over by Rex Illuminatus, which I helped him to cut loose from a Book of Hours I later concealed in the walls of a chapel north-east of our monastery.' Lloret paused dramatically before continuing: 'This truth is known only to myself and your master.' Lloret gripped my hand tightly. 'And now Ruthven has asked me to share it with you.

'Master Sitwell, Illuminatus imbedded a great wisdom in his writing, a language which can only be accessed by a savant – a holy language which allows the individual mortal spirit to communicate with God.' Lloret's face radiated with light. 'A language which would have wrenched power from the Church, putting the Holy Ghost into the mouth of the individual, outside of the structures of the papal edicts. This language renders the speaker a living, breathing vessel of divine creativity. Miracles? Master Sitwell? You have heard of these things?'

I nodded in affirmation.

Lloret smiled softly to himself. 'Before you leave this island you shall see wonders great and terrible, this I swear to you.' The priest drummed his fingers lightly on the table. 'You must find it peculiar, Master Sitwell, that the writings of a long dead alchemist guide your fate.' With that he took my hand in his and I felt the warmth of him, the blood coursing through his veins. I realize now that adventure is as unpredictable as men. Indeed you can only live it, as it comes, when it comes. I thought a great many things as I listened to Lloret, but said none of them. I have struggled to capture all that passed between us, but will attempt to be as accurate as I may be – Lloret has impressed upon me an understanding of the events of the past few weeks, the more unsettling horror contained in his words which I cannot bring myself to repeat even here. Skipping over these lurid, vulgar details I shall reveal what happened in brief. Lloret's voice lowered as he spoke: 'Captain Ruthven told you to deliver an object for him. An object that will save his life. This is a Ruthvenian play on words. What he wishes you to deliver is gnosis, Master Sitwell. Knowledge. He has instructed you to give his knowledge to a woman, a woman who will safeguard this secret, but has no power over his fate. What you shall save is his legacy. The legacy of the object which you carry.'

I nodded. We had discussed the same in his home.

'He has requested that I share his knowledge with you. Are you sure you wish to go down this path?' Lloret asked me. I made such and such assurances and demonstrated my loyalty, though secretly I found it all perplexing in the extreme.

'Brave words,' Lloret commended me. 'Ruthven believes that Illuminatus and the Order are connected by both circumstance and misfortune. This you must understand. In 1376, a mysterious acolyte of Eymerich under the name of "the Duke" formed a secret organization, an underground network of spies that sought out heretics and brutally abused them. A pogrom erupted against Illuminatus resulting in a Papal Bull that banned 120 of his books while censuring his teaching in the Church. A second wave of attack followed swiftly, spurred on by the Duke's success in Rome. Flavius Clemens, a pupil at the Faculty of Theology at the University of Paris, orchestrated the official condemnation of the works of Illuminatus by the Theologians, prohibiting the study of the good man's writing at the University. The results were disastrous.

'In 1396 two factions formed,' Lloret intoned solemnly. 'Those that guard the secret arts of Illuminatus and those that forward the practices of Eymerich's friend the Duke. Their followers have fought us fiercely, with Anti-Illuminatists blocking the publications of his texts, burning manuscripts where possible and creating false books to discredit Illuminatus's name. Of the 277 recorded works of Illuminatus, at least 273 are lost to history. It is a war that continues to be waged in this century, Master Sitwell, with proponents of Illuminatus such as myself fighting to protect his writing every step of the way. To this day, his enemies are still among us, and return.'

A tear welled at the corner of Lloret's eye. He brushed it away in the hopes I did not see it.

'I'm sure the Captain has told you of his theories of the great Illuminatus's immortality?'

I nodded.

Lloret sighed. 'Rex Illuminatus as you call him drank an elixir of philosophical longevity, not a physical one – this is where Ruthven and I have differed. I believe that his ideas are immortal, and thus his soul survives, and not his corporeal form. He was a doctor of the soul, Master Sitwell, not an alchemist of metals. Do not believe that business about the elixir of life. Illuminatus lives in us, we carry him here.' He pointed dramatically to his heart.

'What was it about Illuminatus that called you to him?' the priest enquired. I told him that I had begun reading his work in my studies at Cambridge and that the mystic had appeared in my dreams. I did not mention that I was dabbling in Romantic Hellenism at the time as it did not seem fitting. We spoke at great length about the significance of these dreams, which I have shared with you and will not repeat. I felt very comfortable with the man, whose face inspired the most intense of honesties and whose passion for his God seems most genuine. We drank together, discussing his history in the Church and his vision for the future of Majorca. He was a most hospitable fellow, hungry for the world though he has never left this island. An hour later I asked where he had learnt his English, and he replied entirely from books, which explains his peculiar accent. When the sun set, the rain stopped. Lloret suggested taking a walk through the countryside.

'You are quite safe with me,' Padre Lloret said, the bell tower glittering before us. Padre Lloret put out his hand and touched a stone cross, encouraging me to do the same. 'It is likely Illuminatus walked here, in contemplation,' he said. 'Life may be an ugly thing if you do not steer it well. There are many of us with regrets, and violence is an end to avoid, if God gives you a choice.' Then he paused, catching a glimpse of my ill-humour. 'Come.' He beckoned with his hand, and we wandered down into the forest, retracing our path down to the edge of the town. The storm had passed, and I felt the first wave of relief that I had arrived in this refuge.

'Tomorrow,' Lloret said, as he left me at the doors of the

Charterhouse, 'I will fetch de la Font and her *Vitae Coetana*.' I retired to my rooms and began to write of this to you, with my single foul-smelling candle. I miss you horribly, though this place does offer a certain kind of peace. What have I done, to deserve this purgatory? Though I wished it on myself, I regret the day I left you. Do not cease to write, as I am ever in need of your strength, and your counsel.

Your beloved and ever closer, Sitwell

6 December 1851, Valldemossa, Majorca

Katherine, I have as yet received no response from you – but I assume this is due to troubles in the post, rather than troubles in your heart. But I will regale you with stories! Today I awoke with the sun. As the glowing mass gathered up his skirts to the East, I emerged from my quarters in my slippers and went to sit in our private gardens. The experience was one of rapture. The sky lightened and the birds danced in the bare branches of a silver birch. I felt the weight of the evening's anxieties fall from my shoulders and elected to go for a walk immediately. I took only a few coins, then made my way towards the donkey path to Deià, stopping to buy a lump of sweet potato bread and a hunk of ewe's cheese. For all that I have read Illuminatus's work – all the time spent in libraries and offices and cloisters studying his treatises on Love and God and Man – I have never understood his import until now, when I look out over the sea and the sky, and stop to break bread on the roots of an olive tree – O! Olea europaea! I would sing its praises to you! The bark knotted and streaked with damp, tight winter fruit green and purple, dusted with a fine white powder – the earth about their roots a marvellous blood red clay. I stumbled into a field of such aged olives, their regal branches sheathed in silvery leaves, their bearing scattered, the rock walls about them crumbling ... And – I swear to God! – the olives I have found are as old as the works of Illuminatus if not older. I have walked back through a portal and am here without clocks or edifice or order – free to simply breathe the air. I am stripped away – all ill-thoughts, all trepidations left on the path to this wild church of the World! No wonder works of truth occur to the hermit in his cave, overlooking such majesty! There can be no doubt in his mind that he is in communion with some nebulous maker of things! And though I struggle daily with my own ease of persuasion, my confusion as to the true reasons for my being on this island, I must admit, dear Katherine, I am lifted up and strengthened by my undying faith in the world and my deepest ardour for the keeper of my heart.

  With Love and Admiration,
  Sitwell

8 December 1851, Valldemossa, Majorca

I had just begun my own translation of the alchemist's work when Father Lloret rudely disrupted me. He burst through the doors of my chambers dressed in a black greatcoat over his outer frock. 'Thank God you are safe!' he cried. 'Quick now! We must away at once!' Before I could reply, the priest produced two pistols from beneath his coat – 'Lift your arms, Sitwell!' he ordered, strapping a firearm to each of my hips, before thrusting me a sabre to carry across my back. 'Can you shoot straight?' he asked. 'Our path prevents me from taking fire, but if needs be you must.' I laughed nervously, replying that I might myself be mistaken for an outlaw, bristling as I was with weaponry. The priest put his hand on my shoulder, bringing his face close to mine. 'The worm has turned, Master Sitwell.'

'I beg your pardon?' I stammered.

'Gather your things.' Lloret's voice shook – 'We ride tonight to meet the Nightingale. She will answer all your questions.' I was silenced, much disturbed by his Latin display of emotion. With that we quit my quarters, swearing de la Font to secrecy. The woman's eyes darted to the guns at my waist. Lloret bundled me onto a horse tethered to the Charterhouse before mounting a second steed. Hooves clattered across the cobbled streets. We made our way swiftly, climbing out from the Valley of Moses. The moon not yet risen, the sky black and full of a hundred thousand stars, robes draped in finery. I resolved to calm myself and watch the luminaries flicker, looking up for reassurance. Suddenly Lloret reined his horse to a halt. The hair rose on my neck, I reached for my pistol – no sound had I heard but perhaps he sensed something?

'Look!' Lloret breathed, and pointed. Before my very eyes the Cimmerian darkness parted in the wake of a gauzy haze, like smoke rising from the earth. The haze grew in strength, turning in strides from a shimmering dust to a radiant burst of white gold, emerging as a numinous goddess from the black ridge, harvest orb consuming the sky. The stars winked into shadow, so moved by her presence were they!

'We are graced, Sitwell!' Lloret cried as the moon's celestial gleam caught on the mare's damp eyes. Sweat greeted me from the back of the horse. My muscles burnt, for I had not ridden in many months, and despite being a healthy man, I am not used to passing so swiftly over steep terrain. However, I kept a steady path and the mare was good, taking care she did not fall for we went a way untrodden. We travelled thus for several hours, traversing higher into the sierra, before arriving in a wide clearing, set against the mountains. At the far end of a rocky plateau I discerned the dancing flame of a candle. Steam rising from the chimney of a low stone cottage. Moonlight bled into the yard where chickens slept in their coop. A cattle dog barked twice from inside a barn while a cat mewled plaintively. Lloret dismounted, swinging his boots onto the ground. I did the same and gave the reins of my mare to the priest, who tied the dripping beasts to a bolt beside a drinking trough. The horses lapped thirstily at the water while we removed their saddles, rubbing their sweat down with a blanket, pressing warmth into their soaked rippling muscle before Lloret led them to a tumbledown barn, where he stabled the horses for the night. As we strode across the yard, the cottage door swung open to a vision more beautiful than any I have seen in my travels. You must forgive me for saying so, but it is true. I beheld thick, black hair, knotted as the sea, pulled into a mass behind her ears. Broad sunken eyes with hooded lids like the effigies of saints. She wore a fragile golden thread against her throat, from which hung a little metal bird, delicate wings outstretched across her bosom. Her dress was rustic, rough cotton sleeves cuffed at her elbows and wide, muddied petticoat beneath her skirt. She was not elegant or diminutive, but earthy and strong, with a proud carriage unlike any I had seen on a woman.

'Welcome!' she called into the yard. 'Lloret! Senyor Sitwell! Welcome!'

As she stood in the door frame, illumined by the fire behind her, I felt she was a second moon rising from the mouth of this vast mountain. She was a goddess, stern and foreboding. I tumbled towards her, following Lloret's lead, entranced by the vision, and I could not help but think, as a man, that this is why the priest lends himself to the call of Ruthven's favour. He is in love with this woman, Kitty, as sure as I love you – for what priest or man could withstand such evidence of beauty? But I banished the thought, relegating it to the realm of the intellectual, the spiteful and false, for I trust Lloret in his faith, though I do not understand it. The tenderness I saw on his brow, and the touch of his hand on her arm, made me think again that I had crossed into some different realm, where the rules of conduct were not as I had imagined.

Inside her cottage was unpleasantly dark. The windows were small and tightly shuttered, the kitchen marked by the presence of a metal cauldron bubbling above an open fire. As Lloret and the woman became quickly engrossed in some tête-à-tête, I thought it best to leave them, and gather my nerves outside. I sat beneath the lantern hanging from her door and watched the moon bulge across the heavens, her veil so bright that I could see all the valley's stones and the individual leaves of low scrub. It soothed me to observe this rugged highland glinting like an oiled obsidian mirror. I noted the position of the spring of the serpent, *la font de sa serp*, not far from the stone cottage. Soon enough Lloret threw open the door behind me and demanded that I enter. Here I saw more than I had previously discerned. Canvases and stretched parchment were stacked against the walls of the cottage, dried herbs were strewn from the rafters. A desk had been prepared, hinged drawing board equipped with magnifying glasses and a multitude of quills, two penknives, a cutting stone, a rule and pencils. There was linen paper, filler and ink, and reeds kept in a jar – from which she must cut her own nibs, alongside vials and potions. *Sitwell*, I thought, suddenly afraid, *this woman is a witch*.

'Are you hungry?' She walked towards me. My stomach turned. I stammered that I was, but perhaps put off the idea of food. Lloret remained silent. The woman went to the stove, where a vat of soup was unveiled, and hunks of meat to warm the belly. Lucretia placed a bowl of the festering stew before me. I was immediately repulsed. *Lloret worships this being!* I thought. *But perhaps his mind has been transfigured!* I refused to bring any food to my lips, having decided that Lucretia was magic, like Circe or Morgan le Fay, and that if I ate her fare I would be trapped as a pig in her yard, or worse, become a devotee like the lovesick Lloret.

'Do I frighten you, Senyor Sitwell? You have read too much. I am no faerie. Lloret. Tell the man how much I can bleed.' She pulled up the sleeve of her dress and showed me a scar that ran down to her palm. Lloret pulled a candle closer, so that the light fell on the raised mark. 'Do you think a faerie bleeds?' she asked. I pushed the bowl away, reassuring myself that every demon and witch from time immemorial had said the same.

'You are very rude for a gentleman. Ruthven wrote that you were rude, and rude you are indeed.' She gestured at the priest and they began conversing rapidly in their thick dialect of Catalan. Lloret announced then that I brought a package with me, an offering the woman expected. He got up from the table and strode to our saddlebags, returning with the wrapped bundle. Taking the package from Lloret, she set it on the table and pulled back the cloth. Inside was a sealed golden reliquary box with a panelled roof inlaid with fine enamel. The box was decorated with an intricate pattern of golden fig leaves, embedded with minute glass birds, the craftsmanship of which was wondrous to behold.

'Open it,' she commanded.

I did as I was bidden, removing the metal key from its latch. Before me were several sheets of parchment tied together by a thin black ribbon. The parchment itself was very old, riddled with the remnants of an animal's veins, and looked not unlike a set of leaves sown together. Gilded illuminations glittered in the candlelight, and the Latin letters moved as if they were alive. In an instant, I recognized the penmanship of a master – my own Rex Illuminatus. Immediately I reached for the pages, but Lucretia caught my hand and held it back.

'You must not touch them. They will sear into you. They will speak to you in a thousand voices. These are the Serpent Papers, Sitwell. They are written in the Divine Language, a language like no other on earth.'

'Do you know this tongue?' I asked.

'You could learn it, Sitwell, but the strength of it would devour you.'

Lucretia lifted my hands in hers and kissed them. '*What transpires will be for you to decipher. A riddle of your own.*' Her lips never moved, but I swear I heard her voice sounding within my body. I attempted to pull away, but she held me tightly.

'Listen closely, Master Sitwell,' the priest said. 'She is a worker of many miracles, she is a final treasure whom we call the Nightingale. Ruthven has asked that she show you what she is, that you might understand the nature of the secret you will safeguard.'

As he spoke, Lucretia bowed to each of the four corners of the room, invoking the North, the South, the East, the West, before raising the relic box in her hands above her head.

'*I call you Mystery!*' she cried, pressing the relic box towards the heavens. '*I call you Mendacious One of Red Erythre, Ida — born of wooded dells, mud-bound in stained Marpessus! I follow the deepening river Aidoneus, older than Orpheus, but all have called her Madness! Sisters! Come forth! For I am the Liminal Nothingness! Traverser of the Void!*'

With each name came a gust of wind, blowing the candles so that we were plunged into darkness. Convulsions racked her form, her colour changed and her hair rose — while a warmth like a hundred hands began pulling at my clothes and tugging at my hair. Lucretia's eyes clouded in a stony emptiness as a foreign, female voice entered her mouth. '*As a virgin I was clad in iron, shackled by the strength of fate, I have not lost my sovereignty,*' the voice sang.

I felt a heat rising on my skin, a hum coursing through my veins.

'*You have called me Thrice Great, Two-Faced, Forked Tongue.*' Following this recitation Lucretia commenced to sing in a language unlike any other I have heard before, at first guttural and aspirated like the hissing of a serpent, then dark and soft as the call of the dove. As Lucretia sang, the papers in the golden box began to glow and I swear to you, Katherine, that before my very eyes a flood of light roared up from the parchment and drowned the room with a dazzling radiance – a monstrous effervescence that burnt our hands and faces, filling the dark rafters and shuttered windows, before sinking into the earthen floor as she sang in this language I could not decipher. And the sound! O, that sound! I shall never forget it until the day I die. A powerful throbbing broken by sweet, crystal calls that wrenched at my heart! With each mysterious syllable it seemed to my intoxicated senses that a golden leaf unfurled and golden boughs grew until the radiance was a veritable arbour above us.

'This is alchemy!' I cried – starting from my seat to stand in the golden leaves. 'This is the very wonder Rex Illuminatus spoke of! The fashioning of Gold!'

Lucretia panted, breath heavy before me. What emerged as a glow from her lips and eyes and ears swiftly transformed into a marvellous light, brighter than a thousand flickering candles, a heady gold like the rising of the sun, and it poured out from her neck and throat and chest, lifting her body up off the ground as the light sent out roots to the floor and suddenly her entire form appeared to shatter as a leaf of gold shatters under the hand of the illuminator, bursting into luminescent dust until there was nothing left but the song, a crooning deep song, and from the dust and song there grew a tree of light, the breadth and length of Lucretia's body, split into four branches, and at the top of the branches in place of leaves there was a hanging crescent moon. The figure of the woman flickered in and out of the golden light – while I found myself mute, stupefied into wonder – I could not gather strength to speak, so terrified was I by the spectacle. A single moment seemed interminable, stretching for hours. The woman emerged from the golden tree to put out her hands, and showed them to me. *With this language you can create anything. It is the unutterable alphabet of the imagination. The sound of flux, of Spirit. With it you can read the universe, conjure entire histories, see all futures, live forever, but should you use it coarsely, greedily, inhumanely, the more it shall burn, eating you away until you enter the wind!* Then holding her hands above her chest, she rubbed her palms together, harder and faster she rubbed them, sweat streaming from her brow as a cold shiver ran through my bones, and I felt the urge to abandon everything. To run far away, fast down the mountain valley – away from there! Too soon the voices came again – fiercer, louder – the windows and doors of the cottage burst open with sudden gusts of a howling inferno – light rushing from the woman's fingers until we were all surrounded, and light spun about her until with a great roar it exploded out and covered up my eyes, showering my skin with gold! At once I threw myself down on the floor, trembling with fear.

'Lloret!' I cried in horror. 'What devilry is this?'

In a final gust the siege abated. The light drained from Lucretia and her gaze cleared. She wiped the spittle from her mouth before slumping down in a chair like a dried chaff of wheat.

'Mark me, Sitwell. Mark me well,' she whispered. 'I am in you now. I have bound your blood to mine.'

The lapsed priest bowed his head, kneeling beside me.

'Tell him,' she said fiercely. 'Mikel, you must tell him now.'

Lloret's eyes met mine.

'I have brought you here tonight, Master Sitwell, because I was ordered to do so upon certain eventualities. Eventualities I could not reveal until after the fact. You cannot return to Valldemossa. The Captain has made provisions for your safety. He has given you everything. His wealth, his heritage, his library. You are a rich man. He wishes that you return to London, where his solicitors will pass his estate into your possession.'

'Whatever do you mean?' I rasped.

'The Captain has asked me to inform you in this fashion and not from the papers.' With that dreadful pronouncement, Lloret handed me a crumpled envelope and watched as I read – but I can write no more of this – I must tell you straight and frankly: Captain Ruthven is dead. Worse, he is murdered. Found dangling from a noose in Barcelona, his heart violently removed from his chest, his body burnt. He has sacrificed himself to his enemies. And in doing so he has given me all that they feared the world might find. As his sole benefactor, I must bear this lodestone. I hold the entirety of his estate. And I do not know what to do with my terrible burden! For Ruthven's death has shackled me to his fate ... Dear God, perhaps my writing has endangered your life, alongside mine? You must be swift. Gather up my letters, even the messages of love – you must gather every word that I have sent you since leaving England and place them in the most secret of locations. Tell no one what I have told you. Tell no one, from this point forward, that I have written to you at all. Do not act rashly, you must be strong – on no account should you seek to destroy or burn our correspondence, for it must stand as evidence of what I have witnessed shall Ruthven's murderers ever be brought to justice. I have entered into perdition. My darling, you must keep my secret as your life depended on it, for surely it does now – forgive me, please forgive me – for once you have known what I have known, there is no turning back – but do not fear. Wait word from me, and stand your ground. My God, Katherine. One thing and one thing alone is clear—

BOOK THE THIRD

A Prophet's Holograph

'Divination is fiction applied to life to predict the future.'

'Fiction?' I asked. 'What is that?'

'A novel form of writing.'

'Outside of the canon? There can be no books that do not relate to God,' I said.

Thinking warmly of my Book of Hours.

'Do you not dream in stories?' Philomela asked, signing with her hands.

Rex Illuminatus,
The Alchemical History of Things
1306 CE

Let who says
'The soul's a clean white paper,' rather say,
A palimpsest, a prophet's holograph . . .

Elizabeth Barrett Browning,
Aurora Leigh
1856 CE

I

FACE TO FACE

When he arrives, nearly half an hour late for our evening rendez-vous, Ferran Fons shouts at me across the bar, glowing in his churlishness: '*Hòstia* Anna! You've cut your hair. You look like a boy.' Linen shirt, top three buttons open, chest hair sparse, but present nonetheless. Coffee stain on right pocket.

'How many years since you got our degree?' Fons asks. 'I can't keep track. We give you a diploma and you're ass-over-heels outta here, never to be seen again. And me? You think nothing of me! Deserted! Betrayed! And now? The heavens have sent you again! A drink, girl, a drink!'

Fons lets out a whooping laugh.

'Anna! I'm starving. Beer? Wine? *Pintxos*? What's got you here? In your message you mentioned Hernández?'

'Yes—'

He cuts me off, waving frantically at the *camarero*.

'Maestro!' the waiter cries, and bows, doffing an invisible cap. 'Where would your highness like to sit?' Fons gestures regally. We are moved to our table, his hand paternally on my shoulder.

'In the drinking establishments of this city,' he beams, 'Ferran Fons, and Ferran Fons alone, is King. It is my last pleasure. One of the very few in life. Now – does Oriol Duran know you're in

Barcelona doing this?' Fons asks. A thundering whisper through the back corner where we are seated, separated by an elegant wooden frieze from the other diners. 'You need to be sensitive to him. He loved her deeply and has been very cut up since her death. Ten years later and he's only just recovering. Walking wounded, I'd say. It's a delicate situation and I expect you want to go crashing into things.'

'What makes you think I would do that?'

A waiter appears at our table. Fons smiles, then orders for me, asking for a bottle of cava. I made no move to stop him.

'It's a fragile community here. You haven't lived it with us – so you wouldn't know,' he adds tartly. 'You left. Deserted everything. Got mixed up in books.' He shudders.

'Should I apologize? We've been through this before.'

'No. But this worries me. Your being here now. Don't like it.'

His words hang uncomfortably in the air. Fons frowns and folds his napkin into a triangle. His fingers are thick. My heart goes out to him. There is a black ink circle on his right thumb.

'Have you given any thought to our community?' Ferran blinks. 'We suffered! For Villafranca, and for us, Hernández is a clean slate, done deal, wrapped up. You come back and say you're curi-ous – academically – conducting interviews about her life to be published . . . and the whole investigation starts again.'

I pause, uncertain.

'I don't want to reopen any investigations. That's not why I'm here.'

'Good.'

'But I have to ask one thing, Fons. A decade later. Are you satisfied?'

I look at him directly.

'With what? Cava? Have a drink.'

The waiter uncorks a bottle and pours two glasses. Fons evasive, as always.

'The story. The accounts you had. Does it bother you?'

'I've made peace with it.'

'How?'

'I've moved on.'

'I don't think that's true.'

'Do I look like a man who's suffering?'

Fons bites the knuckle of his thumb.

'How do you want to do this? A séance? Perform a resurrection on a mountaintop?'

'I want to write about it. Revisit everything.'

Fons lets out a low, guttural sound like a growl. Disapproval.

'Alright. A personal account?'

'A history.'

'About what? That night? You're curious about that night?'

'I want to create a running testimony of events – with the clarity of hindsight. Look at what people remember.'

'You do not know her career intimately enough.'

'I want to study it.'

'To prove what point?'

Food arrives. Two hefty bowls of soup. *Pa amb tomàquet.* Bread. I sit very still, studying my plate. *Botifarra negra. Escudella i carn d'olla.* An acquired taste. Fons slurps hungrily. Hunks of black meat floating in a thick bean broth.

'As to that hooligan who carried her, I used to teach his sister.' Fons frowns. 'Núria. Troubled girl.' He turns to me. 'You must watch what you say in this town. Everyone knows everyone, we've all crossed paths, always –' he claps his hand together – 'bumping! Like little atoms, zinging about, coincidences here are collisions. But ... I do think about what happened that summer ... if and when I allow myself.'

'Of course, Fons! You're a sentimentalist. Comes with the territory.'

'Natalia's a myth.' Ferran Fons pushes his chair out from under the table. He waves the waiter down, and asks for wine. 'A very dangerous one. Trust me. It would be better for us all if you let her rest. But you have asked for my services and I admire you! So, I will do what I can. Pull a few strings in the community, etc. Get you an interview. This I can do. However, be warned. I'm more interested in the living than the dead – and I want to keep it that way.' He raps the table with his finger. 'Don't stare at your food. It's impolite.'

Fons orders me a coffee and a *crema catalana*. 'The best in Ciutat Vella.'

Ferran Fons represents something of a mystery. Foul-mouthed, sweet-tempered, and strangely tragic, he has a tendency to lecture for hours without interruption. In class he is harshly critical, but never grades harshly, which his students appreciate and enjoy. When asked about his history, he remains silent. He accepts appointments for office hours but never keeps them. If one were to conduct a survey of information gleaned by his students – gossip exchanged at the university canteen, conversations overheard between whispering dramaturges in the library, an unattractive sighting with a younger woman at the Opera Liceu, etc., etc. – one would arrive at a motley hodgepodge of information. Details are sparse. Age: unknown (mid-fifties?). Wife: award-winning actress Aurora Balmes (a point of infantile excitement among the young). Separated six years ago. Never officially divorced. Daughter, twenty-five. Not on speaking terms (an argument witnessed by two masters students in the university cafeteria). Difficulty relating to women. (Noted tendency to mark down female papers.) Painful romantic. (Caught weeping during student production of Chekhov's *The Cherry Orchard*.)

A British exchange student researching the emergence of modern Catalan folk art in the 1980s made the most pivotal discovery. A peeling black-and-white photograph in a journalist's private collection entitled 'Traditional *festa* of Northern Catalonia'. The picture captured a group of young men holding masks, next to a magnificent metal dragon. Ferran was smiling at the centre, hair tousled. In his heyday, he was a member of a troupe of radical actors called the 'Fire Eaters' or *Tragafuegos*. Thus the British student unwittingly exposed Ferran's point of origin: he was one of *els rurals* – a fire-dancer from a northern village near the Pyrenees. Only the cruellest critics aptly described him as what he was; as a bitter Sevillana said in a late night smash-up at the Bar de Choco: '*Those who can't do, teach.*'

If he's pressed to remember, Ferran Fons will tell you that his office in that fateful summer of 2003 was near the library, a shoebox on the second tier of the drama school. He shares the office with his aged English colleague Professor Tums. On this particular Friday – the last Friday before Natalia Hernández died – Tums is absent, once again taken ill by a predilection for liquor. (Ferran bitterly notes a collection of airport-sized bottles of whisky in the third drawer of the translator's desk.) Tums's expatriate speciality was that of Catalan adaptations of Oscar Wilde (*The Importance of Being Earnest* was on at the Teatre Goya) and he had catapulted to relative fame by insisting in the local nationalist papers that Wilde 'read better in Catalan than he did in his native tongue'. On the opposite side of the office, facing the back wall (age and rank secured both Fons and Tums the window vistas) is the desk of a young postdoc from Madrid who taught *commedia dell'arte* to the undergraduates. Occasionally, when no one was looking, Ferran would rifle through the papers on Marco's desk, to see if the Madrileño had any rival theories to his own beleaguered attempts at cultural criticism. Once satisfied that Marco was another talentless chump employed by the institute to fête the wealthy children of Barcelona's elite, Ferran desisted from illicitly reading Marco's material. Though not before encountering a bland love letter to beautiful Maria, the café girl downstairs who served coffee to the world, was already engaged and, Ferran pleasantly muses, well beyond young Marco's reach.

Satisfied, Ferran Fons bides his time, preparing for the afternoon class. According to his lecture notes, Stanislavski was a Russian Theatrical Genius, Method Acting the bastard child of Poor American Translations – a category of dramatic criticism widespread and constantly growing. Ferran thinks about this often. He hates Poor American Translations – but most of all he hates Commercialization of Art – something he views as sacrosanct. He hopes to express this belief in the three-hour lecture afforded to him by the Institute of Theatre, but that morning, when he drearily arose from the comforts of his bed, he had awakened uninspired.

So he was late. As is often the case.

This afternoon he distracts himself easily. *There is a poster on the Theatre of National Liberation, hanging from the terracotta wall next to the Theatre Café.* From his office, on the second floor of the Institute, he can see the flirtatious edge of her smile, a corner of her right eye, the shadow that devours her cheekbone, the black stain where her jaw joins the flesh of her neck.

Ferran Fons settles into his chair. A knock at the door sounds suddenly, rasping twice at the wood. *Clack. Clack.*

'Silvia,' he groans inside, recognizing his superior's mincing hand. He resigns himself to the torment.

'You're late,' she declares as Ferran opens the door.

'I suppose.'

'It's half past two.'

'Yes.'

Silvia purses her lips.

'Follow me.'

The head of the Performance Department, Silvia Drassanes has her offices on the sixth floor of the Institute. She shares the room – much grander, open plan – with her assistant Caridad and the resident artist (an actress with thin fingers and a foul disposition). Ferran follows Silvia into the elevator morosely, wishing that he too had been ill that day, that he had never come in to teach, that he had stayed firmly where he belonged: in bed.

On the sixth floor, Silvia ushers Ferran towards her desk. She clears her throat.

'Ferran, I want to talk to you about Alexei. Apparently you are behaving quite inappropriately towards him.'

Alexei is a tall Muscovite, broad-shouldered, trained in the Russian Academy of Theatre Arts. To Ferran's irritation, Alexei's appearance at the Institute last autumn is worsened by rumours that his academic nemesis is a direct descendant of the great man himself. In retaliation, Ferran has taken to calling Alexei 'Ivan Vasilievich' in public after the character in Bulgakov's *Black Snow* – a reference which very few of his pupils find entertaining. The sharp-faced woman with pointy-rimmed glasses tuts.

'We're trying to modernize the course structure. Alexei already teaches a seminar on Stanislavski – and with all due respect, Ferran – he is our Russian expert.'

Ferran fiddles with a broken cigarette in his pocket, teasing out the tobacco, ripping the paper into pieces.

'We are rearranging the academic roster.'

A low-flying plane over Tibidabo catches Ferran's attention. He holds it with his eyes, following its trajectory west over Barcelona.

'Ferran?' Silvia breaks his concentration. 'Your attention please. It pains me to have to put things in such concise terms, but the academic committee needs to see a shift in your behaviour. The Institute is changing. You need to find a new place in it.'

Ferran's phone buzzes in his pocket. He meets Silvia's gaze before checking the message that bleeps onto his screen. Every rebellion, no matter how small, is empowering. The left corner of her mouth twitches minutely.

When Fons leaves the office, he sees her again, through the glass windows facing the theatre. The posters of Natalia Hernández went up three weeks ago. (Ferran noted the date in his diary, underlining it twice in red.) Now they follow him everywhere: one hundred and fifty-four hung from Gaudí's lamps lining Las Ramblas and El Passeig de Gràcia. Twenty-seven plastered over the ugly construction walls that barricaded the left side of his apartment in the Barri Gòtic, half of them peeling and sun-faded. He cannot ride a bus or go on the metro without being confronted by her face. Ferran guesses their dimensions: 80 × 120 cm. Dark red foundation. Text: All Caps. Font: a crisp Euphemia UCAS. Standard silk paper in full colour. High gloss. Distended contrast, popped exposure. One photograph. To describe it as an infatuation would be inaccurate. It is more of an *idée fixe*. In the words of Guillermo, his friend and amateur psychothera- pist (an avid reader of Žižek), the girl encapsulates Ferran's own 'subconscious desire for self-perfection'. His fixation on her image is an act of 'non-sexual shrine-making' (Guillermo was careful to underline this point), not dementia or desire.

Why?

Why does she have this power over him? Ferran bites his lower lip. For days he despaired in his office, looking at her for a moment, steel- ing himself against the inevitable. Earlier that week, the longing had been so intense he had to leave school early to seek respite with the therapist Guillermo – so violent, it frightened Ferran – *I'm not myself*, he shuddered, as he packed the contents of his satchel, walked down the flight of stairs, exited the building and marched straight into the arms of Guillermo's chaise longue on Passeig de Sant Gervasi.

'I can't do this any more. She's taunting me.'

'Relocate your energy. Describe your feelings.'

'She sees everything I've lost, what I gave up.'

Guillermo asked him to continue. Earlier that week, Ferran was stopped on his way home from the Institute and swept into a *vaga*

('There was passion,' he told Guillermo, 'real Nationalist passion!'), a demonstration which forced him into the throng of striking railway workers and dump-car drivers, and their children and bright clothes – and the flag – always the flag. Five red stripes of Catalunya and that brilliant yellow, the blazing gold of independence.

'You like the summer,' Guillermo told him. 'You feel more ...' He lifted his hands in the air to prove a point. 'You feel lighter. Freer. Winter weighs on your spirit – I tell you this as a friend –' they decide to have a beer now in the Plaça del Sol – 'not a doctor, OK?'

Ferran explained: it is the dream that makes things complicated. Had it simply disappeared, life would have remained far more intelligible. Now Ferran is perplexed. It has returned. The same lurid notes. The same strange insistence on the soldier, the boy with the blackened eyes and the hands full of limbs and organs. He is wearing an officer's military jacket. It is oversized and he is thin. He will walk through the ruins of an old city, bearing the carnage to a shrine in the burnt-out chambers of a Gothic cathedral. There will be roman pillars knocked to the side. Enormous. They are covered with moss and red ivy. The marble is firm to the touch, and in parts green. When he reaches the shrine he will place his bloody cargo on the ground and take two steps back. Ferran will watch the soldier cross himself and cry.

Ferran does not tell Guillermo about the second dream. The ugly one, so dark and so secret it cannot be shared. The one in which he himself perpetrates actions that make him retch inside, so that he vomits in the bathroom. It's the murders in the papers – he tells Guillermo – the reappearing naked girls in the Raval, the bodies police are putting away with no information – the city is sick, he repeats – my Barcelona – there's something wrong. Guillermo nods. Ferran mutters – *and Barcelona takes to it like an old friend* – his voice breaks, thoughts incomplete – the streets in my dreams – he shudders, sweat dripping from his brow in the chaise longue as the doctor takes notes. Ferran alludes to a terrible urge with a wistful, dramatic flick of the wrist.

Guillermo says things would be worse if Ferran had dreamt his teeth were falling out, which is a sign of either financial troubles or imminent death, neither of which are desirable futures. This offends Ferran. How can the loss of dentures be more significant to the psyche than a solder carrying human remains to a crumbling altar? (Or the vision of a murdered actress, skin glowing in the street?) Ferran questions whether Guillermo is trained at all. He says, 'You're just an Argentine hoax.' Guillermo snaps his tongue against his teeth, making a clicking noise. Ferran feels juvenile, ashamed. He returns to speaking about the girl in the poster, Chekhov, unresolved ambitions.

The dreams return. Ferran thinks it's because he fell asleep staring at the poster of Natalia Hernández. There is now a massive one hanging from the deserted construction scaffolding outside his bedroom window. The dream is identical, only this time it takes place on the platform for the *Ferrocarriles*. There is a girl, small. Auburn hair. She has round eyes and no smile. An oversized military trench coat. Grey. Civil War era perhaps, date unclear, and a battered cap. Around her everything is modern, women wearing beige collared shirts carry elegant leather purses and silent children. The girl makes no eye contact. She stares at the ground or at the ceiling or into nothing. But you watch her incessantly, hypnotically, as the train pulls into the platform, and the electric doors pull open, and she steps gingerly up and over the lip of the platform and enters the train. Once inside things become more uncomfortable. She is hiding her left arm beneath the folds of her trench coat, and you seek to see it, as the train rumbles through the underground. Her weight adjusts suddenly. The train lurches to the side. The coat flies open, revealing the left stump of an arm where the hand has been shorn off. The cut is clean, but the wounds are open, and you see the blood and the chopped white marrow of her bones.

Guillermo recommends that Ferran start writing his dreams down as soon as he wakes up in the morning. 'A dream diary,' he says. 'Keep a detailed account.' Guillermo thinks that Ferran may be having an artistic resurgence prompted by his exposure to the erotic vitality of Natalia Hernández. He asks Ferran if he has fallen in love with the dancer. Back in the safety of his office Ferran promptly feels the urge to confess:

> Guillermo,
> It's true. Everything you say.
> I am in love with the poster of Natalia Hernández.

Ferran stares at the screen. He does not click 'send'. Instead, he saves the draft to his inbox, shuts down his laptop, slips it into his messenger bag, turns off the lights to the office and makes his way down to the cafeteria, where he orders a *cafè amb llet* with one sugar from Maria the bargirl and drinks it slowly. He does not look at his watch once.

After arriving twenty minutes late to his own class that fateful Friday afternoon, Ferran discovers that the entirety of his students was absent and retires elegantly to Bar Xirgu. It's far too close to the lunch hour to be lecturing postgrads on Stanislavski and inter-pretations of Method Acting. (Let them digest at least – he railed at the registrar. *Hòstia, sisplau*, after lunch they're sleepwalking – all of them – they pass out!)

And as for his students (those few who had themselves been on time), they had gone to get coffee, or a smoke, or do something useful, and so when he arrives at classroom S2 P1 nobody is there to listen. Alas. He scribbles a note on the chalkboard. *Find me at Xirgu.* And leaves.

Forty-five minutes and two *cortados* later, Ferran's students congregate around him in the Bar Xirgu, a café of mal-repute just outside the back entrance to the Institut del Teatre. On sunny days, which are most often, the lady of the establishment puts tables outside where the students can sit and smoke cigarettes in the breaks between classes. She sells plain sandwiches popular among the young – *embutits*, made up of dry bread and slices of cured sausage.

Once satisfied that he had successfully squandered half of his three-hour lecture in Xirgu, Ferran decides that it is time to go back inside. He corrals the postgraduates through the metal gates of the Institute of Theatre – that bastion of higher learning – past the doorman on the ground floor and down into the heart of the glass building, beneath the ballet rooms with the lovely high ceilings to where the black-box theatres are, no windows and no natural light, the workshop spaces designed for movement and theory courses: *Stanislavski and Method Acting*.

After debating the appropriateness of Stanislavski's terms in the contemporary zeitgeist, Ferran feels it necessary to workshop his favourite Chekhov passage. Neither Catalan nor Spanish writers have ever managed to capture that intensity, he thinks bitterly. On the spur of the moment, he opens his briefcase and pulls out a battered photocopy of Act One of *The Seagull*.

He hands it to a pretty red-haired French girl in the front row. Once he had entertained great hopes for her. But he has abandoned everything. She has no talent. Now he enjoys simply tormenting her.

'Read it again,' he says.

The girl stumbles over the lines.

'*I am alone. Once in a hundred years my lips are opened, my voice echoes mournfully across the desert earth, and no one hears. And you, poor lights of the marsh, you do not hear me. You are engendered at sunset—*'

'More emotion,' he interrupts, holding his hand out to the classroom. 'Is this the correct response to the text?' A porous silence. Ferran's soul slips out of S2 P1 and relocates itself between the barwoman's breasts in the Xirgu. They are useless, these students.

Boring, vapid, the opposite of stimulating. They are empty of everything except youth, and even that they refused to share with him. Even Núria is absent, he thinks forlornly, scanning the classroom. The one rising star from the abyss of apathy.

The girl reading the lines falters.

'Again?' she asks.

'No! No! No!' Ferran shouts. 'I do not want you to go again. Somebody else read! Please! For God's sake, what do you think she is saying? What do you think she is feeling? Find it.'

He rips the lines from the girl, pressing them into the hands of a gangly boy in the front row. 'Go,' Ferran commands, settling back in his chair to listen.

Where had all the time gone? The grand schemes? The banners lining city streets proclaiming the advent of a new Stanislavski-ism – a Catalan evolution of realism – that far surpassed the moody modernist psycho-babble filling up the theatres of Barcelona. Sadness wells in his lungs, a heavy liquid far worse than the grey malaise he generally encounters there. No! Enough! The boy could not act either.

But she can.

Natalia Hernández can.

And that is everything.

Always the same, always uncontrollable – the perpetual torment!

His heart yearns for salvation, but his mind's eye races back past the long limbs, her tawny skin, the crease of the corner of her mouth, away from the images on the streets, to the portrait emblazoned on his cerebral self – Oh! Oh! Oh! That first almighty vision of the actress Natalia Hernández on stage.

A spotlight illumined a single Edwardian chair, dilapidated, propped up against an antique table. That night there was a typewriter and a blue china vase, a feather-pen and a skull. The professor of drama scribbled details in his diary. A single note

329

struck in the orchestra. The critic next to him murmured an illicit secret in the ear of her husband. She giggled. Followed by the long protracted sigh of a flute. From the floorboards, a figure stirred, obscured in the shadowy folds beyond the frontier of light. Ferran yawned, checking the time on his phone as he switched off the volume. Nothing worse than an oppressive focal point at the beginning of an avant-garde performance. 'Cheap emotional tricks.' Ferran wrote this down, fidgeting in his seat.

In an hour and fifteen minutes he could gracefully leave at intermission, return to his office and finish his article at the Institut del Teatre. If timed correctly, he would then emerge, unscathed, for the end of the show – greeting his colleagues at the reception with the required complimentary graces. His attendance during the first half of the performance was unavoidable. He had students in the act and, as professor, was duty-bound to make an appearance. Still, Agustí raved about this performance. Said it was worth his while. Ferran settled into his chair. *Agustí had questionable taste, of course.*

The shadowy figure hidden beyond the threshold of light moved. A tiny gesture, perfectly executed, a delicate extension of fingers and toes. The hunched form lowered itself to the floor, serpentine, flat. The sigh of the flute returned, filling up the dome of the theatre with a dark Apollonian hunger.

There, in the blackness, the creature turned. Cautious. Uncomfortable. Hands and legs and feet emerged. It stood, then staggered towards the halo of light, the table, the typewriter. A long hand. Protracted fingers reached into the beam, touching it gingerly. Female, almost feline. Something animal and naive, Ferran thought. He settled in his chair. The body unfurled into the half-light, features still obscured. He found that it was beautiful to watch: slow, elegant, introspective.

The tones of the symphony expanded. An angry violin stroke, dangerous and menacing, shattered the calm with a yellow dagger.

The figure danced two steps forward, swayed, then tripped,

collapsing to the ground, now desperate, part blinded, part hungry for the light – Ferran's heart leapt – curving hips pushed the form to the frontline of brightness, where it threw its arms wide. The form hovered for a moment, before stretching its naked feet into the brightness. Then chest, shoulders, hips and legs were bathed in light, revealing a woman, lit with brilliant clarity. Dust from the stage swirled around her like fireflies. Her eyes were round and wide, painted black. Her hair was matted and dirty, her lip stained with violet dye. Streaks of dirt ran across a thin white dress. She breathed. Once. Twice. Ferran watched her chest rise, *up and down*. The woman's frail arms reached out to the focal point of light.

As Ferran watched, he felt his body fall away from him.

He hung suspended, a thought awaiting discovery.

Natalia Hernández's performance was a brief one. It was not the title role or even a supporting one. She represented a type of energy, a malevolent force of sadness destroying the world enclosed by the thin spotlight. At one point, she lifted the type-writer off the desk and smashed it onto the floor, where it shattered into a thousand pieces. She wrote in the air with the quill, and then writhed on the ground. Her legs convulsed, gripped by an electric shock, as she slammed herself into the stage again and again, before singing, recoiling from the darkness. The sound of her body hitting the floorboards so stunned Ferran that he jumped in his seat, gripping the velvet plush of his armrest. He wanted to cry out – cry out to her! – call her name, rescue her from the darkness, from the world. He found himself weep-ing, tears running down his cheeks in rivulets, when she rose up and raced across the stage, leaping and pirouetting, then running – running more and more frantically, like a moth, like a blind thing maddened by the warmth of the light.

The professor looks at his students.

Can they understand this vision?

'Drama,' Ferran says, 'is the art of being alive. Of conveying ... aliveness.'

He swoops his arm round over his chest. His fingers are splayed, and the palm of his hand presses down into the collar of his denim shirt.

The professor breathes slowly. Deliberately.

His chest moves with an uneasy comfort.

Up, down. Up, down.

The classroom rustles, interested. He continues to breathe. The St Petersburg student who has been peeling dirt absently from beneath her fingernails lifts her head momentarily to listen. The sounds of Ferran's breath echoes softly, volume magnified by the darkly angled walls of the black-box theatre. The Valenciano catches the attention of the Russian and nods absently from his chair across the classroom. The professor breathes louder. He closes his eyes, and lifting one finger into the air, points gently upward. His mouth parts. A trickle of saliva rolls to the edge of his lip and hangs there with a static energy. Someone coughs. Silence. The professor's hand moves slightly, a paralysing calm, and then with a screech of action, he jerks his arms wide, flings back his head and screams.

He was asked to take a leave of absence from the Institute that evening.

'Be merry, my girl!' Fons says when he has finished. 'This is cause for celebration! You have returned to the fold! We've missed you at the Institute. I always hoped you'd be a director. But you didn't go into theatre?'

I shake my head.

'But you want to write about Natalia, and the theatre?'

'Yes.'

'So you're still in the theatre,' Fons declares. 'Good. Indirectly, at least. And if you are writing, you are struggling. You haven't sold your soul to commerce. You are one of us. I can be frank. As to gossip!'

Fons adopts a ceremonious whisper:

'Àngel Villafranca has become creative director of the Theatre of National Liberation – would you like to meet him?'

'Yes.'

'And Oriol?'

'Can you arrange it?'

'Can I arrange it? Can I arrange it? Of course! Oriol is an old friend, though he seems to value my company less these days. My dear, this I can do, but only if you promise to be very sensitive, very well behaved. Nothing rude! They are colleagues! Brothers in arms.'

After we finish, Fons invites me to stroll with him through the Raval. I ask him what he knew of that night – if he had been to her last show – *No!* he cries – there were no tickets! I was persona non grata, no room at the inn. A tragedy of fate. *Did you see them that night? Out for drinks? Can you remember anything?*

Fons turns green. 'No. It is painful to remember the slight. They abandoned me. Wanted nothing to do with me – they would not let me near her. Bad politics. We're all over that now. Atenció! Caminem!' He storms on ahead, saying it will calm his nerves. 'My heart is fragile.' He puffs and shakes his head. I relax into the familiar crisp of winter darkness. A brisk roam through the city at night, a *cafè amb llet* from the bookshop behind the university.

'Do you remember if Natalia Hernández had any books or papers she valued? I'd be very interested in getting my hands on something like that.'

'Books!' he shouts. 'Goddesses don't read books! They embody them!'

He pauses, ruminating on something.

'You must come to visit my archive.'

'When?' I ask him.

'*Ara.*' Fons growls, suddenly aggressive. 'Now.'

I check my watch. Fons nods; he hums and haws. I agree. He beams.

'Natalia Hernández represented this city for me, she was made of it, for it . . .' We stand at the corner of Carrer de l'Hospital and the Rambla del Raval. Our breath makes dragons in the air. I watch him closely, out of the corner of my eye, suddenly, inextricably uncomfortable. His thoughts roam across the music halls, the opera houses, lurking on the red tiles of the Mercat de Les Flors, thoughts opaque and musty.

'I have devoted my home to the recording of modernity for future generations of thespians. My therapist encourages me to express myself through this non-sexual form of shrine-making. He says shrines are important to a modern sense of well-being and our culture of anxiety has come as a result of deifying the interests of the individual rather than the collective spirit of the community.'

Ferran Fons leads me up the stairs to his apartment in the Raval.

'I moved five years ago – wanted to be closer to the action. More room. The place is quite special, I think you'll find.' He opens the double wooden doors, painted aquamarine. 'It's very festive, very bright.'

My eyes adjust to the sepulchral darkness as we enter.

'One moment! One moment!' Fons cries as he flicks on the lights. '*Et voilà! Así nació el teatro!*' Four walls covered in human faces – young, old, male, female, all histories, all persuasions, perhaps a hundred portraits? Stacks of books, two wide balconied windows and bright red curtains. Aubergine-coloured lounges at the centre of the room, ornate and baroque, puffed-up armchairs. A glass coffee table laden with architectural monographs, design pamphlets, sharp typography.

'Take your time,' Fons says. 'My salon is dedicated to remembering.'

On the largest wall of his living room, above a black tiled fireplace filled with drying violet orchids, the centrepiece − the treasure of his collection. A poster, recovered I assume from some billboard or the press office of the theatre, of that face emblazoned into the subconscious folds of the city. The wide-open eyes, the shadow like a severance down her nose and brow and jaw, playing on the sheer lines of her face, the plum flesh of her lips parted, her tongue moist against her teeth, open. Waiting. Beckoning. *I have a secret. Just like yours.* The name of her play, the last play, serenading the reader in full caps. 20 JUNE − 10 AUGUST 2003 . . . *The show that Natalia Hernández never closed.* How many of these were tossed aside? Torn down in the wake of her death? Fons has mounted the poster against the wall in the style of an Andy Warhol print, eye-popping, room consuming. *There's nothing else to see but her.* To either side, potted ferns, fecund and dripping. At the centre of the poster, beneath her mouth, a small wooden table perched on a single wooden leg. On this a kitsch figurine of the Virgin Mary and a red burning candle. He has hung pink and orange flowers round the sides of the poster, in the style of a Hindu shrine to Ganesh.

Fons beams.

'I keep the Eternal Flame of Natalia Hernández lit whenever I am home. It's complicated. I would like to have it burning always, but we had an accident when I first put the poster up − I burnt the bottom. Had to have it replaced. Took me ages to find one. An Artistic Disaster. Total Disaster. So now this must be footnoted as the eternally *monitored* flame of Natalia Hernández, the central altar in the Salon of Remembering, primary feature of the Museum of Departed Glory. She is well accompanied −' he opens his arms wide in a swooping gesture – 'by the collected treasures of my dramatic appreciation.'

'She doesn't make you uncomfortable?' I ask.

'No!' he says, aghast. 'Quite the opposite. She demands that I remember to feel alive.'

The walls are covered with a wide-ranging assortment of framed photographs and prints – '*All original,*' he chirps behind me – dipping into a kitchen behind a silk curtain. I hear him turning on the tap. 'I have Federico García Lorca, three weeks before he was shot in 1936!' He shouts. 'A rare Margarida Xirgu, the Catalan actress, on tour in South America. Gandhi in 1948! Oscar Wilde in Paris! And I have the anarchists – Émile Henry! And our very own Santiago Salvador, who so felt the fervour of his cause he threw two bombs into the Opera Liceu!' He whisks through a collection of faces I don't recognize – 'This sub-exhibit is dedicated to Poets-Murdered-Under-Nazi-and-Soviet-Regimes,' he tells me, holding a crystal glass of water in each hand. 'The second collection immortalizes Spanish Republicans assassinated by Fascist forces in the Civil War.'

'And the women?' I ask.

Retracing my steps to the centre of the living room, looking at the wall facing Natalia Hernández.

Garish photographs. Modern.

'The third wall is dedicated to the Assaulted Feminine. I have titled the collection: "Victims of the Unknown Assassin".'

Four rows of three. Twelve photographs. Five vulgar and bright, done by a cheap photographer's studio, hot pinks and nuclear yellows. Souls hidden beneath thick make-up, peroxide blonde hair, lips and brows provocative. I scan down the faces – until I reach one placed in the centre of the quadrant, eye to eye with the poster of Natalia Hernández, a bright pink frame among the cheap painted gold.

'That's Natalia's mother,' I say, pointing at the studio portrait of Cristina Rossinyol.

'Indeed, indeed.' Fons draws each blind shut behind me as I look at their faces.

'And who are these?'

'Victims of a common murderer. Or so I believe. I assumed you might be interested in seeing what I have. The police have no creativity. It takes an urban curator to unearth these beauties – a lifetime of dedication. Have you seen the Raval? Do you think the maître d's of the finest establishments would talk to anyone about the murder of their illegal girls? Ferran Fons –' he pounds his chest – 'is a man of the people. A man whom the ladies of Carrer de Sant Ramon trust.'

'But only three women were murdered alongside Natalia.'

'Three were found,' Ferran says factually. 'Three women, mind you . . .' *He's mad. These are conspiracy theories.* 'My art, my Museum to Departed Glory, juxtaposes theory with image. My more illicit friends, who must remain anonymous for the preservation of our working *relations* – a diplomatic stance if you get me – my *friends* have supplied me with their portraits, though they are not sure of their true names. Here you have dear *Roseanne* and poor *Rosa.*' He points at two girls arranged either side of Cristina. 'These were women found by the police in that week. But I have recorded the deaths of many others. Or rather, disappearances. I find them very unsettling. But what does most of humanity do when a girl who does not exist disappears? She has no papers, no documentation – she might have never been born – what does society do when a girl who has never existed disappears from the streets of a city? They forget. They never know to begin with. But not Ferran Fons. No, he records. He collects the images of their lives, and he records them here, amongst the great and the departed artists who were also disappeared by history.'

337

The girls are arranged above a mahogany chest of drawers decorated with enamel flowers.

'But the true gems of the collection – for the work you are embarking on ...'

He pulls out a drawer. I step back, stunned.

'... rest in here.'

Clipping after clipping. Thousands of newspaper scraps. Photographs yellowed, neatly trimmed. Laid one over the other. He draws them out slowly.

'You are welcome to return. There are more than you can read in an hour.'

I feel my nerves mounting.

'This is me in the *Tragafuegos*. That is Cristina Rossinyol, there is Villafranca.' He turns another over.

'The full company is pictured here. They ran this in the local paper. There is Oriol, Villafranca, Cristina and myself. You would not find it in a typical archive. These were done on the small presses, barely any distribution.'

The faded yellow clipping frames a photograph of the full ensemble. In the picture a much younger Fons, with thick black hair and a broad grin, is holding the head of a papier mâché dragon.

'What role did you have?'

'*El Diablo.*' He pauses. 'I was cast as the Devil ... But things became ...' He slows again, and frowns. '*Fraught*. I gave it up after the first round of shows.'

'Why?'

'I became possessed by something cruel.' He bats a memory away with his hand. My heart skips faster.

'Could you describe that for me?'

He pauses. Chews his lip. I can see the thoughts running across his face.

'Please. Sit,' he says. I make my way back to the sofa, staring at Natalia Hernández. He pulls up a chair behind me. He clears his throat.

'Àngel Villafranca made a pact with the devil that summer.'

He pauses. Eyeing me up.

'He won't say so – no, of course he won't, but the truth is that he sold us out for success. He wanted us to play with things – to push ourselves beyond the normal restrictions of human behaviour.'

I nod.

'At first I didn't listen to the rumours. I was a young actor, at the start of my career, it was an honour to work with his company, but when the devil came to me I took it more seriously. First he entered my dreams. In the beginning he was a striking young man, black hair, blue eyes, exquisitely dressed, like a nineteenth-century English gentleman. He would look at me, talk to me . . . tell me what to do. I listened. I did as I was told, because I thought it was a manifestation of my subconscious helping me in the role – that I was constructing a character – not –' he coughs and clears his throat – 'interacting with a kind of spirit.'

'Have the police ever spoken with you about this?' I ask.

'With me? No.' His eyes narrow. 'Why do you ask?'

'Curiosity.'

He raises an eyebrow.

'I am allergic to authority.'

'When I spoke with the case officer, he said there was no unifying characteristic of the killings,' I lie. *See what he will do.*

Fons sputters. Bright red.

'I know who you're referring to – Inspector Fabregat is a self-preserving fool. There was a hell of a significant "characteristic", as you call it, a *stamp*: the killer gave thought to – was obsessed by . . . tongues . . . No one likes to talk about it, because the suspicion is, the real knowledge was, that it was in-house. *One of us. Took. Each one.*' Fons waves at the wall of women before us. 'Each one with the exception of Cristina. All the rest lost their tongues. Which is why I have decided to immortalize them. Preserved for perpetuity in silence.'

The air inside the shuttered room becomes claustrophobic.

'Do you mind if I take some photographs?'

He nods. 'You're welcome to document the exhibition as you please.'

The camera comes out of my shoulder bag. As I press down on the shutter, his eyes sear into me. *Snap, snap*, goes the camera.

His smile broadens. 'I am an artist, you know.'

I catch his eyes boring into me, as he stands, arms crossed, before the print of Natalia Hernández, she suprahuman. A goddess to be worshipped in solitude.

'You must tell no one what you have seen. I wish to be an anonymous source,' he tells me formally, as he leads me to the door. 'I wish to be known only as the Curator of Departed Glory.'

I accept this. Perturbed. I duck into the metro. Invisible eyes hot on my spine. Skin-coloured tiles, green strips. Sound like a train roaring. A man with a ukulele busking. Through the crowds I sense a presence. *Had Fons followed me from the apartment?* Hunched shoulders. Dark silhouettes. I get out at the next station, change carriages. Making my way north. Again the feeling of being trailed. Of a lingering attachment. I veer through the underground maze, thoughts tumbling and spinning. *No one. There is no one here with you.* And yet I am convinced of being watched.

Oriol Duran stands with his back towards the theatre door, smoking a cigarette slowly, a cheap cup of espresso in his right hand. His curls, the colour of burnt sugar, blond caramel, part to the side, in keeping with the period, with short sideburns from the inner rim of his ears to the neat line of his cheekbone, coiffed at the back of his neck, where his hair is kept neatly ruffled. His eyes owl-specked, ruddy hazel, with shards of honeyed gold, into the depths of which many lovesick women have fallen, but Oriol cannot help this fact (beauty is as beauty does) and, despite the multitudes of fans, the orgiastic presence of his blinking beneficence on the television screens of Spain, his eyes preserve a certain innocence, cloaked in dainty lashes, elongated and doe-like. Oriol's cheeks are smooth and firm like a Roman soldier's, and were he not so small, and slight in form, a sculptor might have rendered him a model for David or Marcus Aurelius.

He hasn't aged at all, I think with a start. *Not a single year, not a single wrinkle. He could be a decade younger than he is.*

'Duran. A pleasure,' he continues. Outstretched hand. Warm grip. I can feel the heat rising on my cheeks – I curse myself – *Don't blush. There's nothing more humiliating.* He waits for my response with eyebrows raised.

'I'm sorry if this comes as a surprise – I always get in early, Fons mentioned you might be here, I asked at the house and . . .'

He shrugs.

'. . . thought I'd catch you.'

His gaze locks onto me. 'We're rehearsing Oscar Wilde. You familiar with *Salomé*?'

I can make out the scenery for the new show – the backdrops and curtains, the wooden sets. The only lights are the exit signs, green above the rows of velvet seats, and two exposed bulbs above either side of the stage doors. *Rest in the quiet.* There is something sad about an unlit theatre. Something ghostly. *The closest thing we have to an experience of death.* Oriol strides to theatre flies and switches on the lights. *Pop! Pop! Pop!* A giant wooden terrace behind me, set above a banqueting hall, to the left of an enormous staircase and an ageing cistern engulfed by a wall of bright green bronze.

Oriol raps the wooden staircase with his knuckle. 'Do you know the play?'

I shake my head. He looks straight into my eyes, again that piercing stare. No shame. A bizarre vulnerability.

'An arresting piece, Wilde's strangest and his best.' His face changes ever so slightly. 'How beautiful is the Princess Salomé tonight!'

I blink. He is reciting lines.

'*Look at the moon. How strange the moon seems. She is like a woman rising from a tomb.*' Oriol comes closer. 'I play John the Baptist.' He draws a line across his neck and makes a rushing sound with his lips. 'Head ends up on a plate. I hope you're not intending to do the same to me. Writers have a tendency towards violence.'

Standing next to me, he is uncomfortably taller than I had imagined. *So close to my skin!* I run my hands through my hair, steady my breath, trying to stop my eyes from covering his features as he stands before me; they strain to linger on the glow of his tawny bearing, his skin a flawless texture like polished sandstone ... I distract myself (*What is he wearing?* A light grey sweatshirt and loose trousers) ... restrain my eyes from dancing down the curve of his bicep, raised veins on the back of delicate hands. Nails immaculately trimmed. I make my introduction. He listens dutifully. 'I'm happy to hear someone is doing a piece on Natalia.' His eyes soften. 'I hadn't spoken to Fons in years – but I agree, it's been too long since someone paid her attention. Fons says you're good. *The American scholar.* You're publishing with Balmes and Sons? That's very fancy for a foreign kid.'

His eyes flick up and down, resting on my chest. I feel the heat rising again on my spine.

'I'm free to talk now. If I like you, you'll get more. But later.'

'Of course,' I stammer. 'I'm all yours.'

Oriol leads me to the edge of the stage. 'Sit?' he asks. Not waiting for an answer, he lowers his body to the floor gracefully and leans back on his hands, legs dangling off the side, taking his cigarettes and BlackBerry out of his rear pocket, stacking them neatly beside him. Oriol hits the interview like a professional; not too rehearsed; he's comfortable. Tone even. I don't ask any questions – he starts with family. *Get a little of his own history out.*

He explains that his mother and father were local politicians killed in a terrorist attack in Madrid ... There was something about the perpetrators being an off-shoot group – inspired maybe by the Baader-Meinhof Gang, the Red Army Faction? An anarcho-communist liberation front that disappeared into Cuba or the Soviet Union. Their car was bombed during a military procession in the capital.

He shrugs as if this were normal. 'Natalia suffered more than I did; she lost her siblings and her parents. She was divorced from her home – she had no relatives and no family money, while I was blessed with aristocratic parentage and grew up surrounded by excess. I was too young to remember much of my parents when they died. Natalia lost parents she remembered and younger siblings. She was much more damaged than I was – but we shared a bond.' Oriol waves his hand generously at the empty seats, gesturing at the proscenium arch behind us. '*The theatre*. My grandfather was draconian. He wanted me to be an athlete; he forced me to compete professionally as a fencer. "*To uphold an old family tradition*." So I did.' His hand twitches in the air, swoops and flies. 'When I was fifteen I took up ballet – in a therapeutic kind of way – teach me some self-control. I was too old to be a dancer, professionally, exclusively, but I took to dance with ferocious appetite. I went to the Institute. They sent me here. I was seventeen when I joined Villafranca's theatre. Natalia was a child who hid in the flies. She watched me, and I watched her. I thought nothing of it for years – you've got to realize, I was eight years older than her. But she grew up, and I stayed the same. It was our secret. You could be anyone! You could slip out of your memories and try another human voice, leave yourself in the dressing room and disappear into the adrenaline, the rush of performing. Of *making*. For that reason I can only perform when I *become* entirely. Natalia understood my sense of isolation. After her parents died, we shared ...' He pauses, looking for the word. 'More than a relationship – how do I put it? A conception – yes – a conception of loss. A great yearning to simultaneously forget ourselves and be embraced by love. *She understood me*. I couldn't talk about it then – we wanted it to be secret. But we fell in love. When she was sixteen then and I was twenty-four. For years I didn't act on it. I waited. We couldn't keep it secret after that. And then she died.'

I look up. His face tragic.

'Natalia would have gone on to be one of the greatest actresses this country ever knew.'

Flecks of green, a dark outer rim to the pupil, and light. Endless light. I reach out to him, feel ... *nothing*. He is empty. Clean.

'I got my first professional job at the theatre just after my grandfather had died.' Oriol rolls up the sleeve on his arm. He notices my eyes drop down to the tattoo. He stretches out his arm. The pale inside flesh is engraved with a small black dog holding a flame in its mouth.

'I got this when I was a kid. An early act of rebellion.' He smiles. 'They have to cover it with make-up every night. Villafranca always asks: *Why don't you get rid of it?* But I like it. Sometimes we do stupid things. It's good to be reminded of them.'

He gazes out into a private storm. I pull my knees closer to my chin. Crouch down. *Listen.*

'I've never understood why she didn't come to me. Why she never told me what she was experiencing. It was like she was frightened of involving me – I don't know. I became convinced it was someone she knew. I saw suspicion everywhere. They flocked to her. They wanted pieces of her. Admirers. Lovers. Fans. I hated them. All of them.' He laughs. 'I was an idiot about it.'

Listen harder. Are you the man I have seen? The man I am looking for? That is all I want. A reflex. An echo. But there is no confirmation. No response. *Nothing.*

⚛

On Friday, 20 June 2003, the Institute of Theatre lights up before him, a six-floor glass exemplar of design. Time passes. The sun has just begun to dip towards the horizon. Long shadows cut across the square like pinstripes. The Plaça de Margarida Xirgu is magnificently desolate, the travelling circus that had occupied it for the last week has left, *thank God*, taking their Russian dancing bears, dwarves and desultory Bearded Lady with them. For ages the yellow tent of the circus had obscured Oriol's view of the trees that lined the square. Now he is free of it. The actor likes to have the space to himself, to inhale slowly and breathe the warm smoke out of his lungs into the calm of the Plaça, interrupted only by the lone

345

skateboarder or stray dog. Behind him the Theatre of National Liberation glows with the self-assurance of power, a powerful building that curves around an oblong *plaça*. The theatre is painted orange and has a bright terracotta tiled roof. On the first floor there is a bistro and bar, with a balcony overlooking the square. The building has a small tower, and three stages, each bigger than the last.

Oriol stands beside the stage door, leaning against the wall of the theatre. Surveying the extent of his kingdom. Oriol has arrived a good thirty minutes before his call. His is a ritual of sorts. First a cleansing of the hands in the men's toilet on the ground floor. Flicking water through his hair, pushing the sweat from his brow. Scraping the dirt from underneath his fingernails. A warm damp towel. A moment of silence, intense and alone, sitting cross-legged on the wooden stage, safe behind closed curtains. Not a meditation – a contemplation (he will tell imagined future biographers) – an assumption of space, claiming every smell of the dusky theatre, every creak in the floorboards, every dead space in the corners, each mysterious darkness turned over and examined. Then a coffee from the battered machine in the green room. Paper cup swirled into light brown espresso, thin crema, congealed milk. Next a cigarette, first of many, smoked alone in the Plaça de Margarida Xirgu, where we find him now, listening to the call of early summer swallows. He will wait here for the producer, Tito, watching each of his fellow actors stroll into the square, crossing the vast expanse, morphing, transforming internally, as they enter the auspicious realm of the theatre. From his vantage point, Oriol can see Ferran approaching. The two men wave to one another, across the vacant swathe of concrete – actor and academic emerging from their respective homes. Oriol studies Ferran as the professor changes his course, moving directly across the square to the bench where Oriol stands languidly, second cigarette stubbed out, gathering his soul into place, finding his centre. The tech run will start soon, those arduous rehearsals when lighting directors map out each painstaking shift in mood. Natalia has yet to appear, but she will come, Oriol is sure, and then the dressing would begin, the hair and make-up, the officious march of the stage manager. The quiet will be gone, he thinks sadly. Oriol lingers for a moment in the evening warmth of *Plaça de Margarida Xirgu*. The trees are green again in the *plaça*. They cast lovely long streaks of shade as the sun begins to press itself low into the horizon of the city. Observing Ferran's arrival, the actor weighs the advantages of a swift departure. A polite retreat behind the thick glass doors of the Theatre of National Liberation to the men's dressing rooms. But something keeps him there. Perhaps it is the general stillness of the moment? An unspoken law that forbids sudden movements? Or a deeper tenderness for Ferran. He does not know. The two men embrace.

Ferran gives Oriol a gentle kiss on each cheek, and claps his hand on his shoulder. They speak in the same accented Catalan.

'How were they today?' Oriol asks.

'Dreadful.'

'Not one with potential? Not one bright spark?'

'They are an absolute void of creative material.'

Oriol laughs. 'You would have said the same of me in my day.'

'No. You were different. *Are* different. From the start.' Oriol blushes and pushes the gold curls of his fringe away from his forehead. One of his more charming characteristics. For the leading role in Milton's *Paradise Lost*, Oriol has grown a blond moustache that he tends ruefully. Oriol believes it makes him look like a pederast. Long ago, Ferran decided that Oriol carried a genus of false innocence, fascinating in a younger man – an uncomfortable emptiness that registered as a yearning for other worlds. ('His energy stretches at the seams of his body,' Ferran once noted, at an early performance in Gràcia, years ago now. 'Oriol Duran's physical work expresses a buoyancy that is uncontainable.') Before fame and

347

fortune found him and removed him evermore from the land of the lowly and mundane, the man had been a sportsman. He remains lithe, sinewy, muscular.

Trained in stage combat, Oriol had been a nationally competitive fencer when he joined the Institute, as a dancer. He later made the transition to the stage at the bequest of Ferran and an old colleague recently passed away – joining the *Tragafuegos*, Ferran's touring troupe that gave folk performances in the villages. The director Àngel Villafranca discovered him then – at a *Petum* in Sant Cugat, dancing the part of the dragon. Oriol Duran, much inspired by the American school of Method Acting, insisted on becoming the character, which ran against the grain of the more traditional approach adopted by his Catalan colleagues. This impressed Villafranca, who looked for something more vivacious, more raw, more daring – he had explained to Ferran – in an actor. *Risk.* Àngel Villafranca said in a hushed undertone, *I want them to risk themselves on stage, body and soul, push the limits – you know – and he does. He has it, Ferran. He has success written into his bones.*

'I need your help, Oriol. They're trying to push me out,' Ferran continues, stumbling through his own reveries.

'Who? Silvia?'

'All of them. I don't know. Silvia delivered the message. I should have a public affair with a student and get it over with nobly.'

'*Molt bé!*' This impresses Oriol. 'You wouldn't dare. You're too square a man for that.'

'Oriol, I'm desperate. They won't be able to make me leave if they see how connected I am. I've taught all of you. I gave Catalonia a new community of actors.'

'Let me think about it.' Oriol frowns. 'I'll have a word with Tito.'

'Tito's back?' Ferran had met the Argentine once before, at a recent benefit for the university. He'd seemed very close friends with Oriol. Powerful fellow. Nice, too. Ferran's pulse quickens.

'He arrived this morning. He's coming to the press gala tonight. You'll be there?'

'No invitation.'

Oriol nods.

'Shame about that. House is full, otherwise I'd grab you a seat.'

Ferran brushes this aside.

'I'm not in a good place, Oriol. All used up. Nothing to say.'

A young woman enters the square, pushing an old perambulator from Carrer de Lleida. A little girl in a pink dress runs circles around her mother. The infant inside the perambulator wails.

'Don't worry about these things. You're an institution, Ferran.' Oriol smiles.

'Maybe. Once. Not any more.'

Ferran's eyes hover over the poster of Natalia Hernández.

'Is she good?'

'You know she's good.'

'No, I mean, does she transform?'

'Did you see her in Casas's *Tennyson*?'

'Yes.'

'She surpasses that.'

Ferran lets out a slow, exhaling whistle. *'Mare meva,'* he says.

'This play will change everything,' Oriol says. 'She'll eclipse all of us.'

The two men stare at the poster.

'You never taught her, did you?'

'No. No. She didn't train at the Institute.' Wistfulness in the corners of Ferran's eyes.

Oriol's attention goes to his watch.

'Nearly seven,' he muses.

Like clockwork, the assistant stage manager emerges from the stage door. A plain girl with a fierce haircut. 'Oriol, your call is up.' She glares at Ferran.

Oriol says goodbye fondly, pressing Ferran's hand. 'I'll do my best,' Oriol reassures him. Ferran offers eloquent thanks and kisses his former pupil on both cheeks. He walks slowly back towards the Institute, heading to the ramp leading to the car park. From the other side of the square, Ferran waves once to Oriol. The actor stubs out his last cigarette. Like mist on a lake, the professor's parting shout wafts across the *plaça*: 'She has a gift, Oriol! She's our future.'

'I got him backstage, that night.' Oriol frowns. 'Out of pity – out of respect. I don't know. I will always regret that choice. He made her uncomfortable; I could feel his eyes on her as we moved, and I hated him for it. I couldn't control the rage. Later that evening, Natalia and I had an argument . . .' His attention drifting away from something distant. 'Once upon a time I had a sense of faith.' He sighs. 'I met Natalia, and I began to believe in something bigger than myself. That's gone now.'

His attention darts again, to the stage behind me.

'You were with her that night, weren't you?'

'Yes.'

I wait. *He doesn't want to talk about it.*

'I think she knew she was going to die.' Oriol sighs deeply. 'But I didn't understand it . . . I didn't understand what she was saying.'

I watch him as his eyes wander over the seats in the theatre.

Oriol has gone very quiet. His legs limp, the energy tightening in his stomach. He looks at his hands, stretching his fingers out in front of him before turning to me.

'I can't really tell you who she was because I don't really know. I don't think I'll ever know.'

'It was a pleasure meeting you today.' Each vowel a tart gem.

I sit up on the telephone, surprised.

'Fons gave me your number.'

'Oh.'

'What are you doing tomorrow?'

I make a vague gesture to my work – a day in the archives.

'Come to our rehearsal. Come and see what we're up to.'

I feel my cheeks flush pink.

'Are you sure that will be alright?'

'Yes. You'll fit right in. I'll meet you at the theatre after lunch tomorrow. Join us for the afternoon.' Oriol Duran perplexes me. *Fragile*, I think. *For all that physical strength, he feels fragile.*

Later I flick through YouTube videos, hunting for a crackling version of the recording. One I have seen before. On the evening following Natalia's death, Oriol Duran was asked to speak at the end of the newscast. The police had agreed and so Oriol was permitted to send his message out to the world. He had not practised the speech; he wanted the emotion to hit home, the words to be unhindered by overfamiliarity. He wanted this to be raw, real, he wanted to help, he decides to do something 'Historical' – or, in the actor's tried and tested drawl, 'Epic', according to the press interview.

'*Increïble.*'

'*Enorme.*'

They would break the news about Natalia Hernández to the public as the bonfires were being cleaned off the beaches and San Juan's day came to a close. Oriol Duran would initiate a national search for the killer. Oriol Duran would give a live speech at the end of the show. After all the remainder of the day's crap they would return to Natalia. The story runs big. Oriol gives his piece as a man suffering the loss of a woman he had loved. He calls on the people of Barcelona, the people of Spain, the people of the world, to come forward with information on the whereabouts of this Adrià Sorra, while he rests at the centre of it all, like an oracle of hope. Oriol's voice echoes out from my computer screen, skittering into my kitchen, Oriol soothing his masses with the ultimate opiate of murder, better than pornography, better than sex, better than anything in the world, the apotheosis of mystery and death and wrongdoing – and I listen, my beating heart open and veins throbbing with the crackling lines of cable. In 2003 the radio waves hummed with the story, and Oriol Duran knows then that this is Big – the camera will swing around, they'll bring him on, and the show – for it was a show – and now! Now! Now! Now! Oriol Duran stands in front of the green screen, and looks directly into the floating camera. He has the stance of a politician. He breathes slowly. He loosens the collar of his cream shirt – he does not wear a tie – which adds to an aura of dishevelled melancholy, honeyed eyes rimmed with stress, golden curls flattened on his forehead. His hands do not rise to his face, but hang at his side. He loosens his spine, and drops his tension to the floor, feels his breath, opens his mouth and speaks. On the beaches wine is uncorked and poured into clear plastic glasses. On the airwaves they replay his message. I watch the face of Oriol Duran tighten and crumple in turn as he begs, prays, demands information!

Information from the age of consumption!

While in the streets they congregate and mourn the revelries of yesterday.

And the sand is warm and dry underneath bare feet.

The rites of la Revetlla de Sant Joan were simple. They smelt of gunpowder and ash. Of burnt skin and cheap red wine.

But tonight, police lights have replaced bonfires on beaches that burn, burn, burn. They turn on the lights of their cars, and station themselves in forensic units facing the place where he entered the ocean.

The sea blacker than crude oil. Slicker and darker and more impossible than the wind, with nothing to say.

'First there was the theatre, and only the theatre.' Tito Sánchez announces boldly. He immediately strikes me as feline. Sanguine. Smiling. Arms wide, breath cigar-fused, broad back plastered to the leather cushions of the restaurant. I have landed in the upscale part of town, north of the tourists, of Las Ramblas, where the well-to-do moved on the Avinguda Diagonal, direct to Madrid. 'This was decided by the men who brought their heads together to organize the 1929 International Exposition. It would be built with a proscenium arch in the style of the Ancients and would boast an architectural feat in which the stage could be submerged with water or rise into the audience on mechanical platforms. A masterwork emulating the great outdoor theatres of the Roman Empire, like the ruins of the coliseum left at Tarragona, over-looking the sea. It would seat 3,500 visitors but – unlike the Greek – they were building higher on the hill, cut simply out of stone – this theatre would represent the excesses of modern engi-neering. The roof would be inlaid with plate gold in the shape of shells, and crystal chandeliers would hang over the heads of the audience that would dim or lighten (depending on the mood, of course) through the latest and most marvellous infrastructure of thin metal cables that carried currents of electricity. Intent on having the finest performance spaces to accommodate the fleets of dancers and acrobats and singers and orators required for the Russian schools of theatre they built the stage with vast wings behind the proscenium, equipped with pulleys and ropes that supported the shell and the red velvet of the safety curtains. This fly system was designed to be the fastest in the world, allowing for the installation of sixteen drops – such that set changes were possible in seven seconds! To this they added a revolving plat-form built in the centre, which would allow for the construction of a spinning set – on which you could interlace three individual universes and have them turn swiftly, thus showing events of multiple characters near simultaneously. A hush fell in the meet-ing room of the organizers of the 1929 International Exposition. The engineers and the directors and producers and architects smiled, for truly they were building the most extraordinary thea-tre in the history of the world.'

He pauses. *Tortilla con espinacas, queso y jamín, muchos gracias – y usted?* Olives and bread arrive. Waiters flit, formal, at the beck of the clientele, blue suits, waistcoats and ties, mistresses chamois-dipped and pearl-earringed, Chanel bags and gold watches. Children uniformed, socks pulled up to knees, skid marks and scars. Hair in pigtails or ruffled under caps. *Tortilla for one. Tortilla for all.*

'When the theatre was completed in 1929,' Sánchez rumbles, Argentine accent like shrapnel, meaning business, 'at the base of the gardens of Montjuïc it had fountains to either side and a mounted wall mosaic, and a series of backdrops painted by Picasso. The first ballet to be performed on the opening night of the expo-sition is the touring Russian *Giselle*. For the next seven years the Theatre of Barcelona's 1929 International Exposition is the best in the world, its glittering lights the finest architectural feat on the Plaça de Margarida Xirgu, before time runs foul and in the midst of something darker, Montjuïc forgets its gardens and becomes once again a fortress, and the theatre fades into nothing before being caught in a fire in 1939 and burnt halfway to the ground.'

A bottle of white wine appears at the table, two glasses.

'I came to Barcelona for the theatre back in 1975. A home away from home. I had some other business at the time – but theatre! Theatre was the passion. Today I am proud to say I am its oldest patron and greatest producer. *Now.*' He folds his hands under his chin like a table, leans into me. 'I don't like journalists. Never have. But, equally, I don't like what happened. Under my watch. As it were. Whole business makes me sick. So. We eat. I talk. You listen. That night is all I'll give you.'

And then?

'You write this, you write this well, and then you fuck off right back where you came from.'

That night, in the reconstructed glory of the Theatre of National Liberation of Liberation, Tito Sánchez takes his seat in his private box, his mouth full-lipped, like a woman's, delicate and sweet. His face round with bright eyes of a rich umber colour. He sports a loose blue dinner jacket, tight against a violet shirt collared with enamel buttons and a barely discernible floral paisley. Grey jeans reveal his rower's thighs, on his left wrist a chrome watch face, plastered to a mottled snakeskin strap. He pours himself a glass of champagne from the carafe on the table to his side and watches the press filing into the audience. There's that smug critic with her long-faced husband and the crooked reviewer from Girona (always good for information). The photographers march into rows. Cameras over shoulders, draped around necks. Àngel Villafranca catches Tito's eye from the balcony with a salute. The director will join Tito for the show – they've already made the arrangements – but for now Villafranca grazes in the crowd. Customary handshakes and greetings for a few. The lights dim. The orchestra begins to play.

A hand on Tito's back. Villafranca slides into the chair beside him. Villafranca is in his late sixties. He has thin, steel-rimmed spectacles and a strong nose. His cheeks are long and hollow. His face bearded. There is very little fat on his body, and his white hair is thick on his forehead. The director is no longer calm, now shaking with nerves.

'It's a relief you're here,' Villafranca breathes, 'to keep me company.' Tito can smell the faint hint of sweat merging with perfume. 'Look at those harpies,' Villafranca whispers, gesturing down at the women in the crowd. 'They're here for my blood, Tito.'

'They won't have it.' Tito offers the man a glass of champagne. *Drink*.

A chord runs through the audience and with a breath they are still.

On stage she wears a black velvet ball gown in the style of a nineteenth-century society lady, hair piled in coils on her head, pearls hanging from her ears. A garland of pansies in her hair rests playfully on curls wafting round her ears and the nape of her neck, pressing gently against her temples. Tito has never seen her so dark before, and the effect is striking. He is drawn into her form, her small hands and feet, her luminous solemn face struggling to hide its light behind a stern smile, her bodice tight around her chest, the swooping neckline of her dress revealing her bronze shoulders and breast.

'Lovely choice.' Tito leans into Villafranca's ear. 'Gorgeous design, very Russian.'

And then Natalia opens her mouth. *She sings!*

The back of Tito's throat is dry. His tongue swells in his mouth. Hers is not a mortal voice. It is divine iridescence. He has heard it before – in rehearsal – but tonight, for the assembled masses, for the journalists and hacks, the critics and their papers, she is unearthly, she is God! Stained glass on the ceiling of the universe. His heart races but at once is still and he feels the warm air leap against his skin as he bathes in the music of her voice, each aria a ripple against his chest. Wild birds do not have so sweet a call! The harshness of it, the pain, like a nightingale calling to the night, she dips and swoops on the air, *up, up, up* her voice soars, and then she calls like a woman lost, like a swallow searching for a lover, and his heart breaks – *Oh for the pain of this woman, this girl, this child* . . . A bath of consciousness lifts his limbs up as if the atmosphere itself were urging him to leap out from his box – but gently, smoothly – the music of her voice an intoxicating promise of flight. Picking up the eddies and streams of his hair. Washing up his ankles. Snaking up his knees. Tickling the back of his thighs. Tito Sánchez is in the midst of summer as she sings the song of *Agua Dulce* – the last song she ever sung in her life – and . . . *My God!* It was as if gold dripped from her tongue, rubies, carbuncles, and you could see the soul of her imagination take shape on the air like an ethereal beast – *a force of nature!* Mountains swoop down below as the earth plunges away from Tito's feet in great crashing waves, rushing and screaming to the far horizon. Caverns and gullies, cliffs sliced out of stone, great pits and undulating green. The surface of the land swirls and dips, arching its back, cutting through his vision. Tito is giddy with vertigo as the breath of her voice catches in the back of his throat. Sun explodes through his eyes, radiating out so that the azure sky turns white and he is blinded by the wilderness of Natalia Hernández. You are coming home, his body tells him, mad with excitement. Churning and leaping through his chest, heart pounding to escape. And, yet, the air is still: uniquely, profoundly, beautifully serene. When had she changed? He wonders – When had she become this? Or was the wilderness always there, beneath the surface and he had never noticed? Never understood?

The audience moves with Tito. Inhales and gasps in unison, as the director wills the world to love her. A sacrifice to the fortune of his own fame. To be part of the realization of greatness – looking out over the faces in the crowd, the open mouths. Tito frowns. The scene changes. A man comes striding across the stage in a suit. A knot forms in Tito's stomach: Oriol wraps his arm around her. Surely the way she looks at him is an act? A performance? Her mouth brushes against his as they dance. His hand on her throat, his hand on her hair, he turns the nightingale round in her black dress, she pirouettes, he lifts her, she falls, fingers on her throat . . . the tenderness . . . Jealousy boils in Tito's stomach, as jealous as every man and woman in the theatre, to see those fingers touch the neck of the nightingale of Barcelona! Tito pushes these thoughts aside. He transcends into the movement of the piece. The theatre.

'What do you think?' Angel leans in to Tito's ear, as the curtains fall for intermission.

'You have a masterpiece.' Tito can barely speak. 'A work of genius.'

After the show, the last show she would ever give, Tito and the critics congregate in the theatre bar. Clara from *La Vanguardia* approaches. She smells of rosé. Tito's nostrils flare.

'Good God, Sr Sánchez!' she brays. 'Barcelona needs a man of your means in these hard times! When I saw your name on the list of producers I just about died. Thank the Lord for private investors! Are you happy with the final product?' She falls into the seat beside him. 'Villafranca is a wily old dog. She'll be a star. No doubt about it.'

Tito nods, scanning the room.

'We're putting her on the front page tomorrow.'

'That's wonderful.' Tito is not interested.

'Not that she even needs my help – she's done enough for herself. I mean the talent – it's unbelievable,' Clara continues.

'Natalia Hernández is an extraordinary young woman . . . I always felt it would only be a matter of time.'

'Oh! Beware! Sr Sánchez, you look like a lovesick schoolboy,' she laughs loudly across the table. 'Have you spoken with Oriol lately?'

'Excuse me?'

'People talk. I'm dying to know!'

Tito nearly chokes on a salted almond. *She's a bitch*, Tito thinks.

'Oh, look!' Clara coos. 'The men of the hour! Àngel! Oriol!' Clara gets up, the folds of her dress falling to the floor around her. She plants two kisses on each cheek. 'How does it feel to be the stars of the night?'

'Glorious!' Oriol shouts, carrying a bottle of wine in his hand. 'Drink up, friends, drink up!' Clara claps her hands.

'Without you, my darling, we would be nothing! Ash on the wind.' Villafranca's voice is sonorous, sweet like thick molasses. He takes a seat beside Tito and whispers in his ear: 'Apologies in advance, old friend. We can abandon shortly.' Tito smiles. No need. Not yet.

'Clara Solana, promise me you'll write well!' Oriol glows. 'Success smells so much sweeter when you're here to celebrate it with us.' He whips Clara into his arms and begins to cavort around the table. His curls more charming than ever. They return breathless, Clara collapsing into giggles beside Tito. She reaches for the wine again.

'Now . . . Oriol Duran . . .' She toys with an empty glass, looking at the actor. 'I want the dirt.'

Oriol raises an eyebrow. Tito's nerves tighten.

'Anything for you, darling.'

'Off the record, of course.' Clara's eyes narrow; she leans her body across the table.

'She's gorgeous, Oriol. Far too young for you, of course, you old goat, but we all know beauty when we see it.'

'Shall I order more drinks?' Oriol asks the table. 'Vodka, Tito? Rum? What shall we have?'

'A little bird told me you've started seeing each other,' Clara interrupts.

Tito takes a long draught of his drink. Oriol's heart beats faster.

'Only on stage.' Oriol smiles. 'I leave the rest to your imagination.'

Villafranca catches Tito's eye. He shakes his head. *Nothing I've seen.*

'Where is she?' Tito asks.

'Oriol Duran, I do not believe you,' Clara continues. She flaps a napkin in his face. 'You're hiding her. Come on! *Dime!* You're Method! We want to know!' She waves to the table. 'We all want to know.'

'Clara,' Villafranca says politely. He puts a hand gently on hers, leans in and says something in her ear. She quietens. Oriol gets up from the table. Tito follows him to the bar.

'What's going on?' Tito asks, trying to hide his discontent.

'Nothing.' Oriol looks him directly in the eye.

'Natalia and I have been friends for a long time.'

'You shouldn't listen to the gossips.' Oriol nods at Clara across the room, deep in conversation with Villafranca. The actor drops his charm, looks sullen. 'Her, particularly. She spins gold out of straw just for entertainment.'

'You humour her.'

'Perhaps.'

'Natalia tells me you've been arguing?'

'No, of course it's not true.' Oriol's mouth forms a stubborn line. 'Have a little faith.'

'I just don't want to see her getting hurt.' Tito's voice catches. Then snaps. He moves his chest towards Oriol's shoulder, leans in to the man's ear. 'You know me, Oriol.' He feels the pulse rise in Oriol's breath – watches the veins tighten in his throat.

Oriol nods.

'Good.' Tito smiles. He pulls away. 'As you were.'

Tito slices into the tortilla elegantly, napkin tucked into his shirt collar; he asks for a second one from the waiter with a snap of his fingers. *You can't be too clean.* He smiles at me.

That night Tito paces in the lobby beyond the theatre bar. Natalia has disappeared. She is not in the leather-covered private booths of the bar. She is not sitting with the others. She could have gone towards the powder room – or maybe she is on the balcony . . . No, she is not there. His feet pound the floor. He remembers the place she liked to hide at the theatre when she was younger, backstage behind the pulleys that held the curtain. He calls to an usher. 'Have you seen Natalia?'

The usher nods, pointing to a stage door. When he steps into the darkness, up the stairs to the wings, Natalia is there. Sitting where he had first found her at seventeen, bare feet pulled up under her, her back to the metal pulley system. Resting against the ropes. She has changed out of her costume, wearing a loose blouse and dark jeans. Her feet are bare against the floor, but her hair is the same, and though she wiped the heavy stage make-up from her face, she has kept the garland of pansies and ringlets about her forehead. Her neck is long and fragrant. She leans her head into the darkness.

Tito says nothing as he sits down beside her.

'It's all changing,' she whispers.

Tito puts his arm around her shoulders. She is frail as a bird – there is no weight to her. Where did the force come from that filled her on stage? Her soul must be so vast. So huge . . . His heart expands. He pulls her close.

'You stole the world tonight.'

'It doesn't matter,' Natalia says. 'It's not real.'

Tito winces as he listens.

'Come out and sit with us.'

'I'd rather stay here.'

'Natalia, there are people out there who want to celebrate you.'

No. She shakes her head. *No.* As he watches, Tito feels helpless. He fumbles in his pocket for a handkerchief – *the girl's been crying.*

'You mustn't be upset, Natalia. Whatever happens. I mean, if anything goes wrong, if something doesn't feel right ...'

She puts a finger to his mouth.

Quiet. Someone has come into the theatre. *Someone is watching them.* Natalia shakes beneath Tito's arm, pushes his hand away. He does not know. Who has she seen? The shadow passes. *Oriol?* No. Natalia shakes her head. *Someone else.* She kisses Tito on the cheek.

'I can take care of myself,' she says. 'I always have.'

▲

Tito presses me into the yellow cab door, flashes a handful of euros at the driver, smacks the hood and leans through the open window. 'Keep her safe.' The driver nods. Then to me: 'Goodbye. Hope it goes well.' Formal. Broken. The cab speeds south, towards the theatre, cutting along side roads, darting down the Eixample grid, the wide, open balconies, sunny for midday, zipping west towards Plaça d'Espanya, the fountains and the madness, then down, towards the sea. Classical music on the radio.

Had I asked Tito enough? No. I think again and again. You're losing grip of them.

'Where did they go next?' A stupid question.

'Natalia excused herself and went into the changing rooms. I wanted her to have an early night, to be fresh for the opening. Oriol and I spoke briefly. He wanted me to come for drinks – to celebrate. You know how actors are.'

'Did you go?'

'No.'

'Why not?'

'I can't remember. I was too tired. I like to keep my distance from the actors' social lives. To not drink with them. Debauchery of that kind is tasteless. Very tasteless. Besides, it was not the opening. Just the preview. The audience had responded well, the critics liked it; there was a standing ovation, even. We knew the press would be good – it was a great achievement. I lost a lot of money in returned tickets ...' His eyes pricked. 'I was saving my celebration until I saw the performance's effect on a real audience. I was right. In the end I went to a funeral.' Tito called a waiter over, and gestured at the table. *Café con leche*, he said. *One.* Our conversation was over.

Outside the Theatre of National Liberation people are laughing. Inside the rehearsal studios the dancers and the actors stretch. Sweatpants run around the stage. Lap after lap. He is joined by an equine nymph with striking musculature who chases after him; they run together, short bursts, sprint then stop, sprint then stop, breathe ... I can feel them breathing. Dance shoes. Beaten leather on black boards ... Smells saccharine and human. *Tap, tap! Crack!* Go to the boards! Arms stretch overhead. Muscle tears. A foot lands. *Breathe.* Wood gives, dust flies into the air. Empty seats hungry and admiring. As I watch the company warm up, the director Àngel Villafranca, stage right, talks to his Salomé. Her large ponytail pulled to the side, chalk scraped across cheek, sweat on brow. It is my first time observing Villafranca in person. Grey as a heron. Glasses aggressive on the bridge of his nose.

'When you kiss him, I want to see desire, pure sexual desire ... This is your conquest, you are destroying his manhood ... in your body, twist – you are a snake.' He gesticulates wildly in the air. 'You are a moonbeam, you are a human manifestation of a violent goddess!'

At six o'clock the actors break. Oriol introduces me to the director. The director's beard wiggles. For a long hard minute he stares at me. He does not say hello. 'You like her, Oriol?' he asks the actor rapidly in Catalan. 'Do we trust her?'

Oriol grins. He nods.

'Excellent. To business.' Villafranca claps me on the shoulder. 'The reading is positive. Oriol is my best judge of character. Now! Come along. Meet the world! Kike! Lydia! Javier! Meet the woman who has come to tell our story! Gather up, family! We are a family! Only when you understand this will you understand us properly. We can help you write this theatre into Natalia's history!'

The director wipes his mouth drily.

'You want another coffee?'

Villafranca scrapes his white shock from his forehead into a wave. His eyebrows a symbiotic species, whiskered, often furrowed. His hands flit about the table, tracing out words or playing with the tip of a black fountain pen he has taken from his interior pocket and placed on the napkin beside an empty cup of coffee.

'Are you sure I cannot get you something?' he asks again, speaking a perfect, fluent English.

'No. Thank you.'

Àngel waves a waiter over, and gestures at the table. 'Cafè amb llet,' he says quickly. He holds up a finger. One. He looks at me, turns to the waiter and asks for two waters. 'You must have something.' Villafranca smiles. 'I feel ridiculous otherwise.'

When the coffee arrives at the table, Villafranca reaches for one of the long, thin packets of sugar and cracks it deliberately in the middle, pouring the contents into his drink. He stirs it slowly.

'I'm an addict.' Villafranca smiles.

He lifts the cup gently to his lips.

'I created her last show for her,' he says, nodding to the picture. 'I wanted to give her the space to explore her artistic talents, her paintings and her visions on the stage. It was a mistake.' Then he pauses, looking sharply across the table at me. 'If we are to continue

365

our discussion, the only thing I ask of you is not to disturb her memory.'

'Of course.'

'As you know, she became my child, as well as my leading actress.'

Villafranca's eyes cloud. 'I raised her in this theatre, as we were building it from the ground. Her parents worked here with me – Natalia was born of the stage and into it, like a creature made of light – she had such luminosity! When she walked onto a darkened stage, the dead space of the theatre came alive. It transformed. One body, illuminated by one spotlight . . . You cannot take your eyes off her. And when she danced . . . Oh, when she danced, the world stood still.'

'She must have been on the verge of becoming extremely successful.'

'She was destined to be a great star.' Àngel takes a decorous sip of his coffee. 'My show would have transformed her life, her career. Recently I have worried that I pushed her too hard. My heart has been hurting. I may have been cruel; as a stand-in father, I asked a great deal. Sometimes, I fear, too much.'

'What do you mean?'

'You cannot make something out of nothing. The notion of conjuring a performance out of air is a farce. Acting is not easy; a talent like hers is a form of transmutation. In the past I have called it alchemy.' Villafranca continues: 'Living with her particular kind of creative energy was a burden . . . I've met very few actors in my time who carry the mark of greatness.' Villafranca looks at me quizzically. 'Do you know what I mean by "greatness"?'

Natalia Hernández came onto this earth in the August of 1981 in the village of Valldemossa on the north coast of the island of Mallorca, in two folds of earth that lead into a gorge that drops five hundred metres to the sea. The time of her birth was summer – and for bad luck she was not born in a hospital. Her mother, nearly two weeks late, collapsed in their country house outside the village. Her husband, hearing the cries, ran in from the garden. The road to the hospital was blocked by a collision. A lorry had been knocked sideways across the thin highway to Palma. The nurse from the village was called, who ran up the trail in the fields, past the olive and apple trees, to the house where Joaquim Hernández had laid his wife across the kitchen table, and then collapsed into tears beside her, blood and water running down the legs of the table. Natalia was their firstborn child. Against the backdrop of a rustic kitchen, with ants running along the rim of the sink, and hunks of meat drying against the open windows, the midwife arrived, with the priest, who began to pray, as did half the village. The midwife reported that a car had been sent for a doctor who lived in a neighbouring village and he would be with them as quick as he could. A cold compress was placed on Cristina's head, as her body rocked against the kitchen table. Many hours later, Natalia Milagros Hernández-Rossinyol was given into the light, with the priest praying all the way beside her. The child emerged with the umbilical cord wrapped around her throat; the doctor cut the flesh and the midwife carried hot water as the priest mumbled under his breath, as the monks of the neighbouring hermitage gathered outside the kitchen door, in the summer sun beneath the olive trees and meditated on the child who had come from the female line of Rossinyol.

At least, this is what I understand from the story the old director is telling me: the concentration of prayer at the moment of her birth, the priest later proclaimed, in conjunction with her genetic inheritance, gave her a close proximity to God. In the summers after her family's death, Natalia would return to the island with her guardian Villafranca. They did not stay in the Hernández house, but rented a little flat in the village, close to the shrine of Santa Catalina Thomas.

It was in this village, on the eve of her sixteenth birthday, in the cloister of the Carthusian monks, that she experienced her first vision. Walking across the garden at the centre of the cloister, she approached a well beneath a statue of a saint. Touching her hands against the cold rock, she leant her young face over the edge and looked into the mouth of the well. A voice behind her spoke her name. She turned, to see an old man, with a blue beard, and a black cap on his head, and a fur ruff round his shoulders, seated on the low wall of the cloister that rimmed the inner garden. He was very old, with lines down his cheeks. She insisted that she had seen his face before – perhaps in her dreams, or in the stories of her mother. When she approached, the old man showed her the gilded book he carried between his hands, a book bound with wide copper clasps. The cover was also made of a copper plate, engraved with strange symbols and letters, in a language she could not recognize. The pages of the book were not of paper or parchment, but of a material like bark. Hours later, Àngel Villafranca found his ward unconscious at the centre of the walled garden facing the square of the Capuchins.

'Natalia is a vessel . . . in the old sense' Villafranca says. 'As a child she was strange, she seemed to have come from other worlds. I can't quite explain it. She had an uncanny ability to access our collective consciousness. For such a small thing, she carried the weight of the universe on her shoulders.'

'But you say that she was happy?'

He laughs bitterly.

'Happiness is a complicated thing for actors – I don't know how to stress this – but she was content. Just as she was also, at times, very sad. She was an orphan. She lost her parents. She suffered from bouts of paranoia. She saw things that did not exist and yet were recognizable in the world around us. She was an Artist. A kaleidoscope of emotion. When a child is forced to learn about death the hard way, it never leaves them.'

'It must have been devastating for her to lose her family so young.'

Villafranca's brow furrows. 'It was a very sorry affair. Their car crashed off the pass to Sant Cugat. Everyone died in the accident. Mother, father, sister, brother. But for me, she was alone in life after that.'

'How did she survive?' I ask. 'There are no reports of her having been in the vehicle at the time of the accident.'

'She had hidden herself in this theatre.' Villafranca's wrinkled face breaks into a smile. 'She was always losing herself in there. Her mother would leave her with me in the mornings ... That particular day the family left to visit a friend in Sant Cugat. When I heard the news, I didn't know what to do. I found her in the wings, sleeping on the rope of the fly system, the coiled pulleys; she'd made a bed for herself in the dark. I held her to my chest, counting the minutes that I could extend the life of her family, before I had to wake the sleeping child and tell her what had happened to her world.'

Villafranca's eyes hold a piercing stare.

I meet his gaze evenly. 'I would like to know more about her mother, Sr Villafranca. Cristina Rossinyol, if I have the name down correctly?'

'That is a long story.' Villafranca checks his watch. 'I will tell you the short version. Another coffee, please.' Villafranca waved the waiter over from the bar. *Two*, he says, to the waiter. 'Even if you don't drink it. Call me old-fashioned, but it is impolite to take coffee alone.'

Villafranca leans into the bench. He has selected a table on the far side of the cafeteria, next to the windows overlooking the square. The coffees arrive at the table. Villafranca speaks quietly. 'I suppose we should start at the beginning. Cristina Rossinyol was born in a village one hundred and sixty kilometres to the south of Barcelona, on the island of Mallorca. She was to be the only child of her parents. Her father was the last of a lineage of dragon-makers. Do you know what that is?'

'No.'

'A dragon-maker is an iron-mason who makes the casts for the fire festivals – our *Correfocs* – when he is not tending pots and pans. Her mother was a religious painter. Before the war the mother's family had been something better. Between the village uprising of 1936 and the culls of the 1940s, both sets of grandparents died. It is not important how or why. Like many things then, it simply happened.

'The year of Cristina's birth was 1950. At that time, our Catalan language was banned. You could not speak it in your home. You could not read it in the papers. You could not study it in school. We were denied our books. Our theatre. Our art. Our history. You cannot understand Cristina's work without understanding this. You cannot imagine how that feels. To not be able to speak a word of your internal tongue. The language of your dreams. It is a prison. Many children born of Cristina's generation lost the Catalan language entirely. Cristina's family, however, kept it alive in their kitchen, passing down the poems and passages of plays that had been memorized. She learnt the language this way through repetition. Through the theatre of the hearth, the old folk stories and songs. Even this was a dangerous pastime. As far as I could tell, she was alone in the world when she arrived in this city, though she had help from the church of Santa Maria del Pi. A young priest named Cançó. I have seen him in passing in the Plaça del Pi. He is an old man like me now.

'Cristina Rossinyol showed a natural artistic flare. In Barcelona she studied restoration and illumination. She was a medievalist, a calligrapher and an avid painter. I discovered her then – I can't remember where or how, it simply happened, like these things do. I sat down for a coffee or a drink as I am doing with you now and she appeared, like an apparition of the future. More beautiful even than her daughter, if you can believe it. I fell in love with her instantly.' He smiles ruefully, and a dreamy haze falls over Villafranca. His concentration drifts. 'Sadly, I was not the first – or last – to do so ...

'At first we became close friends. Cristina brought the talents of the dragon to our radical community, making costumes and carving wooden masks for actors as she had learnt to do in the mountains. We had performances in abandoned railway stations, squats, old factories ... Always in Catalan, always the old stories. For us, drama was the front line of non-violent resistance! When we had a show, word would pass orally, to all members of the Catalan underground. People came individually, often hours earlier than necessary, so they would not be followed. We asked them to take circuitous paths. By the grace of God we were never caught. Our performances were folk-inspired. They were poor, with few props, with Cristina our set designer, costumier, calligrapher, and maker of things. Our moment was perfect and we seized it with gusto. This city was in the midst of throwing off the shackles of Franco, and the theatre put its shoulders to the task. In 1974 I had dreamt of filling the stage with words that the actors would move through as a forest. And in 1975, with the help of Cristina Rossinyol, that dream became a reality. First we built our makeshift theatre. Success followed swiftly. In the late seventies, we came here. Everything you see we made; with the help of devoted engineers and architects, Cristina and I brought this marvellous space back to life.'

'And her husband? Joaquim?'

Villafranca waves his hand dismissively.

'Quim Hernández was just another member of the company. He was much younger, handsome, good with his hands, and an idiot. He didn't deserve her. We grew apart after he married Cristina. He had nothing even close to her genius ...' Villafranca sighs. He takes a sip from his coffee. 'But that is not important. Look around you. The men who built the foundations of this theatre envisioned it as the best in the world. It was a matter of honour to keep that promise. Cristina was determined that our work never lose its connection to the folk roots of the Catalan language. For our opening show – oh, you cannot imagine the crowds – it was as if the people of this city had discovered Mecca. We answered their call with words. Cristina painted towering *Names of Things*, the trees of my forest, in the old Gothic script. It was an enormous success. After that, Cristina and I were inseparable. We began to see each other again as lovers. I only tell you this because I am old, and all the participants are dead. I do not think Joaquim ever knew.'

He looks at me slyly.

'I always believed Natalia was my child. When her family died, fate gave her to me. She became my legal ward. When I lost her, I lost everything. I do not believe that Cristina should have died when she did. If you have read the reports you will see that a second vehicle knocked the car off the road. I am convinced that it was not accidental – that someone was trying to silence the family. It was the final straw in a series of black events that had been plaguing the theatre that year, and we were very shaken. I decided to protect Natalia from that history. I wanted it to be something kept secret. She was only fifteen. I walked away from my position as a director in January 1997. We went abroad. I worked in London for a time and in Paris, also at the Venice Biennale . . .'

'And the theatre?'

'I left it to someone else.' Villafranca checks his watch. 'Are you hungry?'

I shake my head. 'No. But I don't want to keep you.'

'Well, I have another half-hour.' He smiles. 'I am known for being long-winded. It is a terrible habit. I talk and talk – but! I will be as brief as possible, because I want you to understand. Understanding

is crucial. It is gold. And you cannot understand her without knowing this: in the late eighties my company began to tour the smaller
villages of Catalonia. We were interested in reigniting the folk
traditions – I wanted to work with *els tragafuegos*, exploring the
Petum, the gunpowder festivals – you must have heard of these? We
were known as "fire-eaters". Old Fons was with us in the early days,
a fantastic period for theatre – very wild. Best reviews of my career –
we're in the textbooks, my darling. *Visceral Performance*, we called it.
The touring company was very small. It consisted of twelve actors,
our lighting director, a lighting assistant, stage-manager, producer,
two stagehands, myself, Cristina and her husband. Twenty-one in
total. We went in the autumn – in the warm months before winter.
Things were very bohemian, very raw, very creative. For the first
month? Bliss. But as we travelled things began to happen.'

'What do you mean?' I ask.

He sighs dramatically. 'Death chased me like a curse. In the late
eighties we toured the villages near the northern base of the
Pyrenees and suffered a series of quite brutal acts of violence. On
the night of the twenty-first show – I will never forget it! A slaughtered pig laid out the morning after our performance. It had been
quartered – literally quartered into four, and buried, feet up, in the
earth outside around the local church . . . It was absolutely vile, my
dear, just disgusting. And so it continued for the next five performances. At first we thought this might be a reference to local
traditions or customs, a deranged lunatic . . . many of the villages
upheld quite pagan customs, and our work explored rituals of
sacrifice and magic. After a month, the killings ceased. But then we
performed again, this time in the high mountains. Cristina came to
me one night – she said the play had to stop. I told her that we
would not bend under the pressure of a lunatic. We went to the
next village, performed that evening, and after the play a local
farmer found a young woman laid out in the snow.'

My stomach turns.

'The villagers came to us with questions. She was a local healer. She had been to the performance. She had last been seen at our bonfires. We gave our testimony to the police and continued, rather more than shaken, I must say. Cristina broke. She could not take the strain and insisted we put off the show for a few years, but as our company became more famous, I wanted to revisit the themes of those early performances. I became obsessed with the idea of authenticity, of folk-magic. In the early spring of 1996 we launched a nationwide tour with the original cast and crew – Natalia's mother and father among them . . .'

As I listen to him speak, I can almost hear the bonfire crackling, the villagers gathering round the fire set in the central square of the crumbling town, the actors on their makeshift stage, dressed as nymphs and goblins, skin bare, near naked, breasts unclothed, bodies covered in ink. They wear the old masks of wood spirits and witches, there is a good saint and a bad devil, a man-turned-dragon who terrorizes the dancers, nymphs, beautiful girls. The play is simple – a rendering of the old witch dances of San Juan; the fire dancers – *they* dance the dance of the old revellers, which becomes more and more frenzied, whipping the villagers into such a state of excitement, such a state of joy, that the town itself is running and jumping and shouting, skin bare and glistening, tongues kissing, groins moaning, until under Villafranca's expert direction the spectacle morphs into a sexual explosion and the Lord of the Bacchae descends on the crowd while the Devil dances merrily through the flames, the growling bonfire. I can feel the heat on my skin, the ash, the crushed grape and steam . . .

'It was meant to be a release.' Villafranca's eyes narrow. 'A Dionysian celebration of excess and freedom. It became a living nightmare. At the first performance in a decade, another girl was killed, and left in a tree on the side of the road. My actors worked themselves into a state of total panic. We had to cancel overnight despite the fact —' he sighs, a picture of melancholy — 'that the reviews were fantastic, and we returned to Barcelona.'

'And the girl?'

'I don't know who she was,' Villafranca says dismissively. 'I never asked.'

You never asked? You are a strange man.

'Were there any distinguishing characteristics of the killings?'

Villafranca shakes his head. 'Nothing I can remember. I do not like to dwell on these things. But I am very old. For a while I suspected members of my own company.' Villafranca pauses, and then dismisses the idea. 'But that was illogical, a paranoid assumption on my part. My actors are good people — good, good people. We would never hurt a soul. But as you can imagine, it was quite disturbing. Cristina found it profoundly distressing. She became obsessed with discovering who was committing these acts of violence. I tried to dissuade her from probing, but she insisted on asking questions, on returning to the villages after we had left. She would stay for a few days and speak to the women, often taking her family with her. I told her that was mad, but she said we had to stand for *some* principles. In the end I think she got very close to finding out who the murderer was and he ran her off the road. I don't believe the police ever made that connection. I think the national government wanted our theatre to collapse and looked at this as a blessing. As to the murders, they occurred in rural neighbourhoods where the policing perhaps was not strong. It is not an unusual thing. You seem like a sensitive young woman. Hopefully you will be more intelligent than our Guardia. They certainly have done nothing for Natalia.'

I think of Fabregat. What would he feel, listening to this?

Villafranca stirs his spoon in the last dregs of his coffee.

'At the time, I felt extremely guilty. After the birth of Natalia, things had become more difficult for Cristina at the theatre. I probably complicated matters more than was necessary – I wanted her to leave her husband and come and live with me. Instead she made me the guardian of her children in the case of death. I told her that was incredibly morbid. She said we should always be prepared for the unexpected. In the end, it was a gift. I loved Natalia as much as I loved her mother. She changed my life.

'There was a time when her mother wanted Natalia to be an artist – in the painterly sense. When Natalia was a little girl, she was very talented in this arena – in fact, a prodigy. Cristina taught her the art of calligraphy – and her daughter excelled. I suppose this was only natural, given her heritage . . .'

Villafranca drifts off into his memories. I watch him lingering in the thought. Check the time on my watch. 'I brought some of her pictures to show you,' he says. 'They're just little sketches. Her more major pieces are in the galleries – I have a few on my walls, but I think you'll find these more interesting . . .'

He removes a manila envelope from his briefcase, places it gently on the table. He opens his jacket and removes a pack of tissues with which he wipes the tips of his fingers. He opens the envelope carefully. From the envelope he pulls out a sheaf of papers, which he places on the table before me.

'Be careful. Too much handling and they'll get damaged.'

He arranges the papers on the table, making sure the surface is dry before he sets each page down.

'Most of these she painted when she was eighteen.'

Exquisitely delicate, rubbed black chalk, pencil lightly smudged beneath thin washes of pearly colour – a dreamy lilac sky. *Alive.* Images of the theatre, portraits of actors, a church steeple rising out of an urban landscape.

'Who is this?' I ask, lingering on the page furthest from me. A sketch of a man, mid-thirties, warm smile, bright eyes.

A call. I feel a call.

'I don't know.' Villafranca frowns. 'A friend. A man from her imagination. He's very well drawn,' he grumbles. 'Clear, sensitive lines.' He pushes the sketch towards me.

'Do you mind?'

'If you must.' Villafranca nods absently. His eyes glaze over.

I handle the paper gently. Take in the smudged charcoal. I feel forward. *She's signed and dated the image 15 June 2000. She was warm. The day was warm. A dragonfly landed on the pond and laid a thousand infinitesimally small eggs. A man's laughter, loud and ebullient, ever expanding. Echoing on mountains. Deep snow. Somewhere high and far off. An endless night on naked skin. Happiness. Certainly happiness.* The next picture is a sketch of a village church set against mountains and lightly brushed with watercolours, a half-finished painting with brown stains as if it was made *en plein air*. There is another in the series, this time of a house built low and close to the ground with lime-washed walls and a Mediterranean garden painted in silvery greens. In front of the house a man reclines in a chair, a broad-brimmed hat hides his face. He reads with a book in his hands. Beneath this: *Capileira. 18 June 2000.*

Villafranca nods at the inscription. 'Capileira is the last village on the mountain road through the high sierra of Granada. The end of the earth from here. Why she went there . . .' He shakes his head solemnly. 'Who knew who she had met?'

Villafranca watches me as I take pictures of each sketch. Lining them up on the table like soldiers. *Snap. Snap.*

'I'll get you scans,' he says. 'Good quality.'

There is no question of who keeps the originals. He rustles in his briefcase again, producing a pocket phone book, five centimetres by five centimetres, gold-pressed letters, black leather.

'I thought you should have this.' He chews his words factually. 'My housekeeper found it beneath a wardrobe in her summer bedroom in Mallorca when we sold the house two years ago.

Natalia kept it when she was a teenager. Who knows how many secrets she had?' Villafranca shuffles the pictures back into the envelope as I finish. 'But then again, don't we all keep something prisoner?'

He sighs deeply. Shakes his head.

'You must not trust us. Trust none of us at all.'

Voices echo through me. I stop beneath the ornamental bridge connecting the claustrophobic walls of Carrer del Bisbe, each pulling back from the other as the street runs tighter and tighter. I gaze up at the interlocking flowers. A skull smiles down, stone dagger plunged through his bone. I linger for a moment, arching my neck. Looking up. *Fresh air to clear your head.* I walk slowly through the cold, pulling my scarf tight round my shoulders. In my satchel I carry Natalia's pocket address book, hard black leather biting into me. I pass the cathedral, the boulevard busy – darkness charging into the after-noon. Windows like coal fires. Chatter and music. Couples with their legs entwined around barstools. Long-necked flutes of cham-pagne. Short coffees, *cortados* pulled until midnight. A restaurant where the blind serve their clientele in the dark. Molecular cuisine makes its mark in the technicolour foam of El Bulli copycats. The skies are clear. I can see the moon blinking above me, a fragile thin line. She feels far away in the city. Hidden by a cloak of lights, her stars drowned out. Disappeared. In her place, they light the walls of black rock. Shimmering up towards angels. Lances and spears. The scaled spine of a dragon. *A city built for defence.*

I choose a tapas bar. Wooden doors open. Bundles of leather flasks hang over the windows, tied with red string. Full of light, spiralling out on the street. A *camerero* leans with his back against the wall. He lights a cigarette outside. The smoke catches on the sharp night air. 'Quina fred!' He shivers. Blackened barrels along the wall, blue and yellow tiles, flowers, a crowd of people standing, drinking. Along the marble counter, plates of pickled fish, salted olives, sardines, cuts of *jamón íberico, botifarra negra, fuet*, marinated capsicum stuffed with garlic, dried tomatoes shrivelled by the sun. Sandwiches on miniature rolls stacked invitingly. I take a plate and sit at the back. My thoughts flicker. *A serpent and a cross carved on each hand. To witch is to whisper. Whisper as in to hide.* I order a glass of wine. *Too many. Too many. Open Natalia's book.*

And then I see it: a little drawing, a smudge of a serpent biting its tail. Anger builds in me. I want to shout at her: *You cannot be so passive! Why did you accept the terms of this pact? This deliberate silence! One confession, one clear answer, and you would have given the police everything they needed. Unless you yourself were corrupt?*

I want to yell at her:

You are a coward!

But I understand the agony. *She kept a secret.*

Greater than it all.

Her tongue bore the paralysing weight of fear.

There's a mirror in the restaurant across from my table. Divided into gold-rimmed panels, mottled, dusty glass. I see the blurred edges of a human – red nose, androgynous lips. A frown where my face is resting. I push my hair into place nervously. Look away. I will never be pretty. Tomboyish, I scowl, my body neither long nor full, but flat and thin, dwarfed in the heavy clothes of winter, a bland grey turtleneck and brown scarf. I think of Hernández, her dazzling features, her flawless skin. Of the signature ebony curls that formed an impermeable halo of beauty around her. Who would I have been if I had been born with those eyes? Those endless lashes? Who would we all be if our faces were cut from gold?

In alchemy the best key is a simple code. A word or image that hides a true meaning. Or at least it should be. Short. Sweet. Easy to identify for the initiate, a kernel of knowledge that relies merely on obfuscation, a riddle that prompts the code-breaker in a language initially confusing but retrospectively clear. *Painfully obvious.* But you haven't cracked hers – not yet, I remind myself.

You don't have the full picture, I tell myself.

So listen. This night is ripe for listening. Evening settles in my bones. Sun sets too early in winter.

Before me: leafy trunks bedraggled and unclean. The streets empty but for the drunkards and pickpockets who make their trade with the foreign clientele of after-hours bars. Graffiti grins, the face of a leopard. Halal butchers, closed for the night. Red meat hanging from hooks. Veer deeper into the Raval, urban caves formed by a burnt-out complex, bricks falling out of the side of a stairwell, an open, hanging door of a brothel covered in piss. Bar Marsella. The first location marker. At the corner of Carrer de Sant Ramon the prostitutes are out in style – then two blocks to the south towards Drassanes – a back alley near Genet Genet – the hanging gardens of Baluard. The square of the first girl, Rosa, is lined with trees but none of them are flowering now. I saunter to the side, taking a seat on the step of a bar facing the square. Fifteen windows on the square, looking down on the action. *And no one saw anything . . .* Even now, shivering children look down from the railings of the apartments, a woman smoking a cigarette, in a nightdress, watching with dreamy slowness, laundry flapping in the wind, the smell of fish broth burnt on a gas stove. The notion of secrecy was a farce the law clung to, *sobretot*

in this neighbourhood, where the network of informants is vast and news travels faster than light.

And yet, precisely what happened to Rosa has never been clear.

When I turn, I walk towards the square, very slowly, deliberately. Looking towards the municipal trash skips, the cracked cement. The dead borders. Pink plaster. Metal shutters. Four benches facing in. A placard on a stone. *In Loving Memory of Rosa Bonanova 1987–2003.*

Roses planted in scraggy bunches to either side. Bare of blossoms. Brittle and thorny. Still winter. No summer yet. And then I feel him. *Eyes on me.* A man standing at the upper corner of the street. A smear just beyond my field of vision. I look towards him sharply. Focus in. *You.* He waves. My heart ticks. *Striding towards me?*

'*Maca! Querida!* I followed you. You caught me.'

Oriol hides his face behind ornamental, pretty-boy glasses, frames perched behind his ears. Worn black leather loose on his shoulders, jacket smooth as silk.

'I'm sorry! Forgive me! I wanted to know where you would wander.' He comes very close to my neck, breathing in as he kisses each cheek. *A hot flush.* I walk with him slowly. 'I don't want to stay here,' he says. He leans into me, our shoulders touch. *Not so close. An electric pulse in my chest. A scent of arousal.*

He laughs. 'I worry about the foreigners. You can never be too careful around here.' *Bashful.* His mouth is tender. 'What chance!' he says. 'Luck brought me to you.' He smiles, boyish.

As we walk, he plies me with questions.

'I know nothing about you. And you know everything about us.'

I drift above him, keeping myself removed, listening.

'You know where I was born, my family, my house, who I loved, who I lived with, what I suffered. You know my shows, my history, my work. And you? What I know is superficial. You are a writer.

An investigator. You have come here to resuscitate a dead memory. You are clearly an accomplished young woman. Very pretty – yes, Anna – you are pretty, I am a connoisseur of ingénues – did no one ever teach you not to blush? Ah, I have found the weakness of Little Miss Foreigner. What country do you come from? And where do you call home? You intrigue me, *el meu petit misteri.*'

His hand brushes against mine. I retract. *My little mystery.* His hand moves to the small of my back, propels me forward.

'*Tinc curiositat* . . . I want to know more. What you stand for, what makes you tick . . .' He leans into me. Sharp and protective. 'You remind me of her. There's something of her about you, it's uncanny, almost as if she inhabits your eyes – there – I can see her, looking at me from a stranger's face. You unnerve me, Anna.'

We walk forever. I pause and stare up at the buildings ringing Plaça del Pi. *That is the house where Ruthven lived. White on chalky orange.* The exterior façade a bright coral, with portraits of cherubim, wreaths of grain in raised plaster. Paint peeling. Faded glory marked by inlaid flowers on the internal walls and an old teak banister. *Don't go inside.* Below, a knife shop. The doors Sitwell must have walked through with the servant Brass Buckle. The pine he stood under, the night the woman came – today the shop front below displays sharp objects made to look like art. Cooking knives, cutting knives, climbing knives. Knives to skin a lamb or whittle wood. Knives to bone a fish, knives to pull out feathers, knives to carry in a back pocket, hooked knives, jagged knives, smooth knives. Ivory-handled. Ornamental. Chopping blades. All sorts. Everything you can imagine.

Oriol leads me through a winter market. Little stalls with taupe-coloured shelters. Peaks and waves of fabric. At long tables, men in aprons offer sweet marmalades, honeys, beeswax candles. Cured meats.

'Try this –' Oriol gives me a marzipan square covered in candied

383

pine nuts. It is sweet and damp on the tongue. A warm buzz, though hands stay inside pockets, scarves wrapped round cold necks, moisture drips from red noses. I feel his weight drift towards me. He points out gargoyles in the Gothic, a secret fountain, the grave of a philandering bishop, the square of a massacre. He pushes my attention to the ferns growing out of balconies, the sun-faded roofs.

'This is my city,' he says again and again. 'My home. I belong here.'

I hear him calling, a siren-voiced yearning. *Come closer.* He walks quickly – 'The Born? You're staying in the Born?' In the restaurants before the cathedral he buys me a beer and tapas. *Black bread. Salt cracked between forefinger and thumb.* I watch him move his hands, playing a beat on the tablecloth, running fingers through his hair. He is kind. Gentle. *Lonely.* He feels lonely. When we are finished I do not know what to do. I do not want him to know where I live. For privacy. For intimacy with myself; no one from her world can be permitted into mine. I remind myself. *An arm's length. A healthy distance. For clarity's sake.* Another beer. I giggle. *Stupid.* A third. A fourth. At the door to my apartment I stop him. He looks up at the house number, my windows. I put out my hand. 'You're not coming in.' He leans in towards me, body closer – laughing by my ear. 'You really are very pretty for a researcher.' I brush him aside. His lips close to my own. *Oriol Duran—*

I open my mouth to speak when the chuntering rips through me. Chattering down through the crown of my skull. Laughing. Singing. Crying. Louder. They come louder and louder. I lose control of my body, slumping forward onto his shoulder, my face collapsing into his chest, my throat swelling – but I am silent! I keep them out with all my power. *You will not come through – you will not come uninvited.*

I smell the full-bodied man of Oriol – feel the hard muscle of his chest – his body dips under my weight, but he holds me up against him, I grind my teeth together. *You will not come out, not here, not now.* The blood rushes from my forehead, tingling in my elbows and knees and I know that they have come for me – that nothing I do will keep them out. With the familiar certainty of the damned, I accept their presence. These episodes – the doctors say – are psychological side effects of physical relapses caused by a degenerative neurological disorder that has created an epicentre of lesions in the tissue of my brain. The doctors call these psychic constructs *hallucinatory incubi.* That is an idiotic name for them. I am meant to breathe deeply – *relax, damn it, relax* – I am meant to enter the state of sleeping and let them fade away . . .

'You are a funny little thing,' Oriol whispers into my ear. 'You've had too much to drink.' I feel my body lift off the ground, arms around my shoulder and legs. The tangy jingle of keys in the latch.

Remember.

I look closer. Slither of woman in violet darkness. *Think of your family. Of your history. Think of your love, of your happiness. Think of your future, your past, your present.* First there was the theatre and only the theatre. *Yes. That's good. The theatre was the cave.* A watery sheen. She has run to the edge of the stage and waits for the lights to illumine. *Molt bé! Molt bé!* grins a bearded gentleman in spectacles, who lifts her on his shoulders and pirouettes before setting her down on the floorboards. *You were born to dance, my Maca! Querida Estimada, t'estimo! Escolta* . . . sounds like rich *xocolata* and cold water. *We must build the walls here,* he says, *and cover the orchestra pit so they may walk out into the audience and appear to be floating.*

Spotlights explode into her consciousness, supernovas brighter than the loveliest star, and then the floor lights spring out and Dance! With a *pop, pop, pop* and the little girl runs her hands in the liquid gold, watching the shadows as they form on the wall. A red lifeline glows round her fingers and she shrieks and giggles, playing in the dust clouds that rise around the lights, and the steam, for the air inside the theatre is damp. If she holds her hands there long enough and squints, she will see her bones, but the stage manager finds her then and *tsk, tsk*, pulls the little girl into her arms who says to the woman – *Mama! Mama! A kiss on the forehead.* At night she sleeps at the house of her guardian, and by day he brings her to the theatre where she sits in the wings with the pulleys and rope on a fly box and watches the people build new universes, the houses with their swinging doors and chequered tablecloths, the painted mountains and powdered flowers, the installation of the truss with its gels that change the colour of the light and all emotions with a delicious, whirring *click, click! I have made this world for you, and only you, my nightingale.* Her mother whispers in her ear and in that instant, she is gone, swept into the spirit of the wind, leaving the child standing alone in the centre of the darkened stage, staring into a void. In her pocket the girl reaches for the golden dials, the spheres made by her mother, engraved with the magic letters, and spins them intently, watching the combinations as they form.

B, C, D

First there was the theatre and only the theatre / As man is a pen so he is a knife. But tonight it is a dream. She is alone. But this is what she remembers. *Com, Medi, l'Extrem,* and she remarks that the legend is true. That the coming of Love brings a certain quality of Truth. You will see it all. *The secrets of the beloved are revealed in the secrets of the lover / The secrets of the lover are revealed in the secrets of the beloved.* Past–Present–Future. But in the meantime she drifts. *The only rule of history that was any good was the rule taught her by her family. That in the world of the living, past–present–future means one*

386

thing and one thing only: an old maxim of the arts which wove round her thoughts in circles, like a prayer of intent. The ground slopes gently where she rests. The pain, which had been vast, has left her, and now there is only dampness around her ears, growing cold against the stones and the world very quiet beneath her. For a long time she is still. There are sirens in the distance and a car that crosses the upper line of the square. She can feel the cement cold under her fingers. She has been left close to the tree and she is grateful. If she had the movement of her hands, she would reach out and touch it, and hold herself against it – to be so close to something living! She does not want to go, not yet, she lies there and watches the clouds part above her head and tries not to think at all. To be empty and clear and remember her childhood. But – no. The memory is gone. When she closes her eyes, this is what she hears: *Follow. Me.* Two words, spoken soft and low.

I sit bolt upright in bed, pushing the covers away, breaking the dream, and look down at my clothed chest, running my hands over my stomach. My skin clammy and warm, jeans crusted to my legs. *Why have I gone to sleep in my clothes?* The air oppressively hot. I have left the heater on and now it stifles everything. My body rebels against the night. I stand and walk to the tall balcony window that interrupts the exterior wall of my bedroom. I pause here, pressing my forehead into the glass, looking out over the jagged line of Barcelona. A second city, the rooftop gardens, linked exterior patios, laundry lines, gargoyles and church steeples, cranes' nests, a million mismatched TV radials. Hidden from view, I open the balcony windows, stepping out into the cool night air. The roar of the city devours me.

There is a book. She has hidden a book.
But where?

I stumble to the shower, cleaning my hair twice, scrubbing down my body with a hard stone, pushing suds over my chest and legs and arms. Time stretches and slows. I do not know if I am there for minutes or hours but I do not care. I lean my head against the glass of the shower walls and dissolve into the steam. I make a cup of chamomile tea naked in the kitchen, wet feet dripping on the floor. It is only then that I notice the flowers: a bouquet of yellow tulips in an ornamental vase. A folded note in confident English:

CALL ME. LET ME KNOW HOW YOU ARE.
Oriol.
P.S. DOES THIS HAPPEN OFTEN?

Shit, I think. *He got me inside. How long did he stay here? What did he see? Nothing on my desk but a laptop.* I send a quick text, too embarrassed to ask. *Thank you. Sorry to put you in that position.*

He writes back immediately: '*Res, Nena, res.* ALL COOL.'

A second message flashes up: '*I know something about you. You're real.*'

A third: '*You have a bed in the city. A home to sleep in.*' Do I tell Fabregat? *No*, I think. *Too embarrassing. Besides . . .* Two pills into my mouth and swallow with water. *You've got this under control.*

II

A FATE LIKE HERS

I emerge with a pounding migraine. The lights of my apartment are dimmed and I stay flat in my bed, breathing carefully, so as not to forget myself in the repeated hammering on my skull. The plaster on the ceiling has lumps and I make out the shape of a rabbit. The skin around my ears itches, tingling down my back into my wrists. I check my alarm. I've slept through the best hour of the day. *Why? Why do you do this to yourself?* Bare feet on linoleum floor. Outside my barred window rests winter. She renders this city limp like the slit belly of a fish, cold and wet and slippery. A silver sheen to its roofs and radars. A damp, pernicious darkness, even in the afternoon sun. Grey walls consume the light, birthing fungi and rot – the line of mildew running round the corner of my roof. I stumble to the bathroom. The world spins. Something has died in my mouth and buried itself in the stale mulch of day-old liquor. *Is it worth it?* The mirror above the sink is cracked. I'm shocked by the circles under my eyes. Pale formaldehyde skin. *You have come here to locate the palimpsest pages of a book. Nothing more, nothing less. Do not complicate it.* But even I know that is a lie – *You are seduced. You want to know, as much as the others did. You want to understand what would drive a man to murder, and a woman to sacrifice her life and the lives of three others, for that is what I am convinced she did.* I distract myself from the stomping noises coming from the roof. A ghost has moved into the attic above my apartment and started dragging small objects from one side to the other. *Pat, pat, BANG!* goes the ghost. Or the footsteps of pigeons? My head throbs louder. Iron-smelting by my left temple. I run my hands under harsh water. The boiler is not working. My knuckles turn a bright inflamed red. And then I sense it. *A presence in the room.* A wind blows up from nowhere. Sliding through the apartment – rustling my pages – but I know that I have opened no windows, and this wind is dangerous, other-worldly. I shiver, and try to ignore it. *You are summoning things, Anna, and they are coming as you call. Do you follow? Do you follow?*

The wind tugs at my tongue.

Blows around me.

No, I argue back. *You will unseat me. Derange me.*

The headaches come again. Louder. Angry. I clutch at the colours on the air, the threads of indigo and gold – I listen, I feel for them. *Where do you lead?* I ask the pulse and throb. *Out.* To the heart of the Gothic quarter through the square of the Palace of Kings, where many overlapping arches form a wall of empty windows framing the sky. I do not remember leaving the apartment, only that in my quest to follow the golden threads I pass doors hiding *patis dels tarongers*, courtyards filled with orange trees echoing the interior lives of medieval gardeners.

Men in battered shirts roam the streets offering red cans of beer. They approach me carefully, as one who recognizes their quarry, jangling wares against moth-eaten mittens. *Cervesa? Un euro.* When I shake my head no, their voices drop to the language of under-ground exchange, a train of illicit substances: *heroin, coke, speed, hash, ecstasy, meth* . . . the connoisseur's full menu. *Barcelona'll give you anything you want.* But I decline.

I must wait patiently. For the pores behind my ears to open up and the voice to make itself known. Soon she will arrive like a river, smooth stone strapped to my throat, tracing her weight into the lump of my cranial bone, nestling under my hair, swelling in my nodes. Transference is a dangerous pursuit – but this voice is so enticing, so heavy in my throat I cannot help but listen, and if the curiosity is strong enough, a mania sets in where logic – oh! Logic! Mine is tossed to the wayside and retrieved retrospectively. I have come here because *this stranger* felt it was necessary, her communication unspoken, I do not hear her, but I feel her reaching into my heart, impulsive, dictatorial, I feel the cold hard folds of a woman's essence, compact and brown as a walnut.

Walk.

I obey. First I see the shapes emerging, the flickering tremors on the air, the glinting like ripples on the still veneer of the night, the shimmer in my retina. Aromas of modernity – fried oil, moped engine, rose perfume – morph into a stench of smoked animal pelt. I swoon into the wall of the Great Cathedral, staring up at the bowels of a gargoyle. Claws clenched around a spoke of rock. Panicking now, out of control, instinct rattles through me and I take out my phone to call Fabregat. It is difficult to hear myself in these situations. I am still conscious, still sentient, but my voice – that distinguishing characteristic of the soul is often the first symptom of relapse. My weathervane. In severe cases, cross-wiring occurs. Overlapping identities.

'Nena?' Fabregat asks, when the phone picks up. 'What's wrong?'

Nerves bloat behind my ears.

'Where are you?' he asks.

Skin cracking in my ear lobes, spots breaking out with pus.

'We'll find you – Nena, don't move.' But mist already coils along my river Lethe, and I forget myself entirely in the flow of green lanterns, translucent neon glow over covered rivers and veins – the knot of this foreign creature resting on my tongue.

Follow, she commands.

393

I twist and turn through the Gothic maze until I reach a sloping alley, La Baixada de Santa Eulàlia, and then the hulking frigate of the old Basílica of Santa Maria del Pi. Once there was a sacred grove here, filled with halting words, like no normal language – and I remember the deaf man's tongue, round and full-bodied, that Illuminatus heard as he passed through this square on his way to the court of the kings – *the pine of all pines*. In the flesh before me.

Dig, the voice commands. Root of your root. Clay of your clay.

I kneel beneath the tree, ignoring the pedestrians, the buskers, ignoring the barmen and baristas, the clientele, the neighbours in their balconies. I kneel and bend my head and, short of any other tools, begin to dig with my hands in the earth beneath the trunk of the tree. A strength foreign to my own body enters my fingers. It has rained and the earth is muddy about the roots of the pine. The earth comes away easily. I dig and dig and dig, as this other mind directs me, for surely that is what I suffer, until my fingers strike *metal*. I work harder, faster, lust driving me, desire for the hidden object. I rub away the dirt, pull away the form and stop. *An intricately patterned box. Golden fig leaves laid over enamelled metal. Jewelled birds nest in dirt-smeared foliage.* I shake, holding it close to my chest. Rocking back and forth on the ground. *Is this it? Are these they? Is this what you wanted me to find?*

Open it.

I unlatch the hook, yearning for the papers – imagining the folds of parchment, my stolen quire, cut out of the Book of Hours – instead I am met by revulsion. Three brown rags, stained with what looks like earth, wrapped around a pocket edition of a disappointingly modern, dingy little book. Agony bursts through my chest. *What game are you playing?* I turn the book in my hands, leaving the disintegrating rags in the rusty box. A working edition of the *Oresteia*: a trilogy of ancient tragedies produced by the Greek dramatist Aeschylus in 458 BCE. The book well creased. Dented.

Dog-eared. Stained in the same mire as the ugly rags. I peer closer. Passages are underlined. First – *Agamemnon*. Cassandra's story. My heart skips. I keep the pressure down. *Gentle. Be gentle.* Flick back to an inscription on the title page:

To my Cassandra
From your Aureus

Words circled. I skim softly. *Cassandra, high priestess of Apollo, stolen from Troy. Raped. As a maiden she rejected the romantic advances of Apollo, and was cursed by the god. She would bear the burden of divine foresight, but never be understood.* And suddenly it clicks. *Check. Check what is written. The dates in the letters to Fabregat.*

1182–1188. 1312–1317. Coordinates in a play. Latitude and longitude of verse lines. My eyes scan to the line numbers at the side of the page. *Hunting.* I alight on my quarry. *A thin underline below each one. A date. A marker. June 2003.*

Lines 1182–1188:

Flare up once more, my oracle! Clear and sharp
As the wind which blows off the rising sun,
I can feel a deep swell, gathering head
To break at last and bring the dawn of grief.
No more riddles. I will teach you.
Come, bear witness, run and hunt with me.
We trail the old barbaric works of slaughter

Could it be? She was delusional. Mad. I feel the spasm in my belly. *She was waiting for someone like you.*

Lines 1312–1317:

I must be brave.
It is my turn to die.
I address you as the Gates of Death.
I pray it comes with one clear stroke,
No convulsions, the pulses ebbing out
In gentle death, I'll close my eyes and sleep.

In the distance a siren, like a battle cry, whoop-whooping, playful, skipping over rooftop bars, merging with a chorus of voices – the wails and death throes and shouting and chattering, like the incessant squawks of birds, *ca-cawing, shriek-shrieking*. Drilling into my pores, screws biting into my skull, breaking bones, black pustules bubble up, opening like slits, or eyes, unlocking the energy that sits coiled in the base of my spine. And then the line, the invisible line that rushes from the apex of my scalp, down over my nose, through my tongue, and out over my chin. A magic line of palsy. Of division, of rupture. Throbbing round my lips before the left side of my face freezes, falling slack as the brain swells, it pulses and beats, followed by the extraordinary pain, like needles piercing flesh, those familiar microscopic haemorrhages in my ear canal.

Silence. She is coming. I feel her entrance. Ominous. *You've pushed too far.* And then my head throws itself back, my mouth no longer my own, and the voices rattle out of me, tumbling over my tongue as I fight to return into myself, pushing through the fog, begging, thrusting into my lungs! I must return to myself – before I am swallowed up again as the voices yap through me, yearning! Howling for expression.

'Let me hold her!' I bark – clutching the box to my chest – 'I must hold her!' The spirit shunting through my vocal chords is *a woman*. I listen as I speak – yes – a young woman …

Natalia?

The gurgling responds.

Follow.

I stand, facing the tree, unsure. People swirl around me, but I do not take them in because I sense the emergence of that dreadful being. Down she comes, unravelling, moving out of the branches, golden green. The snake descends regally, confident, unafraid, she moves over shoes, gliding round boots and stilettos, over a dog's paw and the point of an umbrella until she reaches me. She is bigger this time, much larger, no longer a garden snake. She is a python.

Are you afraid? The dream voice asks. The snake unhinges her jaw, moving bone away from joint, the scaled rubber grows and grows, mouth trebling in size. At the bottom of her loosened jaw lies a golden fig leaf, like the leaves on the tree I had seen in my dream. *Take it. Place it in on your tongue.* I do as I am told. Reaching my hand into the green snake's mouth, I am hallucinating wildly. *This is madness, far worse than before, I will never come back* . . . but I obey.

I feel the weight of the gold on my tongue, the wide expanse pressed down by the form of the leaf. The snake is gentle. She comes closer, putting her cold head next to my ear lobe; she licks me, once on each side, tongue flicking. She is kind. The experience mesmerizing. The pine tree from which she descended grows in size, the branches bud with glass jars, magnificent amphorae, glittering ornaments. From each one I detect a voice. A chorus of whispers. I listen carefully, no longer afraid, plucking stories from the wind. The first memory is a man's, very old and papery, made of crushed reeds.

'*It was at night as I crossed the desert alone from Chenoboskion to the city of Luxor that I came upon a woman lying on the road. Thinking that the woman had met with some assassin I went to her immediately. She lay on her back, with her arms outstretched to either side in the shape of a cross. Her body was covered in simple earthen robes. She whispered as I knelt beside her: "Do not fear for me. Be gone. I am meant to die." – I knew*

397

then that she had been poisoned by a snake, judging by the wounds in her wrist – a sound drew my attention, and I saw the black form of an asp slither across the moonlit sands. I made a move to kill the creature! She reached to stop me. "Let her return to the desert. Your hands are already bloodied." I held the woman to my chest as the snake's poison raced up her arm. The end drew near, I praying to the Gods for her safe passage to the underworld, while from her lips the woman confessed that she had buried a book she called a secret. I asked, "What is this secret?" She would not answer clearly, saying only: "I have buried this work for eternity, giving our words into the earth, hidden as a seed from those who would destroy us, and like a seed it will emerge and its branches will reach towards the heavens."

With that she blessed me. Her skin fell ashen and cold, the death rattle sounded on her lips, then her mouth opened and she spoke a language I did not recognize that sounded as a call from a nightingale. Each word from her tongue shimmered as though it were born of light. Her voice hung like stars against a black desert sky.

"What language is this?" I asked entranced by the shimmering light. She answered that it was the secret language, a tongue that would heal the sick and cure the dying and turn every lump of ore into gold. As she spoke, the words of her song caused her body to disintegrate into dust, crumbling in my hands as light shone out from her heart, taking the shape of an eagle and then a snake, and then a crescent moon hanging on the air before a final note of gold on which the woman disappeared.'

At some point I must have fallen to my knees. I don't know when, only that I find myself close the ground, and that putting my hand to my nose my fingers come away dark. Through the haze I see a man – *Is he real or part of the dream?* I wonder, thoughts sluggish . . . unreal city looming above me.

I am asleep, I struggle to be sure—

'Give her space,' Fabregat booms, his voice roaring into my

consciousness. I feel the spittle foaming in my mouth. The convulsions in my tongue.

'*Joder!*' he shouts. 'Can we stop the blood?'

A man puts a cloth to my nose – I smell something strange,
chemical and foreign.

'Let her work, damn it.'

'Will she come back from this?' a stranger asks, holding my head
in his hands. His colleague covers my body with a blanket. They
form a wall around me. I see dark trouser legs, scuffed boots. *The
tree of gold.* I lift my hands to my face. Nails rammed with dirt. I feel
my heart beat calm. My vision clears, the snake has gone.

I focus on the imagined figure of a woman. A woman I recognize,
standing in the dark beneath the door to a church behind me. She
is hooded, her hands dirty. A night a decade past.

In Santa Maria del Pi, at the south-western end of the nave, a
wooden door creaks opens. A man appears in the undergarments
of a curate. His skin dark, thick hair on his forearms. Unable to
sleep, he has left the quarters of the clergy and makes his way to
the foot of the wooden Madonna to contemplate her beauty in
the dark. He travels by candlelight, preferring not to illumine the
church, but rather to exist in the comforting presence of God.
All too soon, his silence is roughly disturbed by the panicked
ringing of a bell. The shrill piercing at the public door to the
priest's entrance. It rings again, and again, with such intensity that
the young man feels compelled to answer. The figure of a woman
meets him when he opens the door. Her head and neck hooded
by shadow.

'I took a liberty. I am sorry.'

She stands, hands out by her side, shrouded in a silk scarf. Above her the sky is black.

'I need to see a priest,' she whispers.

'Do you realize what time it is?' he asks. 'You should not be here.'

And with that, she leans forward and whispers in his ear.

The young curate lifts his nightgown above his feet and rushes down the corridor to the quarters of the good priest Canço, shielding the flame of the candle with his hand. He knocks twice on the door with no answer, then, steeling his strength, presses through, making his way to the bedside. Setting the candle beside the priest's book, left open to a page of Genesis, he crosses himself twice before taking both hands and roughly waking the sleeping man.

'There is a woman here to see you!' The young curate's eyes glint in the light of the candle.

'Tell her to come back at six,' Canço groans from his bed, heaving over to his side.

'She asks to confess. She does not have much time.'

'And I have lost much sleep,' Canço grumbles.

'Father, she has said she is dying.'

Father Canço sits up with a start. His breath catches in his throat. He sputters and coughs loudly, lungs heaving under the light of the young priest's candle.

'Where is she?' the priest asks the curate, sitting up in his sheets.

'Please, Father, I have left her near the pulpit. She asks to see you now.'

And the young curate departs. It is a young woman. He can tell by her form, half hidden in the heavy coat. She kneels in the furthest pew by the door. Her face hooded, wet hair evaporating into darkness.

'Do not look at me, I beg of you,' she whispers, as the curate approaches.

'Father Canço is ready.' The young curate averts his eyes, but catches the tips of her fingers as he glances down. Her hands are delicate and fine, more beautiful even than Mother Mary's in the presbytery, carved by master sculptors out of stone.

'*Mercè.*'

Her voice sweeter than incense and honey. The young curate breathes in the warm scent of her skin, damp with rain. Something dark and lustful grows in his chest, a desire long suppressed and carnal; he breathes again and shudders. Walks faster towards the confessional, leading her beneath the deadened lamps.

From just one word. God help me. On those lips I cannot see . . .

The church long and vaulted . . . *Let this pass quickly*, he prays as he leads her down the nave, stone walls flame-licked and bare.

She interrupts his thoughts.

'*The storm has left me lonely tonight. I am glad of your company.*'

She reaches out to touch his arm. He does not remember the rest.

Once inside the confessional, the chinks in the wood are dark, but Father Canço can just make out her form, the curve of her cheek, the pink flesh of her lip against the wooden screen. Her voice is soft, but he can hear the shudder of stress running through it, and a coldness mounts on his hands and fingers, rising up from his knees, a drop in temperature like that experienced with a ghost.

Through the chinks he too catches her scent.

A warm smell like damp leaves and smoke − he banishes the thoughts from his head − perhaps he is still dreaming?

Rallying his strength, the good priest Canço greets his shadowy visitor with the sign of the cross and she follows.

'Bless me, Father, for I have sinned. It has been six days since my last confession.'

'You have given us the sign, we will be of service to you. Now tell me, child, why have you come to us, in the dead of night, to seek forgiveness?'

'I wish to be clean, Father.'

'And under the eyes of God in confession you may be cleansed of all sin.'

'I wish to be pure.'

'Seek penance for your sins and we may purify your soul.'

She opens her mouth and speaks then – of all the things she has seen, of all the horrors and terrors and tribulations, and the priest pulls his habit close round his shoulders and makes the sign of the cross over himself to ward off the evil.

'Who has died?' he asks slowly, when she catches her breath.

He listens close.

'*Three women.*'

'And?'

'*I have done nothing to prevent their murders.*'

The priest feels a cold sweat descend upon him. Even as the words rolled from her tongue, he senses the things of which she confessed walking through the city, noting the profusion of police cars in the square, blood on the corners of Carrer de Sant Ramon – but this – this is far worse than he imagined, and yet the promise must be guarded – ancient as it was – the practice of confession, secret under the sanctity of God.

'And do you desire revenge?' He asks, hearing the steel in her voice.

'I do, Father.'

'And it is for this that you ask forgiveness?'

'Yes.'

'Do you suffer, child?'

She did not respond.

'Have you gone to the police?'

'I have given them the key, but obfuscated its meaning,' she whispers.

'It is a sin to hide the truth,' murmurs the good priest Cançо. 'It may alleviate your suffering to confess to me. The Church can take your cause upon its shoulders. Can you tell me who he is?'

The sounds that comes from her throat terrify the priest. She tries and tries again to utter a man's name, but it is as if she has lost her tongue. Each time she grappled with the words, her head bangs against the wooden slats of the confessional, she screams and spits. The sound rips out of her, echoing into the church, a note from the clearest bell.

'I . . . I am sorry . . .' She chokes. 'Please. Promise me, Father, you will help. I will tell you the only way that you can help me.'

And with that she passes a furled paper through a notch in the screen, a tightly bound scroll, no larger than 5 mm in diameter and 2.5 cm in length. When the girl speaks again it is unlike any language he has ever heard, the cadence of Catalan all but extinguished from her voice; thus she imparts her message in a mysterious tongue that knows no nation, and yet from the vantage point of the priest he understands.

'Rest.' The man's voice comes again. 'Help is coming.'

'Happy hunting.' Fabregat grins like a wolf.

His eyes sharp in the darkness.

Sirens draw closer.

'Chin up, girl,' he whispers as the ambulance arrives.

He strokes my forehead. I gurgle, clutching at his hand.

'Chin up. You're here,' as the medics strap me into the vehicle.

Silence. Let there be silence.

I wake to the whistle and pop of onions in a frying pan, my bedroom door open to the kitchen–living room. Fabregat is doubled over, straining broad beans from a vat of boiling water. He swears under his breath, a large floral apron tied in a bow around his neck.

Merda. Cabrón.

Little whispers of exasperation.

Beneath the daisy-covered apron, the man is dapper, almost formal. Despite the cold, he has stripped down to a shirt and chinos, leaving his shoes at the door. His socks are mismatched, one plaid, the other purple, and he has tossed a rather ungainly panama hat onto the armchair in the living room. A large brown overcoat hangs on a hook by the door. It is an odd combination. He looks for all the world like a dilapidated British tourist, sleeves of a linen shirt rolled up to his elbows, cheeks red with the strain of culinary exertion, a befuddled elephant in the kitchen.

'Nena,' he booms when he sees me lifting my beleaguered self from the sheets. 'You eat like a bird. What is this? A hunger fast? Nothing in the fridge, barely any oil – No garlic! *Ostras! Nena?* I had to buy it all!' He wipes his forehead in exasperation. 'Today we're eating properly. You're going to need a little extra fat.'

Fabregat dumps a lake of olive oil into the frying pan. The onions spit and hiss.

I ask him about the change of style – the panama hat in particular. It doesn't suit him. 'Disguise.' He grins and taps his nose. *Obfuscation.* I don't bother to ask why. Frankly I am not interested.

'What are you making?'

'*Déu dóna favas a qui no té quiexals.*'

I rub my eyes.

'God gave broad beans to the man who has no teeth,' he repeats, looking at me crossly. 'You're having *Favas a la Catalana.* Fabregat-style. *Més pernil, espinacs, pamboli, i bravas . . .*' He points at the steaming mass of desultory beans, and caramelizing flecks of sliced spring onions. *Botifarra negra,* dark blood sausage, heaped on the sideboard, browning bacon crackling on the stove. Grease bubbling. My stomach turns. I open my mouth to speak. He cuts me off with a flourish.

'El Maestro cannot stray from his task.'

'I can't eat that,' I say, pointing to the pan. 'It looks like a war zone.'

'Don't be ridiculous.'

I stumble forward in my pyjamas.

'No really, I can't.'

Fabregat ignores me.

'My wife thinks I'm having an affair. I've told her *No, t'estimo, I love you, la meva estimada . . . Querida,* if you'll only believe me – I've sponsored *una bruixa* and I want the next act to blow my fucking socks off . . . But that sounds even worse.' He laughs and babbles on for a while, about his wife and his son and his dog, all of whom he's leaving to their own devices. He seems happy, oddly so, and I am immediately suspicious. *Does he plan on moving in and babysitting me?*

'Thank you.' I say, tentatively, 'For sticking around.'

He grins at me. I gaze blearily past him.

'You really are a freak. First-class performance,' Fabregat says. 'My boys will have nightmares for weeks.'

He's moved a chair from the living room now and perches at the end of the kitchen table, pleased as an ornamental parrot. He leans forward on his elbows and looks at me.

'Ever consider a career as a circus act?'

'No,' I snap back. 'You're giving me a migraine.'

'It's a shitload of drugs they put you on. Are you usually medicated?'

I shake my head.

'Just in emergencies? That explains the syringes in the refrigerator. Biscuit?' Fabregat asks. 'Wife made these. Almond and chocolate. Very nice.'

He pushes a plate of cookies towards me. I don't want one.

'Drink,' he says firmly. I accept water meekly, gulping down the contents.

'How long have I been like this?'

'Two days. I'm glad to see you're walking.'

'And you've been here the whole time?'

'Someone has. The doctor said we couldn't leave you unattended. You're not very stable, Nena, when you work yourself up into this state. However, I'm pleased.'

'With what?'

'The results.'

'What results?'

He whistles a little tune to himself. *The man's being cagey.*

'You called around eleven o'clock – I got to you at eleven thirty, the ambulance was there fifteen minutes later. A small crowd had gathered – two policemen called by the neighbours who watched you digging! Digging? Nena? You approached the pine in a trance – *como una loca* – the witness's precise wording. Despite the fact that your eyes were closed, you appeared to see clearly. You were speaking in voices – very quickly – many different voices, languages I couldn't understand – it was gobbledygook.' He rocks back and forth on his feet, grinning as he waves his hands in the air and imitates a baby gurgling, 'Only it was fucking spooky, Nena. Freaked the damn lot of us out. The doctor tells me you were technically asleep – but sleepwalking – acting out a dream? You were able to respond to questions but unable to wake up. Is this normal for you?'

'What do you think?'

'If sleepwalking always produces evidence, you're welcome to do it more often.' He takes another bite of his biscuit. 'You're missing out, you know, she's an incredible cook.'

My insides turn. *You should go home. Leave him. Follow your own way. He's a dead weight. An encumbrance. Has nothing to do with you.*

'I looked up your medical records,' Fabregat says simply. 'Well, the doctors did. And I looked on. If you see what I mean.'

Up go the hackles. I cannot help myself. I hope to say something elegant. Respectful. Mature. Instead:

'I quit.'

Fabregat puts down his spatula.

'Come again?'

'I quit.'

'You can't. We haven't finished yet.'

'I have. I'm done.'

He frowns. I glare back at him.

'Do you believe in ghosts, Sr Fabregat?'

'No.'

'But you hired me.'

'Yes.'

'So you must have some instinct. Right there, in your stomach.'

'Instinct, no. Curiosity, yes.' He squints at me. Narrowing his eyes to look closer. As if he wanted to pull back the layers of my chest and examine my heart. 'I like to think the dead are dead. But I'm open to persuasion.'

'Well, because of my *instinct* . . . I quit.'

'What?' he roars. 'You're hallucinating again.'

I lash back. 'My mental health is more important than your hobby.'

'You owe me a week.'

'I don't want to do this any more.'

'A contract is a contract.'

'If I stay,' I cut him off, 'and I mean *if*, what do I get in return? What could you possibly offer me?'

'A blind eye,' Fabregat snaps back. 'A lot of things came out of you in the ambulance, Nena. These papers you're after? You hadn't mentioned anything about them to me. You stole from *the Church*.' He crosses himself twice. 'I could have your grant removed for something like that – and believe me I would if you dicked me around. One phone call to the Diocese and the Ayuntamiento from my highly esteemed and respectable self and *peuuuuuuuuh–*' he whistles – '*adios, Nena.* Anyways, you can't quit now, girl, you've already made history!'

I stare at the inspector blankly.

As the beans cook on the stove, Fabregat pours me another glass of water. 'Take a seat.' He nods at me. 'Catch yourself.'

It comes down to the book.

'The book you pulled out of the earth?' Fabregat grins. But he doesn't need to say. I already know. The book was *hers*.

'Àngel Villafranca has confirmed: a copy of *The Oresteia.* By Aes-chy-luuus.' Fabregat trips over the name. 'The bastard says she knew every line by heart. Where did she get it? I asked. What do you make of the inscription? *To my beautiful Cassandra. From your Aureus.* The old dog feigned ignorance. "I don't know," he said. "Aureus? She never knew a man by the name of Aureus." "But you confirm this book is hers?" Villafranca stumbled, to my delight. I know a liar when I see one,' Fabregat barks. 'And that man will lie all the way to his tomb. He's hiding something, Nena, plain as day.

'But that's not the end of it. Turns out the old battered tin full of rags was not stained by dirt but stained by *la sang*,' he says. The word for blood in Catalan is hard – full of sharp vowel. It has none of the sing-song of the Spanish *sangre*. *Sang* in Fabregat's mouth feels blunt. Honest and direct.

'We think the blood is human. The rags were probably medical gauze used to clean wounds – we don't know whose yet, or what type of cornucopia we're looking at – but give the team a few days –' Fabregat slams the table – 'and we'll be running hard down the tracks. It could be nothing . . . but you asked me about instinct? Hah! My instinct says: *Drive*.

'Drive on, Anna. There's more where this came from. So you keep doing your work, and I'll keep doing mine – and somewhere, we'll meet in the middle.'

Like hell we will.

'*Nena! Entens?* Do you understand?' The joy on his face electric. 'The police have reopened the case. The lives of four women – maybe more – are wrapped up in this. *No t'importa?* Don't you realize what you could do for us? You have a gift. A bloody gift, girl! I have been waiting ten years for this and we're not giving up now. You're a crack, Nena. No one suspects a little *guiri* has teeth. But you do. You definitely do. I want you onside. We –' he pushes up from his seat and pours dark meat over the onions in the pan – 'are working together on this one. So: we clear? I decide when we stop. I run the show. In the meantime: relax. Be grateful. And eat. I'd also ask that you generally try and pull yourself together. Take a shower. *A la taula.* To the table,' he orders. 'Ghosts or no ghosts. *Mata més gent la taula que la guerra.*'

I cannot help but smile at Fabregat's morbid Catalan *refrany*. *Feasting at the table kills more people than war.*

While the inspector naps on the low sofa in the living room, I decide to take matters into my own hands. I place a belated phone call to my friend and colleague the Abbey Librarian. He puts me through to a man who would not give me his name, but deals with the more mystical intrigues of the monkish community on the island. I tell this man about my vision of the girl in the church, and the name that came to me in my trance. Out of all the people in the world, these monks of Mallorca are the only ones who take my lunacy seriously, and for this I am deeply grateful. The voice on the phone asks if the vision had given me a name. Padre Cançó, I reply. A woman came to him ten years ago at Santa Maria del Pi and left him an offering.

'Ah,' says the voice, and its owner thinks for a moment. 'You are certain?'

'Yes.'

A long, meditative pause ensues.

I am summoned cursorily the next morning to a meeting on the far side of the Parc de la Ciutadella, built on the ruins of a panoptic military fortress called the Citadel – raised in the mid-nineteenth century. I enter the park via the Zoological Museum, strolling through the cast-iron gates, winter sun floating like a half-forgotten denarius. I stop for a moment at the great waterfall flanked by winged serpents with a lion's head. The fountains dance, and people swarm to watch. The park is a charged, strange place, full of pained histories and I remember how I arrived in this city and set about educating myself in Catalan history and language. I bought myself an Anglès–Catalan Dictionary and a thick tome entitled *Forgotten Empire: A History of Catalonia and Her Ports*. I learnt a word a day, and read the book overnight. During those first few weeks in the city, I raced through *The Kingdom of Aragon* and *Gothic Spires, Roman Roots*, followed by *Gaudí's Universe*, *The Secret Life of the Black Virgin of Montserrat*, *Els Quatre Gats: Barcelona's Art Legacy* and George Orwell's *Homage to Catalonia*. Later I studied the *Usatges*, or *Usages*, Catalonia's medieval charter of civil rights, which predated the Magna Carta by more than a hundred years. The *Usatges* formed a bill of rights insisting that 'citizens' (though not serfs) existed alongside nobility in the eyes of the law. These keys led to the founding of the *Consell de Cent*, the Council of One Hundred, or the original governing body of Barcelona. I sigh as I walk. *These books were meant to be my salvation.* I did not think murder would bring me back here.

I arrive early at the appointed rendezvous and decide to order an almond milk *horchata*, out of season but still delicious, and a plate of *jamón ibérico* with crushed tomato and bread. The waiter brings me a copy of *La Vanguardia*, which I skim through. Unbeknownst to me, he then retreats into the lobby and places a swift phone call to the clerical offices at Santa Maria del Pi. Fifteen minutes later the bustling figure of Father Cançó heaves out of a taxi and scoots across the road towards the café.

Cançó is round and red as a swollen tomato and wears a white carnation in his button hole. A moth-worn coat amplifies the effect of this bulk, and there is not a hair on his shining head, which sweats despite the cold, insipid sun. When he sees me, he gives a furtive meaningful sigh and shuffles forward, worrying his hands. 'Perdó,' he interjects upon reaching my table, eyes nearly swallowed up by fat. 'But am I speaking with Anna Verco, friend of the Librarian of the Abbey of La Real and the Noble Monks of the Tramuntana Range?'

'You are indeed.'

'Thank God you are here.' The priest gathers wind before exhaling – 'I have a matter of grave importance to discuss with you ... And I fear there might be people listening.'

The café is unpopulated and the waiter absconded entirely.

'I will take a coffee with you. I cannot stay for long. My throat is very dry.'

He pauses, twitching slightly, and smiles the smile of a man who does not want to appear nervous. 'I admire that you are reading the papers. Too few of our citizens read the papers.' The waiter reappears and Cançó orders himself a *cafè amb llet*, a fresh orange juice and a side of *churros* with chocolate.

'I feel, given the circumstances, that a bridge must be made between our distinguished personages. Miss Verco, your illustrious name was delivered to me by a messenger who asked me to reveal my secret upon certain circumstances, which sorrowfully –' the priest crosses himself twice – 'have occurred ...'

Goosebumps on the back of my neck.

Cançó drops his voice to a theatrical whisper: 'It is concerning the murdered girl, Natalia Hernández. Now I would like to hear everything that you claim to have witnessed in your vision.'

'My dear ...' he sighs when I have finished. 'It was all just as you have described. I must affirm the correlation in the positive – proving once again that one can never underestimate the mysterious powers of the delicate sex ...' The priest dipped the end of his *churro* into a bowl of chocolate. 'The woman you witnessed came to my side on the eve of San Juan, 23 June. From her voice I knew that she was young, no older than twenty. One of my novices found her in the church – such a dreadful story – it was very late on La Revetlla, around midnight, if I remember correctly.' The priest takes another bite of his *churro* before continuing: 'She confessed a great deal to me that night ... She called herself a "midwife to murder", insisting that she had drunk blood, blood she could not wipe off her hands. When I asked her to speak the name of her oppressor the devil bit her tongue. She could not utter his name aloud – a terrible thing which I am told occurs only –' he coughs demurely into his hand, then squints up at me – 'when one has had sexual intercourse with the Beast. My dear girl, you must understand that this woman had fallen under the control of a monster – and that in penance she wished to excommunicate herself from Heaven, believing her crimes could have no punishment but the most miserable of self-inflicted deaths.' The priest paused. 'With hindsight I have come to the bitter conclusion – as I am sure you will – that the madwoman who arrived at my door was none other than Natalia Hernández.'

'Why didn't you go to the police?'

Cançó sighs a large, arching sigh.

'Ours was a private matter of the Church. An issue of faith. If we went to the police with every confession we received half this city would be behind bars. However, my agreement before the eyes of God does not stop me from her message. The girl gave me a most puzzling and rather horrible object. I had it blessed with holy water on the off chance that it did something vile.' From the pocket of his coat he removed a small bible, and opened it to a dog-eared page. There, tucked into the fold of the book was a furled piece of parchment.

'Give me your hand,' the priest orders.

I offer up my palm hungrily.

'Miss Verco, I wish to absolve myself of this burden. Each day I have felt guilty. But I believed the time would come. "The Sign of the Sibyl" she called it, and by God —' Canço crosses himself profusely — 'it is surely a mark of the devil, the very thing which bound her tongue, and I am glad to be rid of it.'

My breath sucks in as I turn the scrap over. On one side: the golden ouroboros. Against the opposing face, she has written six illumined letters:

AUREUS

Beneath this, two ornate keys drawn in the shape of an X, their mouths crusted with battered gold leaf.

'That night the girl uttered a great many wild incantations: repeating — *That which she seeks he does not know, and that which she knows he does not seek* . . . and a second line — if I recall correctly — *As a man is a pen so he is a knife* — or something to that effect. After this point, my dear, I am afraid I could not make head nor tail of her ramblings. I thought she was deranged, and did not believe the import of her words. I absolved her of her sins and sent her on her way. My shame will follow me to my grave.' The priest casts his squint down. 'I apologize for not having come forward sooner, but the heavens have their own logic — which I, mere mortal, cannot fathom. I trust also that you will respect my secrecy in this matter. I do not want it getting out. If you have any questions you know where to find me, but I see from your face the object is self-explanatory.'

The priest slurps the last of his juice, throws down a five-euro note and sombrely bids adieu, leaving me speechless in the café, staring with fascination at the shimmering golden serpent in my hand.

Aureus. A scrap of paper handed to a priest in a confessional, accompanied by a myth. The Mark. I redraw her compass, allowing my imagination to follow the lines of her diagram. *Aureus.* I scribble the word again, sound out the syllables. *Au. Re. Us.* From the Latin *aurum* meaning *gold. In figurative speech, meaning glorious, excellent, magnificent.* Followed by the black keys of St Peter, formed like a barrier, a position of defence. Check again for Catholic connotations. *Bishop and Martyr of Mainz, Germany, slaughtered by Huns with his sister. Saint Aureus. Also: Treasure. See: Codex Aureus of St Emmeram, ninth-century Carolingian Book of Gospels.* I drum my fingers on my computer keyboard. Then *Aurelius. Bishop of Carthage and Companion of Saint Augustine of Hippo, active in the fourth century, responsible for the establishment of Christian Doctrine and the eradication of the leading heresies of the time.* Father Canço called it the 'Sign of the Sibyl'. The lead in my pencil breaks. *Click, click,* snagging at the paper. *Again. She meant it as a name. A name. A name.* I am interrupted by the movement of two feuding crows in the branches beyond my window. They squawk and argue bitterly, but I find them reassuring. Wine cold down my throat and warming all at once.

AUREUS

I shift the first three letters.

415

URAEUS

My pen hovers. *Uraeus.* From the Egyptian hieroglyphic: 'rearing cobra', from the Greek, *ouraios* or *on its tail.* The Egyptians celebrated the beauty and wisdom of the snake, and chose it as a symbol of divinity, royalty and power. The cobra could not blink, and thus was an ever-watchful guardian of kings, rearing on the golden Mask of Tutankhamen. The Uraeus may also have been a totem of the ancient goddess *Wadjet,* the snake-headed deity of pre-dynastic Egypt, the life-giving Serpent Womb, protectress of Lower Egypt; her oracle inhabited the city of the region named after her snake-self, *Per-Wadjet* or House of Wadjet – rumoured to have given birth to the oracles of Ancient Greece. Her image was worn for the blessing of women in childbirth. *Wadjet. Derived from the hieroglyphic symbol: Papyrus. Or Papyrus-coloured one. Wadj* meaning *green-coloured* in reference to the leaves of the plant – *Goddess of the famous ancient symbol of the Eye of the Moon, the wadjet, later called the Eye of Horus,* the focal symbol of seven gold, lapis lazuli, carnelian and faience bracelets found in the tombs of the mummy kings, in the pendants of old framed by the rearing carnelian cobra and eagle ... The goddess Wadjet being the two-headed Serpent, or lion-headed matriarch ... an amulet against the evil eye and chthonic protection for safe passage into the under-world, the mark of a king on earth, icon of the dominion and power of Egypt. *Aureus – Uraeus. Connection far-fetched?* I rein myself in. *Focus on the keys.* That symbol is clear. *The Crossed Keys of St Peter, Pope of Rome. Peter the Rock.* Gemini mouths canine, at once a barrier and a seduction. Protecting and revealing.

Then it dawns on me.

I feel a resonance.

Gut-deep. *Act on it.*

On my makeshift desk a glass of wine. Open laptop. The photographs of her face posted on the window. Ashtray with six stubs.

Two half-drunk cups of coffee. I upload the photos from my camera, the sketches she drew as a teenager. *Rest in them.* Little phonebook black on table. Her handwriting so delicate, so quick. I flick through the book.

'*I was always too scared to call these numbers.*' Villafranca's voice breaks my thoughts. '*Every man's name. I thought: "I'll ask each one. Did you do it? Did you drive her mad? Did you love her?" But I didn't want to know this version of my daughter.*'

I return to the picture. *Keys to the city of Rome.* Perhaps they signify something so simple as *Pere* in Catalan? Or *Pedro*? She has not alphabetized by first names, but I am undaunted, and read methodically on through the bulk of the entries until I reach five magic letters in blue pen. *Peter.* I think of the fisherman. The tight skip of her *R* ending with a sharp flourish. To my surprise the spelling is English, the last name *Warren*. Beside his surname she has drawn a tiny set of keys. A landline number. Reach for the phone. *One, two, skip to my Lou. Fly's in the buttermilk, shoo, fly, shoo. There's a little red wagon, paint it blue.* Round and round you go. Dial. Punch the numbers in. Phone next to ear. Mouth open.

Lost my partner, what'll I do? I'll get another one, prettier than you.

Skip, skip, skip to my Lou.

The call rings out. And out again.

Click. Carr-rrink, caaarunk.

'*Hello, you've reached Peter Warren's phone, please leave a message . . .*'

The breath rushes out of me. I call again. No answer. *Not this time*, I decide. *No message.*

Peter Warren. I type his name and 'Barcelona' into Google's search bar. Far down in the results a series of links to articles published in the British travel magazine *Bulldogs Abroad* detailing nightlife in the city. A small photograph of the man is attached to the third article advocating a pub crawl linked to religious heritage sites of the city. Brown skin, broad smile, pixelated features. The fourth article, published in

1998 and reposted on a blog, is a review of a breakout performance by an ingénue, eighteen-year-old *Natalia Hernández*. The writer quotes the actress.

Back at my desk, I dial Fabregat. I hesitate. *Do not tell him about the priest. The scrap of paper. It was left for me – and not for him.* Instead I focus on a hunch – a 'nebulous feeling' – my circus act.

'Good girl!' he shouts down the line.

'Can you do something for me . . . ?' I ask slowly. 'I don't know what your capabilities are but—'

'Out with it! I've not got all day. Barça is on in ten!'

'I have a name for you.'

'Who are we looking for?'

'Peter Warren.'

'Anything else?'

'A telephone number.' I read it out.

'On it.' Fabregat signs off. I shuffle into the kitchen and make a cup of tea, leaning my weight into the countertop. When the water boils I choose chamomile and drop the bag into a yellow cup. Steam rises. A brown stain leaks into the water.

Fabregat calls back almost immediately.

'He left the city ten years ago. Sold an apartment in Gràcia. No residency papers. UK national. Goes back and forth in the summer months. Seems to have come through Border Patrol this year, no record of leaving. Doesn't pay taxes. Scrounger. Does that help? The phone number belongs to a house in Capileira, Cortijo del Piño,' he booms, audibly pleased. 'I'm asking my boys to check it out – any single British males in that town.'

Time slips by me. I find the taste on the air off-putting; Natalia Hernández has emptied me of emotion. I pick up my phone and dial Peter Warren. His voice clicks on: '*Hello, you've reached Peter Warren's phone, please leave a message . . .*'

No response. Irritation boils. Who the hell is this man? What is he up to in Andalusia? *He's here illegally* – no residency papers? A criminal record perhaps? *Nothing serious. A bar fight in Seville in 1989.* Can they find him? Fabregat hunts quickly. Where was he in 1996? The year Cristina died and Villafranca went on tour?

A day passes listlessly. I call the landline again. Obstinate.

'Hello, you've reached Peter Warren's phone . . .'

I leave a message, calm, collected. My name and number. And my interest in speaking to him, euphemistically about his 'time in Barcelona'. Next I consult the Great Oracle Google. *C-A-P-I-L-E-I-R-A.* Image search. *El Cortijo del Piño.* It comes up immediately. A holiday rental in the summer, occupied by the owner in the winter. I forward the details to Fabregat. The town hall next, *tourism*, any hack will do. I get a village number. A local bar. Scribble them down. *How big is the population?*

528.

A village that small? *They'll know him.* Everyone will know him. I call the tourist centre in the town hall and speak to Juan, who agrees that, yes, there is a man who fits that description. *Pedro?*

Is he there now?

Maybe.

Ahora? I ask.

No sé. I don't know. He gets suspicious.

I say I will call back later. Phoning the bar, I hit up a cheery woman with a croaky voice – '*Comó?*' she asks, perplexed. With whom do you want to speak?

I'm trying to reach my uncle. 'His cell phone isn't working. Tell him I want to speak to him urgently. About Natalia.'

'*Un Peet-Tirr Warren. Si. Lo tenemos. El inglés.* The Englishman? I know him. Yes. *Si,*' she adds gently. 'Of course, we will help you. Of course.'

The next morning it's sports bra first, uncomfortable elastic round flesh. Black leggings, baggy long-sleeved shirt, braced for winter, hair tied back, hidden for now. Grab the metro pass, keys, music, stuff it into a pocket, close the door, groggily stumble down the stairs, wipe the sleep from the eyes again, squint, open the inner door, take a second look in the mirror for good measure. This part of the ritual is always a mistake. Face sleep-bloated and worn. Close eyes. A message chimes into my phone. *Notícies? Has esmorzat?* Fabregat wants to know if I have eaten. Ignore reflection, then click, door open, freedom, escape into the road, and *run*. Up past the memorial to the Catalan fallen, the eternally burning flame to the west of the apartment. Salute the gargoyles of Santa Maria del Mar. Street cleaners in their funny green cars brushing the cobbles like mad – and continue running. Up Via Laietana, the great central square of the city – Plaça de Catalunya – just a little bit (mustn't strain the self) into the *Ferrocarriles*. Catch a train, up the mountain to Funicular de Vallvidrera. Vertical. Ride up to the Carretera de las Aigües. Escape train – walk into: dirt, cacti, open earth, sea breeze, sun white bright morning. Tie your shoelace. Now. Breathe. Run. And as you run the city wakes. The sun rises higher in the sky above the sea. *You are alive!* In time with my breath. The sweat stains the small of my back and I feel free of coldness. Light pours over the terracotta rooftops. Dust flies. Thoughts calm.

When I return to my apartment I seat myself at my desk and prepare my work for the day. I have scheduled a call with Bingley to let him know things are moving, carrying forward. At 10 a.m. the phone rings. An unknown number. I pause. Decide. Then pick up. The voice comes like a salutation from the heavens.

'Hello ... ' English syllables I recognize. Precise and clear. 'Peter Warren here.' He pauses. 'I think I might have what you are looking for.'

The Englishman Peter Warren sits on the patio of his country house in the Alpujarra, eighty kilometres south of Granada, up and along the old road that runs past the mass graves of Órgiva and Lanjarón, marked by legends of a holidaying Generalissimo who once bathed in mountain springwater. The wine in Peter Warren's hand is pink, much like his cheeks. Oh, Peter Warren. He is content as a man can be – admiring his Gibraltar Candytuft in his greenhouse (grown from a clipping smuggled in from the littoral flora of the rock) with its many blushing petals, a hazy cloud of violet splayed in concentric circles. He has planted heirloom roses in three varietals: a climbing peach Gloire de Dijon, a bed of Sombreuil, and an Aimée Vibert and they are doing brilliantly, though they will not bloom for many months yet. As he was away for the majority of the last year, Peter Warren hired a local woman from the village, Concha, to come daily and water his plants and she has done a bloody splendid job, has Concha, tending the lavender and the young olive trees at the end of the drive. Peter Warren's patio curves around a 300-year-old pine, which emerges from the ledge below, and shades the house from the late afternoon sun across the valley. The patio is formed of pebbles, arranged in interwoven circles. The house had been his father's, and had only recently received electricity, which pleases Peter Warren. The water that runs from the taps is hard, and the surfaces in the house are positively medieval – but Peter Warren likes these details. The wormwood and fire-blackened rock link him to his father who had loved Spain, and to an old Andalusia near extinction – the land of the Alpujarra, the last strongholds of the Moors and Cante Jondo and by God he loved it. Possibly more than he loved women, possibly more than he loved Barcelona, he loved this house in the mountains so deeply he dreamt of never leaving here and making a vegetable garden and living off the land until he expired in his sleep; whereupon women who adored him in the village would bring his body cured meats and dried flowers as offerings to the dead and the priest would bless him and lay him here in the ground forever.

He leads me quickly into the house. The cedar beams are low. Inside, Peter Warren sits with his back to his desk, turning his chair to face me. I am struck then by how well young Natalia had drawn him. *She was a master.* The desk is a wide slab of oak on metal, circular legs made of old piping, facing the square window cut out of the rock wall of the house and looking into the garden. *Concha, my cleaner.* He nods; through the window I see an old woman opening the cast-iron gate and walk up the cold dirt path to the garden, weaving her way beneath the pine tree.

Sitting with his back to his desk, Peter Warren speaks openly.

'At first I was afraid when you called. I wanted nothing to do with it. Let the past die. Move on. But you can't kill it, can you? I make a point not to answer my phone anyway. When you called again, I thought, damn, this girl is persistent. Then the third, fourth time, and I began to feel guilty.'

Peter's eyes wander to the washerwoman as she gathers a tin watering can in her hand, goes to the old tap to fill the can with water and tends to the icy roses.

'A drink?' he asks me.

Yes, I nod.

Peter Warren returns to the kitchen and pours us two glasses of a sparkling white wine. He takes some dried almonds and cuts a slice of bread with black crust and offers them to me on terracotta plates. He eats slowly. He sits with his back to the desk, where the green Olivetti typewriter of university sleeps solemnly, gathering dust. The sheaf of paper he had placed in its jaws untouched. I feel the noise and darkness of Barcelona fall away from my shoulders with all the satisfaction of a finished thunderstorm.

'I betrayed her.' Peter Warren watches an ant run up to the rim of the terracotta bowl that holds the olives on the wooden table. 'It was not a great betrayal. I did something small, and all the more cruel for that smallness.' Peter Warren wipes his eyes on the back of his hands.

'Don't know what's come over me. Tea is required in moments like this. Sugar?'

I shake my head and thank him. He claps his hands on his knees and stands, his body towering over me.

Peter Warren returns with two steaming cups and sits down beside me on the sofa. He claps me on the knee. 'So,' he says. 'I suppose you'd like to see it?'

'Yes.' Warm liquid slips down my throat.

'Give me five minutes. I've hidden it away somewhere. Didn't want to get it out without company. Brings bad things up.'

That summer, Peter Warren's apartment had been on the fourth floor of a modern brick complex to the north side of Gràcia – west of metro stop Joanic near a florist who specializes in South American orchids. It is small and sparsely decorated. White walls covered by a few theatre posters in black frames, and a remodelled kitchen that had cost him nearly his entire life savings.

Peter's relationship with the young woman now standing in his doorway had been brief – spanning six months, over the autumn and winter of her first year as a trainee actress at the Catalan Institute of Theatre. He is thirteen years older than her. When they met she had been eighteen, stunningly beautiful. (And she remains beautiful: dressed demurely in a grey overcoat, hairpins pull her fringe back, revealing graceful features, gold pendant earrings, the curve of her neck as it dips into the collar of a white lace shirt.)

Peter Warren remembers the date: Monday 23 June. The day before she died.

Natalia Hernández. In the flesh.

Staring at her now, as he had done when they first met, he is filled with a sensation of wonder: he never understood what she saw in him. A British contributor to guidebooks on Spain, Peter Warren spends the bulk of his time composing briefs about restaurants and museums. When not writing, he devotes a great deal of energy to the gym, and an equal number of hours to sunbathing on his balcony. As a consequence, his exceedingly tanned physique is perfect, his chin chiselled, his taste in clothing appropriate and his intellect sharp, if underdeveloped. Three years before she died he'd found Natalia Hernández in a club he was reviewing near his apartment. That night they connected instantly. But like so many things in Peter Warren's life, the love hadn't succeeded.

☽

In the bar of their first encounter, Peter bought Natalia an expensive glass of red wine and a mixed set of starters – assorted *pintxos*, *jamón serrano* on thickly sliced bread, *pan tomàquet*, olives. Later that night, at his place, when they came in from the taxi, he kissed her in the darkness by the mailboxes at the bottom of the stairwell. He kissed her on each floor they walked up, pressing her into the wall, and running his hand up and under the white lace shirt, his fingers straining, reaching for her nipple, tucked under a black bra, the bra she always wore, no padding – thin and cheap, too tight round the edges. The fabric cut into her flesh so that a rich fold spilt out through his fingers, and he ran his hand over this each time she moved.

Things evolved quickly. He loved the smell of her hair, and her youth, the flash of excitement that brought pinkness to her cheeks and lips, the colour of her skin, deep olive, the black depths of her eyes. He loved her age, her suppleness, her softness, it reminded him of being in his early twenties, and brought him strength, confidence, ease.

He took her out to restaurants, to parties, to the theatre, he bought her tickets everywhere, guided her on walking tours of the city, went to her first performances at the Institute, but never introduced her to his friends. She was too young, he told her, he'd find that embarrassing (after all, his friends had known his ex-wife) and the whole thing was so sensitive, so secret, their love should only be between them – Natalia and Peter – artists at large, out on the town.

When they went to the opera, her face was so open and wide that he imagined she was his daughter, and he wanted to hold her to his chest and stroke her hair and tell her that everything was going to be OK, that he was going to be OK, that he'd make it all work with the mortgage and his house and his dependency problems, and that the tropical plant he'd bought from Ikea (she said it was a coconut tree) would survive, even though it had no direct sunlight in the corner of his bedroom, and he never opened the windows – he wanted her to love him in that moment, and he wanted to love her, but not in that ugly untruthful way. Not this time. No. But one morning she found a pearl earring in the sheets. She sat up naked in bed and held it in her hands.

'Who does this belong to?'

'My cleaning lady.'

'Oh,' she said. She put the earring gently on the bedside table, next to his copy of Gaskell's *North and South*. 'You'd better give it to her tomorrow.'

He justified the lying to himself because she was new to the city and needed to learn what it meant to live in an urban hinterland. She needed to learn that you couldn't trust anybody in Barcelona. That it was a city built on secrets. Some of these secrets were so dark and ugly that it wasn't even worth looking for answers, wasn't even worth wanting to know the truth. His life was like that. His decisions were protecting her. Keeping her innocent for as long as possible, before the darkness swallowed her up – as it had swallowed him up, as Barcelona swallowed everyone up. Always had done. For centuries.

When the buzzer rings to his apartment at 14.47 that Monday afternoon Peter Warren does not expect to see her. Her face in front of his is the furthest thing from imaginable in the realm of possibility. Two years have passed of absolute silence between them.

Seven hundred and thirty days of zero communication.

And now?

'Hello, Peter.'

Hello, Peter. So gentle, so demure, so confident. *Hello, Peter* renders him embarrassed, unsure, compromised. His hands shake. A memory flashes into his head. Chocolates in the duty-free zone of Barcelona's airport. The taxi ride back to her unappealing student home. I've brought you these, he said, sheepishly, after a weekend trip away. He presented her with Belgian chocolates, at her door. He'd surprised her. 'I couldn't stop thinking about you.' The memory interrupted his capacity to speak. Overwhelmed him. Subsumed him. At the door to his apartment, today, now, Natalia looks at him, curiously.

'I know I've come at an unusual time.'

'Yes.'

An awkward silence.

'I wasn't sure if you'd still have the same address,' she says.

'Do you want to come up?' he asks, out of politeness.

'No, no, thank you.'

'Doing well, now, aren't you? Haven't been able to get away from your face recently.'

She laughs. 'I hope that's not a bad thing.'

'No. It's good. I like being reminded of how successful you are.'

An off-hand compliment. A grimace.

'I know this is strange, but I'd like you to keep this for me.'

She hands him a crumpled package wrapped in paper.

'Why?'

427

'You're good at keeping secrets, at least for a short while.'

He accepts the package into his hands.

'I can't give it to anybody else,' she says.

'It's been a long time.'

'Yes. Yes it has. So many things have changed.'

He nods. 'Are you happy?'

'Yes . . .' Her voice falters. 'I hope we can see each other more in the future.'

'Yes,' Peter Warren says. 'That would be nice.'

Walking back up the stairs to his flat, Peter feels the sensation of being hit by a truck on a dual carriageway. He is physically attacked. Assaulted. Ill. He might heave or vomit and when he opens the door to his flat and stumbles inside he cannot even muster the strength to make a cup of tea. He falls onto his couch at the centre of the living room and stares at the blank face of his flat-screen TV. He does not turn it on. He sits very still and waits for the storm to pass, holding the brown paper parcel in his hands. But the memories do not leave him. Oh no. Memories inundate Peter Warren. They attack him. Leave him flooded. Broken. Her face, her voice, the tremor in her hands, the slightness of her waist, the tiny mole to the left of her mouth – everything destroys him with a savage pleasure.

'I'd like to take you out to dinner,' he'd said the last time they'd seen each other. That dreaded Sunday in February.

'As a way of apologizing for what has happened between us.' By which he meant his infidelities, his lack of commitment. She'd agreed like a girl in a dream (she was only eighteen to his pronounced thirty-six, he reminded himself, she had no idea what she was doing). And he'd felt comfortable. Like he could get it all back in the bag. Start over. He couldn't believe his luck when she shut the door to her apartment behind her and walked with him out to a restaurant to eat.

'I'd like you to come with me to England,' he said, over dinner, dangling a piece of whitebait on a fork. His hand was shaking. He was trying not to lose control of the fish – not to drop it, not to break her eye contact – maintain calm. He repeated the word 'calm' to himself, but then he remembered that bitch Fiona pulling back the sheets, and how the naked girl beside him had covered her chest with her hands. Of course Natalia hadn't known he was seeing Fiona. Up until that terrible confrontation, his plan (or lack of plan) had gone exceedingly well. Natalia hadn't realized the earring belonged to Fiona, that Fiona even existed, (a triumph of masculine ingenuity in and of itself), let alone was a longstanding lover, someone he couldn't shake off, An obsession. Later, when he smoked a cigarette with Fiona on the balcony by the dead plants, Natalia had come out with all her clothes on, looked at them both and said:

'He isn't worth it. I promise you.'

And she'd left. She'd walked out of the house, leaving him stand-ing there, wrapped in a towel, as Fiona dug her fingernails into his hand. He'd found the whole thing totally out of control. But that didn't stop him from inviting Natalia to dinner that Sunday in February – three weeks later – and asking her the question. Looking at her in the restaurant, he'd been filled with a powerful yearning to kiss her.

Instead he stammered: 'Come with me to London, please, let's start over? Let's leave – I'm a mess, Natalia, I'm a mess without you.'

She stared at him across the salad and white china. Blinked twice. Drank from the glass of cava. He could tell that she was thinking. He wanted her to think. But not to rationalize, he wanted to win her over through an emotional thought process, one in which rationality would logically be put to the side and the heart, that precious, fickle thing, would speak openly.

Maybe she would come with him then.

'Why do you do this?' she asked. 'You already know what the answer is.'

She put her napkin down on the table, stood up, and left.

From that point onward there was no contact.

No emails. No text messages. No phone calls.

Once he had seen her crossing the street in the Raval, and he had shouted her name. She did not turn around, so he chased after her, running down the street until he stopped her, grabbing at her coat sleeve. She had turned to him, and given him such a look of disdain, of disgust, that he could not bring himself to speak. So he let her go. Stood panting on the curb of Carrer de l'Hospital. He watched her walk away.

So why had she chosen him? I ask myself, listening to Peter's story. Perhaps because he was her own secret. That no one would think to look for him? Because he worshipped her? Obeyed her?

In his apartment, Peter Warren unwraps Natalia's package slowly, inspecting its contents. A heavy book. Musty smell. Cracked spine. He turns the book over in his hands. Perhaps she picked it up at one of the dusty libraries of antiquities in the Gothic? One of the backstreets behind the cathedral. On the title page *THE ALCHEMICAL HISTORY OF THINGS* – printed in London in 1855 and complemented by etched illustrations, with a foreword by one Llewellyn Sitwell. She has rebound the book herself, a small issue, cased in calf's leather, cutting blank folia to size, binding period vellum over boards, with gilt borders and titles. The leather is detailed with red and black Moroccan labels, filigree gold leaf, scarlet thread through the spine. Pages trimmed in red. Original endpapers vibrantly marbled. Peter Warren chokes. He feels increasingly nauseous.

Then he remembers that she is performing in a new show at the Theatre of National Liberation. Tag-lined 'An Original Take on Sin' by that ancient director Villafranca. The posters for the production are everywhere. But still. Unease. Yes. There is unease in his stomach. If the twenty-two-year-old Natalia was anything like the eighteen-year-old Natalia, every gesture, every statement was laced with meaning. When he lifts the book off the table, an envelope falls onto the floor. Peter Warren reaches down and picks the envelope up, turning it over in his hands. He tears the letter open with his thumb. Two tickets to the opening night of her performance, and a note that reads:

When the time comes,
you will know what to do.

Peter Warren is puzzled. Maybe she has forgiven him? Maybe her new security means she can trust him again? That she wants him back? Had he never stopped loving her? He wonders how many other people felt that way. How many victims fall in love with her on the stage every single night? She has a power over people that is unearthly, he tells himself, a corrosive, hypnotic beauty. Dangerous. She's bloody dangerous, that's what she is. Peter Warren holds the letter and book in his hands, and experiences a strange dampness welling in the corners of his eyes. And then, without warning, he begins to cry.

I stop beneath an oak tree, settle down into the dust. *Hold the book in your hands.* There is the familiar diagram of the Rex Illuminatus truth machine, heavy lines printed with comfortable precision. The book is divided into sections – the first formed of yellow paper sprinkled with brown dots of mould. The collated writings of Rex Illuminatus. Natalia has undone the stitching and bound her own folios into the core of the 1855 edition of *The Alchemical History of Things.*

The nib of her pen had been metal, and torn in the corner, so that it scratched the stock slightly. Around repeated circular diagrams of the nine-letter alphabet, Natalia has drawn ornate frames of fili-gree leaves, ivy and rose blossoms, interwoven in blue ink, words wrapped in the spiralling skin of a winged snake, now coiling round the outer rim the page, later ending and beginning with the consumption of its tail. There are many drawings, all of which have meaning I am sure, but I do not take the time to analyse, as Fabregat is waiting in the car down the road, and my moment of privacy must be painfully brief. Despite the intensity of her illustrations, the lines of the drawings are not painstakingly deliberate, but light, and swift on the paper, strokes from the pen made with a dextrous speed that catch me in a wave of adrenaline.

For the first time I can see you clearly.

Natalia Hernández.

Exquisite as the finest painting by the greatest master. She has been likened to a renaissance beauty by her critics and extolled as a living work of art by her colleagues. Her lips are plump and red, parting slightly in the middle. Her mouth pulls too much to the sides when she smiles, a lack of symmetry that breaks the golden ratio, but lends her no uncertain charm. Her eyes empty. Skin colder than Persephone. At times it is difficult to look at her, the beholder intoxicated by the markings on her body, her freckles and moles creating a constellation of interest, leading the eye down her check to her neck, to her chest. Her breasts are not full, but round and small. Bones press against her skin, giving her a look of fragility. In repose, it can seem there is barely enough muscle on Natalia Hernández to keep her moving. But this is a deception of the eye. When she works she shakes out her hair before tying it in a tight knot at the back of her neck. She loves the smell of summer storms, the hot moisture on the air. A sky electric and powerful. For a moment I forget anxiety.

To work, to work.

I watch her bend over the draughtsman's table. Her desk filled with jars of pigment. Red mercuric sulphide for vermilion, cinnabar and saffron yellow, an oxidized copper compound for green, lapis lazuli, walnut ink for brown. Hammered gold in leaf. *First there was the rock, and then there was the knife, and after that came everything*, she says to herself, half in a dream. Each tool has a duality, each element a poison: the toxins in her studio, the emulsifiers and thickeners. *Even turpentine can kill a man.* Perish the thought. *Countless pilgrimages here.* Whether in the late darkness of the night, or the early morning. Gum arabic in an alabaster dish. Gouache and sable brushes. The carbon steel of her gilder's blade rests on blue velvet. *Strike the gold leaf with your finger.* She pats gently, then

433

hard, as her mother taught her, forcing the gold to crumble against her fingers. The leaf shatters. She pounds the gold into dust – careful not to rub the powder, adding gum arabic as she goes. Her hands work quickly. *The mixture must not be allowed to dry.*

When the first leaf has lost its sheen, she adds another, tapping it as before. Then a drop of water. She continues for close to an hour, transfixed by the flaking gold, until the battered shell develops a pearl-like lustre. Next: distilled water. She watches as the gum arabic dissolves and gold dust swirls to the surface of the dish. It will set like this overnight, with the liquid removed, and become a base. Hours later she prepares the parchment. The sun rises. She selects a smooth cinnabar pigment, thinned, and dabs lightly at the page, creating a swift under-painting which will guide the gesso and later the placement of the gold shell. Once applied, the shell cannot be removed, else it will smear. She remembers the firm words of her mother. *You must negotiate your space. Set the terms of your design before applying gold. Illumination is performance. The process as ephemeral as a movement across a stage. The form, once cast, could not be recaptured. It is lost. You could not stop and begin anew. No ...* her lines drawn out as combs of light ... *Beauty is precision. Beauty is perfection like a dancer. Perfection has no room for error ...* The tool she has selected is gentle. She applies the gold with the thin tip, avoiding thicker strokes which will crack. A knife in her left hand, a pen in her right. Later she will burnish with a stone. Smooth agate bent in the shape of a dog's tooth.

There is not much more time, she thinks, and prays. *Not much more time until what she has started will be finished, and given out into the world to judge. It is her lasting gift. The most delicate.* Her brush continues working, and as she lays the first lines of gold, she loses herself in the task. On the outer sheet she draws a serpent, followed by a conjoined figure, half man, half monster, in the style of the two-headed Roman god Janus or an Aztec deity. One human profile, cherubic face, dressed in a black frock coat, holds a golden scroll furled like a snail. His forehead is high, chin elegantly bearded, with a thin moustache across his lip, his brow shadowed and melancholy, and his mouth twisted. But this is only half his expression – as his skull and spine are fused to a monster, vastness in pleated mail, a horned bull covered in thick hair from the shoulders up, human chest bare and streaked with tattoos, the face of an ox emblazoned across his chest, and a star at the centre of his forehead. His hand rests in front of him, holding a bloody mass of flesh in balance with the scroll and beneath this the word AUREUS painted in thin red letters and a poem:

> *Beware Flesh-Born-Tongue-Slayer,*
> *Drunk on the Winepress of God*
> *False Watcher at the Gate*
> *I mark murder with his true guise:*
> *Blood heralds his fall like a Light from Heaven*
> *He is the bull dragon.*
> *Goat-Clad Beauty.*

Aureus. I look at the name with a start. *Golden one.* A detail valuable for the inspector, but not for me – even now I am not certain, even now I could be wrong.

Her work is the prelude to a secret. Throw back your head and listen. Fireworks of colour! Heavy incense and raging fires, stone reliefs, the rumble of a subterranean spring. *An extraordinary cacophony of sounds!* Silver moss damp as an old man's moustache.

Abruptly Natalia's illustrations stop. There is a shift I have been waiting for – a hallucination – in a split second I transcend the boundary of the real. Everything I have been seeking comes racing towards me. In the woods, beneath the oak tree, I am a philosopher presented with an ancient orrery, a cartographer surveying a

435

mechanical map of a distant galaxy, for bound into Natalia's copy of *The Alchemical History of Things* rests a set of pages made of membrane. Inside this book she has inserted a single quire of mottled parchment, texture like woven leaves, a dead animal's veins forming a pattern reminiscent of bark. My breath sucks in. I feel the tremors come, the shaking. Within the folds of Natalia's book, amidst the illustrations and thoughts and printed diagrams, the missing pages of the Illuminatis Palimpsest lie as the tomb of an ancient king, sealed into a funereal urn towards the end of the volume, out of sight and tucked away, pages folding into themselves like a dream. The Serpent Papers. My hands tremble as I turn sheets, pulling back the parchment as the wings of a bird. Where before the writing was monastic, ascetic, on this fine quire there is gold. Gold in vast quantities. Redolent, dazzling, burnished gold. Unlike the ordered menagerie, the ruled lines and figures of a liturgical illuminated manuscript, the gold here spurts in chaotic swoops and curves, making a jungle of the palimpsest.

The Illuminatian script is puzzling in an agitated way. *I bring my nose closer. What are the gold letters hiding?* My heart leaps at the sight of milky red impressions, marks of an older hand, the continuing lines of a poem. Much more beautiful than I expected. Suddenly I am terrified. Afraid to touch them. To put my fingers to the sheets of skin, to turn them over. *Will I burn? Will my body be destroyed? Will the voices echo through me?* No. I am my rational, intellectual self. Modern. Unbound. *Turn the leaves over*, I order myself. Mismatched sheets. *One quire, full gathering* – very thin, sheets like tracing paper – through which I have unstitched the binding – a loose thread, finest grain, weaving in and out of the pages ... and the faintest hint, the almost disappeared subtext ... stanzas of a poem, soft smudge of Greek. *Deliciously unknowable.* Above this the alchemist has written in gold:

For Amat, or as he is knowne Ramon Llull, Raimundis Lullius, Raymond Lully in the oulde bookes, I saye the following: it is my owne fault he hath beene robbed of sayntehoode. What I hath done, they saye he hath done. My chymstry, my magick, my philosophie, they hath given it all to him, though they do seek me in secret, robbing me the rights to my artes. I am not of Lully's worlde, but his mere shadowe. I do not holde truck with his religion, and for this they hath persecuted me most crewelly. Once we were freynds. We sought the same answers. We constrewed mirrors seeking the same simbols in fyre and ayre, oyle and bloude. We made wayes of understandyng the cosmos aboute us, a woven tongue for being. His was a ladder to God, leading to the divyne, whereas myne was rooted to the harte, seekyng the divyne spark of man. We practyced the sayme artes, forged the sayme letters, spake the sayme language, though we wrote our thoughts for difrent purposes. Those who hunt me doe mistake us, seeing my worke for his and his worke for myne, they doe give us the sayme name. Illuminatus. But we were not borne one, and we did not dye as one. His worke sought for conversion of the outward world, and so he dyed under the stones of his enymies. I practice my artes for liberation of the soul. To know the essential mater of myselfe, and thereby know others. My choice was Chrysopoeia, the amalgamyng, and so it was I, Rex Illuminatus, who belonged to no one, borne a poore orphan in the rubble of a conquered island . . . It was I who became immortal.

The principal layer of the palimpsest consists of alchemical drawings. Battered down with a stone and sealed with an oil varnish. On the first leaf, inscribed with a steel point and coloured on the vellum is an illustration of a winged snake dressed in glorious detail, encircling an upturned crescent moon on a red shield. On the second leaf, the snake returns, this time appearing crucified on a cross, head impaled by a nail, on the third, a series of snowy mountains leading to a jungle and then a yellow desert formed of the teeming bodies of snakes. Following this, a depiction of a pagan god, a man brandishing his rod around which a bronze serpent coils. The god beats the clouds above his head, but he is hounded by a wraith, a deathly spectre of a skeleton wielding a scythe in raised arms. Death cuts at the god's knees. On the following leaf, a second man, in robes and kingly ruff, surveys a path of gold leading to a palatial temple engulfed in flames; at its centre, amidst the flames, the alchemist has drawn a lone bird, a small nightingale perched on a rose bush. Behind, beasts prowl through dark woods. Dragons and griffons stalk the land. A knife hangs suspended from the clouds. Above this, a winged serpent soars across the sky. The final picture is of a woman holding a book. Beneath, the alchemist has written in clear, pristine Latin:

> 'Tis true without lying, certain and more true that I have encased the writings of the Sibyl in gold and hidden them from her enemies, so that they shall seek and not find, and though circumstance has forced my hand and I have washed the words of her maker, the seed remains in this, its force is above all force – for that which is below is that which is above and what is above is that which is below – and you who shall carry these words in your heart shall do miracles of one thing.

From my wallet I remove a small set of scissors and a blade for cutting paper. There is a way of sewing pages into a book so that they are easily removable, information meant to be collected and relocated. Passed from hand to hand. I make a sharp incision in the binding. *Do it gently. Leave no scars, pull out the connecting thread . . . there, here it comes, easy now.* Made for this precise purpose: to be rescued — lifted out! The leaves pull away like silk. I take a container designed for transporting documents and slip the loose pages into the inner compartment of my bag. I will not give the palimpsest to Fabregat, I will not even show him. I do not want him to know that it exists at all.

Check your book for any marks.

The oak above me smells of ovens and sage. Shale scratches into my legs, I prick my hand on a thorn and suck the blood from my finger, a tiny drop, barely any flavour. *They'll have a field day with this* — I think, snapping it shut. *Preserve your sanity — it's none of your business. Get out of here whole and get out of here quick.* Along the seam of the insert — any incriminating signs of tinkering? *They won't even know to look for it. Take your time. Play the bluff.* I hold the book close to my chest. Dust off my knees. Continue walking down the trail. At the bend in the road before the dirt path reaches the village, I see the car. Parked idly in the dirt curb. Fabregat talking on his mobile phone. His driver eats an apple as he reads the paper. Both men look up as I approach. Fabregat signs off his call.

'Can I see it?'

I hand him the book, freed of its secret burden. *The Alchemical History of Things.* He sniffs. Unimpressed, weight falling against the hood of the car.

'Nothing out of the ordinary? Nothing untoward?' he asks me of Peter.

No. A good man.

Fabregat opens the book, leafs through. He stops at the poem beneath the picture of Aureus and frowns. Looking for clues. Not that he will understand. *That's part of the game*, I want to say. *The game she played with you.* He whistles long and low under his breath. *Disappointed.*

'Cigarette,' he orders in Catalan to the standing policeman behind him. One is offered. A thin trail of smoke weaves up from the burning embers between his fingers. The mountain air cool and clean. The driver gestures to me.

'You want?' Broken English. I shake my head.

'Why doesn't she just name him? Why does she have to be so damn convoluted?' Fabregat swears under his breath as he turns the pages. *Because she didn't want you to solve a murder. She wanted to save a two-thousand-year-old poem. We are working on the pinhead of that decision.*

The policeman watches a goat grazing in the neighbouring field.

'You should wear gloves when you do that,' I remark to Fabregat, reprimanding his broad fingers. 'You'll damage the material.' For a while longer Fabregat doesn't lift his nose from the book. I shade my eyes with my hand. He squints up at me. Satisfied. *Let's go.*

'How close do you think you are?' I ask once we are in the car.

The inspector goes unusually quiet. He leans out the back window as we drive to Granada, air whipping round his ears. Pensive. Waiting for something. The BlackBerry buzzes in his pocket. *An email.* He takes it out and checks it, trying to keep a smile from cracking into the wrinkles around his eyes. It is a genuinely boyish, ebullient grin. Canines burst out. His mouth stretches wide. I ask him what has happened.

'The profiling report on the DNA samples will be coming in this evening. Three of them already match – we've got the blood of each of Las Rosas in there – and the samples will have more to tell. I'm going to pass by the forensics department this evening. Check in with the boys. Get things sorted. Add this –' he taps the book, now safely sealed away – 'to the collection.' He pauses, awkward, about to say something more. A thought retracts.

I look at him quizzically.

'You should go home now,' he says gently. 'I think it would be good for you.'

Is that all? A simple dismissal?

I frown. Unable to control myself.

'You should look after yourself, Nena. Jump on a flight tonight. Surprise that boyfriend of yours.'

I see a door closing. Hear the absoluteness of his tone. There are things waiting for him that he does not want me to belong to. A new phase with no space or time for raving book hunters. Of course it makes sense. My evidence will be controversial. Not even publicly used. Written over. Incorporated into a rational whole with no place for me. *That was always the plan.*

Fine. I set my jaw.

'Senyoreta Stormcloud. You look like you swallowed a lemon. Don't worry so much. You'll get wrinkles early. Look – I already see one growing. If you're not careful you'll end up like me.'

My scowl deepens.

'Of course I'll tell you what happens. It may be a few weeks before there's anything to report. I'm going to nail the bastard properly. Take my time with it. But as soon as we get a match –' he whistles through his teeth – 'you'll never see anything so fast. I'll bring all the shits in, if I have to. Cotton-swab the lot. Tie them up by their ears.'

He reaches out with a paternal hand. I move crossly away. *Don't touch me.*

'But for now . . . I think it's best if we part ways here, Anna. Keep it clean. Wouldn't want you getting mixed up. Overly involved.'

He tries to ease the blow with questions about my work, where I'll head to . . . Perhaps I'd like a ride to the airport? He can get me on a flight tonight – the last one's at 21.55, but they've got earlier options . . . I am angry with myself that I care. Surprised by my own attachment. I was supposed to leave, I was supposed to be in control, to remain aloof. *You're a fool for thinking it mattered.*

'Look, I don't want to beat about the bush with this. I am grateful,' Fabregat says quietly. 'We're closer than we've ever been before – but *imagina't!* I can't have the defence team knowing you had any part in this . . . It would undermine the whole investigation. When we're millimetres – literally – millimetres off.'

Even when I press him he will not tell me more than this. Satisfied, Fabregat hums happily to himself as we leave the mountains for the northbound highway, steamrolling towards Granada airport. He throws his head against the seat rest and shuts his eyes as the car glides down the motorway. *Thoughts elsewhere.* In an instant I am relegated to the libraries and archives, an annotation at the bottom of a forgotten manuscript. I will be an amusing tale at the bar. An oddity rolled out over *pa amb tomàquet* and a *caña. Nena the Circus Act. The bookworm with nosebleeds and hallucinations.*

I push my energy down into my lap. Perhaps I would have shared with him, had he been curious. But now it is painfully apparent that we inhabit separate worlds. I will not be part of this phase of the investigation, which will belong to the serologists and forensic biology departments, to the haemoglobin experts and DNA profilers. It will belong to the police and the court of law, to prosecutors and juries.

Still.

I look at Fabregat. Disappointed.

It was business. Always business.

So you keep quiet, I tell myself. *Leave. Slip away. Just like that. Tonight. Why the hell not? Your things are already packed. He has just given you the out. Disappear like you always wanted.*

I ask for a seven o'clock flight. A car to come and pick me up. Fabregat agrees. All expenses covered. I am legally bound to confidentiality. I will not speak to the press. I will deny all connections to the case. I accept the role of an anonymous informant. I am formal. Contained. As I listen, I envision a box, as the doctors have told me, around my whole body, in which I sit, cross-legged. I am meant to focus on my breath – on silence, protected by this box so that the voices do not come too quickly – but all I can think in my imaginary compartment – all I can think is that they are with me and I will not tell *him.* Deep within my bag, the snaking letters will soon lift themselves off their parchment and wrap round my legs like sweet peas, climbing up and up to my throat shouting: DISCOVERY! FABREGAT! GOLD!

Yes. My tongue tickles. You could turn to him and say:

You and me and Natalia Hernández. Her secret. Ours alone.

You could tell him what you feel. What you read.

But you won't.

My key turns stiffly in the lock to the apartment door on Passeig del Born. I enter the corridor. The simple design of the hallway appeals to my sense of comfort. An obsession with neat lines. After all, stability in personal life – systematic order – these things allow my work to flourish. Order to disorder and back again. I leave my keys in a concave sculpture that doubles as a bowl. For a brief moment I decide to think about nothing. Sit in the emptiness of the unencumbered soul. Take off my shoes in the hall, then socks. Let my feet feel the smooth wood floor. There is time for a cup of tea and a smoke. The car will come soon and whisk me away. I'll come home alone. Quiet and unnoticed, I will slip back into the mountains and evaporate into my studies. The unknown girl at the end of the dirt road. My long duffel suitcase and two black satchels line the corridor, standing to attention like uniformed soldiers. *We'll be ready soon.* I listen to the silence, and sigh deeply. Will it be worth it? The phone interrupts, buzzing loudly in my pocket.

'Hello?'

It is Francesc.

'I've been in an accident.' He says simply. 'I was driving your car – I don't know what happened exactly – someone came up from behind ... they were going so fast, Anna, I can't really remember. They tried to overtake . . . and the next thing I know they've clipped me hard, smashed me right off the edge – I couldn't see the driver, it was all so fast.' He stops. Panting. 'But I'm fine – Anna, I wanted you to know that I'm fine.'

I slump. Unable to process information. I feel dizzy. Light-headed.

'It was a hit and run. They didn't stop. Anna.' His voice breaks.

Standing in the hallway I feel myself disintegrate. The glare of the street lamps invades my shuttered windows.

I'll be with you soon, I tell him. Tongue-tied. *I'm coming home. A few hours away, that's all I am – I'll be there –* and what I want to say I will save for later. Sirens next. A woman's voice – the call snuffs out. I stare at the dull phone in my hand. *It was meant for you.* A dreadful certainty. Signs I have ignored suddenly become actions. I stand paralysed. Unable to respond.

And then I hear it. A presence in the apartment like a waiting. I had not noticed it before. The hair on the back of my neck rises. '*Hola?*' I call. Thinking it may be the landlord. *He has left flowers, after all – or perhaps it is his cleaner?* I walk forward leaving my phone in the corridor with the keys. There is no response. Silence. I wait a minute and listen. Breathe more easily. *It was nothing . . . Just your imagination. You should go out, go for a walk. You are hyped on adrena-line.* Silence again – and then I locate my discomfort – a feeling of cleanliness in the room. Someone has washed their hands. I stand facing the sink. Study the bubbles on the soap.

Recently.

Pulling the crumpled Serpent Papers out of my bag, I open the second drawer in the kitchen island, and shove them beneath a set of napkins. Close the drawer quickly. *No one is taking this from me.* I walk forward to the bedroom, I call out again – *Hello?* Determined to banish my ghost.

Then stop.

Looking down at my feet. At the centre of the living-room floor, initially obscured by the kitchen island and the low Ikea coffee table, lies a fat, dead bird. A large bellied street pigeon, purple and grey, head twisted round, feathers puffed out, vacant bird eyes gazing at me. Ribs snapped open by a sharp blade, the entrails neatly arranged in a shape of a star on the hardwood floor. It reminds me of something I have seen a cat drag in. A creature played with. Dismantled. Organs dark bluish red. Left out for beloveds.

Retrospectively I hear – perhaps in memory alone – a short sharp breath. But mostly I remember the pain. A wailing crack at the side of my head, hands round my throat. As to my sanity? A roar like the raging of a bull between my ears – my own scream silenced, pounding against my face. A gasping lurch for air.

Human fluids, a crease in the sheets where a body has pressed into me. Ants crawl over my breasts. *They want to eat my lungs.* I am struggling to breathe – my chest breaking – and for all I feel I cannot open my eyes – *Please! Let me wake!* But no sound – no sound emerges. Empty as a hollow seed. I reach to my mouth, but where lips once were, black scabs, pus mountains, leading from my nose over boils of broken skin. No lips where lips once were. No tongue to chastise or kiss! A tooth wriggles into my hand and I stare at the shape of my canine, its hard pronged tail – I choke, I cry – *Let me wake.* Like thunder I turn towards the pillow.

I smell him. Cologne, clean and bright. Rose soap. My tongue! My tongue! *Intact!* Hot rivers down my cheeks. I choke – and hear myself choking and choke harder – moving my feet to see if they make sounds – and scrape they do against the sheets. *A dream.* My legs bare white candles – and then nakedness. Nakedness consumes my groin – the base entirety of my form – the vulnerable damp between legs – my heart beats louder – *Wake up! Wake up!* Whiplash round my forehead, an ache in my pelvis – mind dozy, confused – but! With certainty comes the pain. *This is no dream.* I shiver. Panic rising. On the side of my bed, someone has left a robe. Fish swim against the darkness, the cloth catching on the dryness of pricked

447

goose-bumps. *Where am I?* I pull myself up — knees into my chest, shaking — *You have nothing!* I choke — *You can't remember anything. Gather yourself.* I scan the shadows, looking for a form, and then, cumbersome, sight fogged by fear, the lightning rod of pain — drift towards the window before the bed — *Can you climb out?* My hands on the smoked glass leave warm impressions — *No. Too high — you'll break your legs — you'll fall. You have no shoes!* And the city? Ripped away. A thick indigo haze — woods beyond the drive lined with iron-cast lamps, layered with green glass, suspended against the silhouette of bare trees. Fairy lights woven from branch to branch, connecting Moroccan metal work. I can see the opposing side of the house, looping around a central square — built of stone, in the traditional Catalan style, an old manor house, blue urns line the steps, glazed a rich aquamarine, planted with miniature lemon trees. Laden with thorns and unripe fruit. A single lamp hangs from a fixture beneath the tree at the centre of the drive — I see the outline of a bench, the lamps' metalwork casting patterns of light on gravel. My vision hazy, my hearing muffled — *Is that a moaning that I hear? Like a baying at the moon — a male voice, deep and full-throated?*

I am alone.

The hinge behind me creaks, an internal breeze from some open window deep within rushing towards my bareness. I turn and watch the door sway, back and forth, ever so slightly, as if the room were breathing. A dozy tranquillity grips me, a false calm, a dullness between my ears — and instead of moving, I listen — *is that music? Music from the ground floor?* The purple notes of a record player and a man's voice on the radio — Spanish and lilting.

I follow the sounds, each step a momentous effort, my feet recoiling from the cold tiles, the rich carpeted floor, following the black corridor to the electric orange glow emanating from stairs, swirling down and down and down.

Before I reach the door I see him.

A figure striding, animal and handsome, white shirt and gym trousers, hands ruffling wet hair with a towel. *He has been exercising.* With an arm across the bottom of the stairs, he blocks my way. Looks me up and down. Smiles.

'Can I offer you a glass of wine?' he asks.

My vision spins – *You recognize that voice.* Music from some ethereal source ... Miles Davis drifting through the house like wind. In the entryway, an exquisite reproduction of the Black Virgin of Montserrat, fat baby perched on her lap, golden orb clutched in her right hand. A vase of fresh roses, pink and red, on a Victorian table inlaid with ivory and green glass. Every few feet along the black panelled corridor leading to the kitchen, there is a space cut into the wood. Displays for a growing art collection. A silver-plated foil from the Spanish Conquest mounted vertically on the wall, an Etruscan in flowing robes, a bust of Shakespeare. He leads the way swiftly.

'My latest acquisition,' looking over his shoulder, 'is a small sketch of Picasso's ... Made while he was in Paris, the first time of course. Haven't found the right place for it yet – but as soon as it's on the wall ... You have to come back around and I'll show you. Take a proper tour of the house.' I keep my gaze fixed ahead. The kitchen glows like a fire at the end of the long hallway, doors leading to unknown quarters remain firmly closed, as this man walks with a spring in his step.

My mind locks into gear – Old Provençal, *Auriol.* Medieval Latin, *Oryolus – from the golden – Aureus. Painfully obvious.*

'I'm cooking a stew. A lamb from the neighbouring farm.'

My nostrils flare with the smell of red wine, rosemary, pepper.

'It's a very slow process. You have to wait for the meat to fall from the bones, but then it melts in your mouth.' He takes the lid from the pot and stirs the contents slowly.

'I find cooking very calming ... especially after what has happened. It helps to have a distraction ... Try this.' Oriol dips a spoon into the bubbling stew on the stovetop. He leans across to me, holding the spoon out, with a hand beneath to catch the drops. The flavours are rich and full. His fingers nearly touch my lips.

'Fresh oregano makes all the difference. I'm sorry if you're not comfortable.'

Oriol catches my eye.

'Wine then. Red? White? What would you like? Sit.'

I settle myself into the barstool. *Again this strange, dozy acceptance. My mouth fogs around his name – has he bewitched me? Hypnotized or drugged? A dull ache pooling between my legs. Do not think – no, do not think about what could have happened –* I right myself. Both hands on the countertop. *Steady.* Oriol pours two glasses of Rioja, lifting the first to his mouth and inhaling.

'A very pungent bottle. Woody. Reminds me of raspberries. Now –' he smiles, taking me in with his breath – 'I'm ready! You may ask me anything you want. For this evening I'm yours.' Oriol strides across the kitchen to open French windows leading into the garden. *There is nothing I want to ask.* The cold night air flows in. 'Do you hear that?' Oriol's voice lilting. 'You can hear the noises of the forest – I love how loud this stillness is . . . There is nothing louder than the silence of my woods, if you listen closely enough! There is no one for miles, *Querida*.'

Obedient, I shut my eyes and listen for the call of the nightingale, the rustle of the fox, snort of the wild boar. Bats drink from the water of Oriol's fountain, dipping into and out of the sky, and the smell of pine from the garden pervades everything, a thick heady perfume, lavender and thyme, grown fresh in the garden, marrying the earthy aroma wafting from a bowl of pine needles Oriol keeps in the kitchen. He shuts the doors behind him and drifts back towards the stove. He plucks a tomato, brown and overripe, from the wicker basket on the kitchen counter, and slices it through the middle with a knife. He rips two chunks of bread from the baguette he had purchased in town for dinner and toasts it on a metal sheet placed over the open flames of the stove. Next he cracks a garlic clove from its bunch, cutting the end with his knife before prying away the papery skin. My nose tingles with the grease of garlic. Oriol smiles, bending his head down to the table to breathe a deep, all-encompassing scent. When the bread is finished he rubs it with the raw clove, before crushing the tomato and smearing its juices onto the white flesh of the bread, black at the edges.

'A little snack to keep you going,' Oriol says, handing me a piece of blackened bread. 'I'm glad you've come. I wanted to show you,' he says, drying his hands on a dish-towel, 'what I do.' His eyes green-gold and open. 'Would you allow me to share something personal? Something so personal I have never shared it with anyone before?'

I nod.

'I made a copy of your keys, by the way. The night I let you inside. Hope you don't mind.'

His face parts into a beneficent smile.

'As soon as I finish this I'll take you to my studio.' His gaze rests gently on my hands. 'I think you'll find it very special. Very informative. You must understand. What I do, not everyone understands. Above all else, it is an art form. It is an art. I'm here to talk. I want to know how far you've got. What you've discovered. It's important that we are clear about these kinds of tragedies.'

A little rush of energy bursts at the base of my spine.

'You have an open face. Very frank. Honest. Beautiful, really.'

A sliver of heat ripples from my neck up onto my cheeks. Oriol comes towards me, making a dramatic sweep through the air with his hands, as if he were opening a door to another universe. 'After tonight I think I may even be in love with you – but I'll show you everything. All her secrets. You'll see it through her eyes. That's important as a writer, isn't it?'

I nod. He whispers very close to my ear.

'Natalia enjoyed spending time here.'

His mouth near to my skin. Then he touches my neck with his hand, brushing me with such rapidity I barely realize he had moved. My breath quickens.

'You had an ant below your ear.' I watch him crush something black between his fingers, which he then flicks into the air. Very lightly he touches my skin, hooking his finger into the silk along my neckline; he pulls the cloth down, cupping my breast with his hand. His eyes rest on my nipple, hard against the cold. 'Such beauty,' he whispers before catching himself. A pounding thunder between my ears, a rising, choking rock of fear, up and up in my throat – I have no control of my body as he caresses me, his eyes roaming over my shoulder, his breath tightening on the lines of my neck – suddenly he turns.

'She loved the gardens. The azaleas were her favourites. We used to sit on the veranda and run our lines overlooking the flowers.' He pulls away and walks to the window. When he lifts his face his eyes are filled with tears. Oriol points to the garden. 'I can show you, if you like, where she used to work when she stayed here.' He wipes his eyes with the back of his hand. 'Please excuse me,' he says. 'The onions are very strong.'

His face smooth as he returns to the central countertop in the kitchen. He rests both hands out on the wood, splaying his thick fingers wide, then takes up a knife and slices a hunk of cured meat, thin strips he arranges elegantly on an Andalusian plate. My eyes scan the walls behind him. Blue castles and yellow fields.

'I have a secret. Would you like to know?' He laughs. 'You're the only guest tonight. Forgive me.'

I hesitate, he continues talking.

'I thought – Oriol? Who would you like to spend time with? The girl who has come to recover Natalia? The world is such a dangerous place, I would like to keep you safe.'

His eyes linger on me. He does not say the words but I feel him thinking.

'Where's the bathroom?' I ask.

Hand fixed to the base of my spine.

'Cover yourself,' he whispers. 'It's cold. First door on your left.'

I walk in a daze, shut the door, perching on the enamel toilet seat, head in my hands. Time slows. I look up – focusing on a blur left of the bathroom sink . . . a cigarette pack on white enamel – *American Spirits* – I reach out – turn the object over – *So light. I'm slow, what has he put into me?* Don't wait. I feel my breath panicking, crouched on the toilet seat, a wetness between my thighs, my bowels shake and discharge. An ornate mirror and a bowl of potpourri on the marble surface. Nausea rocks at the base of my stomach, my hair dishevelled, a dark blue thumbprint on my neck – a welt like an egg on my fore-head – my lip is split – *don't look* – I think – the dull aches, the throbbing, the pain beneath the fog of this – there are two firm knocks on the bathroom door. My heart races. *Clear as a bell.*

'Are you alright in there?' Oriol asks.

He knocks again, rattles the door handle. Arrange my hair – the key turns in the lock from the outside – Oriol is standing outside the bathroom door. He stares directly into my eyes.

'What were you planning to do in there?'

'Nothing.'

He takes my hand, leads me away, back to the kitchen, the hot stove.

'What have you discovered?'

My temper flares.

'A mix of things.'

'You've finished?' he asks, curious.

'Yes.'

'You were about to go home. When?'

'Tonight.'

'Why?' He pauses. 'Have you found what you're looking for?'

'Yes.'

'Anything *original*?'

'A name.'

'Oh really?'

'*Aureus.*'

'Aureus?' He scowls. 'Means nothing to anybody else.'

'I found a book.'

Oriol picks up the knife beside the cutting board.

'What book?'

'A book she hid.'

Oriol turns the knife in his hand. He sighs once. Deeply. Calculating something. 'She was an artist,' he murmurs. Steam clings to the clear glass lid of the stew. Flames lick the steel pot. Oriol frowns. His hands drop to his side. He goes to the sink. Smiles. 'Everything happens for a reason. She has led you to me.'

I pause, uncertain.

'Best not say anything yet,' he says. 'Such a shame that it had to come to this.'

The water very hot, near scalding. Cutting knife resting on the marble counter beside the sink. His fingers blush pink from the heat. He cleans his cuticles first, pushing back the flesh from his nails, then takes up the knife left limp on the side of the sink and returns to slicing his *fuet*, irregular cuts on a wooden board. Suddenly he stops. He lifts his face to heaven, closes his eyes and mumbles. A prayer? A word of warning? What happens next comes so quickly I barely remember the beginning of the movement. With the speed of a swordsman, Oriol takes the knife and slams the blade through the fingers of my outstretched hand, pinning me to the table. The blade rips through the web of flesh joining my thumb and index finger so cleanly I don't feel any pain – the shock is so great.

Behind him on the stove, the lamb stew bubbles, an open garlic bunch, skin cracked, displays its white flesh to the kitchen.

'Does it make you feel alive? I find pain like that — well ... profound.' The pounding in my head clears.

Oriol takes the knife out of my hand. He examines the blood on the blade.

'I want to know your impulses, your motivations, your desires,' Oriol continues. The smells from the stew are sweet. Sticky and warm. Bouquet of Rioja marrying rosemary.

'What do you want? What did you come for? I want to learn from you.'

Sing-song, playful. I do not respond, feeling the terrible sharp pain in my hand.

In the confusion I see him twofold — a sink where he runs the water hot — my vision sways — the water is running so hot it's scalding. The flesh of his hands turns pink and raw, and yet he keeps them there, scrubbing his fingernails. The soapsuds thick on his hands. *Witness my knife's sharp point.* He looks into the mirror. Smoothes back his hair. His lips part. They are fine and strong. Above him he can hear the music. The tones of techno-grunge. European house. He keeps time with his foot on the tiles. Dries his hands on a towel. Studies his features. There is no doubt in his mind. The players take their places. The river runs its course. And so the thing they had started would come to an end.

How silent is this town! Ho! Murder! Murder! What may you be? Are you of good or evil?

The stones beneath me are very cold and quiet. The ground slopes gently where I rest. I can feel the cement cold underneath me. A pool of dampness wells around my hair in the dark, and I wonder if the clouds will part and I will see the lights of the stars. A dog barks somewhere distant. But not before the horror grips me, and I sway. A hand touching — a hand caressing — I feel a dampness on the place where he entered, a mouth, a tongue — he is tasting the life of me — until, sharp, the pain turns like a screw.

It is not real. In the living room he asks her to wait. She is looking at me. A stranger. *Don't speak,* she says. Alone. I struggle to stand. *Can you help me?* When he comes in, he wears a mask made of burnt leather, thick nostrils folded out over his face. Small slits for eyes.

The mask ties round his head with a buckle, a metal clash against his hair, and ends above the lower lip of his mouth, so that his chin and jaw are visible, shaved and clean. He goes shirtless. *I wanted to show you what I do.* Naked from the waist up, and about his loins, the thin jeans he had worn in town for the night. He will not use them again. He gives the girl a knife and asks her to dip into the blood in a bowl and taste it. First she refuses.

A sacrifice. I found her yesterday. And kept her waiting. For you.

The girl looks at me. *Before we begin.* Life has already gone out of her. He hits her across the back of her head where her hair will hide the bruise, smashing her face down into the bowl, so that her nose touches the blood. When she lifts her face, and he sees her eyes, he sobs, and apologizes. Then he takes her away. I see him from the kitchen, by the roses and chrysanthemums, dragging the girl by her hair. She stumbles down the steps, calling out, *Stop! Stop!* He lifts his head. Smiles back at me. Through the glass.

You can have her if you like.

She's yours if you want her.

He shows me to the door.

See how far you can run.

The girl convulsing. She sobs again.

The forest, we will be safe in the forest.

I take her hand.

Now we are running, running over the grass, past the fountain.

He emerges from the open French windows, aims the gun and fires once. The girl falls – like a ghost felled in the forest, blood and fragments of bones spurt from her head, and over into the black forest she goes, white limbs uprooted, bare and naked as I watch.

I am paralysed. *A deer.* Drunk on horror. I cannot move. *Is she alive?* I sink to my knees. *Are you alive?* Trying to put the pieces of her back together. *I feel him hunting me.* Still wearing his mask, he takes the gun and presses the barrel into my breast, mashing down the flesh. *Leave her,* he snarls. *I wanted you to see what I do.* With his other hand he caresses my ear.

Vomit rises.

This is a nightmare, this is a dream.

It is not real.

Past, present, future. I do not know where I am. If I am watching through Natalia's eyes or my own, or all their eyes. I have exited my body.

I look back but cannot see her. The mask reaches me. I am hallucinating. There is no girl. The blood is my own.

'My darling? Don't you understand?'

He whispers, kissing my neck.

'She was a witch. She was a witch. *Querida.*'

The leather of his mask hard against my skull. 'Don't you understand, my darling, what I am giving you? All that you have asked for I have given you.'

Hard against my cheek, his breath snags against my mouth. There is no point in screaming.

'Come.'

He shouts, pulling my shoulder.

Lifting me up from the ground, he brings his masked face closer.

I am weak.

I am a monster.

'Come!'

That familiar tolling of a bell.

'I could smell it on you.' He drags me panting through the woods. 'It's a scent like camphor and oil, they taught me to smell – a *witch* reeks!'

Twigs crack beneath my feet, the thorns of a bramble rip

457

through my skin, I fall and stumble on the rocks, crashing onto my knees.

I feel the silk scrape away from my chest, he is pulling me by the hands and wrists, the sash falls to the side, and I am naked and terrified.

Deeper we go into the forest, the trees rise up around us and groan, their branches hiding their faces, tangling in the dark, they pull at my skin, the wild boar rushes through the underbrush, following our path, hungry for blood, and the fox watches us from the sidelines, ever curious.

I shout and hurl a rock at the violator, he pulls at my wrist harder until we reach a clearing, too dark for me to discern, I see only that the thorns and trees part and my knees collapse onto gravel as the fear chokes in my throat and I gag on my heart beating in my mouth.

The forest opens. Moonlight streaming into the clearing and between my horror and my fear I catch the flashes of enormous statues; ascending, he drags me towards the carved mouth of a monster, the face of a Titan roaring from a cliff, as the mountain rises above the forest; before me a lake, on which the moonlight glints, flanked by two marble nymphs attacked by stone hunting dogs in noble regalia.

The women's bodies twist and turn away from the animals, which hound at their legs and arms, as he drags me forward, down the path that cuts across the lake to the mouth of the giant, on whose forehead I see, by the light of the moon, a mighty cross and then?

I wake in an enclosed room, cave-like, without windows, marked by black ornamental marble, the lower walls covered in shelves of strange jars. The smell is one of damp soil, water trickling somewhere – water dripping from an underground source. The light is dim round the edges of the room, the focal point of illumination comes from a single hanging chandelier. A dull throbbing in both my hands, followed by a sharp jolt of pain. I cannot bring myself to look down.

'My father put in the modern amenities in 1969. Lighting, electricity.'

Oriol removes his mask. His hair combed to one side. Tawny curls kiss his ears. On his chest a clean white shirt, loose over his collar. Muscles perfect. He is perfection.

About his neck he wears a golden chain, a crest, black cross and crown, flanked by branch and sword. Behind him, an extraordinary, ornamental façade, a baroque devotional, dark metal forms the crucifixion, lit by candles, the crown of thorns weeps behind him.

Above Oriol's head, the dove of the Holy Spirit and a sun-explosion of gold, which joins the columns of marble and splays out into the room. Marble poison black, as are the rock walls. *A sheet of stalactite?*

My vision blurs.

I look up. My breath loud at my temples.

Chest expanding and collapsing. Veins bulging in my wrists, as the blood flows from my brain into the ground, again, before the pain. Whiplash round. Eyes focus and diffuse. *These walls are painted* – my God – *they are even older than the gold* – *murals* – *there are paintings on the walls, swirling shadows at the edges of the light.*

'So?' he asks, very pleased. 'What do you think?'

Against the black cave, shelves made of ornamental wood and red metal. Stacks of leather-bound books. Beneath the dim light of a chandelier, a marble table where instruments have been laid out. I am pulled back into my body by shooting pain. A burning sensation at the palm of my hands, a raw throbbing. A series of blades. Handles of antler and ivory. Two boning knives and an ornamental razor, beside an open book clean on the marble – *all clean* – *no sign of blood. But there are grooves in the rock. A well at the centre.*

Before me – a single clear jar filled with a yellow liquid. Labelled and sealed with a metal cap. White cloth folded behind it, alongside an ornamental tabernacle and a bowl of water.

I hear Oriol's breath slow. He is an enigmatic beauty.

459

'What do you see?'

My mouth dries.

A heaving sensation in my chest – *choke back the rage* – he has painted red shapes on my hands – a cross – my vision tightens. Flesh peeled to the side, all swollen. *A serpent* – he has carved the shape on my left palm, splitting open my flesh, blood dribbles down my fingers onto the floor – pooling on the tiles – revulsion wells in my throat. A gaping hole in the other.

'I have marked you appropriate to what you are.'

His eyes rise to the roof.

'You are in the Sacred Chapel of the Order Dedicated to the Eradication of Heresy and Witchcraft, the Sacred Chapel belonging to my family.' He points to the words written across the ceiling of the cave – *Arise Lord and Judge thine own Cause and dissipate the enemies of faith.* 'It is an honour for you to be here.'

'Why are you telling me this?'

The longer you can keep him talking – but pain dulls the senses. The wounds sting. He walks to the wall beside the baroque chapel.

'What I do is very simple. When we are finished I will show you your tongue, you will sleep. I will wash you and clean you, and then tongueless I will ask you to repent. When you die you will be guaranteed a path to heaven – assuming you believe in that stuff. The sacrifice of your evil will have been made in the shape of your tongue. However ...' He flicks on a light that runs around the outer perimeter of the cave ceiling. 'I want you to understand before we begin. Nothing should be a surprise.'

My eyes adjust to the light, sharpening on the objects – his macabre perversion of scientific methodology.

Oriol strides to the shelves. What I thought were the spines of books are jars – stacks and stacks of jars, uniform, fifteen centimetres in height and ten across, the fluids contained in them of varying colours, in each a mass of brown and pink mud, like a ball of muscle – pain erupts in me – panic swelling in my nerves, the animal pounding at my temples – *calm please be calm.*

Don't let him see!

'Your tongue will join a collection of witch *llenguas* dating back to 1851 when my forefathers perfected the formalin solution I still use today. Simple really. The collection is dated and monitored, every tongue is labelled as you can see here.'

He takes a jar in his hand and holds it up to the light, examining its contents.

'This one was pretty. Rare.'

He meets my gaze directly.

'You will have appropriate company.'

'Do you keep them all?'

'Yes, yes, yes.'

He waves his hand dismissively, returning the jar to its shelf.

'Safely preserved. You will see our whole history here – we have collected the tongues of heretics since 1244 ... Once our glorious and great acts of spiritual cleansing were public affairs – they were theatre. They were spectacle. My ancestors lived them as artists, performing with pomp and grandeur the greatest of sacrifices, for we were purged with the bodies, and we maintained the strength of our heritage by the ritual communion with God. The space is quite opulent. Very beautiful. In 1780, my family received an artist from the court to paint our own basilica of the faithful with our version of the Pentecost. The result is a true work of art. Look up! Have you ever seen such craftsmanship?' The fresco on the ceiling depicts St Dominic seated in a Spanish court, enthroned above a row of dignitaries; before him, Inquisition functionaries, and then military brigades which move a row of convicted heretics towards a fire to be burnt, while on the stakes two victims already meet their fate. Above the heretics the artist has painted rotten tongues similar to those imagined at the Eucharist – while above St Dominic a golden drop of fire rages.

'The fresco is part of my heritage. The tongues of fire represent our immortal Inquisitional language. We seek out the speakers of the devil's craft, and we take their power. If a witch's tongue is buried in the ground, she is reborn.'

He sighs, relaxes in his chair.

'I like you, Anna.'

I wince when he uses my name. *It does not belong to you.* 'You have a good character. Human reaction, if genuine, can be directed – there's always a pulse. You can read it like a signature. Character. It defines how we act. What we do. Natalia Hernández was fickle. I made her famous ... immortal ... but in the end ... in the end she hated me for it. I gave her the most profound gift. But what did she do with this treasured object? She tossed it back into the hands of the police, as if I were trash. She wrote them letters. I don't know how long for, after all I – I shared everything with her,' Oriol snarls, hunching his shoulders like the hackles of a dog. 'Imagine what that does to a man, betrayal of that kind? It exposes your soul. Leaves you naked in the wilderness. Alone. Do you understand loneliness?'

Oriol edges closer.

'There is nothing dirtier than taking your own life.'

He spits at me.

'As a phenomenon? It weakens the spirit. It impairs judgement – I know. The mistakes. The uncleanliness – but I finished her. No one suspected me – involving a stranger was genius. Theatrical genius.'

Oriol exhales, leaning against the table, caressing the air.

'I hated myself for months. I am after all human – sinful – I crave diversion – *the performance* – the stagecraft. Imagine my melancholy; in the theatre I so often repeated violent actions, without the satisfaction of living them.'

With all the majesty of the consummate thespian, Oriol crosses himself twice and opens his arms wide.

'Let the performance begin!'

He shouts.

'*God! Forgive me, but I desire company – as Adam yearned for Eve – Give me someone who could understand!* So I prayed. And God? Always mysterious, forever testing me! He sent you. *Witch.* No! Do not faint. Listen! Lift your face when I speak to you. Woman! I have brought you here to understand and then send you to your maker – below ground, this is the gateway to your return. It is my duty to stamp out heresy, it is the single greatest struggle which now remains to man, the refutation of those heresies which have sprung up in our own day – and introduced confusion! Great confusion! For it seems expedient that we, making an onslaught upon the opinion which constitutes the prime source of contemporary evil, should prove what are the originating principles of this heresy, in order that its offshoots, becoming a matter of general notoriety, may be made the object of universal scorn. And then – if silenced, burnt, destroyed, we will have played a role in ensuring that they should be *forgotten.*' Zeal glistens on his forehead.

'Have you ever studied the muscles of a tongue or given thought to its power? Our soul rests in our hearts, but language comes most often from the larynx, embodied by the tongue. Each one is perfect, every muscle pure – have you ever seen a human tongue?'

I shake my head.

'I will show you yours.'

'How many have you seen?'

He pauses. 'Of my own, twenty-three. Of others – well . . .'

He grins, gesturing to the shelves.

'I have a wealth of resource. I am the sole collector. The last custodian. One hundred and seventy-nine witches. I'm proud to say I have been the most effective.'

He moves closer to the knives on the table.

'And Natalia?' I ask, switching tack. *How far to the door? He hasn't tied me down.* 'Did you not love her?'

Oriol's face darkens, his eyes swell.

'Don't ask me that.'

'But I was certain you loved her – she writes that you loved her, and that she – Oriol – that she loved you?'

Oriol picks up a knife from the table.

'Yes,' he whispers. 'But she betrayed me.'

He bends his head as if to pray, focusing his eyes on the knife he holds in the palm of his hand. My wounds throb. 'Which one?' he asks me, gesturing at the table. 'Which appeals to your taste? This one is good for pricking – this the sharpest, the cleanest – this the most effective – this the slowest, the most laborious.' He picks the jar off the table – holds it up to the light before my eyes, the colourless solution glints like gold. 'Your formalin is already prepared. Your tongue goes in here. But only for a week. I use formaldehyde to lock the tissues in the muscle. Every tongue is unique and I strive to preserve the details.' He opens the jar, holding the fumes beneath my nose, a sharp burning sensation in my nostrils – I gag. 'The liquid is toxic. Once your tongue has set I will rinse it with water. I will hang it and drain it and store it in alcohol with the complete collection.'

He places the jar, open, on the table and shows me the ornamental blade with the antler handle.

'When did you learn?' I ask.

'When I was very young. A boy.' Oriol comes closer, trailing his finger along my cheek. 'Do you understand? I find you more beautiful than the finest ballet. How you will move. How the body responds to pain.'

He picks the smallest boning knife off the table, idly, toying with it in his hand. Gently he watches me – lips open, serene.

'I'll make the choices for you,' he says, pushing the knife into the flesh of my knee; the pain mounts, he pushes the knife edge along the fat of my thighs and looks up beyond my legs, into the dark shadows.

'It is good that you don't fight.'

Oriol breathes deeper.

'You are an enlightened woman ...' His hands move up my thighs, edging closer and closer to my pelvis. 'You will understand that tongues are power – but people? People abuse their instruments. They sully them – they darken them. Women seek the forbidden languages, the devil's language, like all the fallen, you eat from the tree of knowledge and learn a false language – and so your gift is forcibly removed; as God struck the Serpent dumb, I shall do the same to you.' His hands creep higher – his lips close to my ear, breath moist on my neck. 'Women have two mouths – both easily seduced.'

I close my eyes and let him smell me, let him kiss me – and summoning my courage, *wait*, his hands tender, *wait*, I shift my weight towards him very slowly, I reach with my hand and touch his hair. He sighs like a child and moans softly, running my fingers through his hair, he breathes deeper, the cold pressure of his knife against my thigh pushing harder, persistent, calm, soon he'll break the flesh – it is a dance, one he has practised – I let him enter the trance slowly – overwhelmed by pain, I slump forward, my hand reaching down his back, towards the table, straining, ever so gently – until there! I am there! My fingers straining, the glass is mine! The searing rage of my wounded palm burns harder but it is mine! Raising my arm above his head I pause, muscles tense: *Let him lift his face!* Oriol looks up as I bring the jar crashing down with all the strength in the world, onto the Roman chiselled one, the Siren, the Botticelli Angel of Death – those warm and luminous eyes – shattering the glass on his forehead – he roars! The smell is overpowering – the yellow liquid burns my hands – his blood runs with formalin as he jerks backward – the fluids roll into his pupils, the gas rises, his hands go immediately to his eyes – the knife clatters to the ground. His body topples, he roars again, one hand to his eyes and lunges at me, desperate, eyes stuck shut with the milky liquid, I scrape the knife from the floor and lunge away from him, not waiting to help as he rights himself, *run*, leaping out of my chair! Adrenaline drives me forward. I veer down the passage, and I hear a crash, and footsteps pounding after me, stumbling, unsure, but faster! Faster! The fool! The fool! There is not a millisecond of doubt as I run with the weight of the fear against my chest! Desperate for the night I run, for the dark mouth of the cave, driven to the glow of moonlight, searching for an exit as I careen through the curving tunnel I run! I run like hell, lungs yearning for the clean air, the cold night air, my bare feet skidding on damp stone, feeling my way through the tunnel, the cold pressure of fear against my chest, not thinking of the blood, not thinking of the pain – the forest throws up her arms to me – and – No! I do not turn back! I do not look to see the mouth of the cave or if that beast has followed me, though I can hear his breath behind me – I am certain – so faster I run, past the statues, the fountains, across the lake and into the forest I go, pushing into the dark woods, breaking the branches of trees! Now! Sirens! The whirling scream of sirens! I run faster, following the sounds, the crunch of footsteps and the swaying lights, barking dogs attack the forest as I stumble towards the lights! Then – THWAAACK like a bullwhip! Echoing! Careening off stone edges! An explosive ear-cracking barrel-of-a-gun cry!

A singular-definitive-death-whoop shrieking into the forest!

The moon reels. A flutter of wings roars from their nests as I reach the moving shadows and their lights, the ravenous bloodhounds, Fabregat's wolf face stern before the black-coated army – the heavy boots snapping twigs – here come the dogs baying! Yapping! Blood wet against my chest – I keep my secret, stumbling towards them sobbing, holding up my hands. The colour drains from their cheeks.

EPILOGUE

ISLAND

Boat tickets to Mallorca in winter are not expensive. From Barcelona you can get to the island for twenty euros on a good day. All that I have left on myself is the pain in my hands. A low throbbing hum, a sharp needle through my palm, fingers swollen. Listless and heavy. They have been bandaged awkwardly for a day, and still I struggle to move them without hurting, though the sting itself can bring a certain kind of pleasure. I stand on the deck of the ship, and watch Barcelona disappear on the horizon. Insomnia has taken hold and it is difficult to sleep more than five hours. This sleeplessness lends itself to a wild breathless state, coupled with the adrenaline of escape. *Time. You'll need a lot of that for this job.* I return to my cabin. Take a glass of water. Try and sleep. I look to my bandaged hands, holding them up, above my face as I lie on my back. They smell of disinfectant. I move my index finger slowly. *Sting. Sting.* But I like the feeling. *I am alive.* The cuts he made were clean, very surgical, carving out each line of two simple drawings made in flesh – the snake on my left hand, the cross on my right. Stiches in both, but I may keep the scar. Once the wounds heal they tell me I can cover them up – hide them – but first we hope my body will rinse itself of these marks until they are just fine little lines. Fingers twitching, I rifle through the plastic bag I had filled at the chemist, pull out the weapons of a new arsenal. *Perhaps this will help?* I line each eye with a thick black rim, adding smoke to my lids, and heavy strokes of mascara. *Trying to hide the bruise.* A rich, tinted foundation and a light gold bronzer, giving my freckles a more luminescent tan. The crack in my lip unnerves me but I am determined not to recognize myself. I do not want to see *him* on me. I do not want to feel his hands or smell his breath. I do not want to think it is my fault, and I hate the voice inside me that threatens to pull me down. *Down down down.* Brown powder around the rim of my eyelashes darkens the earth in my eyes. *I will not let him dictate my form.* I go to the ship bar to test my disguise. I am electric and drunk, stepping out of my skin again and again, inventing an entire story for myself – the region in Barcelona this false me comes from, her reasons for going to the island. I order three rum and Cokes and drink them too quickly, one after the other, and then a coffee. The bartender asks about my hands. *I broke a mirror.* Bad luck. At the bar I read the evening paper. Across the front page they've splashed Oriol Duran with the tagline: 'FACE OF A KILLER? INQUIRY INTO FATAL SHOOTING'. I scan the lines. *Coroner reports that Oriol Duran's death was instant. Shots fired in self-defence, claims deputy commissioner. Protects rights of officers to anonymity.*

What does a liar look like? I stare at the photograph of Oriol Duran. *A liar looks like you.* A liar hides as much as they reveal. A liar is not afraid to con. A liar tells no one, not even themselves, who they are.

I order another drink. Maybe my hands will stop hurting then. *A liar looks like the face of Inspector Fabregat behind a man with a smoking gun.*

'Couldn't have asked for more.' Fabregat had said, when he broke it down into beats. They came to take me to the airport, and

I was missing. Luckily they already had Oriol's name from the blood. So it was an easy correlation. But what they did not factor in was *where* Oriol had gone. His family home in the woods. And so there were unexpected delays.

Delays that cost me my hands.

'You have to understand that Oriol Duran always touched everything.'

'But why didn't you tell me?'

Fabregat edged closer.

'Before I could sink my teeth in that summer of 2003, the whole thing had been turned off. Duran pushed back, began to put the screw on. Said I was fucking up his reputation. Said I was orchestrating a witch-hunt in the theatrical community. In this city he has power. His friend Sánchez is a rich and influential man. Eventually the calls came in from the top.' Fabregat's face tightened. 'I was wasting time and resources in the wrong places. I had lost my cool. I needed a break. You know the drill. But retired? Did I say that, Nena?'

He had smiled, wolf-like.

'No. I never retired.'

You shot him. I want to shout. *And what will you do with his cave full of women's tongues?*

Fabregat looked through me into something else.

'When you contacted us, I seized the chance to do something bold. Something big, Nena.'

And he wants me to know that he's grateful. My stomach turns. Fabregat was never interested in the meaning of ancient symbols or coded poetry, or the long-dead memories of an English scholar. But he was intrigued by what I represented. A lone girl who matched a profile. Who could be given a cap and cape and sent into the forest.

471

'Of course I knew we could keep you safe.'

My hands throb louder.

'We were just waiting. We wanted to know which one of them would emerge. Would come out to play. Because I was certain he would. You were so like the others, Nena. I knew when I met you . . . You were made of the same stuff.'

The words stick to me. Consume me.

When I return to my room on the ship, I throw up twice in the toilet. On the deck of the ship, after a restless night, I am recovered now, if one can call it that. I watch the sunrise on the landing. This deck is empty. All the sea is mine. Dawn kisses the Mediterranean with light you can only have on water, where the abyss stretches to either side and the sun rises over a straight horizon. The sun already warming, the only thing cold is the sharp wind off the sea, like the thoughts that stalk across my mind, made stronger by the speed of the boat, and the spray lashing up from the waves. Spring is coming, cardigan loose over my shoulders. My bags are packed in the room below, apartment emptied of my belongings. The island of Mallorca rises on the horizon, a blue mound before lilac turrets of cloud. Seagulls flock overhead and there are powdery crests on the waves. The smell of salt and smoke, a rising billow from a bonfire near Dragonera that blankets the white capped waters.

At the port I see him waving. Down where the ship comes in! He calls and laughs, flapping his hat in the wind. *Home. I am home.* Dirt under fingernails, warm hands. When I emerge from the ship, walking down the gangway, he comes running, more stiffly than usual, lifting me up in his arms he kisses me firmly on the lips, then puts me down, blushes and apologizes. I reach out to touch him. His face spattered by a multitude of red scabs, the remnants of cuts made by the broken glass of his windshield. Francesc winces and gently catches my hand, moving it away from his cheek and looks at the bandages. The mark where the blood has begun to soak through.

'Who did this to you?' Francesc asks, his voice colour-tinged. I embrace him, my lips hot on his mouth, I pull him towards me and he picks me up in the air and I feel the hard full chest of him, the mountain earth on his skin, the hint of rosemary in his hair. I do not want to talk about it. Not here. Not ever. I want to pretend it never happened. *You have been working in the garden*, his hand firm on my chest, my dress tugging at his belt. *Was it worth it?* he whispers. I don't tell him yet, but I have made sure it was.

At home I settle into my own desk, my proper desk, my lair facing the garden and the yawning mouth of the valley. Then ritual. I open my brown satchel and remove, with all the tenderness of a lover, my Serpent Papers. The work will be translation. I have not told Fabregat. I have no intention of doing so. I have caught them a killer and paid for it with my hands; I touch the papers, the vellum so delicate – so frail! Francesc interrupts me, standing in the doorway. I can feel him, sandalwood and ash, fresh spring onions and mud from the garden, sage and turmeric, and the musky odour of work, of sweat, of muscle. I turn around. His face very still, his eyes very gentle.

'Let me hold you,' he says. 'I've missed you.'

That night he takes me walking. The moon blinks as we traverse steep shale, snaking through the wood until we reach a ledge above the village. Looking out to the emerald bell tower. *Calm. For once. For a night at least. Maybe more? Then I will tell Bingley. Then I will tell all of them.* Storm clouds part overhead, disintegrating into thin streaks of soot on the sky, pulled back like a fine grey powder. Our waxing moon strikes the spindly Mediterranean trees, illuminating the mound of a ruined mill. Francesc touches a stone cross beside us, a beacon of history emerging from the rock above his village. He encourages me to do the same. I decline.

'You would do well to forget what you have seen in Barcelona.' Francesc's mouth warm behind my ear.

In the afternoons I wander to my desk and sit with the pages of Natalia's parchment – I will do nothing with them yet. There are certain requirements of recovery, both physical and mental, that will keep me from embarking on the project of translation. For the moment I find them comforting. Knowing that they are safe, that we are bound up in each other. From our sanctuary, the papers and I look to the village, the Charterhouse's bell tower coloured a lovely emerald green in bright contrast to the yellow stone of the walls. The bells chime merrily to count the hours, while the leaves of the neighbouring trees have begun to sprout, a smattering of fresh buds against the pines. The hills nestle us to either side, never sheer, never fierce, such that the stillness beckons me; the soul breathes deeply on this mountain. Nothing is fenced in. Nothing is grey. The village emerges from the hills as an organism, a quiet thing at ease with its foundations, and the respect of the breeze and the billowing clouds lend certain wonderment to my walks in the evenings. Where I scramble up the hedgerow, the earth is farmed in terraces. The farmers wind their tomatoes into conical struc- tures resembling a tepee; the orchards filled with apple trees and olives. On a picnic blanket stretched out beneath a bare apple tree, Francesc feeds me two tablespoons of olive oil to ease my diges- tion. He rests his hands on my back and I feel the warmth, the hot circles of energy.

'You need to learn control,' Francesc says, running his hands through my hair. *To listen better. Take advice. Admit you live with it.* I can feel my heart improving despite the cold.

Each night after dinner we receive a call.

Francesc puts his hand over the receiver. 'It's the inspector again.'

'Tell him I need time!' I shout from the bed.

Not yet. I need to drown him out. *To heal. To forget.*

But forgive? I feel the steel in me sharpen.

I am not so sure I can forgive what has followed me here. The night terrors. The added fear in the dark. It is not my fault. I tell myself again and again. *What happened happened. But it is not your fault.*

'*Quick*,' Francesc says in Catalan, 'pull your mirror in.'

I wind down the window, and snap in the rear-view mirror to the side of the car, to allow the vehicle to pass through.

'It's very ...' Francesc takes his hands off the wheel and makes a gesture for 'tight', his palms almost touching. He grabs the wheel again as the car almost hits the rock walls. I laugh!

'But *el miracle* is that it feels wider going out! It's only difficult *ara* – now – driving in. Out not so complicated.'

As he parks the car, he reaches over and kisses me, tucking my hair behind my ear. The walls of the hermitage are mottled yellow, rocks buried in a sandstone cement, pink tiles. Baby palms and ferns wind-swept and tired. Water-streaked bark of the olive tree. Francesc crosses the courtyard briskly, entering the church, pulling away curtains behind the wooden door. The arc is intimate. As my eyes adjust to the dark I follow Francesc's breath, his husky whisper.

A figure stands, emerging from the oak pews, shaking off his hood. A wooden cross and rosary beads about his neck. Fingers dipped in holy water. Warm drops against my forehead.

'*Benvinguda*, Senyoreta Verco. We have been visited by a spirit,' the monk says, the font beside him. 'When you have a moment, I would like your help uncovering who she is.'

'And in payment?' I ask. We speak in the accepted code.

'We have looked through our sources as you requested.'
He hands me a piece of furled paper which reads:

> *In his three houses*
> *Each a beacon find*
> *First there was that*
> *Book, the dismay man's.*

The signature on the back is instantly recognizable. *L. Sitwell.* A creeping warmth. I feel Francesc touch my back. *Steady. Steady. Arm yourself, Miss Verco. We are in the beginning. Treasure hunters embarking on a long journey. Spin, spin goes the world. And so do we.*

We park the car at the bottom of the road. Francesc strides towards our house. I follow. Slowly. Earth damp underfoot. Fields verdant, the clouds crinkling at the edges, basking in new-born plumpness, a lush goose-grey down. Orchids all buried for winter, but the cone-head thyme blossoms in the gardens and the greenery of potted plants and winter vegetables are in no short decline. The air smells of fresh onions and garlic, mud, and the ash of oak fire. I inhale deeply and rejoice in the experience of being alive. *Succumb.* Here, now, only rapture. Intermittently the sun pierces the clouds with a beam of light that cuts across my path beneath the monasteries and stately homes, winding along wide pastures and through pine forests until the land drops away and I am alone on the Serra de Tramuntana, to my left: rocky outcrops plunging into the sea, to my right: the mammoth shards of the ridgeline, stealing the air from a woman's breath so that she feels her mind float away above her and she is lost in the beauty of it all.

ACKNOWLEDGMENTS

This novel could have no finer champions than my editor Jon Riley, his assistant editor Rose Tomaszewska, and the entire team at Quercus. I am truly grateful for the energy and support that has gone into every aspect of the book, from the beautiful design work, to the copyedit, to the earliest stages of drafting and rewriting. Deep thanks also to my editors Iris Tupholme and Lorissa Sengara at HarperCollinsCanada. Felicity Blunt, superstar, agent extraordinaire, has made this process wonderful. *The Serpent Papers* has flown further than I could ever have imagined due to the Foreign Rights team at Curtis Brown, and the creativity and passion of Katie McGowan and Rachel Clements. I am also indebted to Nick Marston, who encouraged me to keep writing many years ago.

The stories of the Sibyl and her sibylline books are recounted as factually as possible. On the subject of the Sibyl and her haunting presence in European history, H. W. Parke's *Sibyls and Sibylline Prophecies* and Jorge Guillermo's *Sibyls: Prophecy and Power in the Ancient World* were indispensable. As to nineteenth- and twentieth-century developments in the history of paganism, I consulted Ronald Hutton's *The Triumph of the Moon: A History of Modern Pagan Witchcraft* and *Grimoires: A History of Magic Books* by Owen Davies, both published by Oxford University Press. E. J. Holmyard's *Alchemy* proved the most entertaining of works on the subject, while William R. Newman's *Promethean Ambitions: Alchemy and the Quest to Perfect Nature* and Lawrence M. Principe's *The Secrets of Alchemy* are extremely insightful. *The Good and Evil Serpent* by James H. Charlesworth kept me reading into many a night. Robert Graves's *The White Goddess* and Sir James George Frazer's *The Golden Bough* have been equally close to hand. The London International Palaeography Summer School and the London Rare Books School offered exceptional courses at Senate House. For those interested in the works of the Catalan writer and mystic Ramon Llull, who serves as inspiration for Rex Illuminatus, I would recommend Anthony Bonner's *Doctor Illuminatus: A Ramon Llull Reader*. All errors, fictions and inventions are my own.

I have been touched by the kindness and hospitality of a great many people across the world. Thanks to Roman and Olga Camps who welcomed me into their family; and Vera Salvat for her friendship and generosity. Special thanks also to Dr Mercè Saumell and the faculty at the Institut del Teatre. Pep Gatell and Nadala Fernández of La Fura dels Baus took me under their wings and showed me the hidden world of their theatre. In memory of J. Martin Evans at Stanford University, who ignited and fuelled my passion for literature, and London's Rosemary Vercoe who, at the venerable age of ninety-three, invited me to stay for two days that turned into several years. To Francine Toon, who read the earliest drafts and encouraged me to dream. The Dodgson family gave me a second home in London, and the most delicious Sunday dinners in Highbury. Sarah and Peter Bellwood have been there since the beginning in Ojai and making bookmarks to match. Marie, David and Jane, thank you. Your wisdom has been invaluable.

I am profoundly indebted to my parents, Stephen and Clarissa, and each of my seven siblings: Joshua, Samuel, Lizzie, Matthew, Rebecca, Catherine, and Isabella. I owe this book to you. Callum. You are everything. My best friend, my great love. Thank you for an extraordinary four years.